**Scarlet Wilson** wrote her first story aged eight and has never stopped. She's worked in the health service for twenty years, having trained as a nurse and a health visitor. Scarlet now works in public health and lives on the West Coast of Scotland with her fiancé and their two sons. Writing medical romances and contemporary romances is a dream come true for her.

**Marion Lennox** has written over one hundred romance novels, and is published in over one hundred countries and thirty languages. Her international awards include the prestigious RITA® Award (twice!) and the *RT Book Reviews* Career Achievement Award for 'a body of work which makes us laugh and teaches us about love'. Marion adores her family, her kayak, her dog, and lying on the beach with a book someone else has written. Heaven!

# ISLAND DOCTOR TO ROYAL BRIDE?

SCARLET WILSON

# THE BABY THEY LONGED FOR

MARION LENNOX

MILLS & BOON

First Published in Great Britain 2019
by Mills & Boon, an imprint of HarperCollins*Publishers*
1 London Bridge Street, London, SE1 9GF

Island Doctor to Royal Bride? © 2019 by Scarlet Wilson

The Baby They Longed For © 2019 by Marion Lennox

ISBN: 978-0-263-26956-7

# ISLAND DOCTOR TO ROYAL BRIDE?

SCARLET WILSON

MILLS & BOON

For my family's own little Princess, Taylor Hyndman.
Love you loads gorgeous girl!

# CHAPTER ONE

PHILIPPE SETTLED INTO his seat and pulled his baseball cap over his eyes. It was a four-hour flight to Temur Sapora, the Malaysian island in the South China Sea, and he intended to sleep the whole way.

Two minutes later an ample gentleman tried to slide into the seat next to him. Philippe looked up briefly, shifting a little to allow the man more room to sit down. It was an instant mistake. The red-faced man instantly started talking. 'Pardon me. I'm a little bigger than the standard-sized airline seat.' He laughed, then stuck out his hand towards Philippe.

'Harry Reacher, I'm from Minneapolis in the US. Are you going to Temur Sapora too?'

Philippe let his practised face slide into place. He didn't say the word *obviously* that was floating around in his head. This aircraft had only one destination.

'Philippe,' he said simply, leaving the last name blank. It didn't matter that this guy was American. His surname was pretty well known worldwide. The whole point of this trip was to remain anonymous—hence why he was heading to an island in the South China Sea that few people had heard of.

'I'm a doctor,' added Harry quickly, pulling a cotton

handkerchief from his pocket and wiping the sweat from his brow. 'I'm going to work at one of the local medical centres for a couple of weeks. They've apparently made huge advances on wound healing.'

'They have?' Now Philippe's curiosity was definitely piqued. He sat up a little in his chair. 'What are they doing?'

There was a spark in Harry's eyes. 'You in the business?'

Philippe nodded. 'I'm a doctor too.'

'Ah-h-h.' Harry gave him a careful stare, which Philippe hoped wasn't a glimmer of recognition. 'You here to work too?'

Philippe shook his head and smiled. 'Absolutely not. This is a holiday. My first in five years. I'm going to lie low for two weeks, drink a few beers and sleep.' He left out the part about needing a bit of time and head space to regroup after his last patient in the ER. That experience would never leave him.

'If this is a holiday, where are all your friends?' Harry looked around in surprise. 'Don't you young guys all go on holidays together?'

Philippe gave a shrug. He had years of experience at avoiding questions he really didn't want to answer. 'Thanks for the compliment but I'm not that young— thirty-one now. And I can guarantee if my friends were with me I wouldn't get a wink of sleep and that's what I need right now. Five years of fifty-hour weeks is enough for anyone. I'm starting another job in a few weeks and just wanted some downtime.'

Harry smiled again. 'And you chose Temur Sapora? It's a little off the beaten track.'

Philippe nodded. 'Which means it's perfect. Beautiful beaches, perfect ocean and an anonymous luxury resort.'

Harry shrugged. 'I guess we all need some downtime.'

'Except you. You're here to work.' He was still curious to hear about the advances in wound healing.

Harry smiled again. 'But it's for selfish reasons. I'm hoping to learn as much as I can and take it back with me. And for me, coming here, it's the trip of a lifetime.' His smile got wider. 'I can't wait.'

Philippe settled back in his seat a little as the 'fasten seat belt' signs lit up. Harry struggled to fit his around his wide girth, eventually closing it with a bit of a squirm. 'Now,' he said. 'Where were we? Ah, yes, let me tell you about the effects of the ointment they've developed on necrotising fasciitis.'

Philippe kept a smile on his face as the plane taxied down the runway and the possibility of sleep slipped further and further from his grasp.

'Harry, are you okay?'

Three hours later Harry was rubbing at his chest again. He'd hardly touched the food when it had come and had been drinking only water. Sweat was pouring off him and his face was getting redder by the second.

'It'll pass. Just a bit of indigestion,' he said.

Philippe shook his head. 'Let me take a proper look at you.' He grabbed his backpack from under the seat in front and pulled out a tiny monitor and a stethoscope. Every doctor's first-aid kit. Before Harry could say any more, Philippe slipped the tiny probe onto his finger.

'Do you have any health conditions I should know about?'

Harry shook his head. 'Just a bit of high blood pressure but it's been under control for the last few years.'

Philippe reached over to touch him. The skin on his

chest was cold and clammy. He positioned the stetho-scope, knowing it was unlikely to help. Harry's lungs were functioning—it was his heart that was having prob-lems.

'I have to be okay,' murmured Harry. 'I'm meeting Arissa Cotter at the medical centre. She's expecting me. They're down a doctor right now so the timing has worked out perfectly.' He gasped as his hand went to his chest. 'She needs me.'

For the first time Philippe could see real fear in Har-ry's eyes. He signalled to one of the air stewards. 'How soon until we land?'

The steward shot an anxious glance at Harry. 'An-other hour.'

'Anywhere closer we can land?'

He shook his head. 'No. Not for a plane this size. There's only the South China Sea. Temur Sapora is the nearest airport from here.'

Philippe grimaced. For the first time he wished he'd taken the royal private jet. It was smaller and could prob-ably have landed on a much shorter airstrip. But he'd wanted to be incognito—he'd wanted to have the chance of having a true holiday before he had to head back home to Corinez to take up his role in spearheading some changes in the healthcare system. The King had trained his children well. One trained in the armed forces to be the next King, one trained as a doctor to help facilitate changes in healthcare, and one trained as an accountant to join the advisory committee on finance.

But bringing the royal jet to Temur Sapora would just have alerted most of the news agencies around the world. Not the kind of holiday he wanted.

'Give me a number for your chest pain, Harry, between one and ten.' He couldn't help it. Moving into complete doctor mode was so natural to him.

The redness started to fade from Harry's face, replaced by a horrible paleness. Harry didn't answer.

Philippe's stomach gave an uncomfortable lurch. As a doctor he'd dealt with many emergencies, but not at thirty thousand feet—and not without any real supplies. He had a horrible sinking feeling that what he needed right now was some kind of anticoagulant to stop the current damage to Harry's heart. This guy was having a heart attack. And those kind of meds weren't available at thirty thousand feet.

Within a few seconds Harry slumped over.

The steward panicked and ran to get their emergency kit and defibrillator. Philippe slid Harry to the floor. The passengers close by were wide-eyed but moved swiftly aside to let Philippe work.

Ten minutes later Philippe ran his fingers through his dark hair and let out an angry sigh. It was impossible. The defibrillator wasn't even picking up a shockable rhythm. CPR was having no effect and they were too far away from landing to continue indefinitely.

He stared down at Harry and withdrew his hands slowly, making a final check of the pulse before he glanced at his watch. 'Time of death, two-fifty-six,' he said as he shook his head. 'I'm sorry, Harry,' he said quietly. 'I guess you're not getting the trip of a lifetime any more.'

# CHAPTER TWO

ARISSA GLANCED AT her watch. It was odd. Harry Reacher's plane had landed hours ago and he should have been here by now.

Her stomach squeezed. She hoped he hadn't had a last-minute change of heart. Getting doctors here was difficult enough. As it was, she used all her own holidays to cover here five weeks a year.

She finished scrubbing her hands at the sink and moved over to the small trolley she had set up. 'Okay, Adilah, let's get a proper look at that finger.'

She pulled on some gloves and touched Adilah's finger to ensure the local anaesthetic had taken effect. Her mother adjusted Adilah on her knee. 'How many stitches do you think it will need?'

Arissa gave a smile. 'I think about four will be enough. That's a nasty cut you gave yourself, Adilah. But I'll have it fixed in no time and it won't hurt a bit.'

Arissa bent down and started making the tiny stitches as she sang a nursery rhyme that her mother had taught her as a child. Adilah smiled and joined in. Within a few minutes Arissa was done, giving the wound a final check and covering it with a small dressing. She pulled out her prescription pad. 'I'm going to give you some antibiotics for Adilah, as the wound was pretty dirty when she got here. She's more liable to infection than most, so hopefully this will keep things at bay.'

Adilah's mother gave a grateful nod. Arissa noted the dark circles under her eyes. Having a five-year-old with leukaemia was taking its toll. 'Bring her back if she shows sign of a temperature or any discharge from the wound. Otherwise try and keep the dressing dry for the next few days. It should heal without any problems.'

There was a movement at the door, and Arissa looked up. Darn it. Another tourist, doubtless looking for the luxury resort that had a similar name to their clinic.

'Give me a minute.' She waved her hand as she moved to dispose of the items on the trolley and wash her hands again.

Instead of waiting at the door the curious tourist stepped inside, nodding at Adilah and her mother as they left and then turning his head from side to side, scanning the clinic area.

Arissa felt her hackles rise. He was likely looking for luxury Egyptian cotton sheets, straw parasols, cocktails and personal waiters. This simple clinic would be something completely outwith his normal environment.

She sighed and turned around, trying her best to paste a smile on her face. 'Are you lost?' Her heart stopped somewhere in her chest. Wow. Okay, Mr Tourist was about to knock Hugh Jackman off her 'if only' list and steal his place.

Dark hair and dark eyes, combined with height and a muscular build. He was dragging some kind of backpack behind him. Not like the usual designer luggage she might have expected.

He was holding a baseball cap in his hand. He tilted his head to the side. 'Arissa Cotter?'

She blinked. This couldn't be her guy. Wasn't Dr Reacher in his sixties? She held her breath for a second. 'Who wants to know?'

Her heart started thudding against her chest as she tried to control her breathing. Was he a reporter? A private investigator? Had the secret she'd tried to hide for the last few years finally tracked her down?

The man crossed the room in three long strides, holding his hand out towards her. 'Philippe…' He paused, then gave the briefest shake of his head. 'I'm afraid I have some bad news for you.'

She didn't like this. She didn't like this at all. She automatically stepped back and he looked a little surprised.

It didn't matter that his eyes were the darkest brown she'd ever seen. Her breath was tangling somewhere inside her, as she wondered if things were about to come crashing down around her.

She didn't answer him. Her words caught somewhere between her chest and throat.

He took a deep breath. 'I'm really sorry to tell you that I was on the plane next to Dr Harry Reacher. He had a heart attack while we were in midair.'

It took a few seconds for the words to process. 'Wh-what?'

Her brain jumped away from the fear. For a few moments she felt utterly selfish. She'd imagined this was all about her. 'Is he in the hospital?'

Something flitted across the eyes of the man calling himself Philippe and she knew instantly what came next. A horrible prickling feeling spread over her skin.

'Oh, no,' were all the words she could form. She took

a deep breath. She'd never had a chance to meet Harry Reacher but his emails over the last few months had brightened her days, his enthusiasm and passion for his work brimming over in every sentence.

The tall stranger was still standing there, watching her with those intense brown eyes. She gave herself a little shake then tried to give him a smile. 'I'm really sorry to hear about Harry. I was looking forward to working with him.' Her heart gave a little twist as she realised she'd need to carry the workload here herself for the next couple of weeks.

He nodded too and ran his hand through his thick dark hair. It was the first time she'd noticed the fatigue in his eyes. 'I'm just sorry I couldn't save him. But, up there…' he let out a sigh '… I had nothing. No drugs, proper equipment. I don't have a doubt what the autopsy will show, but I hate the fact that if we'd actually been on the ground and near a hospital, there might have been a chance to save him.'

It was the way he said the words. As if he had an edge of responsibility for what had happened.

'You had a defib?' She couldn't help but ask, she was curious.

He nodded. 'But no shockable rhythm.'

Arissa pressed her lips together. She knew exactly what that meant. The heart attack must have been catastrophic. Whether they'd been near a hospital or not, it was unlikely that Harry would have survived.

But how many people knew it wasn't a shockable rhythm? She opened her mouth to ask when another priority sprang to mind. Of course.

She straightened up as the logical part of her brain kicked into gear. 'I should contact the hospital. See about making arrangements regarding Harry—speak to the consulate about contacting his relatives.'

'I've taken care of things,' he said, somewhat carefully.

She frowned. 'Really?'

That seemed a little odd. Regulations and red tape were notorious on Temur Sapora. Who on earth was this guy? She looked at him again. There was something vaguely familiar about him, but she couldn't place him at all. His accent was kind of strange. A mix of French, Italian and Spanish. He was definitely from Europe somewhere but she couldn't quite place the rich tone in his voice. Whoever he was, he must have money. The luxury resorts here were for the rich, the very rich and, the very, very rich.

Too expensive and exclusive for anyone less than a millionaire. At some point Temur Sapora would be found by the masses, but luckily that hadn't happened yet. She cringed every time some billionaire businessman mentioned in an interview that they'd visited a 'luxury Malaysian island' putting the spotlight on her home.

Part of her wanted the island to remain unspoiled and undiscovered. But part of her wanted it to share some of the distributed wealth of the rich visitors. The tourist resorts had given jobs to many of her friends. Families that had lived in poverty had started to gain a little income and independence. Healthcare had finally started to become a little more accessible. In the last ten years people around her had flourished. Before, Arissa had had to leave the island to train as a doctor. There was no university here, and the local hospitals weren't properly equipped. But gradual improvements had happened. She was always glad to return now and give back a little to the place she'd left behind. Her last job was in Washington, specialising in paediatrics. But the plane ride back to Temur Sapora with the familiar sight of the turquoise waters and the backdrop of the volcano always made her heart leap a little in her chest. There was no place like home.

There was a crackle above them. The guy started and Arissa gave a rueful smile. She held up one hand. 'Give it a second.'

He looked confused—his muscles tense in his neck, his hands in fists. Was he afraid? A few seconds later another noise thundered from the sky followed by a sudden torrent of rain deluging the roof above them.

A half-smile appeared on his face as he realised what the sound was, and he glanced outside at the rain thudding down on the ground. The raindrops bounced back up and the street quickly collected water. 'It almost sounded like gunfire,' he said softly.

It was a curious thing to say. Arissa glanced at her watch and shook her head. 'It's almost like clockwork.' She put her hands on her hips. 'Every day around midday we have the daily deluge.' She moved a little closer to him, catching a sea-edged scent with a hint of musk. She could feel her senses prickle. Interesting aftershave. She shifted her feet, curious and a little irritated that she'd even noticed. The rain drummed down relentlessly outside, ricocheting off the nearby roofs like a drumbeat. He'd crossed his arms across his body, revealing the muscles in his back visible through his thin cotton T-shirt.

She dragged her eyes deliberately away but immediately found them focusing on his toned, tanned arms. Darn it. What was wrong with her?

She blinked as she took a step forward so she was slightly ahead of him. His eyes were focused firmly on the water rushing past their feet, rapidly turning a sludgy brown as it mixed with the earth from the surrounding streets.

'Is it always like this?'

She nodded. 'Yip. This is normal. Give it fifteen minutes and the sun will come back out.' She took a deep breath and pointed off to the distant volcano, currently with a dark cloud hanging over it. 'Scientists have studied it and can't really explain the phenomenon. When I was little, my *nenek* used to tell me the God of Thunder was a little sad and wanted to remind us he was still there.'

She glanced sideways at him and she could see the amused look on his face. 'And you believed that?'

Instantly she was annoyed. Her eyes went from his face to the designer emblem on the right side of the T-shirt. She recognised it. That T-shirt cost what she'd normally earn in a month. She was right. He was one of the cocky billionaires that usually frequented the local luxury resort. She'd do well to remember that instead of getting lost in a pair of deep brown eyes.

Memories flooded her brain. Someone like him would never relate to someone like her—abandoned as a baby outside a local shop. She'd been one of the lucky ones. She'd been adopted by a local couple and had a warm upbringing, only ending when they'd both died from ill health a few years ago. But she'd had to fight for everything she'd ever achieved. She loved the local stories and traditions of Temur Sapora. A man of privilege would never relate to a place like this.

She spun away and shot over her shoulder, 'Give it fifteen minutes and it'll be finished. Then, you'll be able to get to wherever you're going. If you need a taxi you'll find one at the end of the street.' She licked her lips, reluctantly adding, 'Thanks for letting me know about Harry. Have a nice holiday.'

He looked a bit stunned by her sudden dismissal. But she couldn't worry about that now. She had work to do—more, now that she knew Harry wouldn't be joining her.

She didn't have time to waste exchanging niceties with an anonymous stranger—no matter how nice he smelt.

One day. That was how long he'd been here and he was bored rigid.

The resort was glorious, immaculate and set on a gleaming white sandy beach. Every room had a view of the rippling turquoise ocean. The impeccable staff seemed to anticipate his every need. The beds and sheets were as luxurious as the ones he slept on in the palace. He had everything he could possibly want or need at his fingertips.

He'd picked the resort carefully. It was exactly what he'd wanted. A place he could completely relax and re-focus. He knew after finishing his last job in a busy ER that he'd need a chance to reflect and change pace. His final patient in the ER had brought home to him just how important it was to spearhead the changes his country needed in healthcare. Corinez was a playground for the rich and famous. But not everyone who lived and worked there was rich and famous, and healthcare was something that frequently came bottom of the list on people's daily expenses. After his last case his father had promised him a few weeks' leeway before he returned to help try and develop free maternity care within Corinez.

He'd prepared for this role his whole life. He'd always known this time would come, as had his brother and sister. There was no doubt that Anthony had the hardest role—as the oldest child he was expected to take over from their father when he abdicated next year.

Philippe nodded as one of the personal concierges set a cocktail down next to him. This was his time to reflect, to plan, to take stock of what he'd learned from around the globe and apply it to the services and people in Corinez.

He had to—because paradise had changed a little over the last few years. Corinez had always been known as an island paradise. For the rich it was well known as a tax haven—the casinos flourished. Lots of celebrities had homes in Corinez. But over the last few years things had changed. The recession had hit areas of Corinez like every other country and, while the fabulously rich still existed, the people who struggled were becoming more noticeable, and those were the ones that Philippe wanted to focus on. He firmly believed that everyone was entitled to healthcare. He wanted to introduce a system in Corinez similar to the NHS in the UK. He had to start somewhere and now, more than ever, he knew that maternity care was the place to begin.

So why was he spending his time thinking about the beautiful Malaysian doctor he'd met yesterday?

Most of his dreams last night had been haunted by her dark hair, serious brown eyes, slim frame, pink shirt and dark figure-hugging trousers. He could remember every detail.

When he'd first watched her, he'd admired her easy manner as she'd interacted with the little girl. But from the second she'd realised he was there he'd almost been able to see the shutters go down over her eyes. He'd been surprised by her instantly suspicious gaze. The truth was—he wasn't used to it.

He'd spent his life in two roles. Prince Philippe or Dr

Aronaz. Neither of which was usually met with suspicion. But he hadn't introduced himself to Arissa as either. Which for him was unusual. He was trying hard to keep a low profile. But now he was here?

The clientele were clearly exclusive. He'd recognised an actor hiding from a scandal. An unscrupulous politician. An author who seemed to spend all day furiously typing her latest novel. And several well-known business associates who were obviously trying to take some time to relax—even though they had phones pressed permanently to their ears.

Truth was, he really didn't want to spend time with any of these people. Particularly the blonde actress who seemed to be trying to attract his attention right now. His last experience of a relationship with an actress hadn't gone so well. She'd relished dating a prince. She'd loved the attention. The constant media coverage. What she hadn't loved was how dedicated Philippe was to his work. Or that his plans for the future had included even more work. When he'd refused to choose her over his day job she'd dumped him mercilessly. He wasn't afraid to admit he'd been hurt. He might even have loved her a little, but her hour-long interview about him on prime-time TV had killed that feeling completely. He was wary now. He wasn't ready to put his heart on the line in such an obvious way again. Here, he could just be Philippe, not a prince of Corinez. That felt surprisingly refreshing.

He looked around again. What exactly was he going to do? There was a gym—been there, done that. A business centre—no way. A beauty salon—no. A masseuse—he shuddered. He'd never been one for a stranger's hands on his skin. As for the tennis and squash courts? It was hard to play tennis or squash solo. He stretched out his arms, feeling the sun continue to heat his skin. Arissa's face flooded into his brain again.

He'd seen the disappointment on her face yesterday when she'd realised Dr Reacher wouldn't be joining her. Philippe hadn't even asked what impact that might have on her. To be honest he'd been a little stung by her sudden dismissal.

He wasn't used to being treated like that. Sure, like any doctor he'd dealt with drunk or difficult patients. As a prince he'd dealt with arrogant or obnoxious dignitaries. But Arissa? That was something a little different. It was almost as if he'd done something to offend her—and he was sure that he hadn't.

He straightened on his sunlounger. There was a chance she could be responsible for the clinic on her own. His legs swung off the bed automatically. He took one glance at the bright orange cocktail and shook his head as he grabbed his T-shirt. He could still keep a low profile. He could introduce himself to Arissa with his Dr persona while just leaving out the part he was a prince. Temur Sapora was an island just like Corinez, albeit on the other side of the planet. Thoughts started to form quickly in his head. He could help out while learning more about their health system—treat it as a research trip. He could give her references, leaving out his last job at a hospital in Corinez. If she called there, she would find out instantly he was a prince. The others would only mention him as Philippe Aronaz.

He strode through to his suite, quickly changing as he wondered who he was trying to convince. His real focus was that slight frame and those deep brown eyes. He smiled as he strode out of the door.

No one would turn down a free doctor—would they?

# CHAPTER THREE

ARISSA WAS TIRED. More than tired. The next two days were going to be the busiest. The annual carnival was due to start tomorrow and it looked as if she was going to be the only doctor available for the clinic.

It was unfortunate. She'd hoped to use technology to review some of the cases like Adilah's. There were seven kids on the island with some kind of blood cancer that she could discuss with a specialist back at her training hospital. She'd really wanted to use time to ensure they were getting the best treatments available. But now, as the only doctor at the clinic, she was unlikely to get time to do that.

She stared at the stack of photos in front of her. The clinic had negotiated sponsorship into research regarding the new ointment made from natural substances found on the island that seemed to have remarkable healing abilities. Part of her role was to help with the documentation. But it seemed that the doctor that had been here before her had fallen behind. The work was vital—the sponsorship helped keep this clinic open and full of supplies. She'd need to play catch up. It would have been possible with two doctors—particularly when Harry had been so interested in the subject matter—but now, with just her?

It didn't help that she couldn't find the digital files on the computer. If her predecessor had saved them he must have used the weirdest filing system in the world.

A shadow fell over her desk and she looked up just as her stomach rumbled loudly. Lunch. She'd forgotten about that too.

She frowned as she recognised the face. She couldn't help herself. 'Lost again? Or do you need a doctor?'

He was dressed in light trousers and a pale blue shirt. Relatively smarter than his jeans and T-shirt yesterday.

'Do you?' Was his reply.

Her brain tried to compute, but hunger and fatigue were making her grumpy. 'What?'

'A doctor? Do you need one—you know—to replace Harry for the next two weeks?'

The frown stayed in place. 'Well, of course I do. But it's not likely. So—' she pushed herself up from the chair '—what exactly do you want, Mr...?' She couldn't remember his name from yesterday.

He held out his hand towards her. 'Dr—Dr Aronaz. Here to help—if you want it.'

She stared at the outstretched hand and, slowly, put her hand out to meet his. His grip was firm, his hand warm. She ignored the little buzz up her arm. 'What kind of a doctor are you?'

'Mainly ER, but I do have some surgical experience, and I've had some obstetric experience too.'

'Where did you work?'

'I've worked lots of places.'

'I need specifics.' She couldn't help but fire questions at him. While she was desperate, she wasn't *that* desperate. She didn't want some lazy, rich guy who'd flunked out of every job that he'd had.

'I spent a spell in an ER in Chicago. I can give you my head of department's number. Before that I was in Italy in Verona, before that I was in Sarajevo in Bosnia.'

'Where did you train?'

A smile started to dance around the corners of his lips at her rapid-fire questions. 'I trained at Harvard.'

Of course. Money was practically stamped all over this guy. She shifted her feet. But there was something else. It was old-school money.

Somehow she knew he hadn't had to work as hard as she had to get grants and loans to pursue her dream of being a doctor. In fact, she was quite sure he hadn't had to do that at all.

She was still working to pay off her loans. Goodness knew when that would finally come to an end. But it had been worth it for her. She'd achieved her dream. Her dream of being a doctor. A good doctor—a focused doctor who did the best she could for her patients. She'd even managed to introduce a system for babies who'd been abandoned like her. The safe haven project held a big piece of her heart.

People who'd trained at Harvard probably couldn't begin to understand that. She hated that money made the world go round. As a capable and competent doctor whose reputation went before her, Arissa had had more than one offer of a job if she'd agreed to work entirely privately. She'd also had a few very rich businessmen try and convince her that she wanted to work in their specialist clinics. It was almost as if they didn't understand why anyone wouldn't chase the money, and come exactly where the high salaries were.

But the biggest part of the population didn't have a high salary. As it was, she considered her normal doctor salary to be good. She didn't want to fold and end up working for the rich and famous.

She didn't need the drama. She didn't want the attention—no matter how fleeting. She was an ordinary person. And that was what she wanted to be—an ordinary person, leading an ordinary life. She'd been particularly careful not to let the media know she'd been an abandoned baby herself when she'd set up the safe haven project—she didn't want her story to be the news. This was all about the mothers and babies of now.

She folded her arms across her chest and stared up at Philippe. Mr Old-School Money. He shook his head a little. 'What's wrong? Looked like I'd lost you there. Did I say something to offend you?'

She paused, trying to find words.

Philippe filled the uncomfortable gap. He looked around. 'I'm not quite sure what services you offer in the clinic, but I'm sure my ER experience will be sufficient to give a good service. Harry told me a little of the reasons he was coming here. He was excited about a research project on healing. I'm happy to help with that too. I carried out a few research projects as part of my training.'

It almost sounded as if the guy was trying to schmooze her. And why should he? He'd just offered his doctor services for free for the next two weeks, she should be jumping all over him. But…there was just something she couldn't put her finger on. As if there were something he wasn't quite telling her.

Arissa's instincts had always been good. She'd learned not to ignore them.

'What kind of projects?' She didn't quite mean the way the words came out—as if she didn't quite believe him.

But he kept his cool even though he looked slightly

amused by her questioning. 'I did one in West Africa looking at polio and smallpox vaccination, encouraging uptake. It was hugely successful. I did another in London, working at a specialist centre that diagnosed PoTS—you know, postural orthostatic tachycardia syndrome. Fascinating.'

She pressed her lips together. He'd gone from one end of the spectrum to the other. If the guy actually showed her his résumé she was pretty sure it was far more impressive than hers.

A pager started sounding at her waistband.

Oh, no.

He wrinkled his nose. 'What is it?'

She started moving, crossing her room and grabbing her jacket and keys. 'We need to go. We need to go now.' This was exactly the reason she could do with another doctor. She tried not to smile as she turned her head. 'If you want to start—Dr Aronaz—you start now.'

Philippe was slightly confused. He watched as Arissa changed her flat shoes for a pair of runners and pressed the button on her pager to stop it sounding. A pager in a community clinic? He wasn't quite sure what that meant. Community clinics didn't normally cover any kind of emergency service.

Arissa didn't hang around. She was out of the door in a flash. For the briefest of seconds he'd felt as if he'd had to convince her to let him work alongside her. He still wasn't entirely sure she *had* agreed to it. What was it about him that put her hackles up?

For another few seconds there he'd thought she was almost smiling at him. But, it had vanished in an instant. And she was already climbing into the old-style Jeep that sat outside the clinic. He didn't hesitate. He climbed in next to her.

'Where are we going?'

She didn't answer as she started the car and pulled out onto the road, glancing at her watch.

He looked around him. 'Do we have any supplies?' If they were heading to some kind of accident they'd want a minimum amount of supplies.

She pressed her lips together. 'There's an emergency kit in the back. Hopefully we won't need it.'

He leaned back into the seat, still trying to work out what was going on. The streets of Temur Sapora blurred past. Arissa kept glancing at her watch, going around a few corners practically on two wheels. Philippe gripped the handle on the inside of the door. Wherever it was they were going, she wanted to get there quickly.

He frowned as they pulled up outside a fire and rescue centre. The front door was down, the rescue truck visible through the upper windows. It didn't look as if it was going anywhere. Whatever they were doing it didn't involve other emergency services.

Arissa jumped out of the car and ran over to the wall. A few seconds later another black car pulled up alongside them. A fire and rescue guy jumped out too; he nodded at her. 'Arissa.' His footsteps slowed. 'Let's see what we've got.'

Philippe was more confused by the second. 'What on earth are we doing here?'

Arissa looked over her shoulder towards him. 'Lim, this is Dr Aronaz. My temporary workmate for the next two weeks.' She pulled a key from her pocket. 'Okay?'

Lim gave a nod and stood alongside Philippe, staring at the red panel on the brick wall expectantly.

There was a noise. Something he didn't expect. His stomach clenched. Was that a baby crying? Lim glanced at him, realising his confusion.

He pointed to the pager on his belt, then gestured towards the red panel that Arissa unlocked and pulled towards her.

'This is our safe haven. A place that someone can come and leave their baby. No questions asked. As soon as a baby is left, our pagers go off. We aim to get here within five minutes.'

Philippe couldn't move. He was fascinated. Arissa slowly pulled out the red panel in the wall, and he realised it was a carefully constructed shelf. Inside was a squirming baby, wrapped in a thin cotton blanket. Arissa lifted the baby out gently. 'Hello, honey,' she said quietly, gathering the baby in her arms, and stroking its head with one light finger. The baby instinctively turned its head towards her finger—rooting. Trying to find food. This baby was hungry.

Philippe stepped forward, his curiosity too much for him. Arissa nodded. 'Get me a pack,' she said to Lim, who disappeared and grabbed something from the boot of the Jeep.

Arissa carried the baby over to the Jeep and laid it down gently in the back, opening the blanket and giving the baby a quick visual check. The umbilical cord was tied with a piece of string and the baby was still smeared in some vernix. 'It's practically a newborn,' Philippe said, looking over her shoulder.

'Do you have much experience with newborns?' she asked.

He gave a little shrug. 'I've delivered three babies in the ER.'

She zipped open a tiny pack, pulling out a tympanic thermometer, a collection of wipes, and a tiny finger probe. 'Give me a hand,' she said quickly.

The baby started to squirm. Lim stood back and let Philippe move forward. He pulled a pen torch from his back pocket—it was amazing the things you kept on you when you were a doctor—and leaned forward, doing a quick check of the baby's pupils. They had no idea how this baby had been delivered, or if there had been any trauma. 'Both pupils equal and reactive,' he said, doing a manual APGAR score in his head. The skin colour was good, muscles reactive, the baby kicking as he examined it. He slipped on the finger probe and glanced at the screen for a reading. 'Do you have a stethoscope?' he asked Arissa. She smiled and pulled a bright pink stethoscope from her pocket.

'Don't you believe the monitor?' she asked.

He smiled as he took the stethoscope. 'I like to do things the old-fashioned way,' he said. The monitor reading said a pulse of one-forty and an oxygen saturation of ninety-eight per cent. This baby was doing fine.

He listened for a few seconds, checking the lungs, making sure the baby hadn't inhaled anything untoward during delivery, then listening to the heart, checking for any heart murmurs or any other abnormality. He hoped Arissa couldn't see the beads of sweat breaking out on his forehead. An abandoned baby, albeit in a safe place. This was bringing back so many memories for him—of a baby that wasn't healthy and pink like this one.

The baby let out an angry yelp as he lifted the stethoscope away from its chest. He did one final check. 'Well, she seems like a perfectly healthy little girl.' He inadvertently tucked the stethoscope into his back pocket. 'I just hope mum is doing so well.' His stomach squirmed as he said those words.

Arissa turned her eyes to Lim, who gave them both a nod. 'I'll put the word out. You okay?' he asked.

Arissa nodded as she wrapped the baby back up and put her to her shoulder. 'I think we'll be good. I'll take her back to the hospital and get her admitted and fed.'

Lim unlocked the door to the fire and rescue station and came back out a few minutes later with a car seat in his hand. He nodded towards them both. 'I'll leave you to it. Will let you know if we hear anything.'

He climbed into his black car and disappeared into the distance. Philippe turned to Arissa, his mind whirling. He pointed to the red panel on the fire station. 'What on earth is this?'

Arissa tossed her car keys towards him. 'It's a safe haven. We set it up last year. Someplace safe that a woman can leave her baby. No questions. No prosecutions. An alarm goes off as soon as the panel is opened.' She shook her head as he frowned and looked above the panel. 'Not at the station,' she said and pointed to her belt. 'To our pagers. There's always a doctor and a member of the fire and rescue crew who have the pagers. One, or both of us, aim to get here within five minutes.'

Philippe was still surprised. 'How many babies does this happen to?' Why hadn't he heard of this before? This was exactly the kind of thing he needed to know about. Ideas were already forming in his head.

Arissa gave a shrug. 'There's only been three since we started. But having a safe haven to leave a baby is organised in lots of places.' For a second he thought something flickered across her face but she pressed her lips together, then started talking again. 'When I was a little girl, there was a baby left outside the old clinic. It was there all night. The clinic isn't staffed overnight and I'm not sure that people knew that. Anyway, the baby nearly died. My mother told me about it. Everyone was upset. They never found out whose child it was. But the story stayed with me. And over the years I've often thought it should be something that we should start here.' There was something in the way she said the words that sounded a little off. From the little he knew of her, Arissa normally seemed quite comfortable, but those words had come out hard and stiff.

But Philippe was frozen to the spot as the memories flooded through him again. So many things about this were familiar. Only a few weeks ago something similar had happened in Corinez. But Corinez had a different climate from Temur Sapora. The baby left in Corinez had suffered from hypothermia. It had been touch and go. Philippe had been on duty. He'd spent the next two days trying to revive the child and had failed. He'd never lost a child before and it had moved him in ways he'd never expected. It had seemed such a random act. And it had enforced for him even more the glaring need for free maternal healthcare in Corinez. Had the mother not presented at hospital because she couldn't afford to pay the bill? Maybe she had no help at home. Maybe she hadn't known she was pregnant, or hadn't told anyone. Whatever the reasons were, try as he might, he hadn't been able to track her down to ensure her safety. He'd asked questions around the hospital. It hadn't been the first abandoned baby—but it had been the first who'd been exposed to adverse weather conditions. Maybe it was time to set up a scheme like they had in Temur Sapora?

'They have these all over the world. In France, the

USA, Italy, Hungary, Russia, Japan, Switzerland and the Philippines. They have a whole host of names—baby windows, baby cots, cradles of life, safe havens. But they all have the same function. A safe place for a mother to leave a baby.'

She fitted the car seat into the back of her own car and climbed in next to the baby. Philippe looked at the car keys in his hand and gave a little shake of his head as he climbed into the driver's seat.

'The fire station here isn't always staffed and it's in a quieter street. That's why we decided this was a more appropriate place than the clinic. If someone wants to leave their baby, they won't do it while the world is watching. Our clinic is right in the middle of the main street. The rest of the crew who work here are on call. So, someone will always be able to attend quickly to any baby left in the safe haven.'

He started the engine. 'I take it I'm driving you both to the local hospital?' His brain couldn't stop turning over and over.

Arissa was bending over the baby strapped into the back seat. She looked up and smiled. 'Well, look at that, little Dee, our new doctor is a resident genius.'

He sighed and smiled as he shook his head. 'Dee?'

She nodded as he followed the signs on the road to the local hospital. It was only a few minutes away. 'This is our fourth baby. The first two were boys. We decided just to go with the alphabet. Our first was called Amir, our second Bahari. Our third baby was a girl. We called her Chi-tze, and this time, we'll pick a name beginning with D.'

Now he understood. 'The babies never have a letter or a note? Something to tell you what their name is.'

He was doing his best to keep his eyes on the road. But he couldn't help but glance over his shoulder at the woman with dark curls looking down at the tiny baby. He could see the compassion and empathy in her face, making his stomach twist in a way he just hadn't expected.

She gave a sad kind of smile as she stroked the little girl's face. 'Not yet,' she sighed. 'I wish they would.'

'Have you ever managed to reunite a mother and baby after they left the baby at the safe haven?'

Arissa shook her head. 'I'd love to tell you yes, but the honest answer is no. For two of the babies we never found their mother. Another one, she got admitted with an infection. But...' he could hear the waver in Arissa's voice '...she didn't want to be reunited with her baby. She had a difficult history. Even with the offer of support, she just didn't want to go down that road.'

Philippe turned into the hospital and found a space in the car park. He switched off the engine and turned around. Arissa was talking quietly to the baby. 'So, have you picked a name yet?' he asked quietly.

She glanced over at him. There was a smattering of freckles on her pale brown skin, over her nose. Her eyes were the deepest brown he'd ever seen. It was almost as if they sucked him in, holding him in place. For the briefest of seconds their gazes locked in a way that made him hold his breath.

'I think you should pick the name,' she replied, the edges of her lips turning upwards. 'As long as you stick to the rules and pick something with a D.'

He got out of the car and walked around to her side, opening the door and looking down at the little baby. Her face wrinkled and she let out a yelp. He reached down and picked her up as Arissa released the harness on the car seat. He put the baby on his shoulder and patted her back as she continued to yelp. 'I think she's hungry,' he said with a smile. Then something else crossed his mind. 'We don't even know if she's been fed at all. Maybe we should hurry up with the admission process and prioritise the food.'

Arissa closed the car door and walked alongside him. 'I think we can manage that.' She gave him a wink. 'I might know someone.'

It was the oddest feeling. This morning he'd been lying at a luxury resort with two weeks of fine dining and relaxation ahead of him. Now, he had a tiny newborn baby snuggling into his neck and—from what he could feel—currently trying to latch on to him. A beautiful woman, surrounded by the scent of freesias, was walking next to him and making him strangely curious about her, and this place.

It was the oddest sensation. He'd thought he'd wanted to come here to sort out how he felt about the next part of his career—the next part of his life. But here he was, volunteering to work on a day job. Wanting to spend the next two weeks finding out more about this woman and this place.

He almost laughed out loud. No wonder his ex had complained he couldn't switch off from work. He just didn't want to. Being a doctor and doing his best for other people was ingrained in him, running through his veins in his blood.

As they walked inside the front doors of the hospital he turned to Arissa. 'Hey, I don't know any Malaysian names. I can't pick a name for this little cutie.'

'Give it some thought. You're about to meet a million

new people.' She wagged her finger at him. 'I'll warn you now, they'll all start campaigning for their own name.'

His footsteps faltered a bit. He wasn't quite sure what she meant. 'They'll know we're looking for a name?'

He looked down at the little face. So innocent. So pure. A little girl abandoned by her mother for a million reasons he didn't know about.

Arissa reached over and touched his arm. He almost jerked at the feel of her warm fingers on his skin. 'Our babies are special,' she said softly. 'Everyone in the hospital supports the safe haven project. As soon as they see us, you'll feel like a superstar.'

There was an edge to the way she said the words. A touch of sadness. He looked at her curiously. 'Does the publicity help?'

She shuddered. She actually *shuddered*. 'No. We don't talk outside the hospital about the babies. We don't want to do anything to compromise the safety of the person who has left their baby. It's just internal. Word spreads fast. Everyone always comes to see the new baby.' She sighed. 'There's a lot of love around here. By tomorrow, they'll have an emergency foster carer ready to take her.'

He gave a nod. Did they have all this set up in Corinez? Was this something he could add into his newly purposed health system? His brain was spinning. He had to make some links. He had to talk to some of his advisors—and to some of the staff and ministers he would be working with.

It was weird. He'd resigned himself to this new life. But he'd never really felt the spark of excitement for it that he did now. The truth was he'd felt a little bitter about his future plans. Or maybe bitter was the wrong word, maybe it was overwhelmed. It was easy to work as a doctor somewhere and complain about lack of supplies or long hours. To be tasked with trying to implement change in a system that was so focused on finance? That was something else entirely. Free healthcare—even just maternity systems—would cost Corinez in a way that hadn't been experienced before. He had to pitch things just right.

The one thing he was sure about was that he wanted to do well.

And for the first time, things were starting to take shape in his mind.

Thanks to this. Thanks to Harry. Thanks to Arissa.

Her hand was still on his arm and it tightened a little as they walked through the next set of doors. She gave him a smile. Ahead of them was a whole heap of expectant waiting faces. Nurses, admin staff, kitchen aides and cleaning staff were all standing at the nursing station.

'Word does travel fast, doesn't it?' he said in wonder as they all started walking towards him.

'Welcome to Temur Sapora,' Arissa said as she raised her eyebrows.

Philippe surprised her. Of course, she'd pulled out her phone and emailed and checked his registration and references—which were all glowing. There was a small gap in the dates in his CV. But she wasn't concerned. Lots of doctors took a few months out at some point in their lives. Maybe that was why he was here?

After he'd done the obligatory baby checks under her scrutinising gaze, she'd almost expected him to disappear back to his luxury resort. But no.

He stayed at the hospital while the paediatrician did their own assessment of the little girl then admitted her overnight for observation. Instead of leaving, Philippe settled down in a chair next to the cot in the nursery. He even asked if he could give the baby her first feed, which she gulped hungrily.

He wasn't flustered when crowded by all the other staff who were anxious to see the new baby. In fact, he dealt with it like an old pro, smiling, answering politely and giving everyone a chance to see the new arrival. But what she did notice was the way he expertly circumvented answering specific questions about himself. It made her curious because she recognised the skill—it was something she'd done herself on occasion. How much did she actually know about this guy—apart from the fact he was a real doctor with good references? She made a note to try and find out if he'd been working in the last few months—that was where the gap in his CV was.

Eventually, they were left alone to get the baby settled. She still had half a mind that Philippe would make an excuse and go back to his bed in the luxury resort. But he didn't. He finished feeding the baby and changed her nappy, all the while firing questions at Arissa about the safe haven scheme and the outcomes for babies like this.

They finally settled on a name—suggested by one of the nursing staff—Dian.

Philippe rested back in the wide armchair and nestled Dian into the crook of his arm, stroking his finger across her forehead and down her nose. 'Well, little Dian, you've had an unusual start in this life. But you're here, you're safe, and hopefully your mum is too.'

Arissa could see a million things swirling around in his mind. Part of her wondered if a man who obviously came from money would be judgemental about what led a woman or girl to abandon their baby. But nothing like that came from his lips. All she could read on his face was empathy and part of her heart swelled in her chest at his reactions to little Dian.

In fact, he'd really surprised her. He sat there all night, asking a few questions about what would happen now with Dian, but mainly just holding the baby and talking to her.

'Aren't you tired?' Arissa asked finally.

'Sure.' He shrugged, but his dark brown eyes still had a bit of sparkle in them. 'But no more than usual.' He looked around. 'And this…' he smiled down at Dian '…is different. How many times as a doctor have you cursed yourself because you haven't had enough time to do something? How many times have you wanted a few more hours just to spend with a family, and give them some comfort?' He gave a little nod as he looked at Dian again. 'Tomorrow, Dian will go to a foster family, who'll hopefully have all the time in the world to support her. But for now…' his gaze met hers again '…it's you, and me.' Dian gave a little whimper and he tucked her up onto his shoulder and gently rubbed her back. 'And let's face it—this isn't so bad?' He stretched out his legs and put them on the low table in front of him. 'What else would a guy do? Eat fancy dinners? Drink champagne cocktails?' He winked. 'That is how you think I spend my time, isn't it?'

Her stomach gave a little flip. Maybe it was time to start making her facial expressions less obvious. 'I didn't say that.'

'Yeah.' He nodded, a gleam in his eye. 'You did. But let's just call it getting-to-know-you time.'

Heat rushed into her cheeks and she gave an embarrassed shudder, before biting her bottom lip and trying to get comfortable in the chair next to him.

She didn't want to leave Dian either. It just seemed wrong that this poor little girl would spend her first day on this earth without someone to cuddle her during the night. The hospital staff knew her. They weren't the least surprised to see her settle in for the night, and a few were already casting interested glances in Philippe's direction. By morning, tongues would be wagging. She'd just have to make sure she introduced him formally as the temporary clinic doctor.

He was singing. And it totally wasn't what she'd expected.

But to be honest she wasn't sure what she'd expected at all. All the preconceived ideas she might have had about her upper-class guest were rapidly disappearing out of the window.

They'd come straight here from the hospital and had a quick chat first thing about the types of patients who normally attended the clinic. Temur Sapora had once had a mining industry, so chest complaints were common in the older population. Philippe had volunteered to see all the respiratory complaints and he seemed to be doing well. Until she heard him singing…

She pulled back one of the curtains. 'What is that?' She couldn't help but ask.

Philippe was sitting next to an elderly local man whose shirt was open. Philippe had a stethoscope pressed to the man's chest and both were singing along and laughing. Philippe turned towards her. 'That,' he said in mock horror, 'is Frank Sinatra. You mean you didn't recognise it?' He tutted and shook his head. 'Youngsters these days, Rahim. They don't recognise one of the greats when they hear it.'

Arissa couldn't help the smile on her face. 'Oh, I recognise the greats, but no one could recognise that,' she said.

Rahim erupted in laughter, than started coughing and spluttering. Philippe shot her a look and stood up, moving to the nearby sink to wash his hands. 'It looks like Rahim has another chest infection. We were trying singing to see if it could help his lung capacity.'

He was choosing his words carefully. It was clear that Rahim, like many of the people around here, had chronic obstructive airways disease. His colour was poor and his breathing rapid. Any delay in treatment could end up in a hospital admission. Philippe moved over to the medicine cabinet. 'I'm going to dispense some antibiotics for Rahim to take away with him, so we can get him started on treatment without delay.'

She liked the way he was obviously trying to put the man at ease.

Now she really did smile. He knew that for a patient like Rahim, writing a prescription that would have to be taken to a pharmacy and dispensed wasn't the way to go. More often than not, patients like Rahim wouldn't fill their prescriptions. Some might assume it could be down to cost—and it could be, but not always. Other times some of the older patients didn't want to be a nuisance, or forgot to fill their prescriptions. There was a whole variety of reasons. But Philippe was doing exactly what she would have done—making sure the medicine was in the hands of the patient who required it.

The very fact that she didn't have to explain any of this to Philippe made her wonder about him a little bit more.

She gave him a nod and let him finish, moving on to the next patient.

A few hours later he appeared behind her, an empty coffee cup in his hand. 'Okay, I've snagged a cup. But where do we find the coffee?'

She glanced out at the waiting room that had finally quietened after her morning's immunisation clinic.

She gestured with her head. 'Come on. I'll take you to the magic.'

She led him through to the small kitchen at the back of the clinic, switched on the percolator and flicked open the nearest cupboard, which was stocked from top to bottom with a variety of coffee.

Philippe blinked, then laughed. He lifted his hand. 'What is it? Did some kind of rep come here and give you his whole supply?'

Arissa folded her arms and leaned against the wall, watching him for a few moments. 'Maybe. Or maybe it's just a rule that every doctor that works here has to buy their favourite kind of coffee before they leave.'

His eyes widened. 'Exactly how many doctors have you had working here?'

She gave a sigh. 'A lot. There are no permanent doctors here. Haven't been for years.'

He frowned as he pulled one of the packets of coffee from the cupboard, gave it a quick appreciative sniff and loaded it into the machine. 'So how on earth do you keep things running?'

She shook her head as she grabbed another mug. '*I* don't. We...' she held out her hands '...the community does. I commit all my holidays to working here.'

He stared at her for a few seconds. 'All of your holidays?'

She nodded. 'Sure. Have done for the last five years. Temur Sapora is home. This is where I'd come for my holidays anyway—so why not come here and work? We have lots of volunteers. Though I have to admit that the wound-healing project has definitely been a boost.'

The smell of coffee started to fill the room. 'So, you're telling me that this whole clinic is staffed by volunteers?'

She smiled. 'Yes, and no. There are three permanent nursing staff and two administrators. They're actually the most important people of all—they handle the rota.'

'So, there are more doctors like you?'

She could see just how many questions he wanted to ask.

She nodded. 'There's no university training for medicine on Temur Sapora. Anyone who wants to train as a doctor has to leave.'

He tilted his head to the side. 'And no one wants to come back full time?'

She instantly felt her hackles rise. He probably didn't mean to offend but she couldn't help how she felt.

'Hey.' He moved in front of her, his fingertips connecting with her arm. As she breathed she inhaled his sea-edged aftershave. 'That didn't quite come out the way it should.'

For a few seconds she didn't move, conscious of the expanse of his chest moving up and down under the pale blue shirt right in front of her face. She hadn't realised she was quite so short compared to him. She tipped her head upwards. Now she was this close, she could see the emerging stubble on his jawline—apparent after a night spent in the hospital. It rankled that he still managed to look this good with no real sleep or a change of clothes. It suddenly made her conscious of her own appearance.

His dark brown eyes smiled down at her apologetically. 'Sometimes things just come out a little awkwardly,' he said.

'They didn't seem to earlier. You had all the hospital staff practically sitting in the palm of your hand. Charm seemed like your main offensive.'

'Ouch.' He laughed, then ran his fingers through his dark hair. He hadn't moved. He was still only a few inches from her. 'I guess when I'm tired then the charm slips.' He held out both hands. 'What I meant to say is that I'm impressed. I've only been here two days and I'm impressed already. By the clinic, by the safe haven project. You're making me think about things. Work I could do back home.'

She wrinkled her nose. 'Aren't you supposed to be on holiday?'

'What can I say? I got bored.' The percolator started to bubble and this time he did step back.

It was the oddest sensation. She was almost sorry that he did.

She blinked and turned away, feeling instantly self-conscious. She fumbled in her trouser pocket to find a ponytail band, then tried to capture the errant curls that had escaped around her face. She pulled her hair upwards, then stared down at her wrinkled pink shirt. 'Maybe I should take five minutes and go home and change.'

He handed her a cup of steaming coffee. 'Why? You look fine. Gorgeous as ever.'

Her stomach clenched. The man who'd displaced Hugh Jackman from her 'if only' list had just called her gorgeous. As soon as the thought appeared in her head she pushed it away. She didn't have time to think like that. There was too much work to be done. Too many other things to sort out. He might be a doctor, but he was still a tourist. Temur Sapora would be just a fleeting visit to him. Nothing more. Nothing less.

She pulled herself back to the conversation from earlier. 'If I came back here permanently, then I'd have to work as a generalist. I've spent the last year specialising in Paediatric Oncology. It's where my heart lies. But because there's a smaller population on Temur Sapora there wouldn't be that opportunity to specialise.' The aroma of coffee was drifting around her, overpowering the teasing smell of his aftershave and allowing her to concentrate again. 'It's the same for the rest of my colleagues who volunteer here. One is a surgeon, another a cardiologist, another an endocrinologist. In fact—' she gave a little smile '—we probably cover just about every speciality that there is—and that has its benefits too.'

She glanced through the glass-panelled door to the waiting room outside. It was the first time in days there hadn't been a number of patients waiting to be seen— partly because Philippe was proving so useful. She gave a little nod and sat down on the comfortable sofa in the staff room. 'There's a few children whose cases I can review and treatment plans I can look over while I'm here.'

Philippe settled onto the sofa beside her, his thigh brushing against hers. 'They don't go to the mainland for treatment?'

She shook her head. 'The mainland is a four-hour flight away. The truth is it's expensive, and it's not just the flights. It's the hospital treatment once you get there, and room and board for the families. It all adds up.'

He took a sip of the coffee, sighed and rested back on the sofa, closing his eyes for a second. 'You're right, it does. I guess none of us has really mastered the health-care system yet of our countries.'

It seemed an odd thing to say. She let out a little laugh. 'And why would that be our job? We just have to work in the system. Not design it.'

It was as if she'd just given him a sharp jab. His eyes flew open and he sat bolt upright again. 'What? Oh, of course, yeah. You're right.'

She frowned. 'Dr Aronaz? Are you okay? Do you want to get some sleep?'

He shook his head. For the briefest of seconds he'd had that rabbit-caught-in-the-headlights kind of look. But he seemed to shake it off as quickly as it had appeared. This guy had a real talent for smoothing things over.

Something prickled in the back of her brain. Something vaguely familiar that she just couldn't place. But before she could think about it any more, Philippe had turned to face her. 'Hey, we haven't had a chance to discuss the research project on wound healing yet. Why don't you run me through it and tell me what you need me to do to assist?'

Of course. For the last few days there hadn't really been a chance to keep things as up to date as she wanted. The project was proving really successful and it was vital she made sure the research was recorded accurately. If things worked out, it could eventually lead to better funding for the clinic. She had to keep the long-term goal in mind. She set down her coffee and pulled over a laptop from the nearby counter. 'Sure, let me show you what we're doing...'

# CHAPTER FOUR

HE WAS TIRED. He was more than tired. But being around Arissa was keeping him on his toes. She seemed to be the adrenaline shot that he needed to keep going.

She'd checked his references—of course she had. But he'd been lucky that a quick call to the palace had resulted in them arranging an emergency visa for him to work in Malaysia—so all his credentials had been in order.

The research here was fascinating. The locally made, natural ointment was producing worthy results. He predicted as soon as this research was published there would be a variety of manufacturers vying for their attention.

Leg ulcers were a worldwide problem. Generally a product of old age, a deteriorating circulatory system and lack of mobility, they were one of the most chronic, slow-healing wounds to deal with. Philippe had encountered patients before who'd had leg ulcers for years that sometimes showed a few signs of healing, then broke down all over again. So far the ointment they were using on Temur Sapora was showing remarkable results.

The data collection was meticulous. He'd reviewed six of the patients using the ointment today, and another six patients who were being treated with an alternative ointment. Photographing the wounds, documenting the treatment plans and recording the patients' observations had actually been kind of fun. It had been years since he'd been involved in any kind of research study, and this one had real promise.

He stretched his arms above his head as Arissa came into the room. 'Are you done?'

She put a hand on his shoulder. He nodded. 'Just finished. It's taken me back to my student days, and I forgot how much I love all this stuff.'

She gave a tired smile. 'I just wanted to say thanks. You doing this has given me a chance to review the kids I wanted to.'

He could see the tiny lines around her eyes. 'All good?'

She pressed her lips together. 'One is sicker than I hoped and doesn't seem to have responded well to treatment. I've made some recommendations for changes.'

'Would the kid have done better on the mainland?'

He could see her muscles tense. 'Maybe. Who knows? But the rest of the family wouldn't. There's only Mum. And she has four children. If she'd taken her son to the mainland, she would likely have had to leave the others behind.'

He gave a slow nod. He knew exactly what she didn't want to say. Although many child blood disorders were now curable—not everyone had the same outcome. He could tell this case was bothering her.

He stood up. 'Come on,' he said.

She looked confused. 'What?'

He leaned over and grabbed his jacket, shutting down the computer quickly. 'It's been a long day. I'm going to shout you dinner.'

She shook her head. 'You don't have to do that.'

'Yes, I do. Come on.'

She shook her head again. 'No. It's late, you must be tired. You've already given up your holiday.'

He extended his hand out towards her. 'As have you.'

He wasn't going to listen to any of those half-hearted excuses. He'd only had a glimpse of the type of person that she was—and it was enough. She'd had to move away to study. Her long-term career path couldn't be here—but that didn't mean she wasn't prepared to give up all her holidays in order to pay back a little to the place she called home.

If he was tired—how was she?

When was the last time Arissa Cotter had been pampered? Taken out for dinner? Looked after?

There was something behind those eyes that he hadn't got to the bottom of. And after only a couple of days he couldn't expect to. But that didn't mean that he wasn't curious.

She hadn't taken his hand yet. 'Do you really want to go back home and eat barbecue snack noodles?' he teased.

She sighed, then laughed. 'Actually I planned to have frozen pizza and some candy bars.'

He put one hand on his hip, leaving his other hand deliberately still extended. 'Oh, it was one of those kind of nights.'

She shrugged. 'Maybe. I hadn't quite decided yet.'

'Well, I have. I spotted a restaurant in the next street over I want to try.'

Her tired eyes twinkled. 'Which one?'

He looked directly at his outstretched hand. 'You have to agree to come before I tell you.'

It was almost like a stand-off. She reached for her

denim jacket and put her hand in his. 'How about you let me pick your dinner?'

Right now, he'd agree to any terms. 'What, you know the boss? You get a discount?' he joked.

She rolled her eyes. 'Like you need one.'

His stomach gave a tiny twist. Maybe he wasn't as incognito as he'd thought.


Fifteen minutes later she'd ordered all her favourites. Homemade *roti canai*, *roti telor* and curry chicken, Indonesian fried rice and seafood soup. The aroma made her stomach rumble loudly and he turned towards her and laughed.

She gestured towards the array of dishes on the table. 'You asked for recommendations.'

His eyebrows rose. '*All* of them?'

'Absolutely. Dig in. The food here is the best around.'

Philippe didn't hang around, he filled up his plate and sampled everything.

She couldn't help but watch him. He'd changed just before they came here and the black polo shirt made his eyes seem even darker. He signalled to the waiter for some wine and waited until they both had a glass.

She took a sip and leaned back in her chair.

'When was the last time you actually relaxed?'

'What do you mean?'

'I can practically see the knots in your shoulders.'

She shook her head. 'No, you can't. And I told you, this is what I like to do on my holidays.'

'But then you're never really not working.'

She took in a deep breath. 'I know. But it's what I do. And it's not just me. There are others too.' She ran her fingers up and down the stem of the wine glass. 'It's called giving back. I guess in a world of non-stop technology and the search for perfection it's kind of been forgotten along the way.'

He set down his knife and fork and smiled at her. 'You've no idea how good that is to hear.'

She met his gaze and gave a sad kind of smile. 'I sometimes feel as if life is rushing past.' She held out her hand and looked out of the window to the street outside. Even though it was late at night the streets in Temur Sapora were still vibrant with life. The street markets lasted until late in the evening, packed stalls with brightly coloured strips of red and yellow forming the roofs. Business was brisk and the chatter lively.

'I love this place,' she said quietly. 'I love coming back here.' She took a deep breath then met his watchful gaze. 'But I love my work too.'

'Where are you based now?'

'In Washington. It's great. The team I work with is special. The patients—even more so. I've learned so much.' She kept talking. 'When I come back here I work as a generalist. That's important. I like it. Sometimes, when we specialise, we lose sight of everything else.'

He sat back and looked at her with interest. 'But, when you love something so much, how can you give it up?'

It was the way he said the words, the tiny edge to them that made something inside stand to attention. 'I'm not giving it up,' she said carefully. 'It's still in my heart. I'm just compromising for a few weeks.'

His eyes fixed on his hands on the table. She could tell he was thinking about something else. 'Sometimes we have to do things for other people.' She put her hand on her heart. 'I like that I do that. It keeps me sane. Stops me getting wrapped up in the whirlwind of the world.'

He looked back up to meet her gaze again. Her heart was thudding against her chest. What was it she didn't know about this guy?

It was weird. It was almost as if he had some kind of aura around him. Something weighing him down.

Her fingers drummed lightly on the table. 'I have to do this. I get so wrapped up in my patients that this is the equivalent of a break for me.' She picked up her napkin and twisted it between her fingers. 'When you're dealing with kids with a potentially terminal condition, it's so easy to let it take over. To search everywhere for the possibility of a new treatment or cure. I get so focused on my work that I forget what else is out there sometimes.'

'Isn't that what everyone wants? A doctor who is committed and dedicated?'

She licked her lips, choosing her words carefully. 'But what if you can't let go? What if you miss something important because you can't see outside your own little box?' She twisted the napkin again. 'I learned a few years ago, to take time to take a breath—to take stock. Some people go skiing. Some people go to the beach—like the resort you were staying at. Some people hire a cabin in the mountains to hide out in. Some people turn off the Internet, the phone and read books.'

A hand reached over and covered hers. She hadn't even realised that her hands were trembling. His warm touch encompassed both of her hands and made her suck in a deep, steadying breath.

Here was she worrying about what he wasn't telling her, but wearing her heart on her sleeve instead. He spoke in a low voice. 'But sometimes you come to a place expecting nothing, and get a whole lot more than you bargained for. Sometimes you don't know what you were looking for until it jumps out and finds you.'

She closed her eyes for a second, her heart rate increasing. Was he talking about work, or something else? It seemed ridiculous to imagine that he could be talking about her—they barely knew each other.

But something was in the air between them. She knew it. And she thought he did too.

He just sat for a few minutes, his hand still over hers. When she opened her eyes again he wasn't staring at her. He was looking at the dark sky outside, his mind obviously someplace else.

Instantly she felt embarrassed, pushing any stray imaginary thoughts aside.

But when Philippe met her gaze he just said simply, 'How about we take a walk? I haven't been on the beach yet in Temur Sapora and I hear it's one of your biggest tourist attractions.'

She was glad of the easy diversion. 'Sure, as a resident it's my duty to show you around. A walk on the beach at this time of night will be perfect.'

The restaurant was only a few minutes' stroll from the beach. Arissa bent to unfasten her sandals as they got there. He stopped for a few seconds to watch. She grabbed hold of her dress as it fluttered in the ocean wind.

The edge of the beach was lined with thick green foliage. Philippe brushed against some, sending a host of pink butterflies into the dark purple sky. Arissa let out a little yelp, then stood laughing with her hands wide, letting them flutter against her skin.

Philippe stuck his hands into the pockets of his jeans. It was the most relaxed he'd looked since he'd got there.

They strolled down next to the rippling ocean. There were a few other couples quietly walking on the beach.

'What happens when you go back?' asked Philippe. 'Do you have someone else lined up to work here?'

She nodded as she kicked at the sand with her bare toes. 'I have a colleague who is a surgeon in Texas. He'll cover the two weeks after I leave.'

'And he'll pick up the research study?'

She bit her bottom lip. 'Yes, well, he should. He's the lead researcher. When the study gets published it will be under his name.'

Philippe stopped walking and turned to face her. 'Why would the study be under his name? I've seen all the files on the computer. This is your study. You made the discovery. You applied for the research ethics and grant. You arranged the protocols. Why on earth wouldn't you publish as the lead researcher?'

She sighed and looked out across the dark ocean. The night sky was littered with sparkling stars, reflecting on the midnight-blue rippling water. She ran her fingers through her hair. She was stalling. She knew that. She wasn't exactly sure how to put this into words.

'This study is going well. It's going better than well. I didn't discover this ointment. It's made from natural products found on Temur Sapora. This ointment was something my grandmother used when I was a child, and her grandmother before her. I just decided to do official research to see how well it actually works.'

'*You* decided,' he emphasised.

She reached up and released her curls from their band, allowing them to fall around her shoulders. 'I just pulled things together. That's all.'

He folded his arms across his chest and moved in front

of her, blocking her view of the ocean. The ocean breeze sent his aftershave drifting around her like some sort of protective cloak. His voice was low. 'That's not really an answer. Why don't you want to lead the paper?'

She wrinkled her nose. 'I just…'

'Just?' Now he was smiling, his eyebrows raised. It didn't matter how much she hedged, he wasn't going to let her off with this one.

She sighed again and pointed to the sand. 'Let's sit for a minute.'

He tilted his head to the side and gave her a curious glance then nodded his head. 'Hmm, okay. Let's sit.'

She waited a few seconds until he settled down next to her. She pushed her hand against the cooling sand. It was pressed down hard from the people who'd walked on the beach all day, so she dug her fingers into the sand and pulled some up to run through her fingers.

'So, Dr Arissa Cotter,' he said, 'why on earth wouldn't you want your name on a research paper that's probably going to be widely read, have great acclaim and maybe lead to some money-making opportunities?'

'I don't care about the money,' she said quickly.

He turned his head to face her. 'I might have guessed that already.'

She kept playing with the sand, pressing it between her fingers and letting it grind together. 'The truth is, there's been a whole host of doctors working on this research. The project has lasted around a year. You know that the healing of an ulcer is always a slow process.'

'But not the ulcers you've treated with the ointment,' he said swiftly.

She gave a short laugh. 'Ahh, you've been paying attention. But ulcers we've treated with the placebo—some of them haven't healed at all, so to make a fair comparison I wanted to wait almost a year. I don't want our research to be criticised for short-changing the alternatives.'

'So, the findings are good. Isn't it time to tell the world?'

She nodded her head slowly. 'Yes, it is. But this ointment? It's good. It's *really* good.'

He shook his head again. 'I don't get it. If it was about the money, I could understand you wanting to hold off and get a product licence or patent on the product. But, if it's not about the money, why the delay?'

She pulled a face. 'I don't think this ointment will just do well. I think it will do brilliantly. Just how long has the world waited for something that is more or less guaranteed to heal the biggest chronic leg condition in the world?'

'Exactly. Arissa, what aren't you telling me? Most doctors would be delighted to be part of this research. The prestige you'll get from this alone is amazing.'

She swallowed, her mouth suddenly dry. 'What if I don't want the prestige?' she whispered.

He frowned and reached over to touch her arm. 'What?'

She shook her head. 'I think this research will pretty much explode. There will be conferences and presentations. There will be expectations that I should chat to press about the research and the findings.' She pressed her lips together. 'That's not me. I don't like that. I don't want to be in the public eye.'

He looked stunned. It was the only word to describe the look on his face.

Her stomach was churning. This was personal; it was a bit of herself she didn't like to reveal, but she'd thought he'd understand—chalk it up to anxiety. So many of her friends and colleagues wouldn't dream of being interviewed or standing in front of a room full of people to present research findings. And while that might not be her reason for resisting being lead publisher on the research paper, it was the one she'd fall back on for now.

'That's it?' he queried again.

She nodded. 'There are plenty of other doctors who have worked on this project who would love to be named on the research. I'm happy to step aside. I'm happy to let them deal with all the publicity around it.'

She let out a wry laugh. 'And anyway, my speciality is paediatric oncology, not wound healing.'

But it was clear he wasn't really buying it. 'What you've done here is good. Just about any doctor I know would want to have their name attached to this.'

'Including you?' she snapped. She was getting frustrated now.

He spoke carefully, deep lines appearing on his face as he tried to keep things in check. 'Arissa, this work could be monumental. Headline making.'

'Exactly, and I don't want to make headlines. I'd much rather be in the background.'

It was apparent he didn't understand. 'I just think credit should be given where it is due.'

'Leave it, Philippe.' She was tired. 'I want the research out there. I just don't want to be in the spotlight. I don't want to be in the spotlight at all.'

His face became firm and her stomach flipped a little. For a while it had seemed as if they were about to get to know each other better. The walls around him had come down a bit and she wondered how much more there was to find out about Philippe Aronaz.

But her actions and words had just killed that chance.

She sighed as he stood up and brushed the sand from his trousers. Ever the gentleman, he waited for her to stand up too and put her sandals back on her feet.

The walk home was silent and she blamed herself for the painful awkwardness of it all.

'See you tomorrow?' she said as she finally reached her door. She couldn't help the hopeful tone in her voice.

'Of course.' His answer was perfunctory and delivered with a sharp nod. She watched as he turned and strode down the quiet street.

After a few seconds she rested her head on her door and gave it a half-hearted thump. The guy had given up his holiday to help out at her clinic. He'd offered to help with the research so it didn't fall behind. He didn't need to do any of those things.

He'd taken her to dinner then asked her to go for a walk when it was clear she was still stressed. The guy should be getting nominated for some kind of sainthood. Her?

She'd behaved like Mrs Angry and Mrs Ungrateful. He couldn't possibly understand her feelings because she hadn't wanted to explain. She didn't feel as if she could. She still couldn't put her finger on it.

Maybe it was the fact she was trying to deny how good-looking and charming he actually was. She was fighting any possible attraction for reasons that only she could understand.

It wasn't wise to mix business with pleasure—even for such a short duration. Plus the fact she still thought there was a lot more beneath the surface of Philippe. There was the distinct impression he wasn't telling her everything she might want to know.

Then, there was the underlying class issue. Money was an issue for her. She knew that people who had money acted differently from the rest of the population. She'd seen it. She'd witnessed it. She didn't need or want to be around anyone that might make her feel 'not good enough' even if it was only in her head.

She sighed and looked up at the dark night sky above, fumbling in her pocket for her key. Every bone in her body ached. Her eyelids were heavy.

She couldn't wait to get to bed.

Tomorrow was another day. She would wake with the intention of making sure Philippe knew she was grateful for his assistance.

It was time to start with a clean slate.

# CHAPTER FIVE

PHILIPPE WOKE UP with a growing headache. He wandered over to the glass doors and pulled back the curtains. The turquoise sea was rippling next to the white sand beach decorated by luxury parasols and sunloungers.

He could spend the day there. He could find a book, some sunscreen and lie down for the day, sipping whatever beverage he decided would suit.

It made him want to laugh out loud, because, even with the headache, he knew he would never do it. He rifled through his luggage to find some paracetamol, swallowing them with some water as his concierge showed up with breakfast.

Toast and English breakfast tea. He had decidedly simple tastes.

He glanced at his watch and sat down. It was just past six a.m. His internal body clock just wouldn't let him sleep any longer.

He glanced at his emails, dealing with a few from his father, brother, sister and his personal palace secretary, but, no matter how hard he tried, his thoughts kept drifting back to Arissa and last night.

He'd known that she was overtired. He could tell when she was on edge.

But last night's conversation had gone in a direction he hadn't intended or expected. There had been a real spark of conviction. Determination from Arissa. A real don't-mess-with-me moment.

It set so many alarms pulsing through him.

He was a doctor. He had difficult conversations on a daily basis. He'd always thought he was good at reading signs from his patients. When they were stressed. When they were hiding something. When they were lying.

He'd thought his instincts were normally good. He knew when to push, and when to let something go.

But last night with Arissa it seemed all his usual instincts had flown up into the glittering night sky.

He'd pressed and pressed her when he knew he shouldn't. He just couldn't understand how someone would be part of such an important research project and not want to take any credit for it.

Publishing research was huge in the medical world. Some of his colleagues desperately fought to be involved in studies that they thought could lead to publication and prestige. He'd met people before who genuinely weren't interested in clinical research and just wanted to focus on the job, but he'd never met someone who'd taken part and didn't want to be included in the final result.

It was odd. It was beyond odd. Particularly when, once she had a national platform, she could also use it to talk about the thing that really was true to her heart—the safe haven project. She could find a way to tie the things together. He knew he would.

Her half-hearted explanation of it not being her field hadn't washed with him. Plenty of people changed their speciality or kept an open plan, allowing them to be involved in several projects. It had to be something else—

but right now, particularly when he wasn't being entirely honest himself, he didn't feel in a position to push any further.

Arissa appeared to be entirely unique.

But then he'd already thought that when he'd met her.

Philippe had dated plenty of women. You only had to pick up the gossip magazines of Corinez to see the play-boy prince tag that wasn't entirely unjustified. He might have gone on a bit of a dating frenzy after the actress fiasco. Whether that was to try and get over his hurt, or just to try and get back out there, he wasn't quite sure. Somehow he had a feeling that if Arissa learned of the playboy prince tag she wouldn't be entirely impressed.

It didn't help that his brother, Anthony, had been dat-ing his wife-to-be for practically his entire life. There was no gossip there—no story. So the press had to con-centrate on someone.

He'd spent most of his life in the spotlight. It was part and parcel of being a prince and, although sometimes in-trusive, he'd got used to it.

His stomach growled and he quickly ate the toast, dressing as he drank the tea. It was still before seven as he reached the clinic.

His hand hesitated at the handle of the door. What if Arissa was still in a bad mood? What if she was still un-happy with him? He would have to try and make some amends.

As soon as he pushed open the door his nose wrinkled at the smell—the very enticing smell.

Steam was coming from two coffee cups sitting on the table in the staff room, along with a plate of chocolate croissants. It seemed there was a French bakery some-where in Temur Sapora.

'Oh, you're here.' Arissa halted as she walked over with another plate in her hands. Her hair was loose around her shoulders and she was wearing a green knee-length shirt dress with a simple tie at the waist. As he moved closer the scent of freesias drifted towards him. He'd noticed it before around her, either her shampoo or her perfume.

'Yes, I'm here,' he said carefully. 'Weren't you expecting me?'

She licked her lips and pushed one of the plates towards him. She seemed nervous. 'Yes, well, I'd hoped you'd still come. Here. I brought a peace offering.'

He tried to hide the smile that wanted to appear as relief flooded through him. 'Why would you need a peace offering?'

She gave a forced kind of smile. 'I think I might have been a bit uptight last night. I thought a visit to our French bakery might stop you deciding to withdraw your services.'

He pulled out a chair and sat down, sliding one of the coffees towards him. 'You thought I would withdraw my services?' Now he truly was surprised.

She gave a half-shrug. 'I might have stayed up half the night worrying about it.'

He shook his head and reached over and squeezed her hand. 'Don't be silly. I'm not going to walk away and leave you on your own.' He raised his eyebrows. 'No matter how cranky you are.'

She mimicked his expression, raising her own eyebrows. 'Cranky?' she queried, grabbing one of the chocolate croissants and ripping it in half, revealing the half-melted chocolate.

He nodded as he took a sip of the coffee. 'Oh, yeah,

you're definitely cranky. But, hey, you're stuck with me for the next couple of weeks. I told you. I'm bored.'

He was keeping things simple. If he didn't ask Arissa too many questions, hopefully she would return the favour. It was nice being under the radar for a while and there were benefits to keeping it that way.

The last few months working in one of the hospitals in Corinez had been a different experience from working across the globe. He'd started to take for granted the anonymity of working in other countries. Back home in Corinez everyone knew who he was. Some even addressed him as 'Your Highness'. As much as he wished it wouldn't, it impacted on his work. He'd found things much more difficult back home. But here in Temur Sapora he was regaining the chance of just being Philippe, the regular doctor. Not Philippe, the Prince. And he'd forgotten how much he missed that.

But it seemed that Arissa didn't want to go into too many details herself. She gave a grateful nod and reached for a laptop. 'I have a way to stop you being bored.'

'You do?' He leaned a little closer.

She pulled up some lists of patients. 'There's a number of patients I'd like to review today—and, if you don't mind, there's a few I'd like you to review too.'

Philippe gave a nod and turned the laptop towards him as he glanced over the list of patients. There was a wide variety. A few of them were on the research study, some had already attended the clinic with chest complaints and been asked to return for review. Another few had minor complaints and required stitches removed.

Philippe gave a smile. Nothing here was arduous. 'No problem. Happy to review all these patients, plus any others that appear at the clinic today.' He glanced at the list that Arissa had prepared for herself. It was full of more children with blood disorders. A completely specialised area that he knew she was best to work on herself.

She leaned her head on her hand and he could see her shoulders visibly relax as she tore off another part of the croissant.

He waited until she'd started chewing before he spoke again. 'So, I wondered if we could make a trade.'

She stopped chewing and narrowed her gaze suspiciously. 'What kind of trade?'

'A trade for finding out more about the safe haven scheme.'

'You're genuinely interested?'

'Of course I am. You set it up in your country, I want to see if I can set it up in mine.'

The words were out before he really thought about them. 'What country is that, exactly?' she asked.

He pasted on a smile again. 'Just one of the lesser-known Mediterranean countries. It's not well known but near to France, Italy and Monaco.'

She opened her mouth as if she was going to ask him to be more specific but he cut her off quickly. 'Tell me as much as you can before the patients get here.'

The clinic was busy. The weather had been stormy these last few days and it seemed to have irritated just about anyone with a chest condition. She'd spent the morning dealing with kids and adults with asthma, older patients with chronic obstructive pulmonary disease, and a variety of chest infections.

The nurses were triaging the patients as best they could, and, in the midst of all the chest complaints, they'd had a man with an MI who they'd had to refer on to the hospital, along with a kid with a fractured wrist that required surgery.

She rounded the corner to speak to Philippe about something but stopped as he was bending over a small boy with a lacerated finger. He was speaking quietly but seemed to have really engaged with the child.

'Okay, I'm going to need you to be my really brave champion.' Philippe glanced over his shoulder as if it were a great secret. 'I mean like a superhero.'

The little boy was mesmerised and Philippe started telling him a superhero story to distract him from the stitches. He was finished in a matter of minutes. Then he threw the little boy in the air, declaring him a new champion superhero. They finished with a fist bump and the little boy left the clinic with a wide smile on his face.

She stopped for a second and gave a sigh. It was just another plus point of the guy she was still a bit unsure of.

Philippe was great to work with. No patient was a problem and she trusted his judgement. He seemed to have tireless energy and could last all day on coffee alone. She envied his commitment. And it made her even more curious about him. A guy who could afford to stay at one of the luxury resorts in Temur Sapora was happier slogging his guts out in a community clinic? She couldn't make it up.

But it just made the underlying attraction she felt towards him smoulder even more.

Even watching him from afar was becoming more than a little distracting. He had such a way with the patients, and the few conditions that he came across and was unfamiliar with, he wasn't afraid to come and ask for advice. She liked that. She'd worked with way too many doctors who were arrogant enough never to admit their own lack of knowledge—often to the patient's detriment.

She couldn't quite put her finger on it. There was something about him that wasn't quite off, but just wasn't quite right. Maybe it was her own hang-ups about the rich, the very rich and the very, very rich, that were skewing her normally sound judgement. But whatever it was, the person he was, the *man* he was, was definitely getting under her skin.

Besides the good looks and charm, Philippe Aronaz was, at heart, a good guy. Occasionally he drifted off someplace, as if there was something else on his mind, but most of the time he was focused. He related well to the patients. In fact, it was one of the things that was most impressive about him. He could talk to literally anyone, from cajoling the youngest baby, to having lengthy discussions with some of their most elderly patients. It was almost as if he'd been born to it. And she envied him. She'd had to work hard at that part of herself.

There was always that little part of herself she didn't want to share. She'd shared it once with a colleague at medical school, but the reaction hadn't been good. Her colleague had instantly wanted to do an Internet search on abandoned babies, cross-check with hospital admissions that could be related to childbirth, and search DNA ancestry websites. It almost turned into a personal quest.

They couldn't understand why Arissa didn't want to do all that. They couldn't understand why she wasn't desperate to find out where she came from. Of course, they couldn't begin to realise what it felt like to be abandoned by her mother. To have to spend endless nights wondering if she wasn't good enough, wasn't pretty enough.

Her adoptive parents had told her she was a special

angel sent to them from heaven. They'd filled her with such happiness, but told her honestly about her start in life. Arissa had never wanted to be anyone's 'project'. And after that first reaction of sharing her background, she'd learned to keep quiet.

She'd originally lived in one of the smaller villages in Temur Sapora, so no one in the capital city knew her story. No one questioned her dedication to getting the safe haven project off the ground and she'd managed to keep that part of her past out of the public eye. So, trying to connect with patients—opening herself up to people, even just a little—was something she'd struggled with. So, she'd taken steps to stop closing herself off to her patients and their families. Working in paediatric oncology meant she was exposed to a huge amount of joy and pain—she had to be able to have difficult conversations at any point in the day. She had to give people a spark of hope while keeping things realistic. And sometimes she just had to be there, in body and in mind. And she couldn't do that without connecting with people, without exposing a little of herself.

Watching Philippe do things so easily reminded her how hard she'd found her job for a while. It didn't make her resentful. It just made her a little sad that she'd had that experience.

Philippe appeared behind her as she was finishing some notes on a child she'd just seen.

'I phoned to check on the kid yesterday with the fractured ulna and radius. They had to pin it, but the operation went well.'

'So, no more diving off the rocks and crashing into the sea bed?'

He smiled. 'I think we can safely say his mother will

have him bound to some kind of deckchair for the rest of the holiday.'

Arissa pulled a leaflet from the wall. 'I might give the paed ward a call and ask them to steer him towards the community centre. They have less harmful activities for kids during the day that could stop him getting bored.'

Philippe looked over the leaflet and nodded. 'No worries, I'll do it. Nothing worse than a bored, overactive nine-year-old.'

She gave a grateful smile and picked up the list for this afternoon. It was an immunisation clinic and was packed full. Several of the babies had missed some of their routine vaccinations due to coughs, colds and a bout of chicken pox that had been doing the rounds of the local nursery. She put a star at several of the names, taking note that if they didn't show today, she would give them a follow-up call.

'We should break for lunch. Want me to go and grab something?' Philippe asked.

She laughed. 'What—like yesterday?'

Yesterday he'd gone to grab lunch and couldn't make up his mind, coming back with the most bizarre range of foods she'd ever seen—none of which had gone together.

The muffled scream came out of nowhere and they both froze.

Arissa turned, trying to locate where the sound had come from, but Philippe was quicker, heading straight to the front door of the clinic and out onto the street.

She followed him with rapid steps. He stood for a few seconds until he heard the scream again, then moved across the street,

A few people glanced at them. It was a baby crying.

Babies cried all the time, but the noise put Arissa's teeth on edge.

Outside the grocery store a tired-looking woman had a small baby on her shoulder, patting its back soothingly.

Arissa recognised her instantly. It was Mariam, one of the local mothers who was due to attend with her baby this afternoon.

She shook her head at Arissa. 'Looks like we won't be getting this immunisation either.' She sighed. 'Rosni has been unsettled all night and she's got a bit of a temperature. Her big brother just had chicken pox. I wonder if she's next.'

The baby screamed again, a high–pitched noise, and Philippe held his hands out straight away, giving Arissa a warning glance. 'Would you mind if I take a look at her?' he said.

When Mariam hesitated he quickly explained. 'I'm one of the doctors that's helping Arissa at the clinic. Dr Aronaz. Do you mind if I take a look at your daughter?'

Mariam's brow creased, instantly worried. 'Do you think there's something wrong?'

Philippe's voice was steady. 'Why don't we just give her a check to be on the safe side?'

Prickles ran down Arissa's spine; she didn't like the sound of the scream any more than Philippe did, but it was clear he had something else on his mind.

She gestured across the road and slid her arm around the woman's waist. 'Come on, Mariam. The clinic's open and there's no one there right now. Let's give Rosni a check and see if she's about to come down with chicken pox.'

Arissa was sure that Philippe wouldn't be reacting

like this over a case of chicken pox, but she didn't want to alarm Mariam.

Mariam held out Rosni with slightly shaking hands and Philippe took her quickly and pulled the blanket down that was tucked around her. He gave a nod of his head. 'Let's go over to the clinic.'

It only took a few moments to reach the clinic and set Rosni down on one of the examination tables. Arissa pulled out a tympanic thermometer and pulse oximeter as Philippe gently peeled back Rosni's clothes, speaking to her in a soothing manner.

But Rosni was clearly agitated, her legs and arms flailing wildly and the high-pitched scream continuing.

'Has she fed at all?' he asked Mariam.

Mariam shook her head. 'I tried to feed her all night but she just wasn't interested. I eventually gave her some water this morning—it was all I could get her to take.'

'Have you given her any acetaminophen?'

Mariam shook her head. 'I was just about to buy some. They sell it in the grocery store.'

Philippe continued his examination. When the temperature gauge sounded a few seconds later she turned the screen towards him. The baby's temperature was dangerously high and her heart rate rapid. Rosni continued with the high-pitched wailing as Philippe checked her over. The baby appeared to have bouts of agitation, between periods of sluggishness. Philippe murmured to Arissa, 'Look.' He ran his fingers over the baby's fontanelle. It was bulging slightly.

She started and walked quickly over to one of the locked clinic cupboards. She grabbed some IV antibiotics, some acetaminophen, and some other equipment from the cupboards.

Philippe narrowed his gaze in question. He was still examining Rosni, checking the palms of her hands, soles of her feet and eyes. There was no obvious rash right now, but sometimes in Malaysian children rashes could be difficult to spot. He shook his head.

Mariam was getting more anxious by the minute. 'What's wrong with my baby?'

Arissa gave Philippe a quick nod of her head. It didn't matter that this was her clinic. She'd never had a child with meningitis before and it was clear that Philippe had got this.

He bent to speak to Mariam. 'We have to act quickly, Mariam. I think Rosni might have meningococcal meningitis. I can see from her chart she's had her first vaccination but not the rest.'

'She's been sick. There hasn't been time…'

Philippe put his hand on Mariam's shoulder. 'This isn't your fault. We don't normally see meningitis in babies as young as Rosni. She's just unlucky.'

'You're sure that's what it is?' Mariam's voice was trembling.

He gave a sorry nod. 'I've heard this scream only once before.'

Arissa stepped up alongside him. 'It's important we give Rosni antibiotics as soon as possible. We have them here—for emergency circumstances like these.'

'Shouldn't she go to hospital?'

Arissa nodded. 'Yes, absolutely. But if we call an ambulance now it will still be over an hour before you reach the hospital. We'll start the antibiotics now before we call the ambulance.'

Philippe picked Rosni up and put her on the baby scale for a second, taking a quick note of her weight. It only took a few moments to work out how much of the medicines to give the baby and Philippe found a tiny vein quickly to slide in an IV portal. 'Just as well you've got these,' he said quietly as Arissa bent beside him to assist.

She gave a brief nod. 'Let's just say we've learned over the years to plan for every contingency.' Her shirt was sticking to her back and she gave an uncomfortable shudder. 'But I'm glad I've never had to do this before.'

His hand closed over hers for a few seconds as she passed over the syringe with the antibiotics. His eyes turned to the clock to begin the administration. 'Hopefully this is a one-off,' he said. 'You call the ambulance, then I guess we'll spend the rest of the day contact tracing.'

She sucked in a breath. She hadn't even thought of that. Of course.

She couldn't help but admire how smoothly he'd handled all this. It was likely she would have gone outside to see whose baby had been crying like that—but would she have recognised the signs of meningitis as quickly as Philippe had?

As an ER doc it was likely he'd had cases before. Any case she'd dealt with in paediatrics had already been diagnosed, or been under investigation, by the time they'd got to her. She'd had to perform lumbar punctures to guarantee a diagnosis on small children before, but most of the initial diagnostics had already been recognised.

Arissa made the call for the ambulance, then phoned the referral through to the hospital so they would be ready to expect the patient. She then grabbed a chart to make some notes and went back to Mariam. 'I know you also have a son, Mariam. Are there any other children in the house?'

She shook her head. 'Just my son, Vasan. He's three.'

Arissa took a quick note. 'I'll arrange for some oral antibiotics for your son. Anyone else in the household? Or has Rosni been at nursery?' She tried to be as methodical as possible, taking all the notes she should to ensure that anyone potentially exposed to meningitis would be identified and protected.

Philippe continued the slow and steady administration of the antibiotic, monitoring the baby for any reaction. Rosni was still agitated—the medications taking time to take effect. The ambulance arrived around fifteen minutes later, the paramedic more than capable of dealing with their charge.

By the time the ambulance left Arissa was exhausted. She slumped against the door jamb and took a deep breath.

Philippe sat down at one of the tables and put his head in his hands. She realised instantly he was upset, much more than his calm demeanour had implied. She walked over and, after hesitating for a second, sat down at right angles to him, close enough to touch him.

She reached up her hand, holding it just next to his hand before changing her mind and edging her seat closer. She took both his hands in hers and lowered them to the table. His head was still bowed. So, she took a deep breath and lowered her head so her forehead was against his.

His voice was low, throaty. 'Once you hear the cry you never forget it.'

His breath was warm next to her skin. She could see the faintest tremble in his hands. She licked her lips slowly then asked the question. 'When did you hear the cry before?'

He shivered. His eyes still closed. 'A few years ago in another ER. I'd just come on shift. The woman had been in the waiting room for a few hours.'

Arissa's stomach sank. From his reaction she could almost guess what might have happened. 'How did that baby do?'

He clenched her fingers tightly. 'He made it—but barely. His vaccinations were up to date, but his mum had put him to bed and given him some acetaminophen when he'd developed a fever. She'd brought him in to the ER in the middle of the night when he hadn't settled.'

'And she was still waiting when you came on duty?'

He nodded and winced. 'There had been a road traffic accident, and a house fire. No one had a chance to properly assess the baby.'

She squeezed his hands. 'But you did.'

He shook his head slightly. 'It was almost too late. The baby fitted within a few minutes. It was a few days before we knew if the baby would live or die.' He licked his lips. 'The baby recovered, but there were some long-term effects. He lost his hearing. If I'd got to him quicker...' His voice trailed off.

He stopped talking, his eyes closing again. It was the first time she'd ever seen him shaken. How much had it taken for him to hold things together while Mariam and her baby had been here?

She took a deep breath. 'I'm really sorry to hear about that baby, to hear about how busy the ER was. I'm sorry for him, and the fact that he lost his hearing.' She sucked in another breath. 'But, Philippe, I'm not sorry you heard the cry. I'm not sorry that today you recognised the cry instantly and acted appropriately. If I'd been on my own, it might have taken me a bit longer to reach the diagnosis, and we both know that time is of the essence.' She pulled one of her hands free of his and reached up and touched his cheek. 'You did good today, Philippe. You've probably saved Rosni's life—and the rest of the family that's been exposed.'

He opened his eyes, his lashes only an inch from hers. His dark eyes were so deep, so full of emotion that she blinked back tears. 'You did good today, Philippe. Don't forget that. We all have cases we can't ever forget.'

It was odd. She'd never expected to get so up close and personal with this man who was still a bit of a mystery to her. But this just felt so right. He was her colleague. He was helping her. He had likely just saved a baby's life and that had obviously brought back some hidden memories.

She gave him the smallest smile. 'Thank you,' she whispered. 'You made a difference today. That's all we can ever ask.'

And they sat there, foreheads touching, until the first patient arrived for the vaccination clinic.

# CHAPTER SIX

HE WAS UNSETTLED. If he tried to be rational about things he would put it down to the baby conjuring a wave of memories and emotions and the frustration he'd felt first time around.

But it wasn't the baby. He'd checked on Rosni, and after a few days in hospital she'd made a good recovery thanks to the early administration of antibiotics. None of the other family members or kids at nursery had developed symptoms. So, he should be happy. But he wasn't. He couldn't think straight.

Maybe it was the pressure of the job awaiting him back home. Maybe it was the million and one ideas that were clamouring for space in his head about how he could reform health services in Corinez. He had to start somewhere. His head was swimming. So many things needed to change back home.

But the truth was he knew exactly what was unsettling him. The days were marching on in Temur Sapora and his relationship with Arissa was growing every day. They worked well together, almost anticipating each other's requests, and at the end of each day, they sat down together, debriefed, then generally spent the evening in each other's company.

Sometimes it was dinner in a local restaurant, other times they grabbed a takeaway. Sometimes it was just a walk around the streets or down to the beach. But the more time he spent with the quietly gorgeous, unassuming doctor, the more time he wanted to spend with her. And she still didn't know who he was.

The thing that had initially just been a vague and unimportant secret was beginning to feel like the elephant in the room. Why hadn't he just told her straight away who he was? Now, it felt as if he were deliberately lying to her.

No one had recognised him in Temur Sapora and, for that, he was eternally grateful. But every day he was cautious, quickly checking the Internet for any mentions. It was almost like being off the grid and that had entirely been his intention when he'd come here. But now his intention seemed a little…deceitful.

Part of him was grateful for the chance just to be 'Philippe'. No Prince. No Royal Highness. No one treating him differently at work. No actress waiting on the sidelines. *My Night with the Charming Prince* had been the headline after the interview.

But how would Arissa feel about headlines like that?

As he finished scrubbing his hands in the sink, she appeared at the edge of the door. 'Almost done?'

He nodded. They'd finished work for the day and made plans for dinner. For the first time he was going to see the inside of her home as Arissa had offered to teach him to cook some traditional Malaysian dishes.

Her curls were loose and bouncing on her shoulders, she was wearing flat shoes and a red shirt dress that complemented her skin tone and dark eyes.

He gave a quick nod. 'Let me change my shirt. I

brought another with me.' She raised her eyebrows and smiled as he strode towards the staff room. His cream short-sleeved shirt and jeans were sitting in the corner along with his antiperspirant and aftershave. Two minutes later he was ready and stood next to her as she locked up the clinic.

'It was a good day today,' she murmured.

'It was,' he agreed. The research study results were remarkable. He'd seen a patient today whose leg ulcer had almost completely healed in a few short weeks—a leg ulcer that he'd had for more than four years. The ointment really was working wonders.

Arissa's hand brushed against his as they walked down the main street. 'I've still not heard from the professor of my new hospital,' she said absent-mindedly.

'Isn't it less than a week until you go?'

She nodded. 'I fly out on Sunday. I've filled in endless amounts of paperwork for the recruitment agency and the hospital HR people. It doesn't usually take this long to sort out. I've had a deposit down on my accommodation for the last four months.'

They crossed into the nearby grocery store. Arissa had already pre-ordered supplies so Philippe just paid for them and carried the brown bag. 'Maybe it's just an administration thing. Some places aren't as organised as others. Have you tried to call them?'

She gave a shrug. 'Only about a dozen times. No one seems to answer their phones. I sent another email today though. If I don't get a reply I'll try again tomorrow.'

They turned down a street that ran parallel to the beach. It was lined with small bungalows painted in a variety of colours. Arissa stopped outside a pale yellow one and pulled the keys from her pocket.

'This is a fantastic location,' enthused Philippe. 'You're only a few steps from the beach.'

Arissa nodded. 'Yeah. I love it. This was my parents' house and my grandparents' before that. Most of the houses in this row are generational properties.'

He looked around the bungalow as he stepped inside. From the outside there were two large windows at the front. One was in the main room, which was small but contained a comfortable sofa that gave a great view of the beach, and the back of the room opened out into the kitchen with a small dining table.

Arissa waved over to the left. 'My bedroom and the bathroom are over that side. There's another room that's literally just a broom cupboard. That used to be my bedroom, but I use it as a study now.'

'You never wanted to move?'

She waved a hand towards the view. 'Who wouldn't want to live on the beach? My mum and dad could have moved to a bigger house a number of times over the years, but the beach and the view kept them here.'

Philippe walked over to a framed photo on the wall. It showed a much younger Arissa, between an older man and woman who were both beaming down at her with their arms around her shoulders.

He asked the inevitable question. 'Where are they now?'

She moved towards him, holding out her hands for the brown paper bag. 'Let's just say I was a late—but much-wanted—baby. My mother died of breast cancer a few years ago, and my father had an accident when he was out on one of the fishing boats a few months later.'

'I'm so sorry.'

She gave the briefest nod of her head; one hand

reached up and traced over the figures in the photo for a second. 'I was lucky to have them as long as I did. They were proud of me. Saw me through medical school, and they were the proudest parents in the room at my graduation.' He could see the love on her face, the admiration for two people that at one point had been her whole world.

He watched her for a few moments as he realised how big this was for her. She'd invited him back to her house, to see a part of her that most people wouldn't know. It made the fact he'd been less than straightforward with her rest heavily on his shoulders.

She took the bag and carried it over to the small kitchen. Philippe moved beside her. 'So, you've never wanted to sell up, even though you don't stay here permanently?' He was curious. She only got to spend around six weeks a year here, and he could imagine that over the years this small bungalow had become prime property.

She shook her head. 'Absolutely not. I sometimes rent the place out to some of the visiting doctors—but only if I know them. Otherwise, I just look forward to getting back here five or six weeks a year.'

He turned and took another glance at the view. A burst of yellow sand, followed by endless turquoise ocean. It really was a prime view. The beach was sheltered, in a little inlet, with no other property overlooking it. 'I can imagine you've had offers for a place like this.'

She nodded as she emptied the chicken, noodles, herbs and spices out onto the counter. 'From the developers? Constantly. Particularly since we own not just the bungalows, but the beach too. But the rest of the people in the street feel the same as I do. Staying here is like a family tradition to me. I get to call this piece of paradise mine.' She put one hand up to her chest. 'I might not be here all year round, but it's here whenever I need it.' She met his gaze with her dark brown eyes. 'You can't sell a part of yourself.'

There it was. The connection. It practically zinged in the air between them. Arissa could probably make a fortune if she sold up and moved. But her heart was here. He could see that. She was grounded here. Even though her family were gone. She loved her island—just as he loved his country.

Nowadays so many people were indifferent about where they stayed—flitting about from place to place, prioritising money over so much else. It was refreshing to meet someone who had as much commitment to their home as he did.

'Family traditions are very important where I come from too,' he said softly. He should tell her. He should tell her now about who he really was. But he didn't want to spoil this moment or time between them.

This was the closest he'd felt to someone in, well, for ever. She didn't know him as a prince. She didn't want anything from him, and he liked holding onto that thought. That feeling.

She blinked and licked her lips, before lowering her eyes as she rearranged the ingredients. 'You're the first man I've invited back here in years,' she said slowly.

The air around them seemed heavy. Every breath a little more laboured than the one before. There was a slight tremble in her hands. She was nervous. He was making her nervous.

But somehow he knew it wasn't a bad nervous. Because he felt exactly the same.

'I'm honoured to be here,' he said simply as one of his hands moved over hers. 'Thank you for inviting me.'

The touch of her warm skin against his sent a little buzz up his skin. He liked it. He liked it a lot.

The aroma of freesias drifted towards him. Perfume. She'd put on perfume when he'd changed. His heartbeat quickened.

He wanted to move closer. To slip his hands around her waist and turn her towards him. But it seemed too forward. Too presumptuous.

Arissa's hand moved from under his and she stepped to one side, giving him a smile over her shoulder. Was she deliberately putting a little distance between them?

He wasn't sure. But what he was sure about was that he didn't want to put a foot wrong. He didn't want to step anywhere she didn't want him. She pulled out a wok and sat it on the hotplate. 'Okay, before we start, no allergies?'

He shook his head; he was happy to take her lead. He'd agreed to make her dinner. That was exactly what he would do. 'No allergies, why?'

She grinned. 'Because I like peanuts with my chicken.'

He wrinkled his nose. 'Peanuts?'

She nodded and pointed towards the chopping board and knives. 'Peanuts. Okay, grab your tools and let's get started. I'm famished.'

He looked at the array of ingredients in front of him. He wasn't quite sure where to start, but the chicken seemed like a safe bet so he started chopping that.

'What are you teaching me?' he asked. 'What recipe are we creating?'

She opened a cupboard and lifted out two wine glasses, taking a bottle from the fridge. 'I'm teaching you how to make Malaysian spicy chicken noodles.' She poured the wine. 'But I want you to know that I have an unusual way of teaching.' She took a sip from her wine glass and winked at him.

A smile automatically came to his lips. She was flirting with him, always a good sign. 'What's unusual about your teaching methods?'

She let out a laugh. 'I don't actually do anything. I just watch you do it. I'm like the ultimate lazy tutor.'

He moved from chopping the chicken, to shredding the cabbage and carrots, all the while feeling her gaze on him. He might be a prince, but he'd learned to fend for himself over the years. He wasn't above throwing some ingredients together. And somehow he liked being under her appreciative gaze.

She nodded towards the sesame oil next to the wok and smiled. 'Better get started.' It was as if her gaze was dancing across his skin, leaving tension in the air between them, and he'd never liked it so much.

He shook his head and poured some oil into the already smoking wok, watching while it spat instantly. He added the chicken, the vegetables and some of the baby bok choy, chilli paste, garlic, soy sauce and finally some hokkien noodles. Last thing he wanted to do was mess up dinner.

'Wait!' Arissa smiled. 'You've forgotten my favourites.'

She grabbed a packet of peanuts and sprinkled them over the dish.

He gave a little frown. 'Are you sure these are a good match?'

She raised her eyebrows knowingly as she put out two place settings. 'These are my secret ingredient.'

He dished out the stir-fry into the two white bowls

she'd set next to him and carried them over to the table. 'Do I get to drink my wine now?'

She nodded as he sat down opposite her and he lifted his glass to hers. 'To friends,' he said. 'You've made this holiday a whole lot more…' he wasn't quite sure what word to add—what word would be entirely appropriate '…special,' he finished with a broad smile.

She clinked her glass against his. 'Special,' she repeated as her gaze connected with his. 'To think I could have spent two weeks entirely on my own.' She took a slow breath, as she held his gaze. 'I'm glad you're here.'

'Me too.'

They ate as the sun set on the horizon sending streaks of orange and red across the sky. When they finished they carried their glasses outside and sat on the cooling sand on the beach.

'Last time around you didn't tell me you owned a whole beach,' he joked.

'Last time around I didn't know you that well,' she replied. 'And I don't own the whole beach.' She drew a little square in the sand between them. 'Maybe just, this much.'

He didn't hesitate, he closed his hand over hers, guiding a finger to draw a wider square. 'Or maybe you own a little more. This much?'

She laughed and lay back on the sand. 'Heard of snow angels? How about some sand angels?' She was still smiling; she started swishing her arms and legs over the sand. 'Maybe it's this much.'

He moved over slightly, lying back too and copying her actions. 'Or maybe it's this much!'

She kept laughing as she watched him. He finally stopped and turned around onto his side, putting his head on one hand.

'We have a whole beach to ourselves,' he said conspiratorially. 'Any ideas what to do next?'

She turned to face him, putting her head on her hand too and shaking some sand from her hair as he eyed the rippling ocean.

'No way,' she said firmly.

'Why not?' He couldn't hide the gleam in his eyes and sat up straight. 'Come on.' He pulled his shirt over his head.

She burst out laughing and he looked down and held out his hands. 'What? Too much paunch?' He knew he looked fine; his almost washboard abs had been gained through long hours at work, not long hours in the gym.

She shook her head. 'There's no paunch—' she wagged her finger '—but don't go any further.'

'Why not?' He was being wicked and he knew it. He unfastened his jeans and laughed as she put one hand up to her face and looked away. 'Somehow as a doc, I think you've seen it all before.'

He kicked his jeans off and held out his hand towards her. 'You're telling me, in all the years you've stayed here, you've never gone skinny-dipping in the ocean?'

Her eyes widened. 'Not with anyone watching. Anyhow—' she sat up onto her knees '—I normally use a bathing suit—don't most people?'

He winked as he looked down at his jersey boxer shorts. 'Depends on the occasion.' He checked over his shoulder. The beach was empty and the sun was dipping even lower in the sky, the rainbow of reds and oranges vivid in the dimming light.

'Thought you were introducing me to Temur Sapora,' he teased, his arm still outstretched and not wavering at all.

Her fingers went to the top button on her shirt dress as she started to stand. The little flicker in his stomach grew.

She undid the first button. 'I'm introducing you to *selected* portions of Temur Sapora. Maybe I hadn't decided if you were worthy of this yet?' She was teasing him back. He liked it.

She still hadn't taken his hand. He stepped a little closer. 'What do I need to do to be worthy?' he asked, his voice low.

She blinked, those dark eyes connecting with his. It was mesmerising watching her fingers oh-so-slowly undoing the buttons on her dress, revealing the skin underneath. His breath was definitely faltering.

The red dress dropped to her feet in silence. Her underwear was simple. Black cotton bra and pants. No silk. No lace. He'd never seen anything sexier.

There was a glint in her eye. She pointed over his shoulder. 'See that buoy out there?'

He turned. The orange buoy was bouncing in the currents. He looked sideways at her, knowing what might come next. 'Yes…'

She streaked past him. 'Last one there's the loser!'

He couldn't help but admire her curvy figure as she ran full pelt into the waves—the actions of someone who'd done it time and time before. She hit the water with her arms automatically starting to crawl as he was still standing on the beach.

Her swimming was smooth and practised, and it gave him the kick he needed to run and join her. Philippe had always had a competitive edge but this was one contest he was definitely prepared to lose.

He waded through the ocean, sucking in a breath at how deceptively cold it was at first, then put his head down and started out towards the buoy. Arissa was already halfway there.

He kicked his legs more, his arms slicing through the ocean. Every so often he lifted his head to check the position of both Arissa and the buoy. Her laugh carried over the water towards him. He was catching her, but it was clear she was confident.

He slowed his pace a little. She was relaxing around him, flirting a little and he liked it. He liked her. She was interesting, clearly dedicated to her work and home, but there was real old-fashioned goodness about her that he hadn't seen in years. And it was in everything that she did. Every conversation. Every thought process.

Nowadays, if he said that, it probably wouldn't be seen as a compliment. But he admired how much the people around her mattered to her, because it was exactly how he felt when he was at home too.

So many people were interested in fame and fortune now. Social media and press seemed to dictate even diplomatic processes and business dealings. It wasn't that he was wildly old-fashioned, but he'd become a doctor for a reason—because he liked to deal with *people*.

Nowadays it sometimes felt as if it was turning into an original concept.

She let out a whoop and he looked up to see her laughing and touching the buoy. He was only a few strokes behind and joined her holding onto the bright orange float. 'Cheater.' He laughed as he spat out some water.

'Not at all.' She grinned. 'If you're not fast, you're last.'

He ducked her head under the water and she came up spluttering but still laughing. This time she moved closer, one arm sliding around his neck as she used him as her anchor instead of the buoy.

'Maybe you just need to learn to swim better,' she taunted, her legs wrapping around his waist.

For the first time he was glad of exactly how cold this water was. Not that it was stopping his blood flowing.

'Maybe you've had more practice.' He smiled back. 'Given that you've got your own private beach.'

She tipped her head back, letting some of the water drain from her hair, the curls were still there, just bouncier now. He tried not to stare at the delicate skin on her neck and the base of her throat. It would only lead his eyes to someplace else.

As she tipped her head back up her grin was wide, showing her straight white teeth. 'Is that beach envy I hear in your voice, Dr Aronaz?' She was still teasing. He liked this new side of her. It seemed as if once she'd shed her clothes, she'd also managed to shed that serious cloud that seemed to hang around her. He still hadn't quite got to the bottom of that.

She leaned forward, her lips brushing against the edge of his cheek. 'One more race, then. First back to the beach.'

He froze, still in place in the water; between the feel of her lips on his cheek and the press of her breasts against his chest as she did that, he'd pretty much lost the ability to concentrate at all.

She let go quickly, turning in the water and heading back to shore. He took a few moments, watching her go. When was the last time this had happened to him?

He'd dated plenty of women—he hadn't picked up the title of Playboy Prince for nothing—but he'd never dated anyone that clean took his breath away. He'd just never thought that was possible. More like an old wives' tale that people liked to mention to pretend just 'how in love' they were with their spouse or current partner.

He'd never really believed those sensations actually existed. But here, right in the middle of the cold South China Sea, he'd just had an awakening. He'd learned something new.

And he didn't know quite what to do with it.

She was slicing through the waves like a mermaid and it brought him to his senses. He crawled lazily along behind, no chance of catching up, while his brain churned with a whole host of new emotions.

Philippe Aronaz wasn't used to being wrong-footed. He was always in control.

He watched as Arissa waded out of the water and turned to watch him, shaking her head with her hands on her hips. She picked up the red dress and held it in front of her as he waded out behind her and walked across the sand.

He was conscious of every bead of water dripping from his skin—just as he was conscious of the rivulets of water running down the length of her. 'Come on.' She nodded back towards the bungalow. 'I'll get you a towel.'

She turned and started walking towards the pale yellow house. He was slow to pick up his shirt and jeans as he watched her retreating form dressed only in her underwear.

His mind could go so many places right now. And to be honest, he wanted it to. But deep down, his internal voice was screaming at him. *Don't take things for granted. Don't move too soon.*

Arissa Cotter was special. He didn't want to assume anything. Just because she'd let her guard down a little tonight, and just because she'd moved next to him—touched him—didn't mean anything.

Somehow he wanted to do everything right around her.

He walked slowly back to her house. She met him at the door with a big blue fluffy towel that she thrust towards him. 'Dry off in there.' She gestured towards her bathroom, before disappearing into her bedroom with a towel of her own.

His body almost let out a growl. But he shook his head and took himself into the bathroom, drying off and re-dressing—even though it was the last thing he wanted to do.

By the time he emerged, Arissa was standing in the middle of her living room, dressed in a baggy green T-shirt and jersey shorts. Her hair was still damp and curled around her shoulders.

'Okay?' she asked.

'Of course,' seemed the natural reply. All of a sudden a wave of awkwardness swept over him. He could say something. He could ask the question. He could ask her what she wanted to happen next. But in the dim light of her bungalow, and the small space of her living room, it didn't seem quite right. It almost felt a bit intrusive, and the last thing he wanted her to feel was any pressure.

'Thank you for tonight,' he said softly. 'I had a great time.' He took a few steps towards the door.

'I did too.' Her reply was so quiet he almost didn't hear it, his hand already on the doorknob. He pulled it open. The sun had finally vanished leaving the semi-dark sky sprinkled with glistening white stars.

As he turned back she'd moved right behind him.

He could have stopped. He could have said something clever. But instead he let his instincts take over and he bent, capturing the back of her head in his hands, letting his fingers slide through her damp curls and tugging her mouth towards his.

They both tasted of the ocean, both still smelling of the tang of the sea. But the scent was heady, wrapping around them as her hands slid up around his neck.

She didn't object, her kiss matching his in every way.

His brain was soaring. He wanted more. But he knew right now that he had to step away.

He kept his hands at her head, forcing himself not to move them to her body, but instead bringing one around to the side of her cheek. When their kissing finally slowed he pulled back and licked his lips, catching his breath slowly.

Her cheeks were slightly flushed, her eyes wide, but she didn't make any further move either, just watching him carefully.

He smiled at her and stepped back. 'Goodnight, Arissa,' he said hoarsely.

She gave a little nod of her head. 'Goodnight, Philippe,' she replied. There was a smile on her lips, as if she too was trying to take stock of what had just happened between them.

He turned and headed back down the street, willing himself not to look back, and feeling the blood pulsing through his veins. He couldn't work out if he was crazy, composed, or contrite.

He'd wanted more, but stepping away had been the only truthful thing he could do. She didn't know everything about him yet. He needed to have that conversation, and it wasn't one you had when your arms were wrapped around someone, either in the water or out.

He sighed and looked up at the dark night sky, shaking

his head at himself. First day on this island had seemed so long. Now, two weeks seemed as if they would never possibly be long enough.

## CHAPTER SEVEN

THE NEXT FEW days were a mixture of easy and frustrating.

It was clear that neither of them could forget that kiss.

She'd wondered if things would be slightly awkward between them, but that first morning after, when she'd walked into the clinic, he'd already been there—with coffee and croissants—and he'd just shot her that sexy grin through tired eyes and gestured to the seat beside him. 'I started early.'

So had she. In fact she hadn't slept a wink after that kiss, wondering if she should just have grabbed him by his shirt collar and dragged him back into her house. Instead, she'd slid down the inside of her door once she'd closed it—her legs like jelly, smiling away to herself. It would be so easy to blame the unexpected swim, but she'd known the jelly legs were entirely down to Philippe.

The croissant and coffee had settled her jittering nerves. And Philippe had been entirely *normal*. Not ignore-the-fact-it-happened normal. No, he'd continued to let his hand linger when they touched, she'd occasionally caught him watching her with his sexy smile, but all the while entirely being a gentleman around her.

She wasn't sure whether to laugh or cry.

There was something so nice about being around him,

laughing with him, talking with him. For such a long time she'd been on her own. Between her commitments to home and her commitments to work, she really hadn't had time in her life for anyone else. Philippe made things easy. She didn't need to try. She didn't need to worry about what she was wearing, or how her hair looked, or whether she'd remembered to put make-up on that day.

They'd had lunch and dinner together every day and evening. They hadn't had a second performance of that night-time swim—or of the kiss—but it was weird. She could almost swear that at times the air between them sparkled.

How stupid was that? An entirely rational, educated woman who thought the air might sparkle between her and some guy? It was like flitting back into her eight-year-old self when she'd imagined she'd marry a prince, and ride off on the back of a unicorn across a rainbow, all while the air around her glimmered. Of course at that point, in her dream she hadn't been wearing a princess dress, she'd been wearing a NASA space suit because her intention had been to be an astronaut. Ridiculous.

Part of her knew that Philippe was only here for another few days. To expect anything other than a fleeting friendship would be ridiculous. But other parts of her felt as if this was some old-fashioned kind of courtship. And she couldn't pretend that didn't warm her heart entirely.

She gave a smile and called her last patient into the second vaccination clinic of the week. There was a queue of patients—Philippe had seen half of the children and the time had flown past. He gave a nod as she escorted the mother and baby into her room. 'I'll put the kettle on,' he mouthed before following it with a cheeky wink.

Her heart scattered across her chest and she hid the smile as she focused on her patient. 'Welcome, Ana, it's lovely to see you again.'

He folded his arms as the coffee percolated. He could have gone out to buy some from across the street but that would only have killed time and he couldn't put this off any longer. He had to tell Arissa who he really was.

His stomach was churning. His two weeks were rapidly coming to an end. He knew that he'd be heading off on the plane soon, what he didn't know was whether he'd have a chance to pursue this blossoming relationship with Arissa.

It surprised him just how much he wanted to. Just how important this was to him. They were right at the beginning. Who knew where this could lead? But with him in Corinez, and her heading to the UK, there would be hundreds of miles between them. Could a long-distance relationship actually work? Particularly when they were both so dedicated to their jobs? All he knew for certain was that he wanted to try.

He waited as she saw the last patient out of the clinic and closed the door for lunch.

But before he had a chance to speak she stopped at the computer to check her emails.

Her face fell.

'What's wrong?' he couldn't help but ask.

She was staring at the screen, then shook her head for a few moments and picked up her phone. 'Give me a minute, would you?'

The expression on her face was a mixture of panic and worry. She disappeared into the office with her phone pressed to her ear. The door didn't entirely close.

He paced around outside. Attempting to be busy doing other things and trying his best not to listen, but it was hard not to hear the rising tones of her voice.

After around fifteen minutes she appeared at the doorway, her face drawn.

'What is it, Arissa?' He couldn't help himself. He walked over and put his hands on her arms.

She shook her head. She looked numb. 'There's been a problem with my visa. The agency I'm due to start with in London hasn't applied in time. I needed the visa to secure my post in London at the children's hospital.'

Philippe frowned. Doctors moved to positions in other countries all the time. Visas were always a tricky issue, but usually dealt with promptly and without delay when the paperwork was submitted. 'Have they made a mistake?'

She nodded. 'Oh, yes.'

'Can the hospital sort it out for you?'

She gulped and shook her head. For the first time he thought he could see tears glistening in her eyes. 'No. It's too late. They need someone to start August the first. My visa will never process in time. It was part of the terms and conditions of the contracts that the visa requirement would be met by a certain time. They can't afford to leave posts like this vacant, Philippe. These kids need doctors. They don't have time for delays.' Her voice was shaking now.

Philippe could see the pain in her eyes. 'But they need you. They'll be able to pull some strings. Doctors are a priority around the world. If we can speak to the visa office, I'm sure they'll sort things out for you.'

She shook her head again. 'They won't buy it. As soon

as the hospital were notified my paperwork wasn't agreed in time, they offered the post to someone else.'

She sagged down into a chair. 'For the first time in my life—I don't have a job to go to.'

He could see how upset she was by this. He was upset for her. Most doctors were meticulous planners. They all knew that job visa requirements could take months and generally worked with agencies to ensure all these things were in order well in advance.

He knew how hard she'd been working. Covering the job she'd had in Washington, spending all her holiday time here, and helping document the research. It was no wonder something had slipped. It could happen to the best of people.

But from the look on her face it had never happened to Arissa before.

'I can try and help. Let me see what I can do. Let me try and speak to someone.' He was babbling now and he knew it.

But she shook her head again. Her eyes were vacant when they met with his. 'But the job's gone already. Even if strings were pulled and I got my visa, I wouldn't get this job. The opportunity is gone.'

It was almost as if all the energy had gone from her body. Her shoulders sagged, her head dipped and her breathing got heavier.

He'd never seen her like this.

His mind was whirling around and around. He knew exactly what he should do right now. But the timing just felt so off.

It was inevitable. He'd spent the last two weeks in a bubble that didn't really exist. It was time to tell the truth.

His brain was desperately trying to create a spin on what he was about to reveal.

He took a deep breath. 'Arissa, I know this is a shock. But, maybe this means you have an opportunity to do something different?'

'Different like what? What else is there that I can possibly do?'

He gave her a hesitant smile. 'How about I take you someplace else? A different country. A country that could benefit from your expertise.'

She frowned and shook her head. 'What?' It was clear she had no idea where this was heading.

There were parts of this story that he knew she wouldn't be happy about. He took a few breaths. 'Arissa, have you heard of Corinez?'

She shook her head. 'Where?'

He wasn't offended. While most people in Europe had heard of Corinez, in other continents around the world it wasn't so well known.

'Corinez. It's an island near France, Monaco and Italy.'

A frown creased her brow. 'Corinez? That's the place you're from?'

He nodded. 'I'm due to go back—to start a new job...' he cringed as he said those words '...and I wonder if— until you get things sorted—you would come with me.'

For a few seconds she looked stunned, then confused. The frown in her brow grew even deeper. 'To do what?'

He paused for a moment. 'I have a senior position. One that means I'd be able to look at the possibility of setting up a scheme similar to the safe haven scheme you've set up here.'

It didn't take more than a few seconds for the pieces

to fall into place for Arissa. It wasn't usual for a doctor who'd spent the last few years specialising in an ER to go to a job like that. 'Exactly what kind of job do you have in Corinez?'

'I'm part of an advisory committee.' He kept his reply short.

Her eyes widened. 'An advisory committee for a hospital?'

He hesitated. 'No...an advisory committee for the whole country.'

'Wow. That sounds important.' She gave a little smile. 'I don't mean to be cheeky, but how on earth would you get a job like that?'

He looked up and met her confused gaze. 'I was born into it.'

He waited. She pulled back. 'What on earth does that mean?'

'It means that I was born to be on the advisory committee for overseeing healthcare. My sister was born to do the same for finance, and my brother...' he took another breath '...he was born to be King.'

Silence. So long and so amplified that the breath he was holding almost burst his lungs.

She seemed frozen. Her eyes couldn't get any wider. Finally, she made a kind of stuttering sound. 'So...so... if your brother will be King...that makes you a prince?'

He flinched at the way she said the word—as if it were some kind of awful disease.

He nodded. His heart heavy. Most of his life when he'd dated he'd wondered if people were going out with him *because* he was a prince, not because he was Philippe. Working in the hospital in Corinez had felt almost awkward. People had been ridiculously polite to him, tiptoeing around him when they should have been more worried about providing healthcare.

But coming here had been something again. He'd never had such a blank slate before. And for the first time he'd managed to have a friendship develop and blossom with no underlying knowledge of his true identity. For his part, it wasn't exactly honest—he knew that. But it had felt so freeing—even if it was only a few days.

He knew that the start of the friendship between him and Arissa had been about him. About them.

'Why didn't you tell me?' Her voice was tight.

He ran his hand through his hair. 'Because I came here under the radar, for a holiday. I met Dr Reacher on the plane. When he told me what he was supposed to be doing, then...' he winced '...died, it made me curious.' He gave a smile and held up his hand. 'And then I reached the luxury resort, and within a day...' he pulled a face '...truth is, I was bored. Even if I hadn't met Harry on the plane I would still have come looking for something else to do. A way to volunteer or help.'

'What's the deal with being a prince? Why keep it a secret?'

He wanted to throw his hands up in frustration. No one really understood what it was like. The constant scrutiny. Living your life under the spotlight. Saying hello to a woman and having a story in the press the next day saying that you were getting married.

He gave a slow nod of his head. 'When I'm in Corinez, I'm Prince Philippe, through and through. It's my role. I've been brought up to fulfil that purpose. But I had a few years' leeway—time to come and train as a doctor and gain experience that would help me fulfil my ultimate duty when it was time to go home.'

'And is it time to go home now?'

He closed his eyes for a second. 'It is.' He took a deep breath. 'Come with me.'

The more he thought about things, the more it all made sense in his head. 'Come with me and help me set up a safe haven scheme in Corinez. The last patient I dealt with back home was a baby who'd been abandoned. We don't have a national healthcare system. People have to pay for all medical services, and finances have changed in Corinez. The recession has hit hard. We have more and more incidents of babies being abandoned. I hope to campaign for free maternal healthcare in Corinez—at least to start with. But I also need to put in place a scheme like you have. I need to ensure these babies can be safe, can be looked after.' He leaned forward and grasped her hands. 'And you can help me do that.'

She pulled herself back. 'But…' Nothing else followed. She seemed stuck for words.

'Think of it as a mix between a holiday and a humanitarian effort. I can show you a little of Corinez and you can advise me on the best way to set up the scheme while you get your visa sorted out and look for another job that you really want.'

She was still stunned. He kept going, conscious he was babbling, but he just wanted her to agree. He didn't want to leave here without her. She looked up at him. 'Look at the trouble I've just had with London. Won't I need a visa to work in Corinez—no matter what role I'm doing?'

He waved his hand. 'That's one of the few perks of being a prince. I can sort that for you.' His gaze connected with hers. 'You've already told me that you've got the time here covered. There's no need for you to stay. You could look for some kind of temporary cover or sick-leave type of job—but do you really want that? Why not try something different? Come with me, help me in Corinez. Help me set up the same scheme you have here.'

He hadn't moved his hands. They were still clasped over hers.

'You're a prince,' she said again, looking him square in the eye.

He nodded again and gave her a resigned smile. 'Yes, I'm a prince.'

She wrinkled her nose. 'Where, exactly, is Corinez again?'

'It's near France, Italy and Monaco.'

She blinked. 'What?'

He shook his head. 'Forget it, it's not that important. It's an island. It has mountains that people ski on, it has a casino—no, scratch that, it has *many* casinos—it has a huge port. We laugh and call it the cruise ship depot because so many stop there.'

Arissa let out a long slow breath. 'You're a prince.'

He smiled. 'Yeah, you said that, a few times. I am a prince. It's not gonna change. But what *can* change is what you can help me do. Come with me, Arissa. Come with me to Corinez. Be my champion.'

'Your champion?'

He smiled. 'It's what I always say to my patients when they have to take a deep breath for something.'

It was as if something flicked in her brain. She smiled then spoke carefully. 'This project. I won't be in the spotlight. I won't have to deal with press. I won't have to be…anything?'

She shook her head. His heart gave a lurch. She was considering coming. She was actually considering coming.

He didn't know exactly what was behind this, but it

wasn't the first time she'd told him she didn't want to be in the spotlight. And right now he would agree to anything.

'Arissa, if you agree to come we can focus entirely on the project. You won't need to worry about anything else.'

He could see her holding her breath, and he held his too, waiting for her answer.

'No publicity,' she reiterated.

'No publicity,' he agreed.

She licked her lips and waited a few moments before she replied. 'Okay, then, Prince Philippe, show me your country.'

# CHAPTER EIGHT

SHE COULDN'T HELP but stare out of the window of the plane, still not really believing that she was actually doing this.

Beneath her, Corinez was revealed through smoky clouds. The high mountains, busy harbour and rich city stretched out under her gaze. Philippe was preoccupied, talking to the man who'd appeared and been introduced as Philippe's personal secretary.

All of this was becoming scarily real.

She felt the undercarriage on the plane go down and they glided to a halt on a long runway. There was no Customs. No queues.

Instead they exited the plane straight into a white stretch limousine.

As soon as they stepped onto the tarmac she sensed a change in Philippe. He wasn't just the nonchalant doctor who offered to help out when required.

Now, he was Prince Philippe, and even though he tried to be self-effacing it was apparent the people around him wouldn't allow him to be anything other than their Prince.

He was at ease amongst them. He disappeared for a few moments and the secretary bent to murmur in her ear. 'He has to have a quick chat with our local press, don't worry. He'll only be a few minutes. His Highness is good at giving them exactly what they want, in the minimum time possible.'

He had a strange kind of grin on his face as he said those words and she wasn't quite sure what he meant. The thought of dealing with the press sent uneasy prickles down her spine. But five minutes later Philippe appeared again and they were whisked off in the white limousine.

'I am supposed to call you Your Highness now?' she asked as she sank back into the soft leather upholstery.

He shook his head. 'You call me Philippe—or whatever name you think suits me at the time.'

She gave a half-frown. 'I'm not sure how that will go down with the rest of the people around you.'

He waved his hand. 'Don't worry about them. You're my guest—they know that. If there's anything you need, or want, you just have to say the word.'

She wasn't quite sure how she felt about that either. Arissa had spent her life doing things for herself and sorting herself out. Asking someone else for something wasn't really in her mindset and she wasn't sure it could be.

'When do we start work?' she asked, moving on to a subject she felt more comfortable with.

'As soon as we're settled.' The limousine started climbing a road winding up one of the nearby mountains. He gave her a knowing smile. 'The jet lag usually hits tomorrow, so we'll start the day after that.'

'I'd like to start as soon as we can.'

He kept smiling. 'What can I say?' He nodded his head at her. 'Your wish is my command.'

She watched as the hilly green countryside rapidly started to turn white. 'You have snow at this time of year?'

He leaned over next to her, letting her catch a whiff of his aftershave. 'We have snow all year round if you're high enough up the mountain. It's one of the few places where you can ski all year round. Down in the city can be in the middle of a heatwave, but up in the mountains the snow will still be lying.'

She gave a shiver. 'I'm not entirely sure I've brought the right wardrobe. Summer and winter in the same day?'

His eyes were gleaming. 'Welcome to Corinez.'

She settled back in the seat as the limousine turned through a set of ornate gates and up to a large grey and white stone four-storey palace, complete with turrets.

'You actually live in a palace?' she asked as her eyes tried to take in the view.

He wiggled his hand. 'There's some debate about that. We call it a palace, but apparently it's the same design as some Edwardian castle back in England. Worldwide travel wasn't common then. I think the designer might have thought that no one would realise he'd used the same plans twice.'

Arissa pressed her face closer to the car window. 'It looks beautiful.'

He gave a nod. 'It is. But the gardens are actually my favourite part. There's a fountain, a maze and extensive oriental gardens.'

The car slowly stopped and the chauffeur got out to open the door. Arissa walked up the impressive front steps, her heart tripping a little in her chest. Yip. She was right back in that childhood fantasy. She'd never imagined that she'd actually meet a prince for real—it still hadn't sunk in.

The inside of the castle was just as impressive as the outside. Arissa was led up one side of a curved dual staircase and along an impressive corridor to a suite.

Even though the style was Georgian, parts of the castle were decidedly updated. Arissa's room was decorated in shades of green and gold. The bed was at least six feet across, with sumptuous bedding. The carpet was so thick her feet sank into it and she wiggled her toes in pleasure. The bathroom was bigger than her bedroom back home, as was her dressing room. She gave a little laugh as the palace aide placed her single suitcase in the middle of the dressing room. It looked so lonely there—her clothing wouldn't take up even a tenth of the space in this room.

She smiled as she wandered through the suite, shaking her head at the expanse of it. Someone had run a bath for her already, with lavender scents drifting towards her and purple petals floating on the bathwater. The main windows in the suite looked out over the stunning gardens and even from here she could see the light dusting of snow across them.

She took a breath and sat down on the window ledge. She was here. In Corinez. What on earth was she thinking about?

There were some chocolates on the table in front of her, along with a bottle of wine chilling in a cooler and two glasses. Who had done this? Was it Philippe? Did he mean to come along and join her, or was this standard for any guest?

She just wasn't sure. She moved from the window ledge and sat down in one of the surprisingly comfortable chairs that looked out over the gardens. It was more beautiful than she could ever have imagined. Every little girl's fantasy.

But, for all its beauty and grandeur, somewhere out there—just like at home in Temur Sapora—could be a young girl or woman, contemplating giving up her baby.

A baby like her.

With the light dusting of snow at the very back of the gardens she could understand that where a baby was left could be the difference between life and death.

She had a reason to be here. She had a function. Philippe knew she was committed to the programme—even though he didn't really know her reasons. Those were hers to keep.

She glanced over at the sumptuous bed and breathed in the lavender scent coming from the bathroom, and while for tonight she might enjoy the lifestyle, she wouldn't forget the people she was here to help.

How could she? Arissa was a doctor. And she was an abandoned baby. And no matter the love she'd experienced in her life—that was what she would always be.

# CHAPTER NINE

PHILIPPE KNOCKED ON the door hesitantly, wondering if Arissa had managed to shake off the jet lag.

She opened the door, bright and breezy, wearing jeans and a red shirt. 'Ready to start work?' she asked.

He laughed. 'I wasn't sure you'd be ready.'

She held out her hands. 'I'm ready to see breakfast Corinez-style, and I definitely want to see where you intend to place the safe haven cots.'

He gave a firm nod as his stomach gave a little flip. Even not seeing her last night had been hard. She hadn't answered when he'd knocked on the door, and when he'd dared to peek inside she'd been sleeping soundly beneath the canopy of the large bed.

It had been so tempting to take a step inside—but Philippe would never do a thing like that. He was just happy that his guest was comfortable.

The morning sun gleamed behind her from the large windows, almost creating a halo above her dark curls. He could see every curve in her jeans and fitted shirt. She really had no idea just how gorgeous she was. He loved the fact she was ready to start. He loved her enthusiasm. But more than anything he loved the fact she'd agreed to come to his country with him. Part of him couldn't help but hope she might love it even a little as much as he did. He held out his elbow towards her, inviting her to slip her arm in his. 'Your wish is my command.'

And he meant it.

The journey down into the city was short. He took one of the cars from the palace gardens and waved away their chauffeur and security staff.

He could have gone to one of the many exclusive restaurants, but instead he took her to a well-established commercial coffee shop with chains around the world. Arissa clearly felt at home there as she could rhyme off her order by heart. It seemed that the menu didn't change the world over. The barista only raised one eyebrow when she clearly recognised Philippe, but the merest shake of his head was enough for her to realise not to say anything.

They settled at a table in the corner with their coffee and croissants as Philippe explained some of their surroundings. 'We're in the east side of the city. This has always been the poorer side of the city, but in the last few years things have taken a downward turn. Unemployment has risen and because Corinez doesn't have an adequate social security system in place, or free healthcare, the few cases of abandoned babies has increased in the last year.'

She met his gaze thoughtfully. 'You could have your work cut out for you.'

'That's why you're here.'

'Have you considered someplace that would be central enough for a safe haven cot?'

He nodded. 'I think we're going to go along the same route as yourself and use the fire stations. Our hospital would have been our first option, but, like your clinic, the road to the hospital is too well used, too open. I'm not sure that someone would feel confident to leave their baby at the hospital without fear of being discovered. The whole ethos behind the safe haven is that a woman can leave her child safely and without exposure to herself—no matter how much we'd really like to know who she is, and if she's safe too. Our fire station is in a central area, but not quite as busy—not quite as exposed—and there are always staff based in the station, so the baby wouldn't be left for any long period of time. It makes more sense to arrange for the safe haven to be placed there.'

She nodded. 'Do you have notes about where any of the other abandoned babies have been left in Corinez?'

He nodded. 'I've spoken to my police colleagues. There have been four in the last year. One left near the hospital, but not quite at the main entrance. Another left in a shop doorway in the east end of the city. A third near the fire station, and a fourth in the car park at the back of a local supermarket in the dead of night.'

His heart squeezed; he was worried she might ask the next question he just didn't want to answer. But her brain headed in another direction.

Arissa gulped. 'Have you ever managed to find any of the mothers?'

'Only one. She was admitted to hospital after collapsing in the street. She had a severe infection caused by the birth.'

He could see the next question in her eyes. 'She didn't want to be reunited with her baby. She had some other serious health conditions. The pregnancy had caused enormous strain on her body, and because she had no healthcare…'

He held up his hands and she finished the sentence for him. 'She just couldn't manage.'

He nodded. It was almost as if she could see the pressure he felt hanging above him.

Her fingers brushed against his and he couldn't help it, his fingers twitched and started to intertwine with hers. It seemed natural. It seemed honest. 'What are you going to do about the healthcare system in Corinez?' she asked.

The million-dollar question—or the more than million-euro question as it would turn out to be. He sighed deeply and gave a slow shake of his head. 'It needs to be overhauled. It doesn't meet the needs of our people.' He gave a wry smile. 'Unless, of course, you're a billionaire. We have dozens of private clinics and hospitals. Corinez is like a plastic surgeon's dream—because we have the climate and the geography, lots of people come here to have surgery and recuperate. But because so many investors like to make money from the private hospitals and clinics, it means our national hospital and community clinics are short-changed, in staffing levels and finance.'

'You can't staff your hospitals?'

He leaned his head on one hand. 'Nurses in the private hospitals get paid at a much higher rate than the state hospital. It's hard to keep staff.'

'And you don't have the budget to pay them more?'

He nodded. 'Exactly.'

She leaned back in her chair and looked around. 'You have a lifetime of work here, Philippe.'

He nodded. 'I know I do. I just need to start having courageous conversations with some of our parliament members and some of our investors. I know where I need to start. It has to be maternity care. If I can even persuade them to make that part of the healthcare system free, then we can try to ensure the best start for every child.'

He waited a few moments, conscious that they were now starting to get a few glances from people from the surrounding tables who seemed to be focusing on their intertwined hands.

He stood up quickly. Arissa looked surprised. 'Come on,' he said. 'Let's go and have a look at the fire station, and then I have somewhere I want to take you.'

She looked a little surprised by his sudden move and after a few seconds took his outstretched hand. 'Okay, then, Philippe, like I said before, show me Corinez.'

She loved it. She loved this place already. It was clear that people here respected their Prince—even if they did seem a little obsessed by him.

Everywhere they went there were nudges and side glances. She tried to stay focused. To look at the geography and the people around them. Poverty wasn't evident at the first glance, but dig a little beneath the surface—go to the right places—and it was there to see.

They visited a few community centres and spoke to some of the clientele. She met the chief of the fire and rescue service and was bowled over by his enthusiasm for the project. He immediately agreed to call his equivalent in Temur Sapora.

She liked the fact they were more or less travelling incognito. Philippe handled the busy streets easily and by the time dusk started to fall she couldn't hide the yawn.

'Tired?' he asked as they drove back towards the palace.

She gave a nod. 'I feel as if I need forty winks. But if I do that, I'll probably be up half the night.'

He gave a shrug. 'It doesn't matter. Do it. And if you

want company in the middle of the night you know where I am.'

She wasn't quite sure how he meant that to come out, but tingles were already dancing along her skin.

'I don't need you again until tomorrow afternoon. We're going to visit the state hospital to see if you can give me some ideas of where to start with the overhaul.'

She stifled another yawn and tried not to let her head nod. She couldn't quite believe how exhausted she felt. 'How did I ever get through being a junior doctor?' She shook her head. 'Sometimes we were awake for nearly forty hours.'

'But you weren't crossing two time zones,' he replied. 'Believe me, it makes a difference.'

'I guess it does,' she said as they pulled up to the palace garages. She gave a frown. 'I'm not quite sure how to get to my room from here.'

He parked the car and walked around, opening her door for her. 'Don't worry, I'll show you.'

There was an elevator to take them upstairs. As soon as the doors slid closed Philippe turned to face her. He seemed so far away.

'What do you think of Corinez so far?' She could hear the edge of uncertainty in his voice.

She took a step closer and put her hand on his arm. From here she could smell his aftershave, see the shadow starting to show along his jawline. 'I like it,' she replied honestly. 'And I want to find out more.' She licked her lips and moved even closer. 'And I like it even more that I can see how passionate you are about your country, and how much you want to make things better.'

He looked down at her, his hand sliding behind her waist. 'That's exactly how you are about Temur Sapora.'

He lowered his head so his lips were only inches from hers. His breath warmed her skin. 'Maybe it makes us a good match.'

'Maybe it does,' she agreed as she moved closer until her lips were only millimetres from his. She couldn't help but smile.

'I sense you might be trouble,' he teased.

'I think you might be right.' She smiled as his lips met hers. Every cell in her body started reacting. It had been too long—even though it was only a few days. She moved her hand up to behind his head, letting her fingers run through his thick dark hair. He tasted of coffee, strawberries and apples—all the things they'd eaten today—but it was his smell that enticed her more. She couldn't place it, too many pheromones—or maybe that was exactly what it was, maybe they were more of a match than he thought and his pheromones were hooking her in. She didn't care. All she cared about was this moment. Her body melded to his. She was already tired and somehow leaning against him made her instincts soar.

She didn't even notice when the elevator doors slid open.

What she did notice was someone clearing their throat. Loudly.

They sprang apart and Philippe stiffened. 'Luka.' He nodded to the dark-suited man at the door. 'You're looking for me?'

The man started talking in a low voice, his eyes darting over to Arissa and giving her the most dismissive of glances. She was instantly uncomfortable. She waited a few seconds then slid out of the elevator before the doors closed again and started walking down the corridor, praying she was heading in the right direction.

Her heart was thrumming against her chest, part from the reaction to Philippe and part from the adrenaline coursing through her body in annoyance.

She turned a corner and sighed in relief as she recognised the corridor, finding her room quickly and closing the door behind her. She took off her jacket and shoes and flung herself down on the bed. Her head was spinning.

Last time she'd kissed him he was just Philippe, the doctor who was helping at the clinic. This time she'd kissed Prince Philippe of Corinez. Did it feel different? Her heart told her no, but her brain couldn't quite decide.

And as she closed her eyes, she still wasn't quite sure.

There was a thud. She twitched. A few seconds later there was another. This time she was more awake. She blinked and sat up in bed. What was that?

She'd fallen asleep fully clothed. The room was almost dark, the only light filtering in from outside. She shook her head and stood up. What time was it?

There was yet another thud. This time she located the sound and watched as snow slid down the window.

Really?

She looked out of the window and almost laughed when she realised what had been green grass earlier was now completely covered with snow. It wasn't particularly heavy, so whoever was throwing snowballs must be taking their time to scrounge up enough snow.

She shook her head and opened the old-fashioned window, listening to it creak and hoping it wasn't going to land on the hard slabs below. Five minutes in a palace and she might wreck the place.

Another snowball sailed directly past her ear, this one landing on the carpet in the room. 'Hey!' she shouted, turning around to try and pick up the snow. She scattered the snow back out of the window and leaned out, trying to catch a glimpse of who was outside. Turned out she was looking too far away.

Philippe was directly under her window, dressed in a navy-blue jacket. He had a mischievous look on his face.

'Hey, sleepyhead. Want to go for a walk?'

She leaned her elbows on the window ledge. 'I thought you said I was trouble,' she teased.

'Maybe I like trouble.' He was grinning up at her. He held out his hands and spun around. 'Let me show you the gardens while they're dusted with snow. It never usually comes this far down the mountain this time of year. By morning, I guarantee it will all be gone.'

She shook her head. 'Snow, in the middle of summer. It's definitely weird.'

'Come on.' He waved her down. 'Grab a jacket and some boots and let's go.'

It only took a few moments to get ready. She threw on a whole new set of clothes: new jeans, a green top, a pair of boots and the only thicker jacket she'd brought with her. She laughed as she zipped it. It was navy blue. They'd look like a matching pair.

She made her way down the stairs and out into the cold night air. Philippe had moved nearer the door and was standing waiting for her. 'What time is it?' she asked. She hadn't even had a chance to look at the clock. It felt as if she'd slept for ever. She wrinkled her nose. 'Did I miss dinner?' she asked as she stared up at the black night sky.

He laughed. 'You definitely missed dinner. It's nearly midnight.'

'Is it?' She felt her eyes widen. 'I can't believe I slept so long.'

He leaned over and touched her nose with one cold finger. 'Jet lag. Told you.'

She gave a little yelp and jumped back. 'Hey, you're freezing.'

He reached out and grabbed her hand. 'And I plan on getting you cold too. It's summer. Who can wear gloves in the middle of summer?'

She shivered as his cold hand closed around hers. But she didn't pull away. She didn't want to. 'You obviously should,' she quipped. 'But, hey, I can make the ultimate sacrifice and try and heat you up.'

'I like the sound of that.'

He pulled her closer and put his arm around her shoulders. Even though the air was chilly she was much more conscious of the length of his body next to hers and the heat coming from it.

She shook her head as they started walking across the gardens. 'Can't believe I completely slept through dinner.'

He grinned and shrugged. 'I could have left you to sleep, but I think you'd probably have woken up about three or four in the morning and not be able to get back to sleep. This way, you're up for a few hours and will hopefully get back to sleep before breakfast rolls around.'

'Where are we going for breakfast tomorrow, then?' she asked.

He gave her a sideways glance. 'I thought you might like to sleep a little later.'

'And miss out on breakfast with you?' Her stomach gave a squeeze. Maybe he was trying to let her down gently, or maybe he was just too busy to spend time with her. After all, what did a prince do all day—particularly one who wanted to reform his health service? The reality was he probably didn't have time for her at all.

He started to talk but she shook her head. 'Forget it. You're busy. I get it. I'll just see you at the hospital in the afternoon like we planned.'

They were walking behind a high hedge and turned a corner and she let out a little gasp. 'Wow.'

The gardens were split level. 'Left or right?' he asked.

Beneath them on one side looked like the oriental gardens, even in the dark night she could see the outline of a pagoda, an arched bridge and hear the sounds of waterfalls. On the other side was a large maze. In the dark it looked quite ominous.

'Let's go to the right,' she said. 'Show me around the oriental gardens.'

'Chicken,' he teased as he led her down the steps towards the gardens.

She shook her head. 'Not at all. I just think the oriental gardens look interesting.'

There was only one old-fashioned lamp post at the entrance to the oriental gardens casting a dim light on the path before them. He walked her slowly around the large gardens. Under the stars she could see the pagoda was painted red and gold with intricate styling. The light dusting of snow made it look even more magical.

Philippe showed her the Kwanzan cherry trees, the bamboo, flowering plums and Japanese black pine. He led her across one of the bridges and stopped in the middle, looking down into the dark pond beneath them. 'I'm not sure if you can see but the pond is full of koi—they're known as the fish of emperors.

Arissa bent forward for a better look. 'If there's snow falling, isn't it too cold for them?' she asked. The water rippled as she caught a flick of an orange tail just beneath them.

He nodded. 'When it's cold they tend to gather just under the bridge where it gives more shelter. But we never usually have any problems with them. They're hardy little creatures.'

He moved his arm from her shoulders and took her by the hand, leading her around the pond edges, pointing out the weeping willow trees and water lilies. Eventually the path led them back to the entrance.

He nodded ahead. 'Okay, have you managed to work up enough courage yet for the maze?'

She put one hand on her hip. 'I've got the feeling you'll have a distinct advantage here. You've grown up with this maze. You could probably go through it blindfolded.'

He opened his mouth in teasing horror. 'Were you spying on me when I was a kid?'

'Hardly.' She pressed her lips together for a second. She had to say something. She wasn't sure when else she would get the opportunity. 'I didn't know anything about you, Philippe, because I didn't generally read about princes when I was a kid.'

The air was still around them. He looked down for a second. It was clear he knew where this would be heading. 'Arissa...' he started, letting his voice trail off.

She stepped forward and gave a little shake of her head, pressing her hand to his chest. She wasn't afraid to touch him. She wasn't afraid of familiarity. But she had to let him know how she felt.

'You worked with me for nearly two weeks, Philippe. You never said a word. I felt foolish when you finally told me you were a prince.'

He sighed and nodded his head, waiting a few seconds before lifting his gaze to meet hers. 'I didn't want to ruin anything.'

'With the truth?'

It was obvious he was frustrated. 'I wasn't there to be a prince. I wasn't even there to be a doctor. I went to Temur Sapora for a rest—but you know how that turned out.' He held out his hands. 'I had two weeks of un-planned nothingness. Two weeks to get my head around what had happened here, and the role I was coming back to. Changes have been needed for years, and, although I've always known that, I've never really known where to start. The last few months have made me realise it has to be maternity services. It goes hand in hand with the safe haven work.' He stopped and reached up and ran his hands through her curls. 'And then, there was you.'

He gave her a smile that warmed her all the way to her toes.

'Me?' All of a sudden it was difficult to swallow.

'You. Arissa Cotter. Mrs No Nonsense. Mrs Plans. The woman with a fantastic career path at her feet, but still having a commitment to, and love for the place you came from.'

The edges of her lips turned upwards. 'Isn't that nor-mal?'

He moved his hand to her shoulder. 'Maybe. It's nor-mal for you. And it's normal for me. But for lots of other people...' He shook his head. 'Lots of other people just seem to want to leave their past and home behind them. Like ancient history.'

She took a few seconds to answer. 'But I love my home.'

'And that's part of what I love about you.'

She froze. She knew it was just a figure of speech but she couldn't help but instantly be a little scared. Love was a big word to say around someone.

Philippe didn't seem to notice her tensing. He just kept talking, his hand drifting back to tangle in her hair. 'But it wasn't just that. You seemed to like spending time with me, *just* being me. Not a prince. Not someone who could help change in their country. And I liked that.' He stopped for a second, his gaze locking with hers. 'Because the truth is, for me, that's different. The last few months working in Corinez? People treat me like I'm some kind of special event—not a real doctor. But working with you in Temur Sapora? I loved the anonymity. I loved the fact I was just Philippe. Nothing else. Because here, in Corinez, I never get to just be Philippe. They want Prince Philippe. They don't want me.' He put his hand to his chest again. 'All my life that's who I've been, that's who I'll always be. I've never had the chance to just be Philippe. Coming to Temur Sapora was the first time in thirty years I've had that opportunity.'

He let out a wry laugh. 'And maybe I've got this all wrong, but I think you quite liked Philippe.'

She stood very still for a minute, letting her breath steam in the air between them. She was trying hard to understand what kind of life he'd led. The pressure put on him. Things she'd never once in a lifetime thought about—never had reason to.

She reached up and touched his face. 'You're different here. I noticed it from the second you stepped off the plane. Here, you're Prince Philippe. I thought I already knew you, but I guess I only know part of you.'

He shook his head. 'That's not true. The person at the clinic, the person who tried to cook you dinner, the person who swam in the ocean with you. That's me. That's who I am. You know the real Philippe.'

She shook her head and gave a sad kind of smile. Her

heart felt a little heavy. 'For me to get to know you, I need to know all of you—not just the person you want me to see.'

She could sense he was getting anxious. He thudded his hand against his heart. 'This is the real me. You know me. You met me back on Temur Sapora.'

But she shook her head again. 'I met part of you. Not all of you.' She held out her hands. 'This is the place where you feel most at home. This is where you lived your life and grew up. I know and liked Philippe Aronaz. I've still to make my mind up about Prince Philippe of Corinez.'

She tipped her head to one side. 'You might not know this, but you have a bit of a reputation as being a playboy. Or being on—' she put her fingers in the air '—"the most eligible royals in the world" list.'

He visibly cringed. 'I hate all that stuff.'

'There's a world of pictures out there, Philippe, of you with a gorgeous girl wearing million-dollar jewellery and clothes on your arm. *Lots* of girls.'

He leaned forward and caught her face with his hands. 'But you are more beautiful than all of them.'

She shook her head. 'But that's not me. That won't ever be me. I want to keep doing the job that I love and keep my head down. I don't want to be photographed. I don't want my life picked apart by nosey reporters. I don't want to be one of "those" people who court the media. I'm not sure that part of your life will ever change. And I wouldn't ask you to change your life for me. This, this is your destiny.'

There was silence for a few seconds, because both of them knew that was true.

He spoke slowly, his words almost pleading. 'But

you're here, now. You came halfway around the world with me. For a guy you met in a clinic two weeks ago. That must mean something. Don't give up on something before it's even started. You came here to help me work. Let's do it. Help me. Be a part of the changes I want to make here.'

She could see the enthusiasm emanating from every part of him and it made her ache. From the second she'd looked down from her window tonight, a little part of her had worried.

Things were different here, and, even though she'd expected them to be, it was only now starting to sink in.

She couldn't ever get back the guy she'd kissed and swum in the ocean with. No matter how much she wanted him.

She had no job to go to right now. It made sense to stay here. But the more time she spent in Philippe's company the more she realised she was gradually losing a little part of her heart to him—a guy she could never really be with.

Did she really want to do that?

She licked her lips. 'I'll stay, just for a while. But I'll be applying for other jobs. I need to find another paediatric oncology centre where there is a suitable position—and this time, I'll sort out my own visa.'

There was a flash of disappointment in his eyes and she hated that she'd put it there. But honesty was better.

If she'd known he was a prince would she have let him close to her? Probably not, and that made her stomach twist in a way she didn't like at all. Because this man standing in front of her was the man who'd made electricity flow through her skin. The man who'd kissed her in a way that no one else ever had. She couldn't ignore that. No matter how much other stuff was going on in her head.

She looked around. It was pitch black. They were in the middle of the palace gardens in the dead of night. For a few minutes more she could try to forget about the prince part. She could try and remember the gorgeous man she'd wrapped her legs around in the ocean and raced to the buoy.

She stepped forward and gave him a smile. 'How about, for now, we just be you, and me?'

She saw his shoulders relax. It was as if a weight had just lifted from him. 'Show me your maze, Philippe,' she said quietly, leaving all the titles to the side.

He slid his hand into hers in agreement. 'Come on, then.'

They entered the maze. The hedges were at least eight feet tall; there was no way either of them could see over. 'I should have tried to memorise what this looked like when we were on the steps above,' she murmured.

He gave a laugh. 'Lots of people try to do that. Most of the time it doesn't work.' He turned around so he was walking backwards and facing her.

She wrinkled her nose. 'Isn't there a thing you're supposed to do in mazes?' She held up her hand. 'That's it, if you keep your left hand running along the hedges you'll always find the way out.'

He shook his head. 'Old wives' tale. No truth in it at all.'

'Really?' She was suspicious now, not sure whether to believe him or not. The further they went into the maze, the darker it got. Shadows seemed to lurk around every corner. 'I think I might have preferred this in the daytime,' she joked.

'Oh, come on,' he teased. 'What do you think is in here? Lions, tigers and bears?'

She shook her head at the film reference. 'I was thinking more like goblins, warlocks and trolls.'

'Ouch,' he said. 'What kind of kids' stories did you read?'

'The good ones.'

They kept walking. He backwards and she forwards. It was odd. It was cute. They were shielded from the world. She liked it that way. Here they could be anyone they wanted to be. Here, she could be with anyone she wanted to be.

They turned a corner and the maze changed. There was a paved area with a star in the middle and a wrought-iron bench. 'Is this it? Have we reached the centre?'

He nodded and pulled her down onto the bench. She perched on the edge of his lap. 'So,' she said with a smile on her face. 'Now we've reached the middle, what happens next?'

The words hung in the air between them. They both knew exactly what she meant.

Philippe slid his hands up around her neck. 'How about you make good on the sacrifice you offered to make a little earlier?'

She frowned. 'What one was that?'

He pulled her closer. 'The one where you offered to heat me up,' he whispered, his lips making a trail down the side of her face.

Their skin brushed together. Full of intent. 'Oh, I have a rule,' she said huskily, 'that I always make good on my promises.'

A smile danced across her lips. 'Somehow I like that,' he said as his lips met hers.

And for a few moments she forgot about everything else. About the palace. About the press. And the fact she was kissing a prince. And just concentrated on the man whose lips were setting her world on fire.

# CHAPTER TEN

BY THE TIME afternoon came around she was anxious to get started. The jet lag finally seemed to have eked its way out of her system, and her brain could only focus on how much time she'd spent kissing Philippe last night.

Her brain told her everything about it was wrong. Silly. Nothing could ever come of it. They were almost at opposite ends of a scale.

But her heart? It seemed to defy every piece of logic her brain could throw at her.

She took a quick glance in the mirror and pulled her fitted black suit jacket straight. They were visiting the hospital today so she could give him some feedback and advice about his future plans. She'd decided on the more professional look. She wanted people to take her seriously, to know that she was always committed to providing good health services. She picked up her bag and gave her lips a swipe with rose-coloured lipstick. The knee-length skirt and fitted jacket were smart—she knew that. But her bright blue shirt gave the splash of colour that revealed a bit more of the person that she was. Most professionals would pair the suit with heels but Arissa had spent enough hours in hospitals to know better and she slid on a pair of comfortable flats.

The knock at the door was almost simultaneous with her pulling it open. 'Oh,' she said in surprise.

Philippe was standing in a dark blue suit, paired with pale blue shirt and dark tie. She hadn't seen him since last night and that first sight took her breath away.

He gave a casual grin. 'You're ready. Perfect. Do you need to eat before we go?'

She shook her head. 'Nope. All ready. Let's go. I can't wait to see the hospital.'

He pulled a face. 'There's so much work to be done there. Don't set your expectations too high. I keep telling myself if I want to build a proper health service for the country, I have to start somewhere.' He gestured his elbow towards her and she slid her arm into his.

'Well, that's why I'm here. I've worked in Malaysia, the US, did a spell as a student in England, and have volunteered for Doctors Without Borders in Romania. You've travelled too, you'll have seen enough health service systems to know what you want for Corinez.'

He gave a nod and led her along the corridor. Neither of them mentioned the kiss. Neither of them mentioned the conversation last night.

And to be honest, she was glad.


He knew he was only scratching the surface of the problem. Both in the hospital, and with Arissa.

He'd spent most of last night wondering what he'd done. He'd invited her here because he'd really, really wanted her to come. He couldn't deny the attraction between them. He couldn't pretend that it didn't matter that he knew Arissa liked him for just being him. It meant more than she could ever know.

But some of the things she'd said last night had thrown him sideways. He wasn't *him*. He would never just be *him*. He would always be Prince Philippe—no matter how much he tried to hide from it.

As a child he'd thought it was normal to be photographed and in the media constantly. It hadn't bothered him—more than a few of his teenage misdemeanours had been captured for the world to see. The Playboy Prince tag had been following him around for the last few years as well.

But now, as an adult, when his time of freedom was gone—when his time to return and help shape the healthcare changes had arrived—it was making him more than a little uncomfortable.

For a guy who'd always known who he was and exactly what his role would be, he found himself questioning *everything*.

And that bothered him more than he could ever say out loud. It wasn't even a conversation he could have with anyone else.

But as he showed Arissa around the hospital he got more and more uncomfortable.

She shone. That was the only way he could describe her. She got down on her knees to talk to the kids in the children's unit. She made several suggestions about gaps in services. Both for children and for babies and mothers. She was good at linking pieces of the puzzle together— throwing in things he hadn't yet considered. She challenged him. She made him think.

She talked through the most basic maternity care. Then, they talked about the maternity care he would really like to offer. She helped him make realistic targets and goals. And he needed that. He needed someone to keep him grounded and make the plans in his head into something more tangible.

But they didn't spend all their time in maternity services. Arissa wanted to see around the whole hospital.

She sat for a long time, holding the hand of a war veteran who wanted to reminisce with someone.

The staff and patients loved her. She was relaxed. She knew when to laugh, and when to be serious. He'd always known she would do well here, but seeing how much Arissa got to be herself made him realise how much of a prince-like status he had to keep in place.

Even when they entered the emergency department he couldn't be himself. He walked around, pointing to equipment, suggesting upgrades, suggesting rearranging the trauma room. Several of the members of staff shot him strange looks. Uncomfortable looks. No one questioned him about making suggestions. They all just nodded meekly.

For a few minutes he wished he were back in the clinic in Temur Sapora.

Somewhere he was no longer a prince.

It was different here. Even walking through a department seemed to cause an 'atmosphere'. Something Philippe was becoming more and more aware of.

'What's wrong?' Arissa was in front of him, her wide brown eyes showing a hint of concern. 'Are you okay?'

He gave himself a shake, trying to smooth out the edges he knew he was exposing. 'I'm fine. Just…there's a lot to think about. A lot I'll need to change.'

She nodded. 'This is a huge job, Philippe.' She gave

him a soft smile. 'But remember, you've got a lifetime to change all this. Start small. Start manageable.'

He ran his hands through his hair. 'Like we talked about?'

She nodded. 'You know you want to start with maternity services. Look at your minimum care standards. Look at your population. How many births do you have? Think about numbers. How can you make this realistic? Recruit obstetricians. Recruit midwives. Recruit lab staff for the extra blood work, sonographers for the baby scans. It ties in with the implementation of the safe haven project.'

He knew it all made sense. But he couldn't help but say something else. He'd seen how much she'd thrived in this environment today. 'What about paediatrics? We don't have any specialists like you. We don't have anyone who specialises in paediatric haematology.' Enthusiasm was brimming over in him.

She tilted her head to the side. 'No. But you can include something like that in plans for the future. Tackle maternity services. Then, in a few years, think about children's services.'

He lowered his voice. 'But if I started with paediatrics instead, I could offer you a job. I could get you to stay.'

She blinked. Shock written all over her face. It was clear he had blindsided her.

It was selfish. It was entirely selfish. It was ridiculous. But he couldn't shake the horrible dark cloud at the back of his head that kept whispering to him that soon she would be gone.

But Arissa stepped right up to him, looking him

straight in the face with those big brown eyes. It was almost as if she could read his mind sometimes.

'Philippe,' she said quietly, with the hint of a smile on her lips. 'I love that you're thinking about me—in amongst the world of things you already have to do.'

She shook her head. 'But we both know how important it is that you get this right. You need to take a bit of time to consider everything. Probably write up a business plan. Discuss it with the other members of your committee and decide what is actually feasible.' She licked her lips and gave him a soft smile. 'And not let yourself be influenced by a girl who kissed you in a dark maze at night.'

Darn it. He wanted to kiss her again. She was right— and she was sensible enough to know that, even though he'd said the words out loud, it had only been a flash of an idea. Not anything tangible. At least not right now.

He hated that part.

She held up her hands. 'Maybe, in a few years—' she winked ' we can talk again. You could consider children's services in Corinez.'

She wasn't saying no. His heart gave a leap in his chest.

He slid his hand into hers as pieces in his brain slotted into place. She gave the briefest start of surprise, looking down at their joined hands. Maybe she hadn't expected him to show his affection in public. Before, they'd really been at arm's length while outside the palace. But he couldn't pretend that he wanted to be at arm's length from Arissa.

He could also see the way that everyone who'd come into contact with them had reacted to her.

After a few minutes in her company and listening to her intelligent conversation, the staff and directors of the hospital had looked at her with interest and respect. She seemed to be able to bring out the best in people. She knew how to engage. She knew how to act. And she knew how to listen—one of the biggest skills of a doctor.

Her manner was calm but enthusiastic. She was certainly at home within a hospital environment; it was almost like watching her bloom and grow. Whoever the hospital was in London that had let her slip through their fingers—they were clearly fools.

By the time they'd made their way back to the main entrance of the hospital the sky was beginning to grow dark and they'd stayed there more than three hours longer than originally had been planned.

Philippe gave a grateful smile to the staff that had accompanied them. Not one of them had complained. His own personal secretary had only made a few occasional glances at his watch and disappeared at one point to make a call to obviously reschedule something or another. It was as if everyone was as enthusiastic as he was. Most were full of some sort of ideas—even if they didn't really know where to start.

It seemed that most of the people who worked within the healthcare system in Corinez were ready for change. More than that—they were embracing it. If he could capture what was in the air right now and bottle it things might actually change. And Arissa was a big part of this. She made him stop to consider ways to make it bite-sized and manageable. That was what he needed right now. It was as if she knew him better than he knew himself.

As they slid into the car that had pulled up outside for them he turned to face her.

But before he even had a chance to say a word she leaned across the car and put her head on his shoulder.

'Oh, my goodness, I'm exhausted. It feels like being at the end of a twenty-four-hour shift.' Her hand moved and rested against his chest. Her fingers gave a few anxious drums against his chest wall. 'What do you think? Will you be able to make some plans?'

He stared down at the dark curls directly under his nose as the aroma from her orange shampoo drifted up around him. He couldn't help but inhale. So much of today had been good. So much of the last couple of weeks had made his brain spin.

But the one thing that seemed entirely certain was the warmth and weight of the woman currently lying halfway across him. Their breaths were rising and falling in unison. He liked that. He liked that they seemed so in sync.

Last night it had seemed as if she was trying to take a step back. A step away from him and the life that he was designated to live. Now, he felt in perfect harmony.

'Oh, yes,' he said quietly. 'I hope to be able to make some plans.'

He breathed in slowly. 'Arissa?' He asked the question quietly, conscious that she already had her eyes half closed.

'Hmm?' She raised her head, her eyelids still mainly closed.

'There's something I'd like to ask you to do.'

This time her eyes opened a bit further. 'What?' she asked sleepily.

He smiled. 'There's something on at the palace in a few days. A ball—of sorts.'

She sat up with a confused expression on her face. 'But…'

He held up his hands. 'This isn't a normal royal ball. This one has no publicity, no press. It's just for my mother's oldest friends and family. We can go together and dance, and have fun. Nothing to worry about. You can...' he touched her cheek '...keep your head below the parapet.' He spoke carefully. 'Would you come with me, Arissa?'

She sat a little straighter. 'No press. No publicity. Only your mother's friends?'

He nodded. 'I have to admit my mother has a few friends. There will be a few other members of royal families across Europe.'

'But no press?' she asked again.

He smiled at her. 'No press. You get to have the fun of attending a ball with free-flowing champagne, a small orchestra, and a world of canapés.'

She wrinkled her nose and looked down at her black suit. 'I didn't exactly bring any kind of ball gown with me. In fact, I don't own any kind of ball gown.'

He gave a laugh. 'Well, in that case. I can either take you somewhere to shop and buy you something new, or you could talk to my sister, who has a wardrobe that covers three rooms—or, you can speak to my mother. She has a bit of a collection of ball gowns from throughout the years. Truth is, in other circumstances I think my mother would be known as a hoarder.'

Arissa blinked her tired eyes. 'How long do I have?'

He pulled a face. 'Less than two days,' he admitted.

She raised her eyebrows. 'What?' Now her eyes opened completely. 'Philippe Aronaz, you're giving me less than two days to find a ball gown for an event that will be filled with your family and friends?'

He shifted on the leather seat of the car. 'Yip. That would be about right.'

She nodded her head then gave him a sideways glance.

'Okay, so you're offering to take me to a ball where I can be on your arm, dance my heart out, and not worry about it being in the news?' She folded her hands in her lap. 'I haven't even met your mother yet—how can I ask to wear one of her old gowns?'

He shook his head. 'She's not been here. She's been in Austria. She'll be back tomorrow, and I can promise you right now that she'll be delighted if you wear one of her gowns. Every year she tries to persuade my sister to pick something from her collection.'

Arissa rested her head back on his shoulder. 'Okay, Philippe, you have a room full of dresses and you've invited me to a ball in the palace. It's like you jumped into my childhood and found one of my kids' fairy stories. How on earth could any girl say no to an invitation like that?'

He couldn't help but smile as a warm feeling spread through him. She'd said yes. It was the first time he'd ever taken someone to his mother's annual ball. He'd taken a variety of partners to various palace events throughout the years. Ones when he'd needed someone on his arm, at a time when he'd been expected to court the media. But he'd never taken anyone to his mother's private ball. This one was entirely different. He moved slightly, adjusting Arissa in his arms.

She smiled with her eyes still closed. 'Now, wake me up when we get back to the palace.'

The maid had shown her up to the room on the first floor of the palace. She gave a little gasp as she stepped into the large space. The walls were pale yellow and the large windows allowed light to stream into the room.

On one side of the room, away from the light of the

windows, were row upon row of a multitude of dresses all shrouded in protective covers. The dresses were arranged like a rainbow with one range of colours flowing into the others.

Arissa's mouth fell open as she wandered along the rows, her hands reaching up to touch the odd dress to examine it a little closer.

The maid smiled. 'They're beautiful, aren't they?' She moved alongside Arissa. 'Is there a particular style you like best, or you find the most flattering? Or is there a colour you like best? I know all the dresses,' she said casually. 'I can probably point you in the right direction.'

It was like being the proverbial child in a sweet shop. Arissa's eyes were practically on stalks as she wandered along the rows. 'There's just so many,' she said in wonder. The maid shot her a smile and settled down in a chair in the corner of the room. There was a huge mirror on the wall close to her, along with a circular velvet curtain that swept around to give a private dressing area. This whole room was dedicated to the enjoyment of trying on these dresses. Every little girl's dream.

After a while she shook her head and held out her hands. 'The truth is, I have no idea where to start. I've never been to a ball—I don't know what's suitable and what's not.'

The maid came and stood in front of her, not hiding the fact that her discerning eye was sweeping up and down Arissa's frame.

'Will anything even fit me?' Arissa asked self-consciously.

The maid gave a smile. 'I think just about everything here will fit you. And if it doesn't? No problem. We have a seamstress on hand who can tweak any dress.' She put her hand to her mouth. 'Now...' she said. This time she started to walk around Arissa. 'What's your favourite part of yourself, and your least favourite part?'

Arissa tilted her head.

The maid smiled and continued. 'There's a whole bounty of dresses in here that I think will be perfect. But it's you that's wearing this dress, and you need to love it enough that you feel comfortable in it. There's no point in me making a suggestion of a dress with a low back if you feel self-conscious about showing skin.'

Arissa gave a nod. 'Okay, I understand. Nothing too revealing for me, then, please. And I'm a little on the short side.' She ran her hand across her stomach. 'And this is probably my worst bit, so nothing that clings too much and shows what I had for dinner.'

The maid laughed. She held out her hands to the array of rainbow dresses. 'You still haven't told me your favourite colour.'

Arissa looked down at the red shirt she was wearing today. 'I guess I like all colours. Preferably not black or white.'

The door opened and the maid turned in surprise. 'Your Majesty, forgive me. I wasn't aware you had returned.' She gestured towards Arissa. 'I was just helping Prince Philippe's guest select a dress for the ball.'

Arissa's feet had found themselves frozen to the floor. She watched as an elegant woman with her fine blonde hair swept up in a chignon came into the room. Her eyes met Arissa's and she gave her a wide smile.

'Ah-h, the doctor.' She walked towards Arissa with her arms outstretched. 'So you're the woman my son has been talking about so much.'

'I am?' She was stunned. She wasn't even sure Philippe would have mentioned her at all to his mother.

'Maria Aronaz,' said the woman, clasping Arissa's hands in hers. Panic flooded through Arissa. Was she supposed to bow, curtsey? What did you do around royalty these days? How did you even address them?

Her brain focused on the maid's words. She dipped her head a little. 'It's a pleasure to meet you, Your Majesty. Thank you for welcoming me into your home.'

The woman kept her hands on Arissa's. Her eyes were warm but Arissa knew that the Queen was inspecting her to see if she was worthy of her son's attention. 'You are indeed beautiful,' the Queen said quietly as she squeezed Arissa's hands. 'And I hear that your home is as beautiful as ours.' She was watching Arissa carefully. 'Philippe has an enormous job ahead of him. Probably harder than the roles of his brother and sister.'

Arissa gave an uncomfortable gulp. The role of potential King would be hard enough, and being part of a finance committee wouldn't exactly be easy either. The Queen continued, 'Things are going to have to change in Corinez, and Philippe will have to weather the storm that comes alongside making changes. It would be good if he could have someone alongside him who shared his vision and understood the tasks he had ahead.'

Silence. Arissa couldn't even gulp. What exactly did the Queen mean? Her gaze felt so examining. She patted Arissa's hand. 'You know, he's never brought anyone home for this ball before.'

She turned towards her maid. 'Have you picked something for Arissa yet?'

The maid shook her head. 'Not yet, Your Majesty. That was our next step.'

The Queen pulled her hands back and gave them a little clap. 'Good, I haven't missed the fun part.' She walked up and down the rows, giving the dresses a critical and appraising look. 'No, no, no, too dark, too severe. Too out of fashion.'

The Queen picked out a few dresses. 'This one, this one and, perhaps, this one. Oh, and this one too.'

Arissa was a little stunned and she couldn't help but smile. Every one of the dresses was by a female designer. The Queen waved away the maid and carried the dresses over herself to the curtained area. Red, blue, green and silver. Each one completely different from the other.

She gave a gentle wave of her hand but had an excited gleam in her eyes as she turned around. 'Come on, Arissa, what are you waiting for? Let's try on some dresses.'

Philippe was nervous. He could hear the murmur of voices downstairs. Guests had been arriving for the ball for the last half-hour. His brother and sister were already greeting people on arrival, and normally he would be doing that too. Instead, he'd spent the last thirty minutes immersed in a conference call to three other countries about their maternity services. He was gathering as much information as he could. He had to, if he wanted to make things a success.

He glanced at his watch as he hurried down the corridor towards Arissa's rooms. Her door was wide open and she was silhouetted as she stood at the large window, looking out over the gardens.

His breath caught somewhere in his throat as she spun around towards him. She was wearing a dark green gown with a sequined bodice, gauze shoulders and a fluttering straight tulle skirt. It complemented her skin perfectly. Her only jewellery was a gold choker at her throat. She lifted her fingers to it self-consciously as she took a few steps towards him. 'What do you think? Your mother gave me it to wear.' She glanced downwards. 'Isabella Hugo designed it when she was still up and coming. Isn't it beautiful?' She gave her head a shake, as if she couldn't believe things. 'Your mother was amazing. In fact, she helped me pick this whole outfit.'

She lifted her gaze to meet his. Her hair wasn't coiffed or styled, it was in the natural curls that she always wore and suited her best. She was wearing a little make-up; he could see the mascara opening out her eyes, and the lipstick on her lips. But even wearing the designer dress and the royal jewellery she still looked entirely like Arissa. She still looked entirely his.

'You look amazing,' he whispered as his lips brushed the side of her cheek.

She patted her stomach. 'Thank you, but I'm a bit nervous.'

He took a step back and offered out his arm to her. Right now, what he really wanted to do was kick the door closed behind them both, and keep Arissa all to himself. But this was all part and parcel of what he needed to do next.

He needed to introduce her to the other side of his life. The one that the world would normally see. Tonight was almost like a trial run. She still hadn't told him why she wanted to stay out of the spotlight so much. He didn't want to pry into her life. He wanted her to tell him when, and if, she was ready.

But tonight she would meet his mother's friends and dignitaries from other countries. This ball was always less formal than any other thanks to the privacy surrounding it. He wanted Arissa to be comfortable in his home, and around his family, and this was the best place to start.

His brother and sister were already curious and had only been held off by his excuses of how much work he and Arissa were doing right now.

He smiled. He might have known his mother would manage to circumvent him in one way or another. And the fact that Arissa was currently wearing his great-grandmother's jewellery gave him a feel for how much the Queen must have liked Arissa.

'How did you find my mother?' he asked.

She smiled as she slid her arm through his. 'For a queen, she's surprisingly like most mothers,' she joked. 'But you might have warned me how I was supposed to act around her.'

'Like yourself,' he said quickly. 'And you didn't need any warning. I knew she was going to love you anyway.'

He stopped at the top of the stairs. 'I can see how much she likes you. That choker was my great-grandmother's. It's one of her favourites.'

Arissa's hands went quickly to her throat as her eyes widened. 'It is? Oh, wow. I had no idea. She never said.'

'She wouldn't.' He looked down towards the ballroom. The music drifted up towards them and people were already circulating in the space below. The waiting staff wore red jackets and ties, or white blouses trimmed with red and black waistcoats. Silver trays were held aloft and the staff moved seamlessly amongst the guests.

Arissa shot him a sideways glance. 'It all looks choreographed. Like some elaborate dance.'

He could sense her nerves and bent closer, tilting her

chin up towards his. 'You have nothing to worry about. Tonight is just about mixing with friends. You'll get to meet some of the ministers from the surrounding countries.' A bright laugh carried through the air and Philippe rolled his eyes. 'And you'll get to meet my Aunt Livia, who I guarantee will be the wickedest woman in the room.'

'What about your brother and sister—and your father—what if they don't like me?'

She'd never really seemed nervous like this around him before. He dipped his head and dropped a kiss on her lips. 'They'll love you. Because I do.'

For a second her pupils widened, as if she'd just taken stock of those words. He'd said them out loud without thinking. Something he'd never, ever done in the past. But before he had time to think about it any further there was a noise behind him.

One of the palace staff gave him a nod. 'I'll announce you,' she said briefly.

'Prince Philippe of Aronaz and Dr Arissa Cotter.'

Neither of them had time to think further as all the faces in the ballroom turned upwards to look at them. Arissa slid her arm into his elbow again and he put his hand over hers as they walked down the stairs.

He nodded at a few people on the way down, crossing the ballroom floor towards the area where the King and Queen and the rest of the royal family were congregated.

The crowd parted around them. His brother had an amused grin on his face. His sister was watching Arissa carefully. He could almost see her sizing Arissa up. His mother smiled approvingly and his father stopped the conversation he was in the middle of, to reach out his hands towards them both.

'So this is the lady I've been hearing so much about. It's a pleasure to meet you, Dr Cotter,' said the King.

Before either of them had time to think, the King had kissed Arissa on both cheeks. His sister's eyebrows rose in surprise then she stepped forward and held out her hand. 'Grace Aronaz,' she said, leaving the Princess title to the side.

'And I'm the good-looking one,' said his brother jokingly as he held out his hand to Arissa too. 'Anthony.' He gave Philippe a glance. 'I think my brother has been hiding you from us all. Trying to keep you secret.' He dipped down low and kissed Arissa's hand. 'It's a pleasure to meet you, Dr Cotter. We hope we'll have a chance to get to know you a little better.' He stepped forward and pretended to whisper in her ear. 'And I have a dozen stories on Philippe that you'll be able to use as blackmail material on him.'

Arissa's eyes were wide. Maybe she hadn't expected such a warm welcome. But Philippe wouldn't have expected anything else from his family.

'It's Arissa, please,' she said finally. 'And it's a pleasure to meet you all.'

The music picked up tempo behind them. The King's eyes gleamed. 'Oh, it's that time again. Right, I'm off to find old Aunt Livia, try and stop whatever trouble she is causing and sweep her around the dance floor while I tell her off.'

Philippe looked at Arissa's surprised face. 'I warned you about her. Wait and see—at various points, each one of us will take her around the dance floor before she ruins any of our diplomatic relationships.'

He watched as Anthony grabbed two glasses of champagne from a tray and moved over next to a blonde woman in a silver gown. Grace turned her attentions to an older woman and launched into a long story. And his mother gave him the slightest nod of her head, which he knew was approval.

He wasn't embarrassed to admit the relief that flooded through his body. All of his family liked her—just as he'd known they would. He could only imagine the questions he'd get later when he was on his own.

He gestured towards the white and black dance floor. 'How are your dancing feet? Do you trust me not to stand on your toes?'

She gave him a nervous kind of smile. Her shoulders had relaxed just a little. 'I guess I could risk it,' she said.

He led her to the dance floor and took her into his arms. It was perfect. The music. The dancing. The lights around them gradually lowered, leaving the ballroom illuminated by flickering candlelight. It was an illusion of course—they weren't real candles, but no one really cared.

They toasted with champagne and ate some of the canapés that were offered. As the sky grew dark outside and the temperature in the ballroom rose, the doors to the gardens were opened. The cooler night air didn't deter people from walking outside.

After her initial few minutes of nervousness, Arissa relaxed. Maybe it was the thought of meeting his parents and family, or maybe it was the whole intimidation factor of appearing at a ball with a prince.

She wasn't used to the life that he had. He'd met Arissa in her own life where she was a capable and competent doctor. Rarely fazed and always able to deal with unexpected emergencies. He'd admired her tenacity and just how capable she was, keeping so many balls juggling in the air at once. Most of all he'd admired her 'can do' attitude.

Tonight there had been a flicker of uncertainty and something else. She'd gripped his arm tighter than she ever had before. Part of him hated that it was him that had put her in this position. He'd almost forgotten how intimidating this could all be to someone who hadn't been brought up in this life.

But Arissa had handled things like a pro. She'd helped him manoeuvre a conversation with a difficult diplomat onto something much less flammable. She'd charmed a few of his mother's friends. He tried his best to ignore the knowing glances they all shot him, smiling and moving on to the next group.

By the time it was almost midnight, he was conscious of the fact Arissa was leaning on his arm. 'You okay?' he asked.

She was staring out at the gardens that had been lit tonight with some pale pink and pale blue lights. 'We could have done with those the other night,' she said dreamily.

'But how would I have enticed you into the maze if everything was clearly lit?' he teased.

One eyebrow rose. 'You enticed me?'

'I think so.'

She gave a shrug. 'Okay, I'll give you that. Maybe you did.' She kept looking out into the dark. 'It's beautiful out there.' She sighed.

'It's beautiful in here too,' he said huskily. She turned to face him, his hands going to her waist. 'You did great tonight. How do you feel?'

'Tired,' she admitted, then gave him a confused glance. 'What—was this some kind of test? What if I hadn't done great?'

He shook his head. 'No. No test. I'd never do that. But this…' he held out his hand to the ballroom behind them '…this is part of my life. It always has been and it always will be. I want you to be comfortable when you're around me, and my family.'

She stayed still for a few seconds, her dark brown eyes staring straight at him. 'Why?' she asked in a croaky voice.

Part of him wanted to cringe. This wasn't the place to have this conversation. He hadn't even really thought things through. He was acting on instinct. But every instinct was telling him the woman in his arms was his highest priority right now.

'Because I want you to stay,' he said.

She flinched. She actually flinched and stepped back out of his arms.

Every part of him recoiled. He'd mistimed things. She wasn't ready to hear anything like this. Or, worst case, she didn't feel the same way.

Arissa put her hand up to her chest. 'But I have things to do, Philippe. I have responsibilities back in Temur Sapora—you know that. I need to find a new job.'

His heart twisted in his chest. He knew all this. He'd known all this before he'd asked her to stay. He'd known all this before he'd told her how he felt.

He wanted to take the words back. Not because he didn't mean them—but because she wasn't ready.

Arissa took another few steps back, nearly tripping over the fabric of her dress. 'I…I…need…'

She looked panicked. He hated that. And he hated more that he'd done it to her.

He held up one hand. 'You need some time. You need some space. You're right. I'm sorry.' He shook his head.

'I should never have said anything.' He gave the slightest dip of his head. 'I'm sorry.'

Then he turned and headed back into the crowded ballroom, letting his professional Prince face slide back into place. Nodding at the right people, making all the right gestures, while all the time his heart was back out on the patio with Arissa, breaking over and over again.

## CHAPTER ELEVEN

SHE STARED AT the teapot on the table in front of her. So far she'd had green tea, lemon and ginger and some kind of camomile. None of them had helped the knots in her stomach.

She was sitting bunched up on one of the chairs in her pyjamas with a blanket tucked around her shoulders. She'd seen the sun come up and the gardens gradually come to life.

Her rational brain was doing its best to kick into gear.

When Philippe had looked at her last night all the little jumbled pieces of her brain had slotted into place.

He'd asked her to stay. To stay with him.

It didn't matter it was impossible. It didn't matter it was crazy. What mattered was the intent. The emotion.

It had taken the feet from under her.

Arissa had always been a planner. That was how she'd got through life—meticulous planning. The fact that she'd just had a job pulled from her grasp because of visa details had completely unseated her. Things like that didn't happen to her.

But then, things like Prince Philippe didn't happen to her either.

After a day of being in his company she'd known that

she liked him. His easy manner, his flirting, his work with the patients and interest in the people around him hadn't escaped her notice.

As for the kisses…and the electricity between them? She couldn't pretend it wasn't there.

But Corinez was a whole different story. She'd already told him, but he *was* different here. Not in a bad way, just in a more formal way.

Someone knocked on the door. 'Come in.'

The palace press secretary put her head around the door. 'Dr Cotter,' she said warily.

'Come in,' said Arissa again, waving her hand.

The press secretary took a sideways step into the room. She looked as if this was the last place she wanted to be. She was clutching one of the early morning newspapers in her hands. 'I'm sorry,' she said hesitantly.

'For what?' asked Arissa.

The secretary swallowed nervously and stepped forward. 'I think you should maybe go online.'

Arissa blinked as the newspaper unfolded in her hands. Right in the centre of the front page was a picture of her and Philippe. It had been taken last night. She was wearing the gown that was hanging in the corner of the room and the gold choker that was nestled inside the black velvet box on her table. Philippe had his hand on her cheek and was looking down at her, just as she was looking up at him—as if they were the only two people on this planet.

Her breathing stuttered.

While the picture took her breath away, the headline sent a chill over her skin.

*Why Is Prince Philippe Hiding His New Bride?*

She stumbled to her feet. 'What?'

The press secretary jumped back. 'I'm sorry. There's never been pictures taken at the private ball before. I don't know who would do such a thing. But—' she glanced at the clock; it wasn't even seven o'clock yet '—we have a meeting scheduled in five minutes. We'll release a statement. We'll get to the bottom of this. I just felt I should alert you in the meantime.'

Panic was sweeping over her. Her picture. *Her* picture on the front page of a newspaper.

How long before they found out who she was? How long before they started probing into her background? How long before the headline above her was *Abandoned Baby*? The press secretary glanced at her watch and gave Arissa a sorry nod. 'I'll get back to you,' she said quietly as she left the room.

Arissa started pacing. She couldn't help it. She pulled up her tablet and dabbed in her own name.

Headline after headline.

*The Prince's Bride Dressed in Old Queen's Gown.*

*Arissa Cotter, Who Is She and How Did She Hook the Most Eligible Bachelor in Europe?*

She shuddered. It was happening. Her life being picked apart. How far back would they go?

She flicked on the TV. Immediately she saw her name on the ticker tape running along the bottom of the screen.

A woman dressed in a bright pink suit was talking to the news anchor.

'No one has heard of her,' the woman said, throwing her hands in the air. 'Apparently, she's a doctor. But she can't be a very good one. Why else would she lose the job in London?'

If it were possible, her blood ran cold.

Another woman, dressed in a similar suit, on the other

side of the anchor cut in. 'But maybe she doesn't need to be a doctor any more. After all—' she raised her eyebrows '—she's just hooked a prince.'

Arissa leaned forward and put her head in her hands. No. This couldn't be happening.

Sure enough, they jumped from one subject to another.

'We hardly know a thing about her. Do we have a contact in Temur Sapora who could fill in the gaps?'

'The Queen let her wear one of the dresses from her collection *and* a family heirloom. Should we be reading more into this?'

The other woman's eyes gleamed. 'Could this be our new princess?' She clapped her hands together. 'Oh, we need to find out everything. Who her parents are, where she went to school, what her friends say about her.' She leaned forward conspiratorially. 'What her *patients* say about her.'

Arissa thought she was going to be sick all over the pristine carpet beneath her feet. Every part of her skin prickled. Did the woman even realise what she'd just implied? Not only would they invade Arissa's privacy, but they might also invade her patients' privacy.

She grabbed hold of the side of the bed. She actually felt light-headed.

The news anchor cut the conversation with a wide grin. 'I think we'll leave it there before these two start planning their wedding outfits.' He shot a smile to the camera. 'But why don't *you* tell us what you think of this news? You can send us a message on…'

He recited all the ways to contact the news station as Arissa sagged back down onto the edge of the bed.

Philippe opened the door. No knocking. No waiting. He was dressed in a T-shirt and joggers, his face pale and dark circles under his eyes. There was someone else behind him hovering in the corridor outside.

'Arissa? I'm sorry. I had no idea. No idea that someone would take pictures of us.' He glanced towards the TV screen and frowned as he recognised the TV channel.

She shook her head. But before she got a chance to speak he'd crossed the room and wrapped his arms around her.

She was angry. She was upset. No, she was furious. But his actions completely and utterly disarmed her. She'd expected him to be defensive. To be apologetic.

Her body was tense. Every cell lit up in indignation. But his voice was low. She could feel the tremor in it. He was angry too. He was furious.

He waved to the door. 'Give us a minute.'

The door silently closed.

'I know you didn't want this. My family knew you didn't want to be in the public eye. They respected your wishes. I didn't know anything about it until someone came and found me a few minutes ago. When I find out who did this...which one of our friends betrayed us...' She could actually feel him shaking. 'And if I'm angry, they have no idea what my mother will be like. Hell hath no fury like the Queen of Corinez.'

She pushed herself free of his grasp and sat back on the bed. Her head was swimming.

'I want to get away,' she said blankly. 'I want to get away from this place and all the people in it.'

Philippe flinched as if she'd just thrown a punch. She couldn't help her words. She needed to be blunt.

Her hands twisted in her lap. She couldn't get any heat into them at all. Her whole body was freezing.

'Arissa.' He sat down next to her and she held up her hand to stop him talking.

She shivered. 'I need to tell you something.'

She could see he wanted to say so much, but he gave a wary nod of his head. 'Okay.'

'I never told you why I don't want to be in the spotlight.' She took a few deep breaths. 'It's not for any scandalous reason, or anything that I've done wrong. It's just a part of me that I want to stay private.'

She could tell he still wanted to talk, but she wouldn't let him. She had to finish.

'The safe haven project. There's more than one reason that I'm interested in it.'

'What do you mean?'

Arissa licked her lips. 'I was one of those babies.' She held her breath as she could see the pieces slot into place in his brain.

'What?'

'I was an abandoned baby. The story I told you about one of the babies back home—that was me. I was the baby left outside the old clinic overnight. I was the baby that nearly died. I was lucky, someone found me the next morning and I was treated in hospital. I was adopted by two great people and lived a life where I felt completely loved.' She shook her head. 'But I have no idea who my mother was. I have no idea if she's still alive. I have no idea if having me put her in danger, then or even now. All I know is that I've never gone looking for her, and she's never come looking for me.'

Philippe had gone so pale he looked almost grey. But she couldn't stop talking. Now she'd started she had to get it all out.

A tear slid down her face. 'I understand safe haven in

a way that others might not.' She pressed a hand to her chest. 'Sometimes at night I dream of all the reasons a mother would abandon a baby—and not all of them are about the cost of healthcare. What if they're in an abusive relationship? What if having a baby would put them more at risk? What if they've been raped? What if they have mental health issues? What if they are entirely alone and have no support? There are a million reasons why a mother leaves her baby.'

Her hands were shaking now as she tried to keep a handle on her emotions. 'The safe haven project is so important to me. I go hand in hand with it. But what now, Philippe? What if the press dig deeper, they find out my background? What if I become a focal point for them and safe haven is considered some kind of gimmick, instead of the important service we want it to be? What if, when they focus on me, they intrude into my patients' lives and families with sick children start getting harassed?'

She stopped for a second as Philippe's pale face changed into a frown, then lifted her chin and looked him in the eye. 'I won't do that to my patients, Philippe. I won't expose them to that—having a sick kid is hard enough. Plus, I don't want the safe haven project rubbished.' She put her hand on her chest and looked at him again.

Another tear slipped down her cheek. All those reasons were good reasons. She knew that. But she still hadn't mentioned what was at the heart of it all. She drew herself up. 'But as well as all that, I want privacy, Philippe. I don't want people examining my background. Asking stories around the place I lived when I was a kid. My parents were my parents. That's their spot in my life. They weren't rich. We struggled at times. Do you think I want to be splashed across the papers as the abandoned baby from the poor family? Then I won't be good enough, *they* won't be good enough. I won't have that. I can't have that.' She pointed at the paper. 'These are today's headlines. I can only imagine what they'll say tomorrow if they start digging.'

It was almost as if the world were working against her. A few seconds later she recognised a face on screen. Amal. A little kid she'd worked with in Washington with leukaemia. He was sitting in his wheelchair, beaming at someone. 'I love Dr Arissa,' he said, waving at what seemed like a camera phone.

The feed switched to the news anchor. 'Well, there's a thumbs up from one of her patients,' he said, beaming inanely towards her.

'No,' she breathed as more tears streaked down her face. It was everything she'd feared. 'How on earth did they do that? How did they get hold of Amal so quickly?'

Philippe looked horrified. He glanced at his watch. 'The press pictures must have leaked hours ago when we were all in bed. The story must have gone global.' His brow creased. 'But I have no idea how they found him.'

She turned on Philippe, her voice rising. 'You promised me that there would be no publicity here.' She shook her head, 'And I, like a fool, believed you.' She was angry with herself again. She met his gaze. 'I believed you because I wanted to believe you. Because I trusted you. Because you had me swept up in some kind of—' she threw her hands out in frustration '—made-up fairy tale.'

She walked over to the dressing room and started pulling out her case. Now she'd started she couldn't stop. 'But this isn't for me. This isn't my life.' She couldn't stop shaking her head as she gestured towards the television screen. 'I won't allow them to do that to me—or my patients.'

'Arissa, please stop. I'm sorry. I'm so sorry. I'm sorry that this has happened to you.' He was at her side, holding onto her arm. He looked just as upset as she was.

She'd already flung her suitcase wide and started to throw things haphazardly inside.

Their picture flashed up on the screen together again and she froze. It was that look. That look that had passed between them. His hand on her cheek and her hand on top of it. It made her heart twist inside her chest. There—for all the world to see—was the look of love that had passed between them. It wrenched at her in ways she didn't even want to admit to.

There was another of them midway down the stairs, her arm tucked into his elbow. The smile on his face as he looked at her. One of them dancing in the middle of the ballroom floor with eyes only for each other.

Philippe let out an exasperated sound. 'There's more?'

She'd only seen the first one that had made the newspaper front page. She hadn't seen the rest. Then another flashed up of them on their first day in Corinez, sitting in the coffee shop together, laughing.

He shook his head. 'I thought someone recognised us that day,' he growled.

She'd felt it. She'd felt it every time she was in his company. But now she was seeing it through someone else's eyes. The way they looked at each other, the way they interacted, the way they laughed together, and, instead of making her happy, it made her want to cry.

She couldn't have this. She couldn't live a life that inspected her every breath, her every thought. She couldn't have a life that destroyed the privacy of her patients. She wasn't cut out for this—no matter how much her heart was tearing in two.

Philippe's hand appeared at her arm. 'Let me do something about this. Let me release a statement. I won't let them treat you like this. I won't let them expose your patients like this. They have no right.'

She shook her head. 'But they think they have every right. Isn't that what free speech is about?'

He gestured towards the TV. 'I'll speak to someone at the station. I'll tell them they had no right to use those photographs or to discuss you—or to contact your patients.'

She kept packing her clothes. 'You can't control the world, Philippe. You can't control what people think, and say.' She looked to the TV where the woman in pink was talking incessantly. 'I do a job that I love. I don't want to be pushed out. But I have to protect my patients.' She stepped right up to him. 'I want privacy to live my life. But I *demand* privacy for my patients.' She shook her head. 'And there's no chance of getting it here.'

She gave a wry laugh as another headline flashed up. 'They even had me down as your bride. How ridiculous is that? We've only known each other a few weeks.'

He moved closer, his eyes serious. 'Not that ridiculous.'

Her skin prickled. 'What?'

Philippe sucked in a breath. This day was just snowballing out of control. First the leak, then Arissa's reaction, followed by her revelation. She was an abandoned baby—just like the one he'd treated. The one he'd lost. Arissa could have been lost if someone hadn't come across her. And the thought of that happening made his heart ache. He lowered his head and shook it.

He watched as she continued to throw things haphazardly into her case. Some clothes were missing the case completely. He hated that he'd caused any of this. He was furious that someone from the press had dared to track down one of her patients. She had every right to be angry, and that made him even sadder.

Because all of a sudden, he knew exactly how much Arissa Cotter meant to him. Love. The word he may have mentioned casually, but now he knew just how much he meant it.

After his experience a few years ago he'd thought he'd built an impenetrable wall around his heart. But it seemed he was wrong. Slowly but surely, this beautiful woman with the world of hurt in her eyes had found a way into his heart.

But look what he'd done to her.

He tried to keep his voice steady. 'Where do you plan on going?'

Something flashed across her face. She was angry with him, but she was hurt too.

She shrugged. 'I have no idea.'

He stepped forward and put one hand on the case. 'Wait. At least until tomorrow. The first safe haven cot is getting installed then. Wait and see it through.'

Right now he would try anything to make her stay. Even for one more day. Anything to give himself a bit of time to try and make a plan. A plan to find a way to make things better for Arissa.

He could see from her face that she knew what he was doing. He was trying to use her professional responsibility to will her into staying. 'I'm sure it will all go to plan,' she said, zipping up her case.

'But we need you to see it through. To help with the

final touches. The protocols.' He winced. 'The press releases. The way we get the word out there to those that need it, that there is a safe place to leave your baby—no questions asked.'

There was an edge of desperation to his voice that he couldn't even pretend to hide. The woman that had stolen his heart was standing in front of him hurt and confused, all because he'd asked her to come here and work with him.

This was his fault. His.

He should have known better. People had been curious about him all his life. Of course someone would comment about her—particularly if he showed any interest in her. And the truth was he hadn't tried to hide it because he didn't want to.

His family could see it. All of them had given him knowing looks last night.

He'd been proud to show her off. Proud that his family liked her. Touched that his mother had taken such an interest in her and could obviously see how important she was to him, thus welcoming her into the family.

If he'd thought this through, if he'd planned better, he would have spoken to palace advisors. He would have spoken to Arissa about her reluctance to be in the spotlight. He hadn't understood what it meant to her.

And even though it was too late, now he did.

Arissa bowed her head.

'Don't go, Arissa. Not like this. I care about you.' He stepped closer and said words that a few years ago he'd never thought he'd say again. 'You mean too much to me.'

He could tell from the look in her eyes it wasn't enough. The pictures continued to flash up on the screen behind her.

Pictures that captured for the whole world exactly how much he loved this woman.

But he didn't need the pictures to tell him that. The way his heart was squeezing inside his chest told him all he needed to know.

After the longest time Arissa lifted her head. 'I'll stay until tomorrow. I'll talk over the protocols with the staff at the fire and rescue station as the safe haven cot is being installed and make sure they're clear what to do.' She tilted her chin, her voice gaining an edge of determination. 'But I want absolutely no publicity. I'm happy to help draft a statement for the media around the project but that's it. After that I go.'

He'd pulled at her professional responsibilities. But he hadn't pulled at her heartstrings.

He gave a nod of his head. Right now, he would agree to anything that meant he could hold onto her just a few moments longer.

'I'm sorry about your patient. Our press advisors will contact the TV station and put in an official complaint, along with a warning about talking to any of your other patients.' He meant it. He really did. She had a right to her privacy—as did her patients.

And it was up to him to sort this.

'If we're finished, I'd like to be alone now,' Arissa said, her voice stoic.

He gave a brief nod. 'Of course.'

He hated this. He hated every single part of it. He'd exposed the woman he loved to hurt and he wasn't sure how he could fix this—if he could at all.

# CHAPTER TWELVE

THE ROOM WAS CLAUSTROPHOBIC. Even though it was beautiful, even though it had views of the expansive gardens, it still felt as if the walls were closing in around her. Every pore in her body right now wanted to get out of here.

But the work was important. They'd moved quickly in Corinez to accommodate the safe haven cot. It seemed that if an order came from a prince, things moved at lightning speed.

An older man knocked and came into the room. He was dressed impeccably in black and held out a hand. 'Jacques Feraunt, Head of Security. I am so sorry, Dr Cotter. But, rest assured, we've discovered the leak.'

She pressed her lips together and tried to ignore the tears that were forming in her eyes. 'You have?'

He nodded. 'It seems that one of our members of staff had been hounded and offered a considerable amount of money to try and capture a photograph of you and the Prince.' He shook his head. 'Regrettably, even though all our waiting staff sign non-disclosure agreements, this individual felt unduly pressured. They had health issues for a family member at home and decided that the money could get them the help they needed.' His face was serious. 'They took the pictures on their mobile phone. We traced them this morning, and they've obviously been dismissed. We will be taking further legal action against them, and the newspapers involved.'

She felt numb. It was as if little creatures were crawling up her arms. She was angry, but the circumstances made her question things.

'What kind of health problems?' she asked.

Jacques looked a little surprised by her question. 'Excuse me?'

'What kind of health problems does the family member have?'

He cleared his throat. 'I believe the member of staff's younger sibling has a form of leukaemia.'

She stood up. 'And they can't get treatment?'

Jacques shifted on his feet. He was obviously trying to choose his words carefully. 'Healthcare in Corinez is complicated, Dr Cotter. None of it is free. Everything has to be paid for.'

She murmured to herself, 'And that's what Philippe is trying to change with baby steps.' She looked back out over the gardens, her brain mulling over everything she'd heard.

'Can I have the use of a car?'

Now Jacques was definitely surprised. 'A car?'

She nodded. 'I'd like to meet them. The family. The sick kid. This is my speciality. My life's work. If that kid needs to be seen, and a consultation and treatment plan, then I can do that, I can advise. I can do it for free.'

Jacques looked wary. 'I'm not sure that's wise, Dr Cotter.'

She stepped forward. 'You're in charge of security, are you not?'

He nodded. 'Of course.'

'Then I trust you can arrange this. And I trust you can get me where I need to go safely, and without any publicity.'

He gave a brief nod and she lifted her hand to touch the sleeve of his jacket as she tilted her chin upwards. 'I didn't get where I am in this life by always being wise, Mr Feraunt. I got where I am by being compassionate.'

His mother was waiting when he got back to his room. She was dressed impeccably as always and sitting at his desk. She looked over at his rumpled clothes and raised her brows. 'What are you going to do about this?'

'She wants to leave.' He couldn't stop the words hurtling out of his mouth.

His mother drummed her fingers on the desk; it was clear she was thinking. 'Of course she does,' she said quietly. She licked her lips. 'What about you?'

He moved over and sagged into the oversized chair on the other side of the desk. 'What do you mean—what about me?'

She looked straight at him. 'What's the most important thing to you right now, Philippe? What's your priority?'

It was almost as if the world stopped all around him. Everything. No birds singing. No people moving through the corridors of the palace. The stillness amplified in his ears.

It was almost like a magnifying glass on every aspect of his life.

He'd been born a Prince. He'd embraced it for most of his life. He knew what was expected of him. He knew what his place was. The job ahead would be hard—maybe even impossible. He was starting small with maternity services, but eventually he wanted to change his whole country's healthcare system.

Every hair on his body prickled upwards. But he didn't want to do it alone.

The realisation was startling. It shouldn't be. It had gradually crept over him for the last few weeks, ever since he'd met a dedicated doctor with eyes so deep they pulled him in.

He lifted his head to meet his mother's gaze. He wasn't even afraid to say the words out loud.

'My priority is Arissa.'

His mother nodded. 'How would you feel if she wasn't here?'

The words felt like a sword spearing his heart. It clarified so much for him in an instant. 'Like part of me was missing,' he said softly. He met his mother's gaze. 'I don't want to do any of this without her.'

His mother stayed silent for a few seconds, then she stood slowly. 'I suspected you might say that.'

She walked over and put her hand on his shoulder. 'You're old enough to make your own choices, Philippe, and, whatever you choose to do, I will always be your mother, and I will always love you.' She bent close to his ear. 'I don't ever want my children to feel as if part of them is missing,' she whispered in an emotion-racked voice.

She walked back out of his door, closing it softly behind her.

He sagged his head down onto his hands. What had he done? What was he about to do?

Part of his brain was screaming out in protest— reminding him how much he loved his country and being part of it. But the other part was forming plans about what it really meant to love someone completely—and to put them above anything else.

## CHAPTER THIRTEEN

THE KID WAS SICK. But in a way it was lucky. She was still at a point where treatment could be very effective—if they were lucky, treatment might even provide a cure.

The family had been more than a little surprised when she'd turned up on their doorstep along with some palace security. After some embarrassment and apologies, Arissa had explained who she was. She wasn't just the Prince's latest girlfriend. She was a doctor—a specialist on kids' blood disorders—and if they'd let her, she'd see their child free of charge and assess what was needed.

With Jacques' help and a quick call to the hospital she'd managed to set up privileges and been able to take the family to a quiet consultation room where she'd had access to equipment and tests. A few hours later, once the X-rays and blood work had been back, she'd been able to sit them down and explain exactly the treatment that their daughter required.

Both of their faces had been pale. She didn't blame them. She'd spent much of her doctor life having these kinds of difficult conversations. But, with the right treatment, this child's chance could be good.

She was still angry about everything that had happened. But she wasn't going to show that to them. She'd taken the time to listen to the circumstances and made the decision that she'd do what she could to help.

It was so easy to judge. So easy to be angry. Occasionally, it was right to be angry. But right now, all she could focus on was the face of the little sick kid in front of her.

It had got her thinking all over again.

By the time she got back to the palace she felt like a giant bag of sand that someone had snipped a little hole in, and the life was just draining out of her.

Her phone buzzed in her pocket and she pulled it out. It took a few seconds for her to scan the email she'd just received. It seemed that even though the research hadn't been published yet, news of their findings had got out. She was the contact name for the clinic so the email had come to her. There had been a huge product licence offer made for their ointment. She blinked, her fingers typing furiously. There was only one thing in her mind. None of the doctors involved in this were in it for the money. This kind of money could secure permanent staff for the clinic in Temur Sapora. She forwarded it on to all involved, along with her suggestion, and held her breath.

But she didn't need to. The replies came in fast and furious. Yes after yes.

At last, something was going right.

She collapsed onto her bed. One more day. That was all she had to last. One more day to finish her duties. Then, she'd need to try and find another position. Maybe she could cover sick leave or maternity leave somewhere? This time she would sort out any visa issues herself.

She rested back on the pillows, trying to focus on her next moves. But, try as she might, her head wouldn't let her concentrate. As fatigue crept over her, her mind circled with the pictures of her and Philippe and the way they had captured how they'd been looking at each other.

It preyed on her senses, making her skin tremble and her stomach churn.

Somehow, the thought of being in Philippe's company tomorrow was making her nervous.

But the thought of leaving this place for good and never seeing him again? That made her head swim even more and her heart ache in a way she'd never thought possible.

## CHAPTER FOURTEEN

THE DAY STARTED AWKWARDLY.

Arissa was ready, dressed in dark trousers and suit jacket, her suitcase sitting in the corner of the room.

Philippe looked as if he hadn't slept. He was dressed impeccably as usual, but his handsome face was marred with dark circles and tiny lines around his eyes.

He seemed nervous. 'Arissa.' The smile he gave her was strained. 'Are you ready? I've talked with the captain at the fire and rescue station and the workmen have just arrived.'

She gave a nod of her head. Jacques was standing behind Philippe and gave her a reassuring smile. She'd asked to keep her actions yesterday private and somehow she knew he hadn't betrayed her.

'Let's go, then.' The words came out a little funny. Almost as if she were really saying, *Because I can't wait to get out of here*. She still wasn't sure how she felt about everything.

Philippe shot her a pained glance and answered in his polite tones. 'After you.'

She stared out of the window of the blacked-out limousine as they travelled through the city. A casino she hadn't visited. A large white memorial that she'd no idea what it was for. The bustling port filled with cruise ships, and the bus terminal with buses heading up to the ski resort. So many parts of Corinez she hadn't got to see.

Her throat was dry. She couldn't stomach tea this morning. Her hands jittered in her lap, no matter how much she tried to still them.

Philippe cleared his throat. 'The press secretary got a response about the invasion of privacy into your patient.'

She turned to face him.

He spoke slowly. 'It seems that as soon as the story broke on US news and the photos were released, everyone started talking. News stations asked anyone that knew you to phone in.'

Arissa cringed.

Philippe looked carefully at her. 'Amal called the TV station himself. He was excited. He saw his doctor on the TV and wanted to tell them how brilliant she was. He took his mother's phone and just dialled the number on the screen. His mother didn't even know that he'd done it until later.' Philippe gave a gentle shake of his head. 'The TV station asked him to send a clip and he filmed himself. That's why the clip was wobbly.'

Arissa's mouth was open. She couldn't help it. Of course. Kids were so savvy these days on all social media, and Amal was the original cheeky kid. It was exactly the kind of thing he would do. She sagged back in the seat and swallowed. The press hadn't invaded the privacy of one of her patients. It might still not be entirely above board, but Amal had contacted them.

Philippe continued. 'His mother, of course, contacted the station later. But she didn't withdraw permission for them to use the clip.' He paused for a bit. 'We do think there were a few other dubious enquiries regarding some of your patients. We made a complaint to the national press agency and that's been acknowledged and will be followed up.'

Arissa took a deep breath as the car slid to a halt.

She tried to collect her thoughts. Had she overreacted yesterday? Now she knew Amal had made contact himself. But it sounded as if there could still be a few underlying issues. She knew at heart she wouldn't be able to let those go. Ensuring the privacy of her patients would always be at the forefront in her mind. Philippe climbed out of the car and turned, holding his hand out towards her.

She hesitated for the briefest of seconds before accepting his hand and getting out.

The fire and rescue station was busy. The crew were all enthusiastic about the latest project and anxious to help in any way they could.

'Welcome to bedlam!' said the captain, holding up his hands. 'I keep telling them to leave the workmen to get on with it, but they can't stop talking about the project!'

Arissa smiled. Enthusiasm was good. Enthusiasm was something she could harness.

Philippe had moved over and was locked in a conversation with one of the workmen who was standing with a huge sledgehammer, ready to burst a hole in the wall.

'It's great to see Prince Philippe back.' The captain smiled. 'And great that he's finally getting the opportunity to fulfil his role.'

It was the way he said the words and the familiarity of his gaze towards Philippe.

Arrisa couldn't help but ask. 'You know him?'

The captain nodded. 'Since he was a boy. The King and I served together a thousand years ago in the army.

We've remained friends. I've watched these children grow up.' He sounded vaguely proud.

Curious, she asked, 'And what do you think?'

He smiled at her. 'About Philippe? He's made for this. He's going to make such a difference. Our health service has needed an overhaul for such a long time. He's so invested in this. After his recent experience no wonder.' He put his hand on his chest. 'At heart, Philippe's a doctor. He'll always think like a doctor and act like a doctor. But for his country?' He nodded slowly. 'He knows what has to be done. He knows how hard it will be. I think free maternity care could make the world of difference in Corinez, and I can't think of a single person who could do the job better than he can.'

Pride. It was there in every word. She could see the admiration in the guy's eyes. The respect.

Part of her ached. Because that was exactly how she felt too. She loved him. She admired him. She respected him. None of what had happened had been his fault. Maybe he should have second-guessed the possibility, but could she really have expected him to, when it hadn't happened before?

Something the captain had said intrigued her. 'What happened before?'

The captain gave her a curious look. 'The abandoned baby. It was his last patient.' He shook his head. 'Hypothermia. He'd been left in the cold for too long. Philippe was heartbroken. He spent two days in the hospital at the little boy's bedside.'

Her heart twisted. She didn't want to ask. 'What happened?'

The captain shook his head. 'He didn't make it. We found him just too late.' The man sighed. 'That's why this is so important. We can't ever let that happen again. That's why everyone here is so behind this project.'

Now she understood. Now she understood the occasional far-off look in his eyes. Some of the things he'd said—and why he'd been so interested in the safe haven scheme right from the start. It all just made sense.

Her stomach flipped. And her story. Her story must have affected him too. At the moment she'd told him she'd only been thinking about herself, not realising that Philippe understood in a completely different way—he'd lost a baby just like her. Her heart melted. This project linked them both. As she gazed across the room and watched his passion as he spoke to someone it seemed like fate that their paths had crossed. As if it had been written in the stars.

The captain touched her arm and smiled. 'Dr Cotter, are you ready?'

She didn't have time to think any more. Of course. She was here to talk to them about protocols. She could do that. The captain led her towards the staff room; the smell of coffee and cookies was already drifting towards her. Her stomach growled in appreciation. The captain laughed and shouted over to his staff. 'Come on, guys. Our girl is hungry. Let's not keep her from the food.'

She forced herself to smile as the men filed into the room. Philippe was not among them. It was almost as if he was deliberately trying to stay out of her way. The question was—did she really blame him after how she'd acted yesterday? And how could she make it up to him?

It was officially the worst day of his life. Last night he'd written the statement he was currently holding and spent all the hours in between looking over every word.

What he wanted to do was speak to Arissa. But he didn't want to warn her in advance. At some point today there was a good chance she would walk out of his life for ever.

He was determined that wouldn't happen. But he was equally determined that he had to let her follow her own heart. Her happiness meant more to him than anything.

Things at the fire and rescue centre moved quickly. The workmen literally just smashed a hole in the wall, inserted the premade safe haven cot, then let the technicians ensure it worked exactly the way it should.

As soon as a button was pressed on the outside wall, the cot slid open. A baby could be left inside the cot, along with other items, and the cot closed securely from the outside.

Sensors were everywhere. The cot had lights and heat. It was also accessible from inside the station, so if a baby was placed while the staff were inside, a silent alarm would alert those working. The whole system was designed to give the mother privacy. Nothing alerted until the baby had been left inside and the cot door closed again. From that point on, the fire station silent alarms sounded, along with any attached pagers in case staff were at a fire and rescue situation.

Arissa had made everything go smoothly. She'd reassured all the crew about dealing with a new baby. She'd gone over emergency procedures. Some of the crew had already delivered the odd baby, and knew about the essentials afterwards, but revision was good for everyone.

Links had been established with the local paediatric and social work department to ensure any baby could be quickly checked over then assigned to a temporary foster carer.

Arissa talked with confidence and an easy reassurance—every now and then shooting an anxious glance in his direction. The fire and rescue crew were already enthusiastic; there had only been a few worries, which had easily been ironed out. She told about her own experience of setting up the safe haven cots back in Temur Sapora. She also expressed a sadness that they hadn't managed to find and help all the mothers, but acknowledged that they could only keep an open-door policy in order to protect the privacy and wishes of the mothers.

He listened to every word that she said. Watching her commitment and honesty made him realise the decision he'd made last night was the right one. Things had to be this way.

As the workmen made the finishing touches some invited members of the press started to arrive. Arissa had finished speaking and did her best to fade into the background. That little act still made his insides twist. Every now and then he caught her looking at him. He couldn't work out if she was annoyed with him, or was preparing for her time in Corinez to be over. What he really wanted to do was to go over and put his arms around her. But that wouldn't exactly help her stay incognito. And what Arissa wanted was his first priority.

The captain waved him over as the press settled into their seats. He bent forward and spoke quietly in Philippe's ear. 'I like her,' he said.

Philippe straightened up. The words were unexpected. 'What?'

The captain nodded in Arissa's direction. 'In fact, I more than like her. She's fantastic.' He looked Philippe up and down—in a way that only someone who'd known him all his life could. 'And what's more, I think she's the best thing that could happen to you.'

Philippe's stomach gave a flip. Did he know what Philippe was about to do?

He took a deep breath and looked the captain straight in the eye, a man that knew him better than most. There was a swell of pride in his chest that had been crowded out these last few hours with the fear of letting others down. He took his responsibilities seriously. He looked at the captain's twinkling grey eyes. 'Thank you,' he said proudly. 'I think that too.' He glanced across the busy room towards Arissa. She had her hands folded across her chest as one of the other crew members was talking to her. He had no idea how she'd react to what he was about to do.

But every part of it felt right. He was nervous—and that was unusual for Philippe—but nerves and uncertainty went hand in hand with something new.

Something good.

There was a wave from the front of the room and someone clapped their hands to bring the noise down to a rumble.

Philippe took a deep breath and made his way to the front of the room. His speech was in his pocket—but he didn't need to bring it out. He'd spent most of last night saying it over and over in his head.

He waited until the press members finally stopped talking. He was aware of the inquisitive glances being shot at him. If he gave the press members gathered here today more than half a chance they would bombard him with questions about Arissa.

This was his opportunity to make sure he said what he needed to.

He started quickly. 'Members of the press, I want to thank you for attending today.' He cleared his throat and kept his voice steady. 'You know why I've invited you here today. Over the last few years in Corinez we've had several occasions where an infant—usually a newborn—has been left alone in a public place. Sadly, you all know what happened to the last baby who was left alone, and it's our absolute pledge today to ensure the same thing doesn't happen again. But we also recognise that we have never had services organised to allow a mother to surrender her baby in a safe and anonymous environment.'

He looked up again at the faces fixed on his. 'You all know that I'm a doctor. My greatest wish is that no mother feels as if they have no option but to give up their baby. But I respect an individual's right to choose. Things have changed in the last few years in Corinez, times are hard, and a good friend of mine—' he didn't mention Arissa's name '—enlightened me to the safe haven cot scheme in their country. This scheme is adopted by many countries around the world. France, the USA, Italy, Hungary, Russia, Japan, Switzerland, the Philippines and Temur Sapora in Malaysia, to name but a few. They all run on the same principles that a woman can surrender her baby, no questions asked, with no fear of prosecution.'

He took a few moments as he scanned the faces in the room. 'I wish that we didn't have to do this. But—' he took another breath '—the fact of the matter is, we do.' He held out his hand. 'And we decided that here, at the fire and rescue centre, was the best place to do this.'

He gave a nod as he could see questions forming on the lips of the listeners. 'Our cot has been installed in such a way that a woman can leave her baby someplace warm and safe, and leave without any interference.'

He waited a second. 'We want you to help us get the word out about the new safe haven cot in Corinez. We want everyone to know they can leave their baby in a safe place if they need to do so.'

People started murmuring to each other. One of them shouted out, 'What part did Dr Cotter play in this?'

He could deflect the question. But that wasn't what he wanted to do. 'Dr Cotter has given us the benefit of her own experience of installing a safe haven cot, and has briefed our staff on their roles.'

Other questions started being shouted from all directions but Philippe raised his hand. 'Actually, I'm not finished. I have a further statement you might be interested in.'

His glance went automatically to Arissa, who was watching him from the station kitchen door.

He cleared his throat. 'You all know the challenge that lies ahead. Corinez's healthcare is not currently fit for purpose—it doesn't serve the needs of our population. This safe haven work today is merely the tip of the iceberg.'

He paused to let the listeners consider this. 'My love for my country has always been strong. You all know my intention has been to return to Corinez and take up post as part of our health committee. I have spent the last few years preparing for this role. But recent events have caused me to rethink.'

He kept his gaze steady, fixing on a few in the room who started to shift in their seats uncomfortably.

'Press intrusion is something that my family, and many other royal families across Europe, experience on a daily basis. I have always prided myself on the good relationship that I thought our family had with the press.

But the last few days have made me re-evaluate what that means.

'This week I took pride in bringing the woman that I love—a dedicated and competent doctor—to our country and showing her its beauty and introducing her to the people. Dr Cotter is a private person, she wasn't brought up in the media's glare and has no interest in being there. I assured her when she came here, her privacy would be protected.'

He took a long slow breath. 'It seems I was wrong.' Even though he was emotional he kept his voice as steady as possible. Arissa had moved. She had taken a few steps from the edge of the door towards him. He'd just told the world out loud that he loved her, and her eyes were huge.

'I love my country, I always have and I always will, but I'm a person like everyone else in this room—I'm not just a prince, and I believe that one of the greatest gifts you can find as a human being is love. And after thirty-one years, I've found it.'

This time he turned to face her. He couldn't say any of these words without looking her in the eye, because they were all for her.

'I've found a woman who makes my heart sing. I've found someone that got to know me as Philippe—not as a prince. I've found the face I want to see every morning when I wake up, and every night before I close my eyes. I've found the person I want to spend the rest of my life with, and I'm willing to make sacrifices in order to be with her.'

Arissa's mouth opened. She took a few steps forward.

'The tasks I have ahead are huge—a lifetime's work. My plan was to start—with the agreement of the health committee—on introducing free maternity services within Corinez. And what's abundantly clear is that if I'm to do those tasks, I need the love and support of someone by my side who understands exactly the breadth of my role. I want to work in partnership with the person I love, because I want this to last a lifetime.'

He swallowed, his throat becoming tight, and turned back to face the press. 'Yesterday, we learned that some of Arissa's previous patients had been approached by the media. These issues have been raised with the Independent Press Standards Organisation. Patient-doctor privilege and confidentiality is sacred. No doctor would ever want to expose their patients to invasion of their privacy. Arissa came here because of me. The press is interested in her because of me. She now feels, because of this intrusion, she won't be able to function as a doctor. And if she wants to leave, then I'll be leaving with her.'

He heard her small cry to his side as the press erupted in front of him.

'You can't do this!' one of the reporters shouted.

'What will the King say? The Queen will be furious!' shouted another.

'Who approached the patients?' said another, looking angrily around. 'We'd never do something like that.'

Philippe didn't hesitate. He looked from one to the other. 'I can, and I will. I have spoken to the Queen and have her complete approval. Like any mother on this planet, her overwhelming wish is that her child is happy. The rest of the royal family have given me their unwavering support. Do we really want to examine what the effects of the press attention have resulted in for other royal families? Arissa isn't here to be a princess. She's here to be a doctor. I suggest that we let her.'

He nodded to the reporter who'd shouted out last. 'And I thank you for respecting patient confidentiality.'

The reporter glanced at his neighbours. 'Any self-respecting reporter would do the same. Let's face it,' he said, 'we'll all be a patient ourselves at some point.'

Philippe's voice had gathered strength. He was determined. He could see a few panicked expressions.

'Philippe.' The voice was almost a whisper.

She was at his side, her eyes wet with tears. Her arms folded across her body. 'You can't give up being a prince for me,' she said with a shaking voice.

He smiled and stepped down, sliding his hand into her hair. 'I can. And I will. Tell me where you want to go and I'll come with you. I'll work anywhere in the world. If you want to go back to Temur Sapora permanently, then I'll come with you.'

He could hear the noise roaring behind him. The multiple conversations. Reporters phoning their editors and TV stations.

He ignored every single part of it. The only thing that was important was the woman standing straight in front of him. The woman with the big brown eyes and trembling lips. He didn't have a single doubt about that—and that told him everything he needed to know.

It felt as if she were watching a movie of someone else's life.

Every word peeled back another of the layers she'd shielded herself with.

The role he'd been destined for. Trained for. Prepared for. He was ready to give it all up for her. For love. And he'd told the world.

She'd wanted to talk to him. She'd wanted to talk to

him about some of his suggestions for change, and about the possibility of her helping to create a service for kids like the one she'd seen yesterday. The need was there. It could be the next step in the plan. She could make a difference. Wasn't that what a doctor was for? As long as her patients were protected. Some of the responses in the room were actually heartening. She could see others agreeing with the reporter who'd spoken out last. Maybe raising this issue out loud today, and the report to the IPSO, would be enough to make this stop.

'I wish you'd told me about the baby that died, Philippe. I know how much that must have affected you.'

He blinked and nodded. 'It almost broke me. It's the reason I ended up in Temur Sapora. I was feeling lost when I got there. I knew the job I had to come back and do, and then...' he smiled '...I met you. And it felt like fate. From the very start. Your story and mine, Arissa.' He bent forward and whispered in her ear. 'I know that for others this might seem rash. But nothing about us feels wrong. And I'll do everything I can to make us work.' The fingers in one of his hands intertwined with hers.

She stopped thinking about the other people in the room and put her hand up and touched Philippe's face. 'You have so much work to do here, Philippe. Who else can do it with the passion and dedication that you can? No one else knows this place like you do.'

'I won't have you feeling the way you did the other day. Not because of me. I love you, Arissa. I spoke to my mother last night. She completely understands. She wants me to follow my heart, and my heart is you.'

A tear slid down her cheek. She'd never felt so loved

by a man. So wanted. Her hand slid over his. 'But can you be happy if you aren't here?'

'What I need in this life to be happy is you, Arissa.'

His gaze was so sincere. He wasn't sad. He was smiling. It was almost as if saying the words out loud and making his declaration had taken a weight off his shoulders.

A shout came from the side.

'Corinez needs this reform. The healthcare system has to change. The people of Corinez can't trust anyone as much as they trust you.'

'The Independent Press Standards Organisation will get to the bottom of this. It won't happen again.'

'Arissa, what can we do to persuade *you* to stay?'

The question came from an older man with grey hair. Arissa's skin prickled. The attention was on her.

For a few seconds she couldn't think straight. Then her focus shifted to the man she loved standing in front of her. He'd offered to give up everything for her. What could she give up for him?

Or maybe she didn't need to give up anything, maybe she needed to compromise. That didn't seem quite so terrifying.

She stared at the podium with the microphone. Maybe it was time to take control. To tell her own story. To use the press attention to bring the focus entirely on the safe haven scheme and its value. If she owned her story and told it herself then she wouldn't need to worry about the press revealing it to the world for her.

She closed her eyes for a second and concentrated on the heat of Philippe's skin next to hers. The strength. The passion. This was hers. This was hers to take.

She straightened her back and relaxed her shoulders, purposely pushing them down.

She squeezed Philippe's hand and kept holding it as she stepped up to the podium. She could do this. She could do this for her, and for him.

What kind of life did she want? One where she had to live a life without the man that she loved? Or one where she faced the world and told them the truth?

There it was. She'd admitted it to herself—even though she'd known it for the last few days.

He had more strength and determination than she could ever have dreamed of. He could have walked away from someone like her. Walking away from his country might have never even entered his head. But for Philippe, it had. He was clear. He would stand up for her no matter what.

He tugged at her arm. 'Don't. You don't need to say anything. Don't be forced into the spotlight—I know that's not what you want.'

She reached back and touched his cheek with her free hand. 'Maybe we can both get what we want,' she whispered.

She stood behind the podium and faced the press. They silenced much quicker for her than they had for Philippe.

She lifted her chin. 'Prince Philippe is right. I'm a doctor. That's what I am and what I want to continue to be. But I have a story to tell you. One that I preferred to keep private. But somehow—' she glanced around the room at the expectant faces '—it seems that today might be a good day to tell it.'

She took a few moments to collect her thoughts. 'I was an abandoned baby. Thirty years ago I was left outside an unmanned clinic in Temur Sapora.' She tilted her chin upwards. "I was lucky. I was found. I was sick, but recovered in hospital and was adopted by a loving couple who gave me the best life they could.' She gave a little smile. 'I miss and think about them every day.'

She could see the exchange of glances.

'And here I am. I've grown up, trained as a doctor and now I specialise in children's blood disorders, with a particular focus on cancers. I know there's a need in Corinez. I saw a patient only yesterday who needs accessible treatment that could save their life.' She put her hand on her chest. 'What will it take for me to stay? I know you only ask because you want to keep your Prince. I don't want to keep a prince.' She turned and met his gaze. 'I want to keep the man I fell in love with, Philippe Aronaz.

'I want you all to publicise the safe haven cot. I want you to tell how it can save lives. I want you to reassure women that there is someplace safe that they can leave their babies. And…' she paused and smiled at Philippe '…if the plans for maternity care work out, maybe we will be able to offer all kinds of support to women in need.' She took a final breath. 'And it goes without saying that I expect integrity from every person in the room to respect the rights of any patients that I see.'

His hand moved, releasing her fingers as he changed position and came and stood at her back, slipping one hand over hers. It was almost as if he was moving into a protective stance—and somehow that gave her the reassurance that she needed.

He was there. He was with her. Confidence flowed throughout her body. She turned to face Philippe instead of the press. 'Do you think this can work?'

He leaned forward and put his forehead on hers. It

was as if they were the only two people in the room. They weren't surrounded by TV cameras. There wasn't an array of hungry press people in the room. 'Are you sure, Arissa? I love you. I'll go anywhere with you. I mean that. Don't do anything that will make you unhappy. I don't want that for you.'

He blinked and his long eyelashes brushed against her skin and sent tingles to every part of her. 'Will you be my champion?' she whispered back.

A smile broke out across his face. 'Always,' he murmured.

'Then, we do this together. We can make this work.'

For a few seconds neither of them moved, but then Philippe raised his head, slipped his hand into hers and turned to face the press pack.

'Our press conference for today is over. I think you have what you need. Today is a unique opportunity for us all. Please spread the word about the safe haven scheme and our plans for maternity care.'

It was a moment in history. It had never been her intention to be in this situation but at this second she couldn't be prouder of the man that she loved.

Yes, life would change. But it would change hand in hand with a man that she wanted to be by her side for the rest of her life.

Philippe turned towards her. 'We need to do something,' he said quickly, grabbing her hand and pulling her towards the staff room in the fire and rescue centre.

She was stunned. He ushered the few people that were in the room back outside and closed the door quickly behind them.

'What's wrong?' What on earth was he doing?

He shook his head and stepped up close. 'Nothing

is wrong.' He laughed as he glanced around them, then reached up and touched her cheek. 'I always thought when I did this I would plan. There would be stars. There would be a romantic dinner. A beautiful setting. Maybe even some music.' He held his hands out. 'Instead we have a slightly messy staff room, with a few odd chairs.'

Her stomach flipped. Somehow she knew what was going to happen next. Her heart swelled in her chest as she tried to catch her breath.

Philippe dug down into his pocket and opened a black velvet box as he dropped to one knee. 'Arissa Cotter, I love you. More than I ever knew was possible. You've taught me to trust and love again. I promise that no matter where this road leads I'll be by your side. If we choose to stay here, then know that I also want to help you with your work in Temur Sapora. When you go there, I'll go there. I want to mirror your commitments to your own country. It's part of you, therefore it's part of me. I want you to—'

She bent forward and put a finger to his lips. 'Stop talking, Philippe.' A millisecond of worry flashed across his eyes before she laughed and shook her head. 'My answer is yes. I love you. I love what you just did for me. I love what you've promised me. I hope we never have to leave, but if we do, I'll be leaving with the man I love.' She ran her fingers through his hair. 'I don't care where we are, just as long as we're together.' She glanced down at the ring and her eyes widened. 'Where on earth did you…?'

He pulled the ring from the box. 'This was given to me last night by my mother. It's a family ring, belonged to a former queen.' He slid the yellow-gold ring with a huge square green emerald onto her finger. 'My mother said that as soon as she saw you in that green dress, she knew this ring was meant for you.'

Arissa sucked in a breath as her eyes filled with tears. 'She gave it to you, even though she knew you might leave?'

He nodded as he pulled her towards him. 'They love you, Arissa. Just as much as I do.'

He walked to the door and opened it for the briefest of seconds. 'She said yes!' he shouted before slamming the door closed and pulling her back into his arms.

And as her husband-to-be kissed her, she forgot all about the cheers outside.

# EPILOGUE

'READY?'

Arissa nodded as Philippe's sister, Grace, bent forward to give her a kiss on the cheek. 'See you in a minute, then,' she whispered as she sashayed down the aisle in front of her in her navy maid-of-honour dress.

Arissa breathed in. The music had started. It was time to go.

She stared down at her yellow and orange flowers. A slightly unusual wedding bouquet with half the flowers native to Temur Sapora and half native to Corinez.

She took a deep breath again to relax herself. They were in the private palace chapel. The world knew the wedding was taking place today, but they also knew it was only being attended by family and friends. The press had been promised a kiss from the newly-weds on the palace balcony later.

Her cream lace bodice gown with satin skirts had been chosen with help from the Queen. As the music continued she stepped out onto the aisle.

Sun was streaming through the stained-glass windows at the end of the chapel. But she couldn't focus on the sun. All she could focus on was her handsome prince standing at the end of the aisle, filling out every inch of his dress uniform.

As she reached him he mouthed the words to her, 'You're stunning,' as he lifted her veil and arranged it behind her tiara, which belonged to his mother.

Everything had worked out perfectly. She'd been working at the local hospital for more than a year now—with little interference from the press. The safe haven cot had seen two babies left there—but that was good, because the message was out there. The research from Temur Sapora had finally been published with her name near the bottom of a large list of doctors. But that wasn't the best part. Philippe had helped her set up a non-profit charitable organisation. The ointment had gone into worldwide production helping people around the globe, with profits now feeding into various charities—as well as the clinic in Temur Sapora.

Most importantly, six weeks out of the year saw them both head back to her island to work in the clinic, swim in the sea and sit on the beach. It was the reality check they both needed. It helped them conquer the overwhelming pressures of trying to build a new health system in Corinez.

The music stilled, and Philippe intertwined his pinky with hers as the minister started the service. 'My champion,' he whispered.

She met his gaze and squeezed gently. 'My champion. For always.' Then she bent forward to kiss her husband-to-be. She didn't want to wait a second longer.

\* \* \* \* \*

# THE BABY
# THEY LONGED FOR

MARION LENNOX

MILLS & BOON

# CHAPTER ONE

*HAPPY IS THE bride the sun shines on.*

Happier still was the bride's mother.

Addie's mum had been beaming ever since she'd read the weather forecast. Actually, she'd been beaming from the moment Addie and Gavin had announced their engagement.

Dr Adeline Blair should be beaming, too, but right now she was struggling. In truth, Addie seemed so far away from her normal, workaday self it was like she'd moved into another body.

She didn't belong…here?

Why? Surely everything was perfect. She was about to marry her childhood sweetheart. She was making her mother gloriously happy. With luck, she and Gavin might even have a baby before…

*Don't go there. Not today.*

She glanced sideways at her mum, sitting beside her in the bridal limousine. Cancer. Metastases. Maeve seemed well today, but tomorrow…

*No.*

'This is the happiest day of my life,' Maeve breathed, and Addie hugged her—which, considering the amount of tulle she was wearing, plus the weight of her over-the-top veil, took some doing.

The car pulled to a stop. The church looked picture-postcard perfect. An arch of roses framed the entrance. Guests were presumably tucked up inside, waiting for the arrival of the bride. A photographer stood ready.

Addie had no extra attendants, no bridesmaids. Her mother was being bridal attendant as well as giving her away, an all-in-one package.

In some ways, it was almost her mother's wedding.

'Oh, Addie.' As the chauffeur opened the car doors, her mother's eyes were like stars. 'I can't believe this is happening.'

And Addie finally relaxed. Her mother was happy. Gavin was waiting. She knew she loved him—she always had. The reservations that had prevented this happening years ago were surely dumb.

This was as good as she could make it.

But then…

She lifted the load of tulle from around her ankles, swung herself out of the car—and straight into Noah McPherson.

Noah. Surgical consultant at Sydney Central. Gavin's immediate boss.

Gav's best man.

Noah was tall, dark and imposing in his beautifully cut dinner suit. He was in his early thirties but his skill and gravitas made him seem older. Addie saw lots of gravitas now.

*Why wasn't he with Gav?*

'What's…what's wrong?' she managed, but she knew almost before she spoke.

'Gav can't do it.'

'Can't do…what?'

She couldn't believe this. She was standing in brilliant sunshine, in her fairy-floss dress, and she was asking a question she already knew the answer to. She'd known the answer since she'd seen Noah.

'Gav says he can't marry you,' Noah said, quite gently. 'I'm so sorry.'

Silence.

There should be bells, Addie thought, almost hysterically. Her mother and Gav's mother had organised bell-ringers. Addie had paid for them.

Maybe the bells had moved to her head. She felt like it was about to explode.

Gavin was…*jilting her*? This wasn't real. It didn't happen. It couldn't happen.

'I… Did he give you any explanation?' She was weirdly proud that she'd got the question out without gibbering.

'He did. But you don't want to hear it now.'

'Tell me,' she commanded.

Whoa…

Once upon a time Adeline Blair had had a temper, but not now. She'd had years of living in a house where every outburst would be greeted with, 'Oh, Addie, what would your father say? You'll break my heart even more.' Her mother's tears had pretty much shoved Addie's temper into a dark cellar, tethered it with chains and left it to its own devices.

But right now she could feel the chains snapping. 'Tell me,' she hissed again, and Noah flinched.

'Addie, we can do this later. We can find somewhere private—'

'I need to know now. Tell me why.'

He took a deep breath and visibly braced. 'Gav said… all his life he's been ruled by women. Their grief and their need. And now your mum's ill… He couldn't tell you. He didn't wish you—or your mother or his—any more unhappiness, but he's decided that he can't keep on being needed. He wants his own life.'

'His own life.'

'That's what he said.'

'So he's decided…' Temper or not, she was struggling to find her voice. She had to try a couple of times before she succeeded. 'He decided to wait to tell me until five minutes before he was due to marry me? And then he didn't even tell me himself?' She was fighting rising hysteria. Stay calm, she told herself, but herself refused to listen.

'I guess… Look, would you like me to drive you anywhere?'

'Go jump,' she hissed. 'He didn't even have the courage to phone?'

'He thought you'd talk him out of it.' He considered his words. 'Or into it. Whatever.'

'He sees me as what…the enemy?'

'Maybe you need to see it from his point of view.' It seemed like Noah was trying to make this whole scenario logical. 'He says you depend on him. He doesn't want to hurt you, but he feels like he's been blackmailed by your mother's illness. By your need.'

What the… 'He w-wants to m-marry me,' she stammered. 'He's been asking me almost once a week since I was seven.'

'Maybe he thought you'd never say yes. I don't know. All I know is that he's finally realised that he can't go through with it. He says he can't be controlled any more by what he calls…'

'What he calls what?' She didn't recognise herself. She didn't recognise the anger.

'Addie…'

'What d-did he call me?' Addie stammered.

'Not only you. I think it's you, your mum, his mum.'

'So what did he call…*us*?'

'This isn't helpful.'

'Say it.'

He sighed—and then he said it. 'He called you…a monstrous regiment of women.'

Silence.

People were starting to make their way out of the church, wondering what was happening. Rebecca was way out front. Rebecca was Noah's wife, wheelchair bound and beautiful beyond belief. She was also the source of any vitriolic hospital gossip she could find. Right now her face was alive with speculation. Pleasure?

All their hospital friends were behind her.

Gavin's mum was with them. Lorna looked appalled.

Her mum was beside her, looking ashen.

'You've been with Gav for the entire morning, listening to this drivel,' Addie managed at last, struggling to keep her voice from being heard by anyone else. 'He doesn't want to be needed? I've cared for his mum as well as mine, for as long as I can remember. And now… You work with me and you didn't even have the decency to warn me…'

The chains were definitely snapped now, and her package of temper, bundled up and controlled for all these years, was suddenly running amuck. All she could see was crimson.

'Addie, I'm sorry.'

'Of course you're sorry,' she said, distantly now. 'That's why everyone's heading this way. Everyone's sorry. Oh, and here's Rebecca, ready to soak up every detail. Explain it to your wife, will you. And everyone else. A monstrous regiment of women? His mum? My mum? Me?'

'Addie…' He put a hand on her shoulder.

And then Adeline Blair did what she'd never done in her life and would never do again.

She struck his hand, and, as he didn't release her, she shoved away. And as he instinctively held on—to comfort, maybe, who knew?—she reached out and slapped his smug, sorry face, a slap so hard the sound rang out over the churchyard to the town beyond.

And Dr Adeline Blair, dutiful daughter, doting fiancée, or ex-fiancée, jilted bride—oh, and obstetrician as well—hitched up her bridal gown, tugged off her veil and kicked off her stupid satin shoes.

'Look after Mum,' she called over her shoulder to Gavin's mother, because even then she was a dutiful daughter.

And then she ran.

# CHAPTER TWO

*Three years later*

'WE'RE VERY GLAD to welcome you to the staff. Six months is great. Have you seen enough of the hospital? Terrific set-up, isn't it? Let's show you to the doctors' residence and get you settled.'

Noah had looked at this place on the internet and liked what he'd seen. Now, in reality, the hospital met his expectations and more. It was small but it seemed excellent.

Currawong Bay was two hours' drive from Sydney, tucked between mountains and sea on New South Wales' south coast. It was a hazardous drive to the next major medical centre, or a fast helicopter flight if weather conditions permitted, so the hospital was geared to independence. For the last few weeks that independence had been compromised. They'd been lacking a surgeon.

Luckily the role of temporary surgeon was a job Noah needed. It was six months before his court case could be heard. Until then he had no access to his daughter.

No. Seven-year-old Sophie was not his daughter, he told himself, for what must surely be the thousandth time. She was the daughter of his ex-wife and he had no legal claim.

But how could he stop caring for a child he'd loved since she was a toddler? He couldn't, which was why he'd needed to leave Sydney. He needed a busy, hands-on workload to keep him sane.

'There's only one other occupant in our doctors' house.' Henry, the hospital's middle-aged administrator, was bluff and genial. 'But the house is good. Because of our isolation we're often dependent on locums, and this helps attract them. The place is set up to give privacy. It's right on site. You can share the living rooms, or stick to your own rooms if you wish to be by yourself.'

'Who's living there now?' He hadn't planned on sharing at all. The advertisement had said self-contained quarters. How did that fit?

'Our obstetrician.' Henry seemed oblivious to his qualms. 'She's been here for almost three years now and because of the nature of her work the doctors' house is a good fit. Hopefully she'll be home now. Come through and I'll introduce you.'

But then Henry's phone rang. He took the call, glancing out at the gorgeous day outside. When the call ended he sighed but the sigh didn't sound too unhappy. 'Sorry, Noah, but there's been a hitch. One of my golfing mates forgot his anniversary tonight, so tee off has been brought forward.'

It was Saturday afternoon. The bay was a glistening sheet of sapphire, the golf course lying enticingly in the distance. This had to be one of the most beautiful places for a hospital in the world. Henry's choice was obvious.

'If you head down the veranda and across the walkway, third door on your left, you'll find everything you need,' he said hurriedly. 'You're expected. Introduce yourself and make yourself at home. Settle in, explore the bay, do what you want until we start throwing work at you on Monday. By the way, do you play golf? No? Shame. Gotta go, though. Welcome to Currawong.'

He was gone and Noah was left to his own devices.

Which suited him fine.

He walked out to the veranda and took a few moments to soak in the view. This was a good decision, he thought. A busy country hospital in a beautiful place. All types of surgery. A great place to live until the courts came down on his side.

Please…

Meanwhile he had a housemate.

That wasn't great. He'd prefer to be by himself. He needed to get his head sorted.

To prepare himself for losing Sophie?

He walked slowly along the veranda, taking time to appreciate the wicker armchairs set out for recuperating patients to sit in the sun and admire the view to the beach beyond. The doctors' accommodation was linked to the hospital by a breezeway, a separate house, simple, wooden, with wide French windows opening to the sea.

A window at the far end was open, the curtains wafting out in the breeze.

He reached the door, raised his hand to knock and then paused.

A moan… Stifled. Coming from the window at the end.

Was his housemate ill?

Knocking and demanding entrance if she was vomiting didn't seem such a great idea.

The glass doors led to what looked like a living room. No one was inside. He tried the door and found it unlocked.

The house was old-fashioned, furnished for comfort

rather than style, with high ceilings, worn wooden floors and faded rugs. The living room was full of overstuffed furniture, big, comfortable, homey.

A vase of crimson poppies sat on the sideboard. They still had a band around their stems, looking like whoever had put them in the vase hadn't had the energy to let them free. He looked around, liking what he saw—and then there was another groan.

Uh-oh. This wasn't a gastro-type groan. He'd been a doctor long enough to differentiate.

This was pain. Sharp pain.

And even as he thought it, the door opened. A woman stood framed in the doorway, slight, mousy-brown hair, heavy glasses, wearing a faded nightgown.

Clutching her stomach.

'Who—?' She stopped at what was obviously her bedroom door and seemed to gather strength. 'Who…?'

'I'm Noah McPherson.' He frowned with concern. She was bending with pain, and while he watched, one hand went from her stomach to her shoulder. 'Surgeon.'

'Surgeon,' she gasped. And then she paused and tried to focus. 'Oh, hell… Noah?'

And he got it. He'd worked with her. He'd watched her as a jilted bride. She'd slapped him, hard.

'Addie,' he said blankly.

But she was no longer listening. She was clutching her side, focussing inward. 'Noah…' She struggled to find words. 'Oh, help. Noah, I don't want… Of all the people… But I think I need…' Her knees seemed to buckle and she dropped to a crouch.

And any confusion he was feeling faded in the face of medical need. He stooped before her, pushing the tangle of curls back from her eyes. 'What's happening? Addie, tell me.'

'I think… No, I know that I'm pregnant,' she gasped, struggling to breathe. 'Test…positive. Ten weeks. I haven't had an ultrasound yet but now…pain like you wouldn't believe. My shoulder hurts. And… I've started… I've started to bleed. I've had…endometriosis. It's a risk and these are classic symptoms. I think my pregnancy's ectopic. I want her so much. Oh, Noah, I'm losing my baby.'

His brief tour of the hospital with Henry had been enough for him to find the right people, fast, and without exception Currawong Bay's nursing staff were appalled.

No one seemed to have guessed Addie was pregnant. From the orderly who came running to help him get her across to the hospital, to the nurses, even to the hospital cook who appeared from the kitchen because she couldn't believe what she'd just heard, they were horrified.

Noah was horrified himself, but he had to put his dismay on the backburner. The hospital used the town's family doctors as backup. They could care for their own patients when they were in hospital, but it seemed none had specific surgical training.

If this was indeed an ectopic pregnancy, then this was his call.

'I need…a scan,' Addie breathed as they wheeled her along the veranda.

'I'm onto it,' he told her. He touched her face, lightly, in an attempt at reassurance. 'Addie, let me do the worrying. You know I'm a surgeon. I might not know as much as you do about pregnancy complications but I know enough to cope with this. Trust me?'

'I… Yes.' And she caught his hand. For a moment he thought it was to push it away but instead it turned into a death grip as more pain hit. 'I don't…have a choice.'

She didn't. It was, indeed, an ectopic pregnancy.

A scan showed an embryo growing in the right fallopian tube rather than the womb. Such pregnancies were doomed from the start, and internal bleeding was now threatening her life.

He didn't have to explain it to Addie. She watched the screen with him, her face racked with distress. Pain relief was kicking in. The nurses were prepped, the theatre was ready but they were waiting for the anaesthetist. Apparently he was on his way, pulled from his son's football game.

'I wanted this baby so much,' she breathed. 'Oh, Noah… I have endometriosis. Scarring. If the other tube's damaged…'

She'd know the odds. Rupture meant an increased risk of future infertility, and if she already suffered from endometriosis the odds were even worse. It was a hard call, treating a doctor, Noah thought. It was impossible to reassure her when she knew the facts.

She'd also know that he was a second-best doctor right now. What she needed was a specialist obstetrician, and the hospital had only one. Addie.

But if Noah hadn't decided to come a couple of days early there wouldn't be any surgeon within an hour's reach. For the first time Noah was hit with the drama of country medical practice. Him or no one.

'Please…' Addie was weeping in her distress. Once more her hand caught his. 'I know I've lost my baby but I can't…please, I can't be infertile.'

'I'll do what I can,' he said gently. 'Addie, you know I

can make no promises.' He was administering pre-meds, willing the unknown anaesthetist to hurry.

'You can repair the tube.' Her voice was blurred from the drugs and pain and shock. 'You must. Please.'

He knew he couldn't. So must she if she was thinking straight. If they'd caught things before the rupture then maybe but now…

'Addie, you know…'

'I do,' she whispered. 'But please… I'm sorry I slapped you.'

And that made him smile. Of all things to be thinking… 'If I'd been you that day, I might have slapped me, too.'

'It should have been Gav.' She took a deep breath, fighting for strength, but there was still spirit. 'To let me get to the church… Toe rags, both of you.'

'We were indeed toe rags,' he said gravely. 'Addie, is there anyone we should be contacting? You need some support. Your mum?' He hesitated. 'The baby's father?'

'No.' It was a harsh snap.

He wanted to stop but he had to know. Addie was suffering internal bleeding. Where the hell was the anaesthetist? If they didn't get in soon… 'Addie, we need next of kin at least.'

'Next of kin's this baby.'

'Addie…'

'There's no one,' she snapped. 'Mum died three years ago. Gav's mother doesn't speak to me, and Gav's long gone. And this baby's father is a number from a sperm bank. So if I die on the operating table feel free to donate everything to the local cats' home. But, oh, Noah…' Her voice shattered on a sob and her grip on his hand tightened. He was no friend but he knew her from the past and it seemed that right now he was all she had.

'You will… The tubes… You will try.'

'I will.'

'Despite the slap.'

'Maybe even a little because of the slap,' he said ruefully. 'You were treated appallingly that day.'

And then he looked up as a redheaded beanpole burst through the door.

'Hey,' the beanpole said, heading for Noah and holding out his hand in greeting. 'You'll be our new surgeon. Noah? I'm Cliff Brooks, anaesthetist.' He grasped Noah's hand and then turned his attention to the patient. And stilled in shock. 'What the…? Addie!'

'It's ectopic,' Addie said weakly. 'I'm… I was… Oh, Cliff, it's ectopic.'

'Bugger,' Cliff said, and then added a couple more expletives for good measure. 'We didn't even know… I'm so sorry, love.' He then proceeded to be entirely unprofessional by stooping and giving Addie a hug.

'Hell, Ad, this is the pits but don't worry. I'll be watching our new surgeon every step of the way. Let's get you into Theatre and get things cleared. And if you want to be pregnant… This'll just be a blip. Maryanne had two miscarriages before she had Michael, and now we have four boys. Hiccups are what happens when you start a family. Don't cry, love, don't cry.'

So he hugged and Noah turned away and headed for the sinks. He felt like he'd felt on Addie's wedding day. Helpless. And…he had no right to comfort her, so why did it seem so wrong that it wasn't him who did the hugging?

\* \* \*

An ectopic pregnancy was always a grief. Growing in the fallopian tubes instead of in the womb, there was no chance a baby could survive. Someday someone might figure a way such a pregnancy could be transplanted to the womb, Noah thought, but that day was a long way off.

By the time of the rupture, the embryo was lifeless. The pressure was on to save the mother. Preserving fertility had to come second. When a woman had a complete family and there was no need to try and make future pregnancies viable, the surgery was much simpler but now... Noah was calling on skills he barely had.

Cliff was good. Noah had checked out the credentials of his anaesthetist before taking on the job, but he'd never worked with him. The fact that he was personally involved could have been a worry, but from the moment he'd released Addie from the hug Cliff had turned pure professional.

'You focus on your end. Leave everything else to me,' Cliff growled, and at least Noah could stop thinking about blood pressure, about the logistics of keeping a haemorrhaging patient alive, and focus purely on the technical.

Except he couldn't quite, because this was Addie.

Separation of personal to professional...how hard was that? He'd glanced at Cliff as Addie had slipped under, and he'd seen grimness in the man's expression. He wasn't the only one caught in personal distress for the woman they were operating on.

But why did he feel like this?

In truth he'd only had a working relationship, with Gavin as well as Addie. He'd been Gavin's boss but he'd been surprised to be asked to be best man. Gavin had obviously kept his life compartmentalised. Work, home and stuff-that-no-one-was-to-know-about. Until after the wedding fiasco when the hospital grapevine had practically exploded.

Addie had kept to herself, too, but where Gavin's lesser-known compartment had turned out to be spectacular, Addie's seemed anything but. The grapevine said that she worked and she looked after her mother. At the hospital she and Noah had occasionally operated or consulted together, but he'd thought her quiet, almost mousy. Technically skilled. Conscientious. Nothing special.

He'd operated on colleagues before, men and women he'd known far better than this. So now…why was it so hard to block out the thought of Addie's distress, the sight of her face, bleached by fear and shock?

He had to block it out. Her life depended on it.

The first part of the surgery was straightforward. An incision, finding the source of the bleeding, removing the unviable pregnancy. There was inflammation around it, and bleeding from the rupture.

'Possible to do a salpingotomy?' Cliff queried as Noah cleared and tried to see what he was left with.

Salpingotomy was the removal of the damaged embryo and then microscopic repair and preservation of the fallopian tube. He looked at the damage under his hands and shook his head. Such microscopic surgery took real obstetric skill, skills he wasn't sure he possessed. There wasn't time to transfer her to Sydney for a specialist obstetric surgeon to take over, but even if there had been…

'Not possible,' he growled. 'There's too much damage to preserve it.' It had to be a salpingectomy, the complete removal of the tube. 'Future fertility rates aren't so different,' he muttered, talking to himself rather than to Cliff.

Cliff gave him a searching look and then nodded and went back to his monitors.

There was the sound of a sob from somewhere behind him—from one of the nurses.

So Addie was loved? She'd been working in this hospital for three years. A small hospital where people had come to know her.

He worked on, but as he did he was increasingly aware of the tension around him.

'We didn't even know she was pregnant,' the theatre nurse, Heidi, a woman in her fifties, muttered as he completed the removal of the damaged tube. 'There's never been a hint of a guy. She's been going back and forth to Sydney but only ever overnight. She never takes holidays. We thought…' She swallowed, biting back what she thought. 'The other tube?'

'Looks good,' he muttered, and felt a ripple of relief through the theatre.

'It's still awful.' Heidi was still looking distressed. 'Chances of successful pregnancy after…'

'It's better than death,' Cliff said roughly. 'The chances aren't zero. Leave it, Heidi. We all need to be positive, for Addie's sake.'

Noah was closing, carefully ensuring everything that could be done was done. If he'd been able to preserve the tube Addie would be facing constant monitoring over the next few weeks, to ensure there was no further growth in the tube, but at least now it was straightforward.

She'd recover. She'd get on with life.

Just as she had after the wedding, he thought. Just

as she had after being humiliated to the socks, standing jilted at a church with everyone she loved around her.

Everyone she loved?

Who loved Addie?

It was none of his business, he told himself. Addie was now a recovering patient. His patient. He needed to invoke professional detachment.

Like that was going to happen.

Cliff was reversing the anaesthetic. Heidi was leaning over Addie, ready to reassure her the minute she came around. A couple of other nurses stood in the background, looking distressed and concerned.

These were her people now. They were...all she had?

Regardless, they were here for her. He, on the other hand, was part of a nightmare from a distant past, and now he'd be part of today's nightmare.

He stepped away from the table, feeling almost light-headed. There was nothing else he could do.

'I'll leave her to you,' he told the staff. 'I... Look after her. Constant obs. Don't leave her for a moment. I'll check back in an hour or so but I'm on the end of the phone if I'm needed before then.'

'Yeah, you need to unpack and settle,' Cliff said, roughly though, and Noah knew how deeply all those around the table were affected. 'Thanks, mate. You don't know how grateful we are that you were here for us.'

Us?

He looked down again at Addie and thought, This is your family. The hospital staff.

It was all she had?

Why did that feel so bad?

'Do you have everything you need?' Heidi asked, and he pulled himself together.

'Yes. Thank you. I won't be far away. Keep continual obs on her until I say not.' He'd already said it but it seemed important to say it again. She couldn't be left alone.

'Of course we will,' Heidi told him, and turned back to Addie. Noah was free to go.

After cleaning up post-op, he walked out onto the veranda and then further, out to the cliffs overlooking the beach.

Addie had lost her baby.

*A baby...*

*Sophie...*

For a moment he felt so dizzy he thought he'd be ill.

How could he ever have thought he could get away from this grief through work? He should have taken a job as a street cleaner for six months. Anything.

To lose a child...

'Get a grip,' he told himself, fiercely, as if it was important to make himself hear. 'You can't stop being a doctor because you've lost...'

'I haven't lost. Not yet.'

It felt like he had. Where was Sophie now? If he didn't win...

'Move on,' he told himself harshly. 'One step in front of the other, for as long as it takes.'

The grief was with her almost before she woke, almost before she remembered why she was grieving. It washed across her like a great black wave, swallowing all.

'Hey.' Heidi was holding her hand. 'Hey, Addie. You're okay.'

'My baby... I've lost...'

'Oh, Addie, we're so sorry. Yes, you've lost the baby

but our new surgeon was wonderful. He's so skilled. He thinks…we all think that things will be fine.'

*Fine.* She let the word roll around her head as reality seeped back.

Noah was here, and he thought things were fine.

She should have hit him harder.

He unpacked, headed back out to the veranda and thought about a walk, but first he needed to check on Addie again. She should be on the other side of the anaesthetic, and the reality of what had happened would be sinking in.

There'd been no call from the nurses so things must be okay physically. But not only had she lost her baby, she'd know the chances of future pregnancies were now reduced. Future pregnancies weren't impossible but it'd be a concern adding to the grief of her loss.

The nurses would look after her. They knew her and cared for her. As for him… He'd been there when she'd been jilted. He'd been there when she'd lost her baby. He was someone she could well never wish to see again, he conceded, but she might have questions. He owed it to her to answer them if she did.

To lose a child… If someone could answer *his* questions…

Don't go there, he told himself savagely. He needed to block it. This was all about Addie.

He headed back into the hospital and a young nurse turned from the phone at the front desk, greeting him with relief.

'Mr McPherson. We were hoping you might not have left the hospital. We have a ten-year-old coming in from down the coast. He fell trying to reach a bird's nest and his dad thinks he's broken his leg. He should be here in about twenty minutes. I know you're not supposed to start until Monday, but seeing you're here…'

So much for taking the weekend to get acclimatised, he thought ruefully. Work started now.

But…was work Addie?

Professionally only, he told himself.

He'd come to Currawong Bay to put a failed marriage behind him and to cope with an interminable wait. And Addie? Had she come here for the same reason? If so, the last person she'd want to see would be him, but for now he was her doctor. She'd have to wear it. She'd had enough pain today to mean the little more his presence added shouldn't make too much difference.

Addie lay back on the pillows and stared at the ceiling and thought…blank.

Nothing, nothing and nothing.

She might have known it would never work. For the last few weeks she'd been gloriously, ridiculously happy. The first twinges of morning sickness had been met with joy. She was going to be part of a family.

Admittedly it'd be a very small family—one mother and one baby—but it would be a family nonetheless. Here, in this hospital, she had the support around her to make it happen. This was a lovely little community and they'd welcomed her with open arms. There was one grumpy nurse administrator but she'd even been able to manoeuvre that into a working relationship. In the three years she'd been here she'd helped deliver countless babies, she'd made good friends, and she knew she could count on the staff and the community to help her.

Except now she wouldn't need them. Her hands fell to

her tummy, to the wad of dressing where a tiny bump had been before, and she felt her eyes fill with tears.

She wouldn't cry. She never cried, not when Gavin had jilted her, not when her mum had died, not ever.

Oh, but her baby...

'Can I come in?' It was a light tap and Noah McPherson was at the door.

Of all the people to see her cry... Noah. She swiped the tears from her face and fought for dignity. The surge of anger she'd felt as she'd emerged from the anaesthetic had faded. It wasn't his fault Gavin had jilted her. It wasn't his fault she'd lost her baby.

He was a doctor, nothing more.

A doctor she'd hit. On top of everything else she was now cringing with remembered humiliation.

'Of course,' she managed. The junior nurse who'd been sitting beside her looked a query at Noah and then slipped away, leaving her alone with a man...who'd saved her life?

A man she'd hit.

'They tell me...you did a good job,' she said, struggling to find words. 'The best you could.'

'Addie, I'm so sorry you've lost your baby.'

He didn't need to be sympathetic. She didn't want him to be sympathetic.

She wanted her mum. Anyone. No one.

Not Noah.

'It's okay.'

'I'm very sure it's not,' he said gently. 'I can't imagine how you're feeling. Can I sit down?'

'I... Of course.' What else was there to say?

He sat on the chair the nurse had just vacated. For a moment she thought he was intending to reach out and take her hand and she hauled it under the covers pre-emptively. She saw him wince.

'I need to talk to you as your doctor,' he told her. 'That's all. Can you stand it?'

'Of…of course I can.'

He nodded, gravely. 'There's not a lot of good news but there is some. Addie…your baby… You know it was tragic chance that she started developing in the fallopian tube.'

'She?' she whispered. *Her baby…*

'That's an assumption,' he said gravely. 'I thought you said her. Am I right?'

'I did…think of her as a girl,' she said grudgingly, and her hands felt the dressing again. 'I…I know it's dumb but I was already thinking… Rose for my grandmother? But that's crazy.'

'It's not crazy at all,' he said gently. 'Rose. That's who she was. She was real, a baby who sadly started growing where she had no chance of survival.'

She could hardly speak. *She. Her baby.* He'd even said her name, a name that she'd almost felt silly for dreaming of. And for some reason it helped. For the last few weeks, filled with wonder and anticipation, she'd been talking to the tiny bump she could scarcely feel. And, yes, she knew she was a girl. At some primeval level…

Or was that because she had so little knowledge of boys? Her family had always been women. Well, two women, herself and her mum.

So many emotions… She wasn't thinking straight. The anaesthetic was still making its effects felt. She lay back on the pillows and closed her eyes.

'Addie…'

'Mmm…' She wanted to be left alone, in her cocoon of grief. Life felt…barren. She wanted… She wanted…

'Addie, let's talk practicalities,' Noah said, strongly now, and regardless of what she wanted he reached out and took her hand. He held it strongly, a warm, firm hold, the reassurance of one human being touching another. She didn't want it but, oh…she needed it. She should pull away but she didn't. Practicalities? Something solid?

Something solid like Noah, she thought, and his hand…helped.

'We might be able to preserve your embryo for burial if that's what you wish,' Noah told her. 'It'll need to go to Pathology but after that… There might be something. If you wish.'

'I…' It was something. Something to hold to. The remnants of her dream? A place to mourn? 'I do wish.'

'Then I'll try to make it happen. No promises but I'll do my best. For now, though, Addie, can we talk through the results of the surgery? Or do you want to leave it until later?'

'Now.' It was scarcely a whisper. How hard was this?

'Then I need to tell you that I had to remove the entire tube,' he told her, in that gentle but professional voice that was somehow what she needed. 'It was ruptured, and even if I'd managed to suture it, chances are there'd be microscopic embryonic tissue I couldn't remove, tissue that might cause even more problems in the future. So that's grim news. But, Addie, I checked the other tube and it's perfect. Perfect, Addie.'

'It doesn't mean…' She stopped. Her words had been a whisper and they faded out, but he knew what she'd been about to say.

'It doesn't mean future pregnancies are assured,' he

finished for her. 'We both know that. But it does mean future pregnancies are possible. More than possible. You need to give yourself a couple of months to let your body heal, and let yourself heal, too, but then there's no reason why you shouldn't try again.'

He saw her face close in pain. This was one of the hardest conversations…talking about a future pregnancy when she'd barely started her grieving over this one. But this was his job, laying out the facts. The facts needed to be implanted, to be there when she needed them.

'You're an obstetrician,' he said gently. 'You know the odds better than I do, but for now you don't need to think of them. Put them away for later. For now, just focus on you, on what you need, and on your grief for your tiny daughter.'

'You sound like you think she was real?'

'Isn't she real, Addie? Your Rose?'

He watched her face. This was the hardest part, he thought.

He remembered past lectures, dry as dust, the technicalities of surgical removal of ectopic pregnancies. But he'd sat in the lectures and looked at the diagrams of the baby developing in the fallopian tubes and he'd thought… it involved a death. A loss. A grief. No matter what happened to cause the end of a pregnancy, there must still be grief. He'd understood it then, he'd had it enforced later from harsh, brutal experience and now, watching Addie's face, he knew it even more strongly.

'She was…my daughter,' she whispered. 'For such a short time.'

'And she was loved,' he said gently. 'And she'll always be a part of you. But for now…' The look of strain on her face was almost unbearable. 'You need to sleep.

Do what your body tells you, Addie. The nurse will be coming back. If you need anything more, I'm within calling distance.'

'I…I know,' she muttered. 'Oh, Noah… I slapped you.'

'You're welcome to slap me again if it helps,' he told her, and smiled. 'Anything you want, just not as long as it stops you sleeping.' And then he paused. Someone had knocked on the ward door. A head poked around, Henry, the hospital administrator, his face puckered in concern. Things must be pretty bad to haul him from his golf, Noah thought, but as he surged into the room he remembered the distress on the faces of the theatre staff and he knew that Addie was indeed loved.

It made him feel better—sort of—but it also made him feel…bleak.

Why? He wasn't sure. But Henry was stooping to give Addie a careful kiss and the feeling of bleakness intensified.

'I'll leave you to Henry,' he managed. 'No more than five minutes, though, Henry, and the nurse needs to return before you leave. Addie needs to sleep.'

'She needs to sleep for months,' Henry said roundly. 'We've been telling her and telling her. Long weekends, that's all she'll ever take. Cliff rang me and I was never more shocked. Yes, I know it's hard to get staff to cover but, Addie, you now have no choice. We're running you out of town. Dr McPherson's shown he's more than capable of dealing with obstetric drama and we'll put in a call for an emergency locum to cover for you. You're heading to Sydney or wherever you want, maybe the Gold Coast, maybe further north, the Great Barrier Reef, somewhere you can lie in the sun for a couple of months and let your body recover.'

'A couple of months!' Addie sounded horrified.

'Absolutely,' Henry told her. 'At a quick calculation, you're due for nine weeks' leave, plus sick leave. So we're not taking no for an answer. My family has an apartment overlooking the beach on the Gold Coast if you want, or you could choose an alternative. Just not here. Addie, you could almost learn to play golf in two months. There's a life skill. But rest is paramount. Isn't that right, Dr McPherson?'

'You do need to rest,' Noah concurred.

'There. It's all settled. No argument. The nurses are out there planning and Morvena's already contacting locums. For the next few weeks we don't need you.'

And then Heidi appeared in the doorway with meds and Henry turned to Heidi and started discussing the pros and cons of Gold Coast versus Great Barrier Reef and it was time for Noah to back away. From her...family?

'Two more minutes and then sleep,' he said warningly, and got a nod of distracted agreement from Heidi and Henry.

Addie didn't need him any more. He was free to go.

Free.

That was what he had to get used to.

# CHAPTER THREE

*Two months later*

SHE SHOULD HAVE moved on. Maybe she should have started a new life altogether, but she'd already been there, done that, got the T-shirt.

A two-month break had changed a lot of things. But she knew she could move forward in Currawong.

During the whole time she'd been convalescing, the hospital staff, the Currawong mums she'd delivered, sometimes seemingly the whole community, had kept in touch as much as she wanted.

Currawong felt like home.

There was the hitch that Noah McPherson would still be living in the doctors' quarters. He'd been with her during two of the worst moments in her life. His presence made her feel...vulnerable.

She'd slapped him when he'd been nothing but a messenger for Gavin's cowardly retreat. For that she felt embarrassment and guilt.

He'd saved her life, but that also meant he'd been with her when she'd lost her baby. He'd seen her raw and exposed.

But he'd been kind. He'd also been professional and that was the way their relationship needed to go forward.

She'd written him a polite note, apologising once again for the slap and thanking him for his medical intervention.

During the last couple of months, she'd occasionally found herself thinking about him. His concern at the wedding, so harshly rewarded by her over-the-top reaction. His skill and his kindness when she'd lost her baby.

The feel of his hand...

Yeah, and that was entirely unprofessional. Professional was what she needed to be.

Moving on... The new, professional Addie.

She unlocked the door to the doctors' quarters and tugged her crimson, sparkly wheelie suitcase inside. Tugged? Not so much. This beauty wheeled at a touch. She let it go and watched in satisfaction as it freewheeled halfway across the sitting room. Nice. Her luggage was part of her new look, her revamp, her declaration to the world that she was moving on. This community needed a dedicated obstetrician and that's what they'd get.

Albeit a sparkly one.

She hadn't gone completely sparkly. Just a touch. She was wearing a rainbow-coloured sun frock, cinched at the waist. She'd let her hair fly free. Her now silver-blonde hair was streaked with soft amethyst streaks. She was wearing oversized amethyst earrings and a single drop necklace, and her brand-new glasses had a hint of amethyst in their silver rims.

She checked herself in the mirror above the hallstand and was pleased to approve.

And then she saw Noah. The fly in her ointment. This place was home...but Noah? A ghost from her past?

Her intention to stay completely professional flew out the window. Memories of that appalling wedding... Memories of her loss...

He'd signed on for six months. That meant he was here for four more months.

Maybe it was time she got herself her own place to live. The convenience of being right at the hospital for obstetric emergencies had kept her here, but there were alternatives.

'Addie...' He was dressed in chinos and a short-sleeved shirt, with a stethoscope dangling from his side pocket. He looked vaguely rumpled, as if he'd had a long day.

Tuesday was a normal day for scheduled surgery, she remembered. He'd probably have kept that routine, and such a day was often hard for a surgeon. Schedules didn't take into account unscheduled stuff that happened in a town like this.

'Hi,' she managed, trying not to think he looked tired. Or...gorgeous? How inappropriate was that?

'Welcome back.'

'Thank you. I'm pleased to be back.' She sounded absurdly formal. They both did.

'You look...well.'

So much for all the money she'd spent on her transformation. *Well?* But, then, what did she expect?

While she'd been convalescing she'd been in touch with a couple of friends from back in Sydney. Noah's name had...just happened...to come up. Apparently there'd been a vitriolic end to his marriage. Was that why Noah had turned his back on his ascendant career to come to Currawong? Loss? Grief?

She thought fleetingly of Noah's wife. Ex-wife? Even

in a wheelchair Rebecca had looked stunning. In comparison, *well* was as good as Addie could expect.

'I am well,' she managed.

'Can I give you a hand with your luggage?'

At least here was safe ground. 'No need,' she said airily. She walked across the room, turned the suitcase until it was facing her bedroom door and kicked it again. A little too hard and a little off course. It zoomed across the polished boards, slammed into the bookcase and a vase toppled off and smashed onto the floor.

Silence.

'I never liked that vase anyway,' Addie said at last, looking down at the mess of broken crockery.

'Designer ware,' Noah agreed. 'Supplied by Bland R Us. I'm sure we can find something less sterile in Theatre.'

'Maybe a bedpan with cactus planted inside…'

'It'd have more personality,' he agreed, and she came close to a chuckle. And then she took a deep breath. The time had come. The time was now. 'I have a confession.'

'A confession?'

'I… We may have to put away…some stuff.' She looked down at the floor rug and grimaced. 'Like this. This has to go.'

'I can understand the vase getting in the way of your luggage,' he said cautiously. 'But…the rug?'

'I'm afraid it'll get eaten.'

More silence. And then… 'Uh-oh,' Noah said.

'I know I should have asked you.' She was talking too fast, her tongue tripping over the words. 'I know the lease says no pets and I thought…well, to be honest, I knew if I rang the hospital board and asked they'd say no—Morvena will have a fit!—but if I presented them with a *fait accompli* then they'll have to wear it. They haven't found anyone to replace me, have they?'

'Locums,' he said, frowning. 'They're not trying to replace you.'

'I doubt they can.' She said it with satisfaction. 'The good thing about working in such a remote area is they need to put up with who they can get.'

'Like me,' Noah said, and Addie cast him a suspicious look. If she didn't know better she'd think she heard laughter.

Actually, there might be laughter. Noah McPherson was way over-qualified for the job here. That Currawong Bay had his services for six months was amazing.

Six months.

Four more months of sharing a house...

'What have you done?' And there was no mistaking the laughter now. Those deep grey eyes were twinkling straight at her. She couldn't help responding. She smiled back and suddenly she felt as she had when she'd walked from the hair salon with her hair coloured. Like the world was opening up before her. With colour?

Well, that was dumb. There was no way Noah McPherson should have that effect on anyone.

'You'll have to see.' She crossed to her bedroom door and pushed her badly behaved suitcase inside.

'You have something that can eat mats in your suitcase?'

'I... No.' She kicked off her high heels because, okay, she'd made a statement and she was home now. It was time to move on to the next thing. But she was home... with Noah?

Daisy would help. Hopefully. Nothing like a Daisy to ease tension. 'You want to see?' she asked.

'I want to see.'

'Okay,' she said, striving to sound nonchalant and not anxious at all. 'Let's go meet Daisy.'

Daisy was quite possibly the cutest golden retriever puppy Noah had ever seen.

Addie had obviously decided to unpack before introducing Daisy to her new home. Daisy was therefore currently tied to a veranda post surrounded by dog bed, dog bowls, dog toys...

And oldies.

The veranda was the preferred snoozing place for the residents of the nursing-home section of the hospital. It overlooked the sea and was protected from the prevailing winds. The big wicker chairs were usually filled with snoozers, soaking up the warmth of late summer.

No one was snoozing now. There was a cluster of oldies surrounding a pint-sized bundle of pup.

Was there anything cuter than a golden retriever puppy? Noah didn't think so, and Daisy wasn't about to change his mind. She looked about ten or twelve weeks old, and she was wriggling all over. Still tied to her veranda post—the oldies obviously hadn't ventured to untie her, although they were clearly longing to—she was tugging to the length of her leash so she could wiggle and lick and greet as many new friends as fitted into her orbit.

His first thought? Sophie would love this puppy.

No. He shoved the thought away, hard. Four months to wait...

'Oh!' Addie was sounding dismayed as she hurried forward toward the clustered oldies. 'I didn't mean to disturb you. You guys are supposed to be asleep.'

They weren't asleep now. Without exception, the residents of the nursing home had migrated to the doctors' house end of the veranda. Bill Harrison, ex farmer, was crouched on the ground, enticing Daisy to crawl onto knees that had been destroyed by eighty years of heaving hay bales. But it was doubtful if he was even feeling his knees. He was intent on unclipping Daisy's leash and his attention was on the pup.

'There's all the sleep in the world where I'm headed,' he growled now. 'Bugger naps. Where'd you get this one, Addie? She's a beauty.'

'She is, isn't she?' Addie beamed and plonked herself down on her knees with Bill. 'I've only had her since this morning. I picked her up on the way home, from a breeder in Sydney. I shouldn't have her here, but I thought you guys might be able to help look after her.'

'Us?' It was Ruby May Alderstone, a long-retired schoolteacher, shrivelled from years of rheumatoid arthritis and usually grim from constant pain. But now she was smiling, stooping from her wheelchair to click her fingers to entice Daisy to come to her.

'Only if you want,' Addie said.

Daisy launched herself from Bill's knees to Addie's, reached up and licked, throat to forehead, a great, slurpy dog kiss, and Addie giggled and held.

And Noah thought, I know why she's bought this dog.

He still didn't have a handle on Addie Blair. He'd worked with her occasionally back in Sydney when she'd been a newly qualified obstetrician, engaged to be married to one of his surgical colleagues. He'd thought her plain, mousy, competent. The couple of times she'd been in Theatre with him she hadn't joined in the general theatre banter. He'd thought her...boring. The fact that she had been engaged to Gavin had cemented that thought.

Then he'd seen her at what was supposed to be her wedding. She'd been beautiful that day, but beautiful in a strange way. It was as if she'd been dressed by others, transformed into a Barbie-type caricature of the real Addie. The boring Addie had still been underneath.

Then she'd slapped him and he'd seen fire behind the bland exterior. For the first time he'd seen spirit.

That spirit had seemed extinguished two months ago—and why wouldn't it have been? The Addie he'd seen in the hospital bed had seemed like she'd had the life snuffed out of her. He'd felt desperately sorry for her, but there'd been nothing he could do.

But now…she'd done something for herself. Not something. Some things. She'd come back perky and fresh and defiant. Her outfit was a far cry from the sensible Addie he'd first met, but it hadn't taken her back to the Barbie Addie of her wedding day. Her clothes, her accessories looked like they'd been chosen with care, and chosen…for fun? Her sun dress was fun and flirty. Her hair looked great.

She hadn't abandoned her glasses, as she'd done for the wedding, but she'd changed them for slightly oversized ones, with silver rims and hints of colour.

She was cuddling the wriggling Daisy and she was laughing and he thought…

Physician, heal thyself?

And then she turned a little and he saw a glimpse of what was behind. She was holding Daisy as if she needed her.

The loss was still with her, then. Disguised, but bone deep.

'What is *that* doing here?'

He glanced along the veranda. Uh-oh. Morvena.

Morvena Harris was the nurse administrator of Currawong Hospital. She was well into her sixties but she showed no sign of retirement, or even slowing down. She ran the little hospital with ruthless efficiency, and, it had to be said, with skill. The staff reluctantly respected her. Patients might sometimes feel they were being bossed into recovering but recover they did.

If there was a medical need, Morvena pulled out all stops to make sure her patients lacked nothing, but there was the rub. *Her* patients. *Her* hospital. *Her* rules.

Noah had already had a run-in with her over visiting times. A young mum, a dairy farmer, had been in with appendicitis and the only time her husband had been able to bring his kids to visit had been after milking, late at night. Which was later than the rules stipulated.

'You can visit your wife, but the children can't come,' Morvena had decreed. 'You can't guarantee they won't be noisy.'

Noah had looked at their distress and put his foot down. Morvena still hadn't forgiven him.

It didn't make it any better that she was Henry's mother-in-law. The affable Henry was like putty in his bossy mother-in-law's hands. What Morvena wanted, Morvena usually got.

Now she was looking at Daisy as if she were a bad smell. A very bad smell. Then she glanced at Noah. He couldn't wipe the smile off his face fast enough, and her expression darkened. As if suspecting mass insubordination?

'Who brought that animal onto the premises?'

'She's mine.' Addie looked up at Morvena and smiled, but Noah could see the shakiness behind the smile. This was defiance but defiance could only go so far. 'Hi, Morvena. This is Daisy. She's going to live with me.'

'Not here, she's not,' Morvena decreed. 'Dogs shed. Allergies present a nightmare. You know the rules, Dr Blair.'

'I've already rung a couple of my young mums,' Addie told her. 'They've offered to organise a roster for runs during the day. She won't be a problem. We can keep her in the yard behind the doctors' house.'

'She can't live on hospital premises,' Morvena snapped. 'The doctors' accommodation is hospital property. End of story.'

'Then I'll find my own apartment.' She tilted her chin and Noah wondered how many run-ins Addie had had with Morvena in the past. A few, by the look of things. Morvena was looking at Addie with the same kind of belligerence Noah had thought was reserved for him.

But was there fear behind Addie's defiance? Fear that something else was to be snatched from her?

Something settled inside him, something hard and unassailable. There was little he could do for Addie, but he could do this.

'She shouldn't be confined to the doctors' house yard,' he said, and Morvena gave a surprised nod of satisfaction.

'I'm glad you agree. Now—'

'She needs to be out here.'

'What—?'

'Daisy's a companion dog,' he said, inexorably. 'Her place is with patients.'

He was watching the Daisy in question turn from Addie to Ruby. The ex-schoolteacher bent with difficulty so she could pat the soft little ears and Daisy responded by trying to turn a complete circle on the wheelchair footrest. She failed, fell sideways, lay for a stunned moment on the veranda and then looked up and around with what Noah swore was a grin. Like, *That was what I meant to do all along.* The circle around Daisy convulsed in laughter. A couple of nurses, further down the veranda and obviously on their break, edged up to see.

'A companion dog…' Morvena snorted. 'What nonsense. They have to be trained. That dog—'

'Was obviously bred to be a companion dog,' Noah said. 'And you must have read the literature, Morvena. The effect of a companion dog on depression and anxiety in long-term residents of nursing homes can't be understated. It's associated with increased social interaction, increased confidence, decreasing levels of isolation and, most of all, fun.'

'If we wanted a trained companion dog we'd have organised one,' she snapped back at him. 'A proper one. With a proper accredited owner.'

'And you'd pay for it how?'

There was the rub. This little hospital ran on a shoestring. It might be excellent and well equipped, but there was no money for extras.

'And you do realise our nursing home advertising brochure is misleading,' Noah went on, pushing his point hard, while Addie and the elderly residents watched in a certain amount of awe. 'The brochure clearly states that activities are organised morning and afternoon. Lorna comes every morning to organise excursions and games, but the afternoon, Morvena?'

'The brochure was printed years ago,' Morvena snapped.

'And it's still being given to potential residents. The people here could sue for false representation.'

There was a shocked hush. Everyone held their breath. Morvena was staring at Noah as if he had two heads. Such defiance was obviously unheard of in her reign.

Addie was staring at him, too, her eyes wide, looking...hornswoggled.

'Hey, we could, too.' That was Bert Nanbor, a Vietnam veteran who'd managed life without a leg until a farm accident two years back had seen him lose the other. 'I came in after reading that brochure and I've sat on this veranda bored stupid every afternoon since. And allergies...' He snorted. 'This is outside. There's plenty of fresh air to blow allergies away, and we all have our own rooms. Anyone with allergies doesn't need to share. But even then... Allergies... Never had 'em in my day. Anyone here got allergies?'

There was a chorus of rebuttal. The nurses up the back were hiding their mouths with their hands. Stifling giggles.

'And we'll help you train him, Doc,' Bert added, turning his attention to Addie. 'Almost everyone here comes from farms and we know dogs. Bill here used to train working dogs, didn't you, Bill? This little lass looks smart as paint. We could have her herding sheep in no time.' And then he grinned. 'Or herding Mrs Rowbotham's hens. It's time those hens learned discipline.'

Addie had been trying to keep a straight face but she lost it now. She chuckled—and Noah glanced across at her and thought... Wow.

The chuckle transformed her. It lit her within.

Had he ever heard her chuckle?

He thought back to the serious colleague he'd worked with before her failed wedding. She'd been sober, conscientious, seemingly almost bowed down by the responsibility of getting things right.

Gavin had told him of the death of her father, and of Gavin's own father. Apparently they'd been engineers, working on a major bridge construction together. The bridge had collapsed when she and Gavin had been toddlers. According to Gavin, he and Addie had then been practically raised together, their mothers united by common grief.

'That's why we're getting married,' Gavin had told him, in those last desperate moments of justification, before Gavin had disappeared and left him facing the failed wedding farce that had followed. 'Addie's mother has cancer. My mum's gutted and she needs me to do the right thing. This was meant to keep all of them happy.'

Yeah, right. Good one, Gavin.

He'd lost touch with Addie after the wedding. She'd quietly left the hospital and he'd been caught up in his own worries. But now... The Currawong hospital grapevine—which spread to Noah whether he willed it or not—was good, and Addie had been here for almost three years. But the grapevine didn't know why—or even how—she'd become pregnant. There was communal disgust that it hadn't guessed.

In that appalling few moments before surgery, she'd told him she'd used donated sperm. Why? Had the experience with Gavin turned her off men for life?

Conscientious. Boring.

Watching her now... Was there a different Addie underneath?

He turned his attention deliberately back to the pup. What business of his was Addie's life?

'You realise Mrs Rowbotham is the hospital housekeeper and weekend cook,' she was saying, stifling chuckles as she tried to respond to Bert. 'Eggs from her chooks feed the hospital.'

'There's no reason why that'll change,' Bert said blithely. 'If I was their size and I had this pup on my tail, I might lay an egg myself.'

It was too much. Everyone laughed, and Addie's chuckle was glorious, a lovely, tinkling laugh that seemed…

To be setting something free?

'You still can't keep the dog,' Morvena snapped, sounding driven against the ropes. 'It's against the rules.'

Addie's face fell but Noah thought, No one's going to mess with that chuckle on my watch.

'Then the rules change,' he growled back. 'Or I send a brochure to the Board of Health and complain of misrepresentation. Our advertising offers activities each afternoon but the advertisement's misleading. Here's Dr Blair, offering the use of her puppy for free. We accept or I act.'

'You wouldn't dare…'

'The consequences being? You'll sack me? Or Henry will sack me? I'm only here until my permanent replacement arrives in four months and there are lots of other places I can go. If you have a queue of surgeons waiting to take my place…'

'They sweated trying to find a locum for Addie, and they've had no responses trying to find a permanent surgeon.' Bert was obviously soaking in the drama. 'Currawong without a surgeon…geez, Morvena, you'd have to close the acute hospital and send everyone except us oldies to Sydney. All for a bit of fluff that never hurt anyone.'

But the fluff in question had been getting bored. He'd wandered along the veranda to greet the one person he hadn't met yet. Morvena. Morvena was wearing sensible pumps, with sensible laces. Tied in bows. Daisy spotted the bows, quivered, crouched—and pounced.

Morvena shrieked. She raised her foot to kick Daisy away but Noah was there before her, diving along the veranda almost before Morvena reacted. By the time her shoe was aimed, Noah had scooped up the recalcitrant pup and was heading back to dump it in Addie's arms.

'Requirement number one,' he said. 'There'll need to be a gated playpen where only those who don't mind being chewed enter. It'll need to be easily accessed by wheelchairs, though. Any of you guys any good at building?'

'I used to be,' Bert said reluctantly. 'Can't do much without legs.'

'Woodwork's something you should be doing if you're bored in the afternoons,' Morvena said, glaring at everyone. 'The men's shed. You know the local citizens' group set it up. It's full of tools and benches suitable for wheelchairs but you never use it.' She glared at Noah, defiantly. 'We have all sorts of occupational aids no one uses.'

'Then isn't it lucky Daisy's here to encourage us to use them?' Noah said blandly. 'Bert, do you reckon you could whip up some sort of a doggie playpen. Bill?'

'I used to enjoy woodwork.' It was Ruby May, interspersing hesitantly from her wheelchair. 'It's years since I held a hammer, but I bet I still can. If the men do the bits that need strength, I'd love to help.'

'Excellent,' Noah said, tucking Daisy under one arm. 'Give me a list of what you need and I'll head down to the hardware store. I'm happy to cover costs.'

'There's no need,' Addie started, but he quelled her with a look. There was a need but the need wasn't purely

Addie's and Daisy's. She saw it, too, and gave a faint smile. And to give her her due, so did Morvena.

'You do woodwork?' she demanded of Ruby May.

'All my life,' Ruby said simply. 'Mum taught me.'

'You never join in any of the activities.'

'Knitting with my arthritic fingers? Bingo?' Ruby snorted. 'Would you?'

'But the shed…'

'It's got a sign on it saying "Men's Shed",' Ruby told her. 'No one invited me there.'

'Well, we're inviting you,' Bert said roundly. 'The sign comes down. Isn't that right, guys? And I'm covering the costs of the wood. No, don't argue,' he told Addie as she made an instinctive protest. 'What use is money if I can't have fun?' He chuckled. 'Fun… There should be more of it. We can keep her, can't we, Morvena?'

'Oh, for heaven's sake…' But Morvena had been trounced and she finally had the grace to admit it. Her sigh resounded along the veranda. 'But it's a responsibility, Dr Blair. If anyone gets hurt, if there's any damage, it's your responsibility.'

'It's our responsibility,' Noah added. He smiled at Addie, and surprised…the glimmer of tears? That spoke of fragility. She wasn't completely recovered, then.

He felt a pang of something that should be concern for someone who'd been his patient—but it was more than that.

Concern for a colleague?

Possibly more than that, too. He was feeling an almost overwhelming urge to step forward and hug her, hold her tight, sandwich-squeeze her and her wriggling puppy until the look of strain around her eyes eased.

Instead he turned business-like. 'Addie, you take

Daisy and introduce her to her new home,' he told her. 'Tell her the back bedroom's mine and if I find her under the covers then all bets are off. She'll be booted out to Bert's bedroom before you can say woof. Right, we need a list. Ruby May, if I grab a pen and paper, can you tell us what we need? I have time before evening ward rounds. As long as there's no emergency, I can fit in a trip to the local hardware store. Addie, can you be trusted to keep the monster under control until I get back?'

'I can do that,' she told him, and even though she was smiling there was still the glimmer of tears behind her eyes. 'Thank you. Thank you all.'

'And special thanks to Morvena,' Noah said, and grinned at Morvena and kept grinning until that dour lady was forced to give a tight smile in response. 'Addie, medically, you, me and Morvena, we're a force to be reckoned with. And Daisy, too. Our medical team has just been increased by one.'

Morvena gave a snort of disgust and turned on her heel. There was a ripple of laughter through the ranks but it was short-lived. The residents had a project and Noah could see each and every one of them figuring how they could play a part.

Excellent.

And Addie?

She was smiling, too, and that was even more excellent.

His fast trip to the hardware store turned out to be not so fast because Bert and Ruby May insisted on coming with him. He had an SUV with roof racks—he had a kayak he used in his spare time—so he could fit wheelchairs, plus elderly companions in crime and still have room to accommodate the extensive shopping list.

'How big is this playpen?' he demanded, astounded, as piles of timber were loaded onto his roof rack, but Ruby and Bert just chuckled. 'Leave it to us, Doc,' Bert told him. 'You fix people. We fix playpens.'

And the extra time was worth it, he decided as he unloaded the timber into the workshop and watched the residents' delight. It was even worth the fact that he had to push back his evening ward round, and then cope with a farmer's kid who'd got in the way of a cow with a mean kick.

By eleven that night he was exhausted but in a good way. The laughter, the enjoyment of Ruby May and Bert, the anticipation rippling through the nursing home were still making him smile. He headed back along the veranda to the doctors' accommodation, pushed open the door and there was something else to make him smile.

An advantage of living in the doctors' quarters was that cleaning was provided. Mrs Rowbotham came in every morning and bustled about, worrying about 'her doctors'. She religiously cleaned the fireplace, set the fire and tut-tutted when he hadn't used it.

Noah hardly did use it. The days were warm. Occasionally the nights got chilly but he tended to work late, eat dinner on the veranda and then crash. But the fire was being used now. Addie had piled cushions onto the rug and had nestled there with her pup. The main light was off, and her face was lit by the flicker of the fire's embers.

Daisy was curled in the crook of her arm. She looked— they both looked—supremely, completely at peace. Neither of them stirred as he came in. He stood for a moment looking down at them, watching Addie's face. She looked young and very vulnerable. She looked…beautiful.

She'd get cold if she stayed there as the fire died, he thought, trying to drag his thoughts back to practical. After all, she was his patient—or she had been. She wouldn't be his colleague until next Monday when she officially started work again. So…if she was his patient it was his duty to look after her.

Should he wake her? Steer her to bed?

He didn't have the heart. Instead he headed for the blanket box and fetched one of Mrs Rowbotham's stash of fluffy comforters. He pulled out the softest, a pile of pink angora, and carried it silently back to the pair beside the fire.

He stooped and spread it gently across them. Daisy stirred, wiggled her tail gently and then closed her eyes again, as much to say, Don't you dare disturb this, this is perfect.

It was indeed perfect. He tucked the rug in and stayed for a moment looking down at them.

Addie's eyes flickered open. Met his. Smiled. It was a smile that reflected Daisy's.

'Thank you,' she whispered, as he tucked her in, and he could tell she was still ninety percent asleep. Dreaming? And as if in a dream, her hand came up and her fingers touched his face, a feather touch, maybe to see if he was real?

'You are a very nice man, Noah McPherson. Has anyone ever told you that?'

There was no need to reply. Addie's eyes fluttered closed. Her hand sank and he tucked it under the rug.

She smiled in her sleep. He had an almost overwhelming urge to stoop and kiss her goodnight.

He did no such thing. Once upon a time Noah McPherson's heart had been open to beauty, to gentleness, to love. Now he stepped back and made a silent vow.

He'd given his heart once and it was still cracked wide open. Who was going down that road again?

Not him. He left the room and went to bed.

# CHAPTER FOUR

ADDIE SPENT THE next few days catching up on work. The hospital had managed to get a locum while she'd been away but there'd been little follow-up with patients with long-term concerns. There were pap-smear reminders, follow-ups with gynae, making sure pre-term mums were up to date with what they needed. She settled into her office and worked methodically through her files.

Her life settled into some sort of order. With the addition of her puppy.

Daisy was like a battery-driven toy without an off switch. She woke at dawn, full on, tearing around the doctors' house, chewing socks, chair legs, toes, anything she could get her teeth into before Addie did her regular lurch to save whatever precious thing she was trying to devour.

Every morning she pleaded to be allowed into Noah's room, but even if Addie had allowed it, by dawn Noah was out. He'd kayak or maybe run. The first morning after her arrival, when she took Daisy outside, she saw him down on the beach. He was running hard, almost as if he was exorcising demons.

She wondered about him. She knew so little.

He'd been Gavin's boss. In truth she'd been surprised

when Gav had asked him to be best man as they hadn't seemed close, but then Gav had been a bit of a loner. Or she'd thought he was. It turned out there'd been a whole other side…

Whatever, thinking about Noah…

She knew he'd been married. She'd known Rebecca, but where was his wife now? He was no longer wearing a ring but surely the grapevine would have known if she'd died. Rebecca had been in a wheelchair but that was down to being injured in a past car accident. Nothing presently life-threatening.

So where was she now? It wasn't the sort of question she could easily ask. *Excuse me, but what have you done with your wife?*

And it was none of her business.

Their routine settled. Every morning Addie played with the pup in the back yard. By the time Noah returned from his run, Daisy was tiring. Noah sat at the kitchen table and ate cereal while Daisy snuggled onto his knee.

And every morning Addie thought… A guy who'd just run… Who'd showered and was still damp but looked… who looked…

Yeah, there was a route she wasn't taking. *He* was none of her business.

After breakfast she scooped Daisy up and headed over to the hospital. Daisy slept in her office, and when she woke she'd let her out onto the veranda.

There was 'stuff' happening on the veranda. The oldies were building a 'playpen', with wide gates and a ramp down from the veranda with wheelchair access. They were wrangling Daisy as they worked. Until the playpen was built Daisy still needed to be on a leash but they were having fun, being busy, being happy…

Sometimes Noah was out there, in breaks in his surgery, popping out to check that all was well.

To be happy, too?

It might be none of her business but the questions still came at her. Why was he here? A six-month locum while he got his divorce sorted? There were much more challenging jobs he could be doing, in any of Australia's cities. Why spend six months in such an out-of-the-way place as here?

Was he running, like she was? She'd come here after her wedding had gone wrong, after her mother's death. She'd wanted to run from everything that had reminded her of pain.

As the days passed, she found her thoughts drifting back to that time pre-wedding. To Noah.

It was no crime to wonder, she decided.

She thought back to the woman who'd been Noah's wife. She'd met Rebecca, both in her role as part-time receptionist at Sydney Central, and then at a couple of pre-wedding functions Gavin had arranged. Her impression had been that she was beautiful, opinionated and selfish, often seeming ready to manipulate her situation in order to get what she wanted.

Rebecca had summed *her* up in a glance and had made it clear what she thought of the ordinary little woman who'd made medicine her life. Being a surgeon's wife was much more important, Rebecca's attitude implied. Addie thought Rebecca herself had seemed bored—and often patronising to the man who'd been her husband.

For the life of her Addie couldn't see why Noah would be heartbroken at leaving such a marriage.

But that was her judgement, and her judgement only. Who could see what really happened inside a marriage?

And now…

Noah seemed a man in charge of his world, a man who had everything. But looking at him out on the veranda, watching him play with Daisy, helping the oldies put a gate into position…

There were shadows.

The shallow Rebecca must have had something she could only guess at.

Yeah, like sexiness and beauty and the ability to put people like her in her place, Addie thought, and tried to turn her attention back to her patient files.

But her attention kept straying to the man outside.

To Noah.

To none of her business?

Addie had brought the hospital to life, Noah thought as the week went on—and it wasn't just her puppy.

While she'd been away, he'd been aware that she'd been missed, that there was genuine affection for her. Now… Watching her move through the hospital, taking time to talk to everyone who'd like to talk, including those who weren't her patients, it was as if the hospital had regained something precious. Something good had returned.

With benefits, for Daisy was definitely a benefit. The pup was being snuck into the wards to visit those who couldn't get onto the veranda, and Noah could pretty much guess where Addie and Daisy were by the laughter that echoed down the corridors.

On Friday night he met her coming out of the room of Edith Oddie, an elderly woman he'd operated on for oesophageal obstruction. Cancer was killing her fast. Noah had managed to clear the obstruction, but secondaries were appearing everywhere. For the last few days she'd been almost comatose, but as Addie emerged from her room with a suspiciously wiggly mound under an oversized cardigan, Noah was astounded to hear a crackly wheeze of laughter from the room she'd just left.

He stopped short and Addie looked up at him with a guilty grin. 'Not guilty, your honour,' she said before he could say a word.

'So you're not carrying a puppy under that cardigan?'

She gave a whirl like a three-year-old in a party dress, and the oversized cardigan flared out around her. It had moth holes in the hem.

'Three bucks from the welfare shop,' she told him. 'You like it?'

'Very nice. Moth holes being the new black. And bumps that wriggle…this season's latest accessory?'

'You guessed it.'

'Morvena would have kittens if she saw…'

'I bet she wouldn't. Kittens… *Ew*, allergies! And saw what?' she asked, all innocence. 'That I've decided bumps and moth holes are the new me?'

'I thought you'd decided on a whole new you when you came back here.'

Her face fell a bit. 'That obvious, huh?'

'Everyone's talking about it. Addie of the makeover.'

'I had to do something to cheer me up.' She sounded defensive. The bump wriggled under her breast and she heaved it closer. 'A makeover and Daisy. What else does a girl need?'

A baby, Noah thought, but he didn't say it. It hung, though, between the two of them.

'Don't look like that,' she said at last. 'I'm okay.'

'I know you're okay.' He smiled, pushing back an al-

most overwhelming urge to reach out and touch her. He
didn't, though. Instead he motioned to the door behind
them. 'Edith just laughed.'

'And so did her kids and grandkids.' She grimaced.
'They're a lovely family. I'm glad I got back before...'
She hesitated. 'It'll be soon, won't it?'

'A couple of days.'

'Brian will be heartbroken. Do you know they've been
married for fifty years? Fifty!' She shrugged and made a
visible effort to put away the greyness that went with the
profession. 'Me, I couldn't even manage a day.'

'I managed almost five before the divorce,' he told her,
trying to match her insouciance, but he obviously failed.
Her face creased in sympathy.

'I'm sorry. About you and Rebecca.'

'Don't be.' The words came out harsh but there was
no way he could stop it. 'We should never...' He stopped,
appalled at what he'd said. This was personal.

But Addie didn't appear to notice—or maybe she did.
Her non-pup-wrangling hand came out and touched his
arm.

'There's isn't such a thing as *should never* where love's
concerned,' she said gently. 'I read that somewhere. You
just...do.' Then she stepped away, blushing, as if the
words she'd spoken had been far too personal. 'Like me
and Daisy,' she managed. 'Love at first sight.'

'And like you and Gavin?'

'Love at first sight? That would have been when I was
two.' She peeped a smile that told him she was indeed
over Gavin. 'My judgement may not have been completely formed. My mother tells me he nobly offered to
share his lolly and I was smitten.'

'A true hero,' Noah agreed.

'And you and Rebecca?'

'I was driving a sports car.' He tried to make it sound like a joke. The words sounded hollow but she smiled.

'She fell for your car?'

'Like you fell for a lollipop.'

'Lollipop versus sports car. That must explain the difference in the lengths of our marital harmony.' They were both heading back to the doctors' house. She tucked her arm conspiratorially into his, which felt a bit inappropriate—until he saw Morvena bearing down on them. Then he understood. The contact allowed their combined arms to disguise the bump.

Blessedly Daisy didn't wriggle. Morvena passed with a cursory 'Goodnight' and the danger was past.

But then… Her arm was still in his. He didn't remove it. Why should he? It felt… It felt…

'I have a favour to ask,' she said, and he forced his thoughts from the direction he most definitely didn't wish them to go, and tried to focus.

'Yes?' he said, with caution.

'And that,' she said with asperity, 'is the tone of a colleague expecting to be landed with a ward full of patients while I swan off for the weekend. Which isn't true. I'm not swanning off anywhere. But, Noah…'

'But…' He couldn't help it. He still sounded cautious.

'I know this sounds daft.' Her voice had suddenly lost all confidence. 'And maybe it is daft. But you said…you emailed me when I was away and asked…'

And he knew. 'I asked you what you wanted for your baby.' He was with her now, understanding the hesitation. And the need for touch?

'I… It was good of you. I know most hospitals…'

'Most hospitals ask, if they can.' Embryos at the stage

of Addie's pregnancy were so small there was often nothing to retrieve. But there had been something, and he'd made sure it hadn't been discarded from Pathology—that it had been kept until she'd made her choice.

'I said if it was possible…'

'It was possible,' he told her. 'That's why I emailed.'

'I know. And thank you.' Her voice broke a little but she forged on. 'You found out. You said she could be buried in the section of the cemetery or that you could organise for a cremation. And I said, yes, please to cremation, and Mr Rowlins brought the ashes to me this morning. In a tiny box with a rose carved into the lid. Which I gather you organised? He said you paid, and of course I'll pay you back. I'm so grateful.'

'You don't need to be grateful and you don't need to pay.'

'I do,' she said, firmly now. 'But now… I know it's an imposition but I wondered… Noah, there's a place where Currawong Creek meets the bay. I used to sit there and talk to her when I first found out that I was pregnant. I want her ashes there. And I thought… I wondered…'

'You wondered if I'd like to come with you?' And he got that, too.

Most people at funerals held onto someone. Most people needed someone.

But why had she asked him?

'Addie, there's no one else?' he queried. She'd lived here for almost three years. She had so many friends. Family? He knew her mother had died. He'd never heard of anyone else but, then, he hardly knew this woman.

'You were there for me,' she said simply. 'And you tried.' She gave a tired smile. 'And, yes, I have friends but they might…they might cry and I don't think I'm up to crying. Not any more.'

He understood. She needed someone to make the emptiness less…empty, but she didn't need to share her emotion. Well, he was good at that. Rebecca had been a world-class teacher. 'Let's do it,' he said simply. 'We can go there now if you like.'

'Now?'

'It's not sunset for another hour. I've finished work for the day. Would you like that, Addie?'

'I think so.' She took a deep breath. 'Yes. Yes, I would. Could you wait until I ask Heidi if she can look after Daisy for the evening?'

'We don't want her pouncing on ash,' Noah said gravely, and she managed a smile, oddly warmed by his humour.

'She would.'

'She definitely would. Shall I meet you in ten minutes on the veranda?'

'Yes, please. That would be…kind.'


Currawong Bay was a vast, sweeping spread of tidal flats, a sheen of sapphire water at high tide and a magnificent expanse of rock pools and glistening sand when the tide was low. It was a mecca for tourists, but mostly they gathered at the town end of the bay. If you want peace on a beach in Australia, walk a hundred yards from a car park, Noah thought as he and Addie walked silently along the path across the dunes. With so much beach space, few could be bothered walking further.

It had been a gorgeous day and the bay below the town was dotted with kids and mums and dads playing in the shallows, eating fish and chips, or simply savouring the beauty of the place. Five minutes' walk from the car park, the beach was much less populated. The odd dog walker was tossing sticks into the waves. Fishermen were setting up their lines for a night of hope.

Fifteen minutes' walk from the town there was no one.

Noah had run here during the last couple of months, using the space and peace of the place to try and come to terms with his interminable wait. He wasn't sure if it helped but it surely didn't harm, and he knew the path so well now that he was sure where Addie was going.

Sure enough, as the track veered right along the bluff she branched left, onto a rough, semi-overgrown path that ran along a trickling creek.

Two hundred yards from the beach the creek bed rose sharply, water rippling over rocks worn smooth by thousands of years. Then the bluff loomed above them and the creek became a waterfall, not so high, maybe fifteen feet or so. There was not much water at this time of the year but enough to form a constant, falling shower into a freshwater pool. Ferns hung lazily over the water and soft moss covered the rocks.

This was Addie's place? Noah had found this place, too.

'You know it,' Addie said on a note of discovery as they reached the water's edge, and he thought she must have read it in his face.

'It's part of my favourite run.'

'Which explains why the track isn't completely overgrown. I had to bush-bash my way in when I first found it.'

'It's worth bush-bashing,' he said, and she smiled. Like a co-conspirator. Someone who'd discovered that a little-known love was shared.

'I swim here,' she said. 'Whenever I can.'

'Me, too.'

'Skinny dipping?' Her smile grew wider.

'Why not? There's no one to see.'

'But now you know my secret. No skinny dipping for me for the next four months.'

'Four months?'

'Isn't that when you leave?'

'So it is.' Leaving was the least of it, but right now he didn't want to think about the end point. 'But no skinny dipping?' he asked, moving on fast. 'That'd be a shame. How about we agree to wear leper bells to warn each other we're coming.'

'I'm not sure you can buy leper bells any more,' she said cautiously.

'Sure you can. I'll put in a pharmacy request this very evening.'

'Can you imagine the reaction of the bureaucrats in Canberra when that rolls onto their database?' She grinned. 'You'll have the entire bay in quarantine before you can blink.'

'That might be interesting.'

'That might be chaos,' she said severely. 'We had enough trouble when Jason Kimber came home from overseas with measles.'

'Town shut down?'

'Almost,' she said. 'The mayor had a four-week-old son who hadn't been immunised, and the thought of measles was almost too much for him. It's a serious disease and we had containment organised fast, but our mayor was all for evacuation, which could have spread measles across all Australia. Can you imagine if we hinted at leprosy?'

'Maybe not, then,' he said gravely. 'Maybe just a cooee

as we reach the last bend will have to be enough.' He glanced at the box in her hands and then at her face. 'Addie, do you want to do this alone? Would you like me to hold your hand while you say something? Stand beside you? Disappear for a bit?'

'I… No.'

'You want me to just shut up and…*be*?'

She gave him a shamefaced smile. 'You understand. Yes, please. Noah, I shouldn't have asked, but…'

'It's a privilege to be here,' he said simply.

He backed away, and settled on a rock a few feet back from her. Giving her space.

Letting her be.

It was time.

Except…it wasn't. Would it ever be time?

Addie stared down at the water. She felt the weight of the box in her hands and it was nothing compared to the grief in her heart.

It felt…overwhelming.

Noah had left her, not going far but far enough to give her privacy. She'd thought she wanted it but now…

The box in her hands… What it represented… Noah or not, she'd never felt so alone.

'I don't know that I can,' she whispered.

And she wasn't alone. Noah responded, his voice gentle, his words almost an echo of what was in her heart. 'Then you don't need to,' he said. 'Addie, there's no pressure to do anything at all. If you feel like you need to keep your daughter's ashes with you, then that's what you should do.'

'I need to let her go.'

'Then take your time. There's all the time in the world.'

'I want… Noah, I don't know what I want.'

She closed her eyes. She let her thoughts wander. She talked.

'You know my father died when I was two?' she asked, maybe talking to Noah, maybe talking to herself.

'Gavin told me.'

'Did he tell you how dependent my mum was from them on? Over and over she told me, "If it wasn't for you, Addie, I'd kill myself." Fancy saying that to a child, but she did. "I want to be with your father," she'd say. Every time I disappointed her she'd say, "I'm only here because of you." I loved her and I'm sure she loved me but…no child should be raised with that sort of pressure.'

'They shouldn't,' Noah said, but still it was like an echo. He was asking no questions. Her thoughts could go where they willed.

She was gazing down at the waterlilies now, but she wasn't seeing them. She was seeing the barrenness of her past. She needed to talk about it.

What was it about this time, this place? This man? Why did she need to explain? She had no idea. She only knew the words were coming.

'So after the Gavin fiasco, after the pain of Mum's grief at our failed wedding, her illness, her death, I made a vow. I'd never depend on anyone like that. More, I'd never let anyone depend on me. Mum needed me to stay alive and that need almost crushed me. Then, when need was gone, it was like I was just…adrift.'

'And then?'

It was a question but a quiet one. If she wanted to stop, right now, she sensed there'd be no pressure at all.

Strangely it made her want to keep going.

'I quit my job after…after the mess of the wedding,'

she said. 'I guess you already know that. I think Mum was more gutted than I was. It was almost like she'd been holding the cancer at bay until the wedding, and she got sick fast. Then, after her death…'

She paused. Stared at the water again. Stared at the box.

'Don't tell me unless you want to,' Noah said gently.

'I do want to. Isn't that strange? You've been with me at two of the worst times of my life and now…it's like I don't have any secrets.'

'Addie…'

'I want to explain.' Was she talking to Noah? Somehow it didn't feel like it. She was standing by the water's edge, holding her box, talking or not talking to a man sitting on a rock behind her. A man she hardly knew.

It didn't make sense but the need to talk was almost overpowering.

'After Mum died I was struggling to come to terms with who I was. I'd been so busy, so caught up in work, in care, in grief. And then, after Mum's death, there was nothing. And one morning I woke up and thought how wonderful would it be to love without…dependency?'

'Kids are pretty dependent,' Noah said wryly, and she managed a smile. But not at him. He was simply her sounding board, in the background.

'Yes, but not for ever,' she said. 'As a doctor I've seen so many mums with babies, toddlers, young children. I see total love—but there's more. Good parents, normal parents, they love their kids but even when they're tiny they're already launching them into their own lives. In so many ways they're teaching them to be free. And I can do that. Or…I thought I could.' She stared down at the little box and her grip tightened.

'So you decided to have a baby.'

'I did.' It was practically a whisper. 'But how? Dating left me cold. After Gavin… I thought I knew him so well. Would you go down that road again?'

'I guess not.' His tone was suddenly dry and she had a flash of compunction. Rebecca… His wife…

'I'm sorry. I shouldn't…'

'Don't be sorry,' he said, roughly this time. 'Addie, this is about you. Tell me what happened.'

She turned and shot him a grateful look, but then went back to staring down into the water. 'I'm an obstetrician,' she said. 'I have friends who…well, the long and short of it was that I queue-jumped for sperm donation—but it didn't work.'

'Because?'

'Because of the endometriosis. At least, that's what they said.' She shrugged. 'So then I thought I'd get a job in the country, away from everything. I settled here and then decided to keep trying. Again and again. Finally I moved onto IVF. So many attempts. In the end I think I was just pig stubborn.'

'Because you wanted this baby so much.'

'I did.' She shrugged. 'And what's left? A tiny pile of ash, and it's time to let her go.'

Silence. He let her be while her thoughts drifted on.

'I can do this,' she said at last. 'I have a life. I have Currawong, a job I love, a community that needs me. I have an adorable dog called Daisy. I have a life where I'm not dependent on anyone and, apart from professionally, no one's dependent on me. I can be happy.'

'I'm sure you can be.'

'I just have to do this.'

'If you really want to.'

'This is what I want.'

'Then do it,' he said softly. 'Do it with love.'

He went back to being a silent, watchful sentry. Addie sat on the moss by the waterfall and gave herself a few moments of quiet. Of peace.

Of love?

A wood pigeon was cooing in the trees above her head, almost a lullaby. The water was trickling into the pool at her feet and a carpet of waterlilies wobbled in the faint current. She could see a fat, mottled frog on a lily pad, waiting for unsuspecting insects.

This was the right place.

The place to scatter her dreams?

Behind her Noah was now completely silent. She shouldn't have asked him to come but she was now desperately glad that she had. As well as being with her, he was her link to the future, to her work, to Daisy, to the world she had to get back to.

And by letting her talk…he'd stopped the grey from descending. Who knew what could have happened if he hadn't been here? It'd be so easy to slip into the water with…

Um, not. That was her mother talking, not her. Besides, suiciding in three feet of water with frogs wasn't exactly an option.

She almost smiled. She almost turned and shared the thought with Noah.

Maybe not. It was enough that he was waiting to walk her home.

It was time to move on.

She shifted down the rock and unfastened the brass clasp on her box. The tiny container was beautiful, something she could keep and treasure. Had Noah guessed that? This wasn't a time to be thinking of Noah but she was still aware of his presence. It was something solid. Something to be trusted.

He seemed someone who somehow, weirdly, understood.

Her box was open now, revealing the tiny bag containing the ashes. She lifted the bag out and held it for a long moment. She thought…for ten weeks I was blessed. My daughter was real.

She waited until the heat from her hand warmed the ashes. It was all she could do. She let them go. They drifted slowly, settled, disappeared among the water lilies. The frog gave a gentle croak and leaped into the water. Ripples spread outward and then faded.

The evening's peace settled once again over the pool.

She was left with nothing.

She sat surrounded by bleakness, but suddenly Noah was there, slipping silently to sit beside her. He sat, his body just touching, shoulder to shoulder.

It was okay. She didn't want hugging or emotion, but the brushing of his body against hers was…necessary.

It grounded her. Gave her strength? Who knew? It was a strange concept but the emptiness inside receded.

She turned to Noah and she smiled. 'Thank you, Noah. Time to go home?'

'Is this your home, Addie?'

She thought of this pool, of the beach, of the place she worked in, of the community who cared, of all the oldies caring for Daisy, of Mrs Rowbotham who bossed and worried her, of the nurses and other doctors who cared for her. Even the scary Morvena…

She turned back to the pool. The ashes had disappeared, absorbed into the life of this tranquil place.

'It is my home,' she whispered. 'I know it.' She caught herself. 'And how about you, Noah? Where's your home?'

A shadow crossed his face that she didn't understand, but he was pushing himself to his feet, giving her his hand so he could help her up, so she didn't slip on the moss. Gathering himself into himself?

'Who knows,' he said lightly. 'For four more months it's here. Home is just…where I am.'

That's not home at all, she thought, but she couldn't say it. He was moving on. Getting ready to go.

Where?

The walk home was made in silence. Addie seemed lost in her own thoughts, and Noah…

There were so many thoughts in his head he had no hope of coming to terms with any of them.

He'd come here to support Addie. He'd left feeling shattered himself.

Too many memories…

Rebecca. His wife. A woman who'd been gutted because she couldn't get rid of a baby. A woman who treated a child as disposable—a child he was fighting for.

His lawyers had told him the chances of winning a court case were small. That he had to move on.

He couldn't without fighting, but if he lost, where was home then?

He couldn't think of it. If he didn't know where Sophie was…

Home was nowhere.

# CHAPTER FIVE

It seemed churlish to get back to the hospital, say 'See you later' and leave it at that. But medicine had a way of filling spaces even when he didn't want them to be filled.

So Noah spent an hour suturing an eight-year-old's leg after a vicious dog bite. He spent another half an hour re-assuring almost hysterical parents that he was sure their son wouldn't carry long-term scars—that was why the suturing had taken an hour. He then spent more time with council officers and police, making statements that would be used to deal with a dog that had been left to roam at will on the beach where the kid had been playing.

He fielded an aggressive call from the dog's owner, demanding that he change his statements, accusing him of blowing up 'mere scratches' into serious injuries.

He'd dealt with this kind of situation before and he'd had Heidi take photographs every step of the way. He called the police again to keep them up to speed on the owner's aggression.

He checked in on Edith Oddie and found her slipping fast. 'But the puppy did her so much good,' her husband told him. 'Imagine…this afternoon she woke and she laughed. With all her girls here. I think…' He glanced at Edie's peaceful but unresponsive face. 'I think it's almost over but this afternoon she laughed…'

Tears were slipping down his face, but they were tears of acceptance, tears of peace.

Noah walked away and for some reason the conversation with Addie came back to him.

*Fifty years married.*

Some couples made it.

He walked back to the doctors' house and there was something heavy inside him. He thought of Edith's hand, held warmly, gently by her husband of so many years.

So much love…

He gave himself a mental shake. He didn't get emotionally involved. Or not more involved than he already was. There was no room. Four more months and he was out of here, no matter what happened. He pushed open the door of the doctors' house with decision—and decision was knocked out of him.

Addie had lit the fire and was sitting beside it, cuddling a sleepy Daisy.

'I know it's not cold,' she said, almost defensively, as he walked in. 'But the fire's good.'

'The fire's excellent.' He sounded cautious and he wasn't sure why.

'There's lasagne in the oven. Mrs Rowbotham left it. I heated it all so it might have dried out a bit. Sorry.' She waved a glass at him. 'But there's wine and you're welcome to share my fire.'

He hesitated. The night…the fire…the woman… The scene he'd just come from. This was intimacy he wasn't sure how to handle.

Addie…

Why had he been asked to share what had been such

a personal moment this afternoon? He'd thought it was because he was separate—because she knew he wouldn't let emotion hold sway. It was an entirely reasonable explanation but now, looking down at her, he wasn't so sure that emotion could be contained.

Oh, for… This was ridiculous. She was a colleague. She'd asked him for a favour and now she was asking him to share her fire while he ate lasagne. And drank wine.

Maybe wine wasn't such a good idea.

But that was crazy, too. He was off duty as of now. One of the family doctors was on call tonight. He'd been inundated while Addie had been away and he'd had to make rules to give him time off. From Friday night, only the most dire emergencies saw him being called.

He could have a glass of wine.

So why was he hesitating?

He wasn't. It'd be dumb.

So he organised his meal, then settled in the armchair by the fire. Addie handed him a glass of wine and settled again, lying by the fire with her puppy.

'Thank you for today.'

'I don't need thanks,' he said brusquely. 'It was a privilege.'

There was silence while he ate, while he took his plate back to the kitchen, while he thought about whether he should leave her to her fire and her puppy and go to bed.

He came back to the fire, looked at the armchair and looked at the cushions on the rug, and then, as if he was someone he hardly knew, he slipped down onto the floor beside her.

Dumb? Of course it was but the scene was like a siren's song, infinitely enticing.

This woman was a colleague. He had no wish to get

close. He had no wish to get close to any woman, but this evening there'd been grief and there'd been courage, and it seemed wrong to end it with a curt goodnight and leave her to her thoughts.

To her loneliness or his?

Whatever, he slipped down beside her, settled, re-filled his wine glass, and stroked a puppy ear himself. Sleeping puppies were excellent for soothing all sorts of things. Daisy had obviously had a wild time with Heidi and Heidi's dogs. Right now, in sleep, she was giving Addie comfort.

She was curled on Addie's knee. He stroked her soft ear and it almost seemed like...

Um, not. If he couldn't get his mind away from that, then he needed to back away fast.

He stopped stroking Daisy and pushed himself back a little. He should retreat to the armchair, but he'd only just sat down and she might think...

What he was thinking?

What he had no business thinking.

There was silence for a while, broken only by the crackle of the flames. Things seemed to settle. Deepen? Become...something he didn't understand?

'Will you try for another baby?' he heard himself say, and then thought, Whoa, you have no business asking that. But she was gazing at the flames, fondling the ears of her sleeping puppy with one hand, holding her wine glass with the other, and it was almost as if the question was an extension of the night. A night where boundaries had been set aside?

Grief did that.

He thought of her face as she'd let the ashes drift into

the water and he thought of his daughter. She hadn't been wanted but she was wanted now. Sophie.

*She was not his.*

And suddenly she wasn't looking at the flames.

'Noah? What's wrong?'

'I...' He shook himself. 'Nothing. I asked...'

'You did ask.' But she was still watching him, her attention deflected from the flames. From her own circumstances. She hesitated and he knew there were other questions.

Questions he didn't want to face himself.

'I don't know about trying again,' she told him at last, but she was still watchful. 'With my endometritis and after the IVF thing... It took so many trips to Sydney, so many failed attempts. I wanted it so much but then what happened...'

'It shouldn't happen again.'

'You don't know that, and the endometritis is still there. My chances of conceiving again... It took over two years. I'm not sure if I could bear it.'

'You're a strong woman, Addie Blair.'

'Strength only carries you so far. And honestly? I think strength is an illusion. People say you're strong because you don't crumble, but sometimes that feels almost dishonest. Because you crumble inside.'

'Is that how you feel now?'

'Like my insides are filled with something that's shattered? It's how I felt two months ago. I've hauled it together, glued it back in place but it's like broken china. What do they say? "That which doesn't kill us makes us stronger?" I don't think so. It just makes us better at gluing up the cracks. The damage is still there.'

'And it hurts.'

'It hurts,' she said softly. 'So, no, I doubt I have the courage to try again.' She stooped and buried her face briefly in her puppy's soft fur. 'Daisy's it. Me and Daisy and the world.'

And then she raised her face and met his gaze full on. And something changed.

This was no longer about her, her gaze said. Her gaze locked to his, firm, kind yet inexorable.

'And now,' she said softly, but her tone said there was to be no quarter given. 'What about you?'

'What about me?'

'You get it,' she said softly. 'You get my grief over my baby in a way no one else does. Maybe that was why I asked you to come with me this afternoon. Yes, I knew you wouldn't break down on me or give me platitudes, but right from the moment of the ectopic diagnosis, I saw my grief reflected in you. And this afternoon... I watched my baby's ashes drifting away and I turned and saw you, and what I saw...' She shook her head. 'Noah, maybe it's not for me to ask but if you want to tell me...'

Did he want to tell her?

He hadn't told anyone. No one, apart from an explosion in his lawyer's office when grief and anger had built to eruption when the lawyer had read the last of Rebecca's demands. And her ultimatum.

He'd decided to stick it out, to fight, but his lawyers were telling him fighting had every chance of failing.

He had no choice. Useless or not, he had to try.

'You don't have to tell me,' Addie said. 'Only if you want to.' And then she reached over and took his wine glass, setting it and hers carefully on the hearth. As if clearing the path for whatever lay before them. 'Only if you can.'

'I don't talk about it.'

'Because you're a guy,' she said, wisely. 'Of course. It's so much more manly to keep that stuff to yourself.'

'Like you telling everyone you were having IVF...'

She conceded, giving a rueful smile. 'Touché.' She hesitated again. 'But I have told you now,' she said. 'And it helped. It...helps.'

Yeah, but he didn't talk. Since when had talking solved anything? And Rebecca's threats still hung over his head. But she was watching him, waiting. She was...trusting?

The firelight was flickering on her face. The warmth, the wine...

This woman...

The barriers of years slipped a little and he didn't reach for them and shore them up.

Could he trust, too?

'Rebecca and I...we weren't a great match,' he said, and for a while he didn't say anything else. And neither did she. She simply sat. Just letting the night—and the trust?—settle.

The urge to talk was almost overwhelming.

Why? In five long years he'd never spoken but to-night...things had changed.

He talked.

'Rebecca was...well, you've met her,' he said. 'When she's at her best she's almost irresistible.'

'Yeah?'

He flashed her a look, saw the hint of laughter and smiled back. 'Okay, that was man-speak,' he said. 'But, believe me, she was, and I was ripe for irresistible. From the time I started med school I had my head in my work. I took big student loans, I worked nights to cover costs.

I had a couple of relationships but they fell by the way-side fast. Even after I qualified as a general surgeon, I didn't stop driving myself. I was so damned ambitious. I headed to the UK for further training and then applied for the job at Sydney Central. That involved responsibility as well as skill and I was stressed. The first day on the job I met Beck.'

'I've seen Rebecca at her most charming,' Addie said, and he caught the note of dryness. Rebecca would never have bothered to be charming to Addie.

So he had to explain. He sought for the right words, words he barely understood himself. 'She can be lovely,' he said. 'But lovely's all on the outside. I was still caught up in the sheer effort of work, relieved that I was home and settled, but stressed by the responsibility of my new job. Beck was bubbly, effervescent, fun, and very, very beautiful, and I'd had my head in my work for so long it was like emerging into another world.

'I was too dumb to see it was financial security and the prestige of my job that she wanted. Given time, surely I would have realised, but I never had time. We were only a few weeks into dating when she was injured.'

He paused. He should stop now, he thought.

'So...do you want to tell me what happened?' she asked, and stopping wasn't an option.

'I crashed the car.' He closed his eyes, remembering the nightmare. 'We'd gone out to dinner with a couple of my new colleagues. She'd behaved beautifully but as soon as we were in the car she changed. The night had been boring, she said, so now it was her turn. She wanted to go on to a nightclub. It was one in the morning and I was on duty at eight. I refused and she kicked up a fuss. A real fuss. Beck having a tantrum... I thought it was just the wine—she was certainly tipsy—but it was the real Rebecca showing through. It was quite a show and in the end she tried to slap me.'

'Story of your life, women trying to hit you,' Addie murmured.

He paused and he even found himself smiling. The pressure eased still further. He could tell her—but the smile disappeared.

'So I got distracted. It was raining, with sleet over the road. I cornered too fast, clipped the kerb and the car tipped. Beck hadn't fastened her seat belt and was thrown out.'

'Oh, Noah...'

The crackle of the fire helped as well, he thought. It was like a background of peace. This woman, this place, it seemed an oasis, as if the outside world was blocked out. It didn't seem as if he was exposing himself, his regrets, his anger. This was just...Addie.

'Paraplegia?' she queried. 'I don't know how complete. No one ever said...'

'And Rebecca never said either,' he said, remembering the shock, the diagnosis, the struggle to get her to attend rehab. 'She broke her spine at S4 but it was an incomplete break. When the swelling went down, feeling returned. Not completely but enough to make walking possible. By then. though, she'd cast herself firmly in the role of victim and she wasn't letting go. I know that sounds harsh, but it's true.

'Rehab was hard. The physios were asking her to do things that hurt and if there's one thing Rebecca won't do it's push herself anywhere it doesn't suit her. A month after the accident she'd remodelled herself. Doctor's girlfriend, damaged by stupid, careless doctor. Wheelchair bound. A woman who could spend her life being beautiful and making her man feel guilty. A woman who could make her man do exactly what she wanted.'

'Oh, Noah…'

'And she *could* walk,' he said, almost savagely. 'She can. If there's anything she wants badly enough she'll get it. Put a designer handbag just out of reach and she'll be on her feet and grasping. But no one's to know that.'

He shrugged, his face bleak. 'It doesn't matter, though. The truth is that she has suffered damage. The chances of her walking without a limp are remote and a woman with a limp doesn't suit Beck's desired image. Not enough sympathy. She loves her part-time job at Reception at Sydney Central, being the beautiful one in a wheelchair, three half-days of collecting gossip, vitriol, stuff she can use about anyone. The rest of the time…it's massages, beauticians, long lunches, making Rebecca beautiful for ever. And then…there's Sophie. Her little girl.'

He stopped, hearing the anger and bleakness in his voice, trying as he'd tried for so many years to hold it back.

'Sophie?' Addie said, obviously confused. 'Rebecca's child? I didn't know she had a child.'

'No one did,' he said flatly. 'But when Rebecca was in hospital, I was suddenly the one in charge.' He was talking to the flames now, caught in horror from years ago. He wanted to block it out, but for some reason he couldn't stop talking. 'Beck's alienated her family. They live in Canada but she moved on from them years ago. She has no one, so the hospital ended up putting me down as next of kin. Referring to me. While Beck was out of it with painkillers, they gave me her phone. I was using her contacts, trying to locate any friends or family who might care, when there was a call from Child Welfare. They needed to talk to her. They told me she had a twelve-month-old daughter. Sophie.'

'But there's never been any talk of a child.'

'That's because Beck simply cut her out of her existence,' he told her. 'From what I found out, two years before she met me she was going out with a guy with lots of money but no scruples. She thought pregnancy would force him to marry her, or at least give her whopping financial support. She got pregnant. She didn't bother with any of the tests because, well, why would she? This baby was simply a means to an end. But Sophie's father has even fewer morals than Rebecca. He disappeared overseas. It was too late to terminate the pregnancy and Sophie was born with Down's syndrome.'

'Oh, no!'

'And don't bother feeling sorry for Rebecca,' he said, roughly now. 'The Rebeccas of this world move on and move on fast. She wanted to get rid of it any way she could. Adoption was hard because she'd named the father on the birth certificate and no one could contact him. It involved hassle and Beck was never one to bother with hassle. So Sophie was placed in foster care. That's where I came in. The call was from Social Welfare saying Sophie's foster parents had a family drama and couldn't keep her. Rebecca was in and out of a drugged stupor and I felt responsible. So Rebecca emerged at last to have me by her bedside holding a beautiful, cherubic little girl, Sophie, a baby who twisted her way into my heart without even trying.'

'Oh, wow...'

'So then I copped a sob story,' he told her. 'How this guy, the baby's father, had fleeced Rebecca for everything she had. How she couldn't afford to keep her beautiful Sophie. And how much she was depending on me. And when Social Welfare moved in, asking questions, she simply clung to me and said, we'll be okay, we're a family, Noah's marrying me.'

*'You didn't even propose?'*

'I didn't have to. Come on, Addie, you know the rules. Successful doctor smashes car, leaves his girlfriend in a wheelchair, a woman with a baby, a woman totally dependent. The car crash was my fault, Addie, and I accepted the consequences. And besides…' he gave a rueful smile '…I *had* fallen head over heels in love. But it was with Sophie.'

'Your little girl.'

'Except she wasn't.' The bleakness slammed back. 'The moment Beck came home from hospital she demanded Sophie go back into foster care. And to be honest I had to concede it was…almost sensible. Beck was struggling with rehab and the bills were mounting. I'd put myself through med school, then spent a fortune on further training overseas. I had debts up to my ears. I had to go back to work and I had to find somewhere suitable for Rebecca to live. I couldn't afford to pay for a carer for Beck, plus a carer for Sophie.

'So we agreed—temporarily—to use foster care. With access. But pretty soon I realised I was the only one caring about access. I brought Sophie home again and again, but Beck would have nothing to do with her. Once she'd used her to wedge me into marriage, she didn't want to know about her. She never talked about her. I wasn't permitted to talk about her. It was like she didn't exist.'

'Hell, Noah…'

'It was, and I should have walked long before I did.

But I still felt responsible and there was now the overriding complication that if I walked I'd have no access to Sophie. Beck soon realised it, and held the threat over my head. And sometimes… The days when I collected Sophie, held her, played with her in the park…' He stopped and smiled, remembering. A hand tucked into his. A little face lighting up as she held up her arms to be picked up when he arrived to collect her.

'I couldn't leave,' he said, and it was all he could say.

'So what happened next?' she asked, slowly, cautiously.

'We lived like that until last year. A marriage that wasn't a marriage. Beck played her poor-little-me role to the outside world and I did what I needed to do to get by. Sophie's new foster parents turned out to be lovely. I was seeing her when I could, but burying everything else in my work. But then we were notified that Harold and Beth—her foster parents—had decided they were too old to continue. They were reluctantly relinquishing her at the end of the year, and Sophie would have to change foster parents—again. I was appalled, but Beck said, "So what?"'

He shook his head, trying to block the remembrance of that night, holding the letter, seeing Sophie being discarded yet again.

'I saw red,' he admitted. 'I told Beck that Sophie was coming home, like it or not. I wouldn't stay in the sham of a marriage if I couldn't care for her. And, as Beck's husband, as Sophie's stepfather, I was applying for legal adoption.'

'Good…good for you,' Addie said, a trifle unsteadily. 'I think.'

'Yeah, holding a gun to someone's head is such a good

idea,' he said bleakly. 'Or not. We had the worst row but finally she agreed. Or I thought she'd agreed. She gave me details of Sophie's biological father and signed forms allowing the authorities to contact him. He signed the waivers. Everything looked like it was going ahead. When the adoption went through we'd bring her home. I told her if Beck wanted, we'd tell people she was my daughter, not Beck's. Or I'd say she had no former connection to either of us. Whatever Beck wanted. But obviously Beck didn't like it. Her agreement was just playing for time.'

Silence. Addie didn't comment. Her expression was carefully neutral. Too neutral. Was she feeling his pain?

Because pain was suddenly there, in spades.

He wanted to stop but he'd gone this far. He had to force himself to tell her the rest.

'After she signed the adoption papers she seemed… wired. I thought it was just the prospect of Sophie coming to live with us but obviously her worries went deeper. She refused to talk about Sophie being with us. She refused to let me bring her home until my application for formal adoption was approved, and with no authority I had to accept. So I threw myself into my work and waited. While Beck…thought of another way.'

'Another way?' It was a flat question, echoing bleakness. As if Addie knew what was coming?

'I was at a conference in Denver when she told me,' he said. 'By phone. She was drunk and laughing. Triumphant. Apparently she'd met…someone she describes as her perfect man. He's twenty years older than she is, wealthy beyond belief, someone who obviously loves the poor-little-me image. She told me she was filing for divorce. Irreconcilable differences. I can't fault her there.'

'Oh, Noah...'

'So when I got home I expected she'd have moved out. But she was still there, sitting at the kitchen bench, drinking wine. She'd just come from the beautician. She looked stunning. Beautiful. Smug. And she was waiting to tell me that she had all her ducks lined up in a row, and none of them included Sophie.'

He was hardly talking to Addie now. He was seeing the woman he'd cared for for so long. Looking at her smugness. Feeling the desolation of what she'd done in the past and was doing now.

'I walked in and she put her glass down on the bench, tilted her chin, arched those beautiful eyebrows and threw it at me. Her new man cared for her much better than I did. He had money but she wanted two-thirds of my assets. I'd done this to her legs and apparently I still owed her, big time. And, by the way, she'd notified Social Services that we'd split. The adoption was off.'

And that had been the thing that had gutted him. That still gutted him. He'd never felt such anger. Such helplessness.

'But if you still wanted it...' Addie whispered. 'Why wouldn't she let you proceed?'

He had to force himself to go on. To make himself say the words.

'She said Sophie was nothing to do with me. She was vitriolic, hissing hatred. But she said...I'd be her ex-husband and if I stayed in Sydney and adopted her, sometime in the future someone could figure it out. Did I think she wanted a mutant appearing from her past? And when I said I'd move, take Sophie to another city if she wanted, it was like a dam burst. The fury... She blamed me for her legs. She even blamed me for Sophie.'

'No…'

'She kept calling her a mutant. She said she should have aborted her and it was my fault she was still saddled with threats of contact now. She wanted nothing to do with her and nothing to do with me. And I could no longer have access. Also I had to shut up. She knows how much I love Sophie and she has that covered. She has a second passport—Canadian. If I made a fuss she'd take her overseas and stage a breakdown. That's what she's done here, playing the foster system. She said she'd dump her on any foster system that'd have her, and she wouldn't even have to tell me. If I knew what's good for me, I'd shut up. Get myself a new life but don't mess with hers.'

Addie was watching him, her face telling him she was appalled. As well she might be. Why on earth had he shared? He'd suppressed his grief, shoving it on the back burner, using anger, coldness, action to move forward. Now it was exposed and he felt raw. He could read Addie's face and the feelings he had were reflected there.

'So that was that,' he said, bleakly now, like the past was something he couldn't escape from. 'I walked back out and I haven't seen her since. Neither have I seen Sophie.'

'So where is she?' Addie whispered. 'Where is she now?'

'She's still with the foster parents who love her. That's the one good thing but it's small comfort. After this mess, Harold and Beth agreed to keep fostering for twelve more months. They're wonderful but they're elderly. Harold's been diagnosed with a heart condition and any minute now Sophie will have to be moved. I've had access, played with her, loved her for five years…'

'Oh, Noah…'

'But I can't go near her,' he said, still bleakly. 'The next time I went…Beck said she'd put a block on my access. Even though she doesn't want her, she won't let me near. Legally I have no rights. But I've decided to fight. I don't have a choice. The social workers seem to be on my side, even though their hands are tied. I've consulted lawyers and reinstated my adoption application. The court hearing's in four months and I'll fight until every avenue's exhausted. Meanwhile, legally I can't go near her. That's why I'm here. I can't bear to be so close and not see her.'

'But I still don't understand. Why doesn't she want you to have access?'

'It's not logical. Maybe part of it's punishment, for someone who damaged her legs. More probably she thinks it'll get out. Sophie's existence has always been kept secret. It doesn't suit Beck's image to have deserted her daughter. I suspect her new man doesn't know about Sophie either. She'll never accept any promise I make. To Beck, promises mean nothing.'

'But you could tell anyway.'

'And let her take her who knows where? For revenge. She's perfectly capable of it.'

'Oh, Noah…'

He shrugged. 'So that's it,' he managed. 'I'll stay here until the court case. If I win I'll head back to Sydney. If I lose my application for adoption I'll still fight for access but if I don't get that… There's a neurology training programme in London that…might keep me busy. But I'm sorry I told you. Before the case comes to court Beck has complete control. Even now, telling anyone risks everything, and I had no right to land it on you.'

'Noah, you do have the right,' she whispered, and before he knew what she intended she leaned forward and took his face in her hands. 'Of course you do. Noah…'

She faltered as if looking for words, but there were no words. They both knew that.

The silence intensified. The fire crackled next to them. Daisy had slid off Addie's knees and onto the rug and Noah noticed. He noticed a tiny wrinkle between Addie's eyes, a crease of worry. She shouldn't worry. This was his grief. His…

'Noah, don't,' she whispered, and she leaned forward, just slightly, just enough.

And she drew his face to hers and she kissed him.

It was supposed to be a whisper kiss.

Actually, it wasn't supposed to be a kiss at all. She'd had no intention, no desire, no thought of kissing anyone, much less Noah, a colleague, a man who'd seen her at her most vulnerable.

A man she'd used for his strength.

A man who didn't need a kiss. Even a fleeting kiss. A kiss of comfort.

But this kiss was not of her making. It was an instinctive, almost primeval response to pain, and she'd moved before her head caught up with what her body was about to do.

What her mouth was about to do.

Her mouth intended to kiss him.

Even then the kiss should have been a brush of lips against cheek. She should never have aimed for his mouth. She surely didn't intend to.

But it happened.

Her mouth brushed his and his hands came up. In defence? To put her away? Who knew, because forces bigger than both of them seemed to be in play.

Instead of putting her away, his hands caught her face, his fingers cradled her cheeks—and the feather kiss became...

A kiss.

A kiss to change the world?

There was a stupid thing to think but somehow she was no longer thinking.

There was only this moment.

There was only Noah.

There was only need.

For in that one blinding moment, things changed. One moment they were by the fire, colleagues, maybe even friends, but a man and a woman who didn't know each other very well. A man and woman who'd experienced past pain and acknowledged each other's grief.

Addie was a woman who'd spent most of her life doing what was expected of her. Caring for her dependent mother. Carrying her mother's grief. Agreeing to marry a man she'd thought she trusted, a man who had been part of that expectation.

And Noah? He was a man who'd been in a bleak and loveless marriage, who'd been treated in the worst possible way.

Maybe there should be bleakness between them. Maybe this night should be one of reflected grief.

But there was no grief now. Not in this cocoon of firelight, of warmth, of wine.

Not in the touch of two mouths meeting, or in the way Noah's hands cupped her face.

Not in the way her body responded.

She needed...

Him?

She didn't know. She was beyond knowing. All she knew was that she needed this moment, she needed his touch.

*She needed his body.*

And he felt the same. She knew it as surely as night followed day. His kiss was deepening, deepening and she felt she was drowning in it.

And she wanted to drown. She wanted to sink into this man's body, to take what she needed from him, and to give what he needed from her. The loneliness, the grief, the bleakness of the last months, no, the last years, had somehow melted. For in this moment there was only Noah and his mouth on hers and his lovely hands drawing her closer.

'Addie...' His voice was a ragged whisper, and she could hear the desire in it. The naked need. 'Addie, we shouldn't. We...'

'We can.' Somehow she made herself answer. 'Noah, right now, we need each other.'

There seemed no room for more words, because something larger than either of them had taken over. Desire had built to a point where it couldn't be gainsaid.

Addie spent half her professional life dealing with the consequences of desire. She should have had far more sense than to let herself sink into this blissful abandonment.

But this wasn't sense. This wasn't even Addie. This was a moment out of frame, and she was suddenly a woman she hardly knew. She was the responsible one, the carer, but right now...to hell with consequences.

Daisy stirred and yawned, a great, goofy yawn, and it

gave them pause. Noah broke away. He looked down at the pup in the firelight and smiled. And such a smile…

It was tender, it was loving, it was all the things Addie most wanted, had dreamed of…

The smile was for the pup on the floor beside the fire. Of course it was. But it didn't matter.

And then he was gathering her into his arms, tightly, fiercely. Amazingly the smile was still there. For her?

And neither had to say what their intentions were. They knew.

'You're sure?' he whispered.

'I'm sure.' How could he ask?

'I haven't…hell, Addie, I don't even have condoms. I could… The pharmacy…'

Stopping now? Heading to a locked pharmacy and trying to find what they wanted?

And for what? If she wasn't so immersed in need she could have laughed. 'I have endometriosis and a history of impossibility of conceiving,' she managed. 'No luck with straight sperm donation. Two years with a petri dish. Plus I haven't even started my cycles yet. And yes, I know better. But surely…' Dear heaven, she wanted him so much. 'Surely we can risk…'

'We shouldn't.' But she heard it in his voice. He needed this moment—this night—as much as she did.

'I know we shouldn't,' she whispered. 'But we're con-senting adults and…we can. Let's just, for once in our lives, be totally, absolutely irresponsible.'

He chuckled and with that the moment of defence—of sense?—slipped away. 'Let's,' he said.

And then there was only each other.

'Your bed or mine?' His voice was husky with desire

as he rose to his feet, with Addie somehow magically cradled in his arms.

'How about both?' she managed. 'One after the other?'

# CHAPTER SIX

SHE WOKE IN the small hours to whimpering.

They were in Noah's bed. She was spooned against his body, cocooned in half-sleep, encased in pleasure. In happiness? Who knew, but it surely felt like it.

It was still dark outside and there was a puppy whimpering by the bed. Noah stirred and chuckled as he realised what the problem was. He kissed her gently, tenderly, meltingly, and then set her back from him.

'Needs must,' he murmured, and rose.

'Come back to me,' she heard herself say, and couldn't believe it was she who'd said it.

'Never doubt it.' She heard the smile in his voice, the smile that melted her heart, the smile she'd dissolved into.

And then he was gone, scooping up Daisy on the way out. She heard him open and close the refrigerator door. She heard him murmur to the pup.

She didn't stir.

Daisy was her puppy. Her responsibility. But right now responsibility was nowhere. This wasn't Addie the responsible, Addie the dutiful. This Addie felt almost wanton, outrageous…free.

What was it about this man?

It wasn't this man, she told herself. It was this moment.

The circumstances. The moment was fleeting but she'd take it with both hands and hold on tight.

And then he was back, sliding down onto the sheets beside her, gloriously naked. His skin was against hers and it was the most magnificent feeling, erotic and wondrous.

He tugged her against him, chuckling into her ear.

'Sorted,' he said. 'Or…sort of.'

'Sort of?'

'We may have puddles to attend to later, but I decided they could wait.' His mouth started doing amazing things to her ear. 'Everything can wait. It has to.'

And she felt herself smile and the smile was huge. It seemed to envelop all of her. She turned so she was hard against him, her breasts crushed against his chest, her arms holding him. Her smile just seemed to grow wider.

'We have more urgent matters to attend to,' she managed, and proceeded to attend to them. With diligence. With laughter.

With love?

Morning happened, even when you willed it away with every fibre of your being.

Morning and reality.

She woke and she was still ensconced in the warmth, the incredible sensation of being one with this man, the feeling of his whole body cradling hers. It felt like she was on an island, a sanctuary, a place where time had stopped. There was only this man. She felt…

Loved? That word had crept into her heart in the small hours.

But it was morning. Time for reality.

And love? The word was enough to pull her out of her fantasy, to have her body stiffen, to have fear step in.

And he felt it. Of course he did. Was there any nuance this man didn't get? He was awake in an instant, drawing back, concerned.

'Addie…'

'What have we done?' she whispered.

'Acted like two teenagers without the benefit of sex ed classes?' He smiled, that gorgeous smile that did her head in. 'And now we're remembering what Mrs Nottle told us in Sixth Grade. Or Professor Clancy in First Year Med.'

'That you never, ever sleep with someone without the checks.' Despite herself, she was smiling. 'I'm not sure about you, but I had a Professor Yardman. She was insistent we head straight to the nearest clinic the moment we thought about holding hands and got ourselves tested for everything from dandruff to bubonic plague. And then we demand certification from at least three practicing medicos that our intended partner was free of the same things.'

'And then take all steps, up to and possibly including building brick walls, to prevent pregnancy.' His smile faded, concern overriding laughter. 'Addie…'

'I wouldn't worry.' She couldn't keep the trace of bitterness from her voice. 'The health stuff is okay from my side. I was checked within an inch of my life before IVF. And pregnancy? Fat chance of that.'

'Health is okay from my side, too,' he said, but his eyes were still worried. 'But, Addie…'

She got it. With his history… With Rebecca's betrayal… Of course he'd be gutted if anything happened. And they had been stupid.

'There's always the morning-after pill to make sure,'

she told him. She sighed and tugged back a little more. 'We *were* dumb. We were needful.'

His hand rested on her waist and the feel of him... 'Addie, it was a great night. An amazing night. We could maybe...'

But reality was now crashing in from all sides. What had they been thinking? There were no maybes.

'We couldn't.' She knew what had to be said. 'Noah, don't even think about letting guilt push this further. We were both emotional. We drank wine when our senses were heightened. We took what we needed. And I did... I did need it, Noah. In truth, I loved it.' She sighed again. 'Confession. I've never had a one-night stand before but I know what it is. This. No strings attached. Moving on.' She managed to get her smile back in place. 'And you know what? It was amazing. Fabulous. Just what the doctor ordered. But it's over and I believe Daisy needs breakfast.'

'You really want to move on as if nothing's happened?'

'I... Yes.' But his hands were still on her waist.

'Addie?'

'Mmm.'

'I gave Daisy a snack at three a.m. She can wait a little longer for breakfast.'

'Noah?'

'Mmm.'

Say it, she thought. Say you don't want this.

But...maybe she could say it after she let herself dissolve in his body one last time?

How could she not?

A one-night stand should last at least until breakfast.

Medical imperatives were there even when you least wanted them. Two hours later the phone rang. A local farmer had rolled his farm bike and was on his way in with a crush injury. Cliff was already on his way to act as anaesthetist. Noah was needed.

He showered and disappeared. 'Sorry, love, to leave you with the puddles. What sort of irresponsible people leave puppies in the living room unattended?' He kissed her briefly, hard, and left in a hurry.

She was left with…regrets? Confusion?

Peace.

Mostly peace, she thought. Despite the lurch of sadness Noah's story had brought to her world, the night before seemed to have settled something deep within her. This wasn't a relationship that would go further. She knew that. Neither of them wanted it. But they'd been together in the right place, at the right time, giving comfort when comfort had been needed.

The age of comfort of loving.

Love? That word was still hovering.

It had been loving, she thought as she showered, much slower, much more languorously than Noah's fast ablutions. She had no urgent cases. She gave herself time to emerge from the night with peace.

Her world was waiting for her, her mums and babies, her ladies with gynae problems, the world as she knew it. But her world had changed.

Why?

Because she felt…

'Like a woman,' she whispered, soaping herself, feeling the warmth of the water slip over her skin, savouring the sensation of feeling like…

She'd been loved.

She wasn't in love. That was a crazy thing to think. After all, how well did she know the man? Hardly at all.

And yet he'd loved her.

*Making love...* She'd heard that phrase time and time again, often by teens, accidently pregnant. 'We only made love that one time, Doc. I never thought...'

She'd never thought either. That she could be so irresponsible. That she could sink so deeply, so fast.

Irresponsible...

She thought fleetingly of patients, the teenage girls she'd seen so many times in her career.

Pregnant.

'It was just the one time, Doc.'

Pregnant? It had taken four rounds of IVF before she'd conceived. The chances of pregnancy were...

Not nil. She'd told Noah she'd take the morning-after pill. It was only sensible to cover all bases, and now it was time she was sensible.

She dressed and made toast and coffee and took Daisy out onto the veranda. Daisy's friends weren't outside yet but she made the most of the space, haring along the veranda so fast she fell over her own feet. She attacked the doormat like it was the world's most vicious snake and it was her duty to kill it. She hared back to Addie and bounced, then raced off again as if to ask why she wasn't joining in. This morning was delicious. The world was waiting.

The trip to the pharmacy was waiting. The morning-after pill.

But Addie was having a conversation with herself.

*It's dumb. I'll never be pregnant.*

*It's responsible. You know there's a slight chance...*

'A chance.' She said the last two words out loud and Daisy bounced straight back to her as if she'd been called. Addie lifted her and hugged, hard.

Why was she hesitating?

Did she not want to take the pill? Did she not want to make sure?

Where was her head going? She couldn't handle any more useless hope. The grief of another failed pregnancy could well tear her apart. She'd decided—sensibly—to move on.

Hadn't she?

Maybe she hadn't moved far enough.

'This is nuts,' she said, and Daisy looked anxious. 'There's no decision to make. It doesn't matter if I take the pill or not. But...if by some chance it does matter, I don't want...'

She faltered. She didn't want...what? If by some miracle...

She let Daisy slip down to the ground, and unconsciously her hands moved to her belly.

What was she thinking?

What was she risking?

'My head's not working any more,' she told Daisy, but Daisy was distracted and no longer listening.

Addie stood and stared out to the horizon. There was a fishing boat, way off, almost too small to see.

Her hands held her belly tighter.

'I can't do it,' she said, softly now but with resolution. 'To risk...'

See, there was the problem. She didn't know what she was risking.

Disaster all over again?

This was crazy. She was overreacting, to say the least. Noah would say she was overreacting.

*Noah.*

She glanced along to the far end of the veranda, to the

Taj Mahal of puppy playpens built by the oldies—with Noah's help—and she knew what she had to do. At least she knew the first step. 'It's Saturday morning,' she told Daisy. 'I have stuff to do and I need to do it now, because staying in this house one more night with Noah McPherson is just plain dangerous. And I need to decide...'

She paused again. Regrouped. Figured it out.

'Okay, that's not fair,' she said to herself at last. 'There's been too much of *I singular* in Noah's life already. And in my life? This time, *we* need to make a decision. Go get the pill, Addie Blair, and then move on with your life.'

Saturday was busy. The weather was amazing. Locals and tourists alike were making the most of it and Noah was coping with the consequences.

Two kids collided in the surf with their boogie boards. One had a broken nose and fractured cheekbone, the other had a dislocated collar bone.

A dad showing off his new Oriental kite to his kids hadn't figured the power and strength of his new toy. The owl-like kite had done a nose dive and split the side of his face. All the young father could think of was his kids, though, so while Noah stitched his face he muttered over and over again, 'Thank God they weren't underneath. What was I thinking?'

He went away with his face bandaged, clutching his wife, clutching his kids, and Noah watched him go and thought...

Yeah, not a good thought. He'd moved on from that particular fantasy.

But he'd slept with Addie...

A thirty-year-old was brought in from the beach, a

drunken jet-ski rider with the brains of a rather small newt. He'd tried to make his jet-ski jump over a sand bank and even the paramedics were shaking their heads over his idiocy. He had broken ribs and femur. Noah was having trouble trying to differentiate drunkenness from concussion. Anaesthesia for drunks was incredibly fraught, so he and Cliff were kept busy for what was left of the afternoon.

By the time he finished he was dead tired but he headed back to the doctors' house with a sense of anticipation. Fish and chips on the back step with Addie? It sounded good to him. If she wasn't doing anything…

She wasn't there.

He opened the door and no puppy launched itself across the room to meet him. There was no dog basket by the fire. Not a single puppy toy.

Addie's bedroom door was open. The bed was stripped, the blankets neatly folded. Her dresser was bare.

He walked slowly across and pushed the door wider.

Nothing. No clothes. No personal belongings. No bright, shiny suitcase.

The room was stripped as if she'd never been here.

And his gut gave a sickening lurch. Had she run? Because of him?

She'd been happy. He could have sworn he'd left her happy. The memory of the night before was all around him.

It had been dumb. He knew that. It had been spontaneous and stupid and…wonderful.

It had made him feel like he hadn't felt in…for ever?

He shouldn't have left her. He should have stayed this morning and talked.

And now she'd gone? This reeked of fear. Hell, did

she think he was going to try and jump her? Push himself on her? Push past the boundaries they both knew were in place?

He stood in the empty bedroom and felt sick.

Finally he turned and headed back to the living room. There was a note on the mantel. He snatched it and read with hands that weren't quite steady. The thought of her heading away in fear was doing his head in.

She hadn't. It wasn't quite that bad.

*Dear Noah.*

*Or should I make that Darling Noah after last night?*

*It was truly awesome, wasn't it? Just exactly what I needed and wanted and, oh, I loved it. But, wow, did we get carried away! We made love like out-of-control teenagers. I can't believe we were both that dumb.*

*But, to be honest, I don't regret it for a minute. Maybe it was what we both needed—good honest sex, no holds barred, a letting go for both of us before we move on.*

*But we do need to move on, Noah. We both do, and getting more enmeshed with each other will help neither of us. You have four months to go before whatever happens with Sophie, and you move on to wherever that decision takes you. I need to take up my role again, working in this community with commitment.*

*Noah, I need to get my head into that space again, and the bottom line, the truth I faced this morning, is that I can't get my head into that space if I continue sharing a house with you.*

*Something happened last night that took me way out of control. The thought of what we shared last night... Well, control doesn't come into it. One glass of wine—or even no glass of wine—and I run a very real chance of jumping you—and that's a crazy thought. I can't believe I'm admitting I'm scared, but I am, and therefore I'm taking steps to prevent it.*

*So I've rented a cottage. This is no big deal, Noah. No sacrifice. It's a wee cottage only two blocks from the hospital. Three minutes' walk. It's little, it's comfy and it has a spectacular view of the sea.*

*I thought about renting it when I first came here, but there was a bit of pressure to use the doctors' house and it did seem sensible. But I checked this morning and it's still available. It's fully furnished. The owners are happy for me to take it for four months, with the option of longer if I love it. As I suspect I might.*

*So me and my puppy and my new suitcase have gone down the road and that's us settled.*

*And you... Noah, you have a great place to stay for four months, too. We get to meet as colleagues—and, I hope, friends. But no more. We need to keep our hands and bodies under control. Sensible R Us.*

*Please don't think I'm making sacrifices, Noah. Believe it or not, I'm much happier today than I was yesterday. Sex with you blew away ghosts I hardly knew I had. So, thank you and let's move on.*

*But, Noah, I do need to talk to you about something very specific, and what I have to say can't be*

*said over the phone. Would you consider fish and*
*chips at my place? No wine!!! Directions below.*
  *If you can't make it, don't worry, I'll catch up*
*with you in the morning, but it needs to be soon.*
  *Addie*


He stood and stared at the note for a long time. It was
a sensible note. A note designed to make him feel okay.

If she'd told him her intentions he would have offered
to leave himself—he *would* have left himself—but she'd
clearly had somewhere in mind where she could go.

He looked around the tidy, empty house and he felt...
Desolate?

Surely that was the wrong word. One night of sex did
not a relationship make. Addie was being sensible and
he had to match it.

She wanted to talk to him.

Fish and chips. Addie.

On the surface, it seemed a good plan. They had to
become...friends? Nothing more.

'So she's made it easy for you.' He spoke out loud
and the room echoed. 'She's put us where we can become friends.'

*If that's all you can have*...the voice whispered at the
back of his head, and he put it firmly aside.

Addie.

*Why did she want to talk to him?*

Friends.

Fish and chips.

He pulled out his phone. The hospital secretary had
filled his list of colleague contacts and Addie was there.

She answered on the second ring.

'Noah?' She sounded uncertain. Scared even? But

he could hear her collect herself, gather her containment. 'Hi.'

Deep breath. Keep it as she wanted it, he told her *Friends.*

'How's the house?' he managed.

'Great. Fully furnished. We're all settled, and you should see the view from my back step.'

'Excellent.'

'But...' She sounded scared. 'I still... Noah, I do need to talk.'

'Half an hour? Your back step? But you're right about no wine,' he told her. 'Not even a beer. You've made a sensible choice, Addie, and I concur. It's time we started acting like adults. Fish and chips on the back step and then back to our respective homes.'

'You bring the fish and chips. I'll supply the soda water.'

'A Saturday night to end all Saturday nights,' he said dryly, but he had to agree. They were both being...sensible. 'I'll put on my button-up shirt and my sensible boots and be right over.'

# CHAPTER SEVEN

HER BACK STEP was gorgeous. Fabulous even. When she'd first thought of moving here she'd contacted the local realtor and he'd suggested this cottage. It was a simple cottage, with one bedroom, a kitchen/living room and basic bathroom, built to accommodate an elderly couple who came here occasionally to fish. But the couple had grown even more elderly. They could no longer travel from Sydney but were holding onto the house in the hope that their busy adult children might one day find time to use it. They paid cleaners to keep it neat, but they didn't much like the idea of tourists short-term renting.

Which meant the little cottage sat unoccupied, which was a shame. It had a gorgeous log fire. It had a lawn that ran down almost to the beach.

It had a view from the back step that took her breath away.

She sat there now, looking at the reflected rays of sunset over the ocean.

She waited.

Daisy had been tearing around, investigating every nook and cranny of her new home. She'd passed out now in her basket on the veranda. Happy.

And Addie was waiting for Noah.

For a friend, she reminded herself. Nothing more.

Except…

Don't go there.

More and more, she knew that she must.

And then he was there, opening the side gate, smiling a welcome, and she thought, *This* is the entire problem. This smile…

'You should have rung the doorbell,' she complained as Daisy lifted a weary head to investigate, decided it was only Noah and she could go back to sleep.

*Only Noah.*

'You did say your back step.' He paused and looked out at the sea, taking in the sweeping vista before him. 'Wow. I'm getting why you moved.'

'I hope you do.'

'I do.' He came and sat beside her. There was an ancient settee on the veranda and a table of sorts but the steps seemed somehow…better. She shifted a little, allowing him to set down his aromatic white package between them. Was there a more enticing smell in the world than hot fish and chips? She retrieved glasses and soda water from behind her, and a handful of paper napkins.

'Dinner's ready,' she said in contentment, and that was suddenly how she felt.

Like the night had settled. Like it was going to be okay.

Except…what she had to say.

Not yet.

They ate in silence, but not because there was tension. In fact, it was almost the opposite. What had happened between them should have created expectations, worry and, yes, sexual arousal, and maybe it had, but for some reason here in this place, for this moment, it had dissipated. All that was left was peace.

And food. Currawong fish and chipper had a reputation nationwide. Deservedly.

They ate tiny fillets of flathead, which was, in Addie's opinion, the world's most delicious fish, with a homemade tartare sauce that was mouthwatering. 'And it's sustainable,' Addie murmured as she popped the third piece into her mouth, and Noah grinned as he did the same.

'Excellent. Take nothing but photographs. Leave nothing but footprints.'

'And tread lightly on the planet,' she agreed as she eyed a gorgeous, buttery scallop. 'These are in season for such a short time but yum!'

The chips were magnificent as well, crisp, golden and so moreish she could have eaten twice as much, but there were fried onion rings and tiny potato cakes and a crisp garden salad so she had to somehow organise her priorities. Some of the chips had to be abandoned. With regret.

And then Noah produced tubs of chocolate ice cream. The ice cream had been slowly melting while they tackled the fish and chips. Now it'd reached the semi-solid state where it was creamy and melty. Even though Addie was full, the ice cream slithered into the edges.

Fantastic.

She ate and Noah ate, too, but she was aware he was watching her.

The sexual tension hadn't gone away. It was zinging in at the edges. Disguised as the taste of melting chocolate on her tongue?

She should focus on that rather than on Noah.

Like that was possible.

Finally she scraped the last of her ice cream from her tub and put it aside. Done.

And she needed to be done with the tension.

'I should make a pot of tea,' she said. 'Though I suspect I'll waddle as I walk inside and it's not a good look for a colleague.'

He chuckled and that was a good sound. A great sound. She loved his chuckle.

This should be okay, she thought. This was the start of acting…like friends. All she had to do was say goodnight and go inside.

But first there was the imperative.

Did she have to ask?

She knew she did.

Oh, but she didn't want to.

Her heart was screaming at her to do nothing, say nothing, but she'd been sensible all day. Her head was telling her to go on being sensible. Her heart had had its turn last night, and look at the mess that had landed her in. It was time for her head to say it like it was.

The sunset had faded. A crescent moon was rising over the horizon. She could just see the evening star.

No. It's Venus, she thought, or was it Jupiter? She could never remember. Either way it was a planet, not a star. So it's not an 'evening star' at all, she told herself. Get real.

And reality was?

Break the silence.

Say it.

'Noah, I didn't just ask you here for fish and chips.'

'You know, I guessed that,' he said, and she heard a hint of laughter. She loved that laughter. It did something…

Um, not. Focus on…not laughter.

'The reason I asked you here…' She sounded a bit desperate but that was how she was feeling. But she had to say it like it was.

'Noah, what was between us, what happened last night…we were well out of control and, to be honest, remembering the way I responded to you, it terrifies me. That's why I moved out. Neither of us are in the market for relationships. You need to be focussed on your access fight for Sophie. I've only just pulled myself together.'

'I understand. I felt bad until I saw this place but now…it makes sense.'

'But that's not all.' How to make herself say these next few words?

'Not?'

'No.' Deep breath. 'Noah, this morning…I went down to pharmacy and got the morning-after pill. I promised you I'd take it. That promise stands—if you want it. But now…I'm asking if you'll…reconsider.'

And she tugged the pill packet out of her jeans pocket and laid it on the step between them.

What followed was silence. A really long silence. It stretched out between them while the evening star got itself a few mates.

They were sitting on the middle step, with the detritus of their makeshift picnic between them. And now a foil container.

What had she just landed him with?

A tiny possibility. The remotest of chances.

Why did it feel huge?

'Noah, this isn't fair,' she managed at last. She knew it wasn't. 'After all you've been through with Rebecca, with the way you've been manipulated, the last thing you need is me doing the same. I should just take it, move

on. But I find… Noah, I can't make myself do it. No
without…asking.'

'You want to be pregnant?' Despite the lengthy silence
his words were a blast of pure shock.

Say it like it was. 'Yes.' This much at least she knew
for a fact. 'I do.'

'You're kidding.' His voice turned to incredulity. *You
planned this?'*

'Of…course I didn't,' she managed. 'Noah, we both
know that. You must know it.'

For a moment she thought he'd get up, walk away,
kick something. The look on his face was indescribable.

Fleetingly she remembered the moment she'd slapped
him. She'd been out of control. That's how Noah looked
now.

But there was no slap. There was only more silence.
She watched as he visibly sorted through what she'd said.

Finally he nodded. The incredulous look on his face
faded. It seemed her version of last night's events had
been accepted.

'I know that.'

Her world settled, a little. 'We just…'

'Came together out of mutual need.' The menace had
gone, but the shock was still there. His voice turned calm
again. Almost thoughtful. 'So…if a pregnancy comes of
last night, you want to go through with it?'

She found she was shaking. She had to pull herself
together. She had to explain.

'Noah, after the ectopic… After so many tries with
IVF, so much failure, I thought I'd moved on. My pup,
my suitcase and my new hairstyle, they were supposed
to be the beginnings of my way forward. It was only this
morning, staring at the pill, I thought, What am I doing?

The possibility of pregnancy is so remote that it's almost laughable, but to kill that tiny chance… I thought, What if I am pregnant? And it was like a shaft of light.'

He was staring at her as if he was staring at a future she'd just complicated a thousandfold.

'But I'd be the father,' he said blankly.

'You would.' She'd been thinking of this all day. Now she had to work out how to get her thoughts out there.

She glanced at him and then glanced away again. She had to say this without emotion, and looking at his face didn't help.

'Noah, if I was…then this *would* be your baby. That's why this has to be your decision, whether I take it or not. That's why I asked you to come tonight. I think…likely or not, the decision to proceed has to be yours as well.'

He was looking at her blankly, as if he could scarcely understand what she was saying. 'What…? Addie, I can't make you take it. It's your body.'

'It is, but if you ask me to take it then I will. And honestly… I'd take it with no regrets. Noah, I might go back to IVF. I might try again with sperm donation. What I do will be nothing to do with you. But this one slim chance…it's your call. No matter what, I hope we'll still be colleagues. Still…friends? All I'll be doing by taking the pill is preventing something that probably won't happen anyway.'

'So…you're asking me, why?'

'I should have taken it this morning. It was only… suddenly it seemed big. And it did seem…as if it wasn't just my decision.'

'And if you don't take it?' His voice seemed to be coming from far away. 'If you are pregnant?'

'Then you'd have to decide how much you wanted

to be involved.' She'd thought this through while she'd packed and moved, while she'd made up her new bed, while she'd sat on the back step and stared at nothing. 'If it does, if I am...you'd be within your rights...no, you'd be welcome to be a proper dad. To be as involved as you want. Noah, I understand Sophie's your priority and I respect that. We could work around it. Figure it out as we went along. But, Noah, I'm not Rebecca. I would never use a child to manipulate or control.'

'You have thought this through.'

'I've had all day,' she said ruefully. 'And my head's been spinning. But I also need to say... Noah, what's between you and me...our lovemaking...that was a one-time thing. I have no intention or wish to develop a relationship beyond co-parenting, and if you didn't want to co-parent then that's okay, too. I had things organised in my head before I got pregnant last time. I think I'll make a decent single mum. I have huge community support, so I'd never think less of you if you don't want contact. Neither will I think less of you if you sit with me now while I swallow this pill. And I will take it. If that's... what you want.'

But then...the shaking got worse.

Despite the warmth of the evening, the comfort of the food, she couldn't stop the tremors. What was she asking of him? What sort of decision? She had every right to do this for herself, she thought, but she had no right to do it to Noah.

But suddenly his hand was over hers, his fingers encircling, warm, firm, strong. His hand held in a grip that was a message all by itself.

'You'd love to be pregnant.'

'Yes,' she said truthfully. 'But it's not my right—'

'If you had it...' His words cut her off '...I couldn't walk away. Addie, regardless of how our baby was conceived, I would care for you. I'd care for you both.'

'Like you were forced to care for Rebecca?' Where had that come from?

'No, I—'

'See, that's what I don't want.' Suddenly a new set of emotions were surfacing. She hauled her hand away from his as if it burned. 'Noah, you could care for our baby all you want—but not for me.' This situation was doing her head in. Was he offering...what he'd just walked away from?

Of course he was. This was Noah the honourable. Noah who'd tried to explain away Gavin's appalling behaviour. Noah who'd rung the day after the wedding fiasco to 'see if there's any way I can help...' Noah who'd stuck to his horrible wife. Noah who'd been betrayed in the most horrible way, and yet here he was with his hand up again.

*I would care for you.*

She should be impressed. She should think what a noble man.

Instead...

'I don't need to be cared for,' she managed, and she couldn't prevent a spurt of anger. 'Noah, thank you, but I don't want it.'

And then she caught herself. The last thing Noah deserved was anger—it was totally unjustified—but it'd been a huge day. She was overwrought and there was something about him that threatened her precious control.

He scared her?

The whole situation scared her. She had to haul herself together.

She had to explain her almost visceral response to his offer to care.

The truth? It seemed this was the night for it.

'Noah, you don't get it and you need to,' she managed. 'Caring's been my whole life. From the moment my dad died I was the carer. "Hug me, Addie," Mum would say. "Without you I couldn't go on." And... "Study hard, Addie. Your father was so smart and you're all I have left of him." And then Gavin... "Addie, marry Gavin... You'd make all our dreams come true. You can't bring your father back, but to have his grandchildren... I could go to my grave happy..."'

Somehow she hauled herself back from the emotions threatening to overwhelm her. 'Noah, I suspect you know what I'm talking about. I can imagine the guilt Rebecca exposed you to, because I was exposed to it, too. And here you are, offering more of the same. You'll care for me and a possible baby because you're honourable. Noah, I don't want or need your care. You need to make a decision, but my need doesn't come into it.'

That brought more silence.

In the stillness Daisy woke. She'd been in her basket near the door. Now she wriggled across the veranda on her belly, as if she was unsure of her welcome. Addie was dimly aware of her but too caught in the moment to do anything about it. Unchecked, the little dog slithered over to the top step, wriggled her head down to the chip wrapper, seized a chip and bolted back to her basket.

Neither of them noticed.

The silence went on.

The little foil packet lay untouched.

'You don't think,' Noah said at last, and astonishingly

there was suddenly a trace of a smile in his voice, 'you might be overreacting?'

Of course she was, but she wasn't backing down.

'All I'm saying is that I went into the IVF process with planning in place, with my future as a single mum sorted. So now…if anything were to happen, don't you dare think of me as an obligation. You have plans, too, Noah. If you don't get custody of Sophie, if it ends up that you can't even get access, then maybe it's time you had life as a carefree bachelor. You surely deserve it. So, Noah, if you want me to take the pill, I will. Here and now, while you watch me. Or tomorrow morning if you need time to think about it. You…we…have a forty-eight-hour window to decide.'

And that was enough. He was too close. She was feeling too emotional.

'Please…let's leave it,' she said, almost roughly. 'If you need to, think about it overnight. Know that whatever you decide there'll be no regrets. No blame. We'll both move on. But for now I need to go to bed.'

But then Daisy, emboldened by her initial slithery hunt, decided that discretion was for dummies. The chip had been delicious. She did another tummy-on-the-ground foray to the top step, but then looked down, saw Addie's hand poised to wrap the remaining chips—and made a flying bid to rescue the lot.

Puppy and chips and paper went flying, the pup somersaulting down the last four stairs. She lay stunned at the bottom, her legs in the air. A chip landed on her chin.

The chip went down the hatch, her tail gave an enormous wiggle like she'd just achieved something spectacular and she rolled over and proceeded to pounce on the remains.

It was so comical they both had to laugh, and it was what they both needed. Over-the-top emotion receded as they cleared the mess. When it was done, Noah's face was calm again. Under control.

'We're talking of a situation that in all probability won't happen,' he said. 'Let's keep it calm.'

'Let's.' Maybe she should say more but it was all she could think of.

'I need to head back to the hospital.'

'I… Yes. Thank you for the fish and chips.'

'Thank you for the hospitality.'

They stood, motionless. She'd picked Daisy up. She had her in her arms and she was holding her almost like a shield.

Why?

Because she wanted…what? She was afraid of what? She was afraid of what she was feeling.

The pregnancy issue aside, what she was feeling right now…

She wanted more of what she'd had last night.

Which was why she'd moved out of the doctors' house.

'Goodnight, Noah,' she managed. 'And don't…please don't build this into a big deal. It's nothing. Just let me know.'

'It's not nothing.'

'I won't be pregnant.'

'Even if you aren't pregnant, it's still *not nothing*.' He put a hand out and cupped her face, a gesture of…what? She didn't know. All she knew was that his touch made her whole body quiver. She had to step back and she did.

'It's not nothing and you know it,' he said gently. 'And you know what? There's also a part of me that'd accept pregnancy with joy. But let's worry about tomorrow when tomorrow comes.' He smiled into her eyes, that mesmeric smile that did something to her heart that she'd never felt before. 'Meanwhile, I don't know about you but I had very little sleep last night. Let's do better tonight.'

And he chucked Daisy under one of her soft ears. He smiled again at Addie, a smile directed straight at her.

And then he took the foil packet and tucked it into his top pocket. 'I'll take this with me,' he said. 'Pharmacy can dispose of a drug we have no need of.'

He walked home along the cliff path, his hands deep in his pockets, his thoughts back in the little house he'd just left. He'd left his car at the hospital because it was a five-minute walk via the fish shop and he'd needed to walk. He needed a walk even more now. He took the long route around the headland, a thirty-minute hike, and even that wasn't long enough to get his head together.

What had just happened?

It hadn't just happened, though, he thought. It had happened last night, when he'd taken Addie into his bed, into her bed. And she'd taken him. The sex had been mind-blowing, the release of years of frustration, anger, need. The release of years of…caring?

But now the caring was right back with him. His concern for her…

She probably wasn't pregnant but if she was, she'd made her decision. And he'd made his.

She…they…wanted a baby.

He paused and stared out over the blackness of the ocean. The moon created a sliver of silver over the waves but the water still looked dark, empty, threatening.

His baby.

Addie.

'You're talking of something that won't happen,' he told himself, but that sounded wrong, too.

And yet…it was probably right. He'd done a statistics unit once to help with research he was undertaking. He understood odds.

The odds said he was out here talking to himself about something that would never happen.

But if it did…

'Then you'll cope with it,' he said, still aloud. But then…she'd already made a declaration that she wouldn't need him.

Would he be sidelined again in a child's life?

She'd sworn that he wouldn't, and somehow he believed her.

So…did he want her to be pregnant? Wasn't his life complicated enough?

'Yes, it is. So why take the pill home with you?'

Because she wants a baby, he argued within himself.

'Do you? Are you trying to replace Sophie?'

The thought made his gut clench and he knew it wasn't true. Sophie was irreplaceable and always would be.

'You're being dumb,' he said, still out loud. 'Let's not dramatise something that won't happen. This is not a worry.'

He moved on, but as he did so he thought it wasn't exactly worry.

It was more like…hope?

# CHAPTER EIGHT

*Ten days later...*

IT'S SAID THE *gods laugh at those who play the odds.*

The odds said she couldn't be pregnant.

Someone up there was definitely laughing.

She walked out to the back step, increasingly her favourite place in the world, and sat down.

Hard.

Daisy bolted across the lawn to join her. Addie laid the plastic tester aside—carefully, as if it might break. She took her little dog into her arms and hugged.

And started to shake.

She'd been down this road before and it had ended in heartbreak. But hope was lying beside her in the form of two blue lines on a piece of plastic.

She set Daisy down. The little dog headed off into the garden to see if she could dig down to a cricket chirping just under the lawn surface. She should stop her. Who needed holes in lawns? But she wasn't thinking of the lawn now. She picked up the sliver of plastic again and the lines were still there. She was pregnant and all she could feel was terror.

Terror for herself?

'Please…' It was a desperate whisper from somewhere deep within her. It was a plea and a prayer and an admission that she was way out of control. She'd never meant this. She could have stopped it. She should have…

No. She dropped the plastic and her hands went to her belly, instinctively, in the way of mothers the world over.

Her baby.

Please…

She'd have to tell Noah. This decision had been his as well as hers.

*This was his baby.*

But…but…

There was no reason to tell him. Not yet. She was literally days into her pregnancy. The problem with increasingly sophisticated pregnancy tests was that they confirmed pregnancy ridiculously early. She knew better than anyone the odds of miscarriage. Most miscarriages occurred almost before the mother suspected she was pregnant. If there was a problem, a woman's body was wired to rid itself of a non-viable pregnancy, clearing the way to start again.

But please… Not this time. Let there be no problem.

She did have to tell Noah.

Tell him what? She was talking to herself almost hysterically. Should she tell him that she was two minutes pregnant?

She should wait and see.

But she knew she couldn't. It was his right to know.

And that was doing her head in. She wanted this baby so much, and somehow she'd dragged him right in. Noah, with his overblown sense of obligation, his friendship. His…his…

She couldn't go there. There was so much about Noah

she didn't understand, so much that almost frightened her. She wasn't in control when he was around.

So many emotions…

Daisy got bored and started pouncing on her knees from the steps above. Over and over. Every time she pounced, Addie picked her up and set her down, which suited Daisy fine.

Babies liked repetition.

Baby…

Her mind seemed like it was caught in an out-of-control spin that left her feeling almost nauseous. She should be joyously happy, but there were so many unknowns. So much fear.

And Noah.

Noah's baby.

Where to go from here?

Pretend things were normal? Wait and see? Decisions seemed impossible and when her phone rang she was almost grateful.

What she needed until she had her head under control was work. A lovely birth, with no major complications but tricky enough to take her mind off what she could barely hope to think about. She had three mums due to give birth about now. Hopefully one was about to oblige.

'Addie?'

But it was Noah and simply by the way he said her name she knew this wasn't a friendly chat. Neither was it a call about a normal delivery. There was urgency behind the two syllables.

Medicine. Her world. She was already shoving her feet back into her shoes, heading indoors with the phone in her hand. 'Give.'

'Car accident,' he told her. 'Car clipped a lorry and

rolled. They're bringing them in now. Briana and Tom Danvers. Briana's suffered multiple injuries and Morvena says she's one of yours. The paramedics say she's in final trimester.'

Addie knew her. She'd seen her two days ago for her prenatal check. Bouncy and confident, Briana had been the picture of health, and the pregnancy was totally normal. 'She's thirty-four weeks,' she said, grabbing her car keys.

'They're thinking foetal distress. They couldn't get a heartbeat at first but it's there now. It could be inexperience that had them not hearing, or stress, but we need you here.'

'Of course. Where's the ambulance? Can I meet it on the way?' She didn't say—she didn't have to say—that the most common injury to a baby in a car crash was placental abruption. If the placenta completely separated from the uterus then death of the baby was inevitable, but if there was a heartbeat now, that hadn't happened. A likely scenario was partial abruption, which meant a partial tear. If the oxygen supply was blocked for any length of time, or even intermittently...

She had to reach her fast.

'They'll be here in five minutes.'

Five minutes meant there was no advantage to meeting the ambulance for roadside intervention. 'I'm on my way. Other injuries?'

'Tom has lacerations, concussion, query broken collar bone. Briana has a broken wrist and chest injuries. Breathing issues. Query broken ribs. The pregnancy means they haven't been able to give her anything.'

'They can give her morphine if they need to. There's crossover but it's better than having her in agony. Airway stabilisation's a priority but they know that. I'm there in three minutes. Or less.'

And she was out the front door, leaving a bewildered Daisy looking sadly after her. Addie had been about to take her over to spend the afternoon with the oldies but there was no time to organise it now. 'I'll be with you before the ambulance.'

Morvena might be autocratic, dogmatic, even ruthless, but in a crisis there was no one doctors depended on more than a good nurse manager. She'd obviously mustered the troops. Addie reached the hospital before the ambulance arrived, and two other cars were screeching into the car park. Cliff, the anaesthetist, and Rob Holloway, the youngest of the town's family physicians.

Four doctors. Cliff and Rob for Tom, Noah and her for Briana? Swap Cliff when needed? If Tom's brain injury was severe it'd have to be Noah and Cliff with Tom, and Rob with her. She was already playing out an emergency Caesar, planning resources.

She headed straight for the trauma room. Noah was before her. Cliff and Rob had veered off to Emergency admissions. There was no greeting. There was no time for anything but what lay ahead.

'Briana's ours,' Noah snapped. 'The paramedics say she's short of breath and they can feel broken ribs. There's also blocked circulation to the arm, plus the foetal problems. I'm scrubbing for an immediate thoracostomy if that's necessary. Our priorities are assessment, breathing, baby, wrist.'

Her skill was babies. Delivering babies. Fast. Noah was the generalist and this was his call.

She nodded her agreement. Noah was prioritising on

the paramedic's information but it was a reasonable call.
They could change their minds after initial assessment
but it settled them all to have an initial plan, to know
what they were facing.

Morvena was standing in the background, holding her
phone, waiting for orders. Addie might have had puppy
issues with this woman, but she had no issues now.

'I need everything for a stressed premmie,' she told
her. 'Incubator, the works. See if you can get one of the
other GPs in, in case we need help with the baby. Warm
everything. And ring the flying neonatal squad from Sydney. We can always call them off if we don't need them.'

'Already done,' Morvena said.

'Tell them to add another doctor to the flying squad,'
Noah told her. 'A trauma specialist as well as a paediatrician. If we need to evacuate a distressed premmie and
a mum with breathing problems, plus Tom with possible
head injuries, we'll need full medical support.'

'If a thoracostomy tube's needed, can we evacuate
by air?' Addie asked tentatively. This was not her spe-
cialty so she needed to ask. Did they need to organise a
road ambulance as back-up? Noah gave her a swift nod
of acknowledgement. Doctors questioning each other
was never a problem—it made for far fewer mistakes.

'It's okay,' he told her. 'As long as the tube's in situ and
they fly at low altitude there's no problem. Morvena…'

'I'm onto it,' Morvena said. 'I'll ring in more nurses.'

She wheeled away. Addie headed for the sinks.

Two minutes later the scream of the ambulance siren
filled the silence of the valley and it was on.

The paramedics' assessment had been—was—totally ac-
curate. They wheeled Briana in first and one look showed

she was in deadly trouble. She was breathing fast. Her chest was heaving with effort, and her eyes were wide with panic. Noah was already in scrubs, gloved. While Noah watched, Addie pushed away the thermal blanket they'd used to keep her warm, then carefully removed the collar the paramedics had used in case of neck fracture. They both looked at her trachea and the shift was obvious. It was displaced, moved to the side.

Tension pneumothorax.

The paramedics had already slit her T-shirt. A light feel of her chest suggested the likelihood of rib fracture. Piercing of the lung. Air was obviously escaping, building up in the chest and causing the lungs to collapse.

There was also the complication of her left wrist. Briana's hand was pallid, cold and pulseless.

Circulation?

Breathing first.

Addie was examining her ribs, gently feeling, focussing on the break. Briana was wild-eyed, terrified, frantic. To not be able to breathe…

Addie took her good hand and held it, taking a sliver of a moment to give human contact, to make Briana feel like she was being held. That the fight was no longer hers.

'You're okay now, Briana. Safe. Try and relax while we ease your breathing.'

'Briana, the reason you're having trouble breathing is that you have air in your chest.' Noah's voice followed hers, deep, calm, steady. They were both in Briana's line of vision, but her gaze locked on Noah. 'It looks like you've broken a rib and it's letting air in, squashing your lung. It feels terrifying but it's easy to fix. The first thing we'll do—what I'll do now—is put a tube into your chest to let the air out.'

'But Tom…' It was a frantic gasp.

'Tom's okay.' Once again his calm, deep voice got through. This wasn't a voice that could be argued with. 'He's copped a few cuts and bruises and a broken collar bone but we think he'll be fine. Dr Holloway and Dr Brooks are taking care of him but they're not bringing him in here. He's bleeding a bit and Morvena doesn't like blood on her nice clean trauma room, do you, Morvena?'

There was a snort from that lady behind them and Addie almost smiled. But…

'My baby…' Briana gasped.

'Yep, we'll check on her, too,' Noah said calmly. 'Her? Him? Do we know?'

'H-her.'

'Nice,' Noah said, and smiled. 'The ambulance officers have checked on your baby's heartbeat, and it's nice and loud.' There was no point in telling her there could be a problem. 'So our first priority is to get your breathing sorted. You have a broken wrist, too, Briana, and you need to let us sort it, but that comes second. I'm about to pop a needle in to get rid of the extra air in your lung. Then X-ray. Then we'll look at your wrist. It must be hurting like hell. We can fix that. Okay with you, Briana?'

He was gazing straight down at Briana, eyes locked on hers, and Addie saw the moment the panic eased.

Trust…

Briana trusted this man, and why wouldn't she? There was no hesitation, only certainty that this was the way to go.

He'd downplayed nothing. He'd told the exact truth. Too much air in your lung, let's get rid of it. Your baby's alive, we'll check on her. Your wrist is broken, we'll fix it.

'We need to do a bit of undressing,' Noah told Briana, and he summoned one of his gorgeous smiles. 'It's undignified, I know, but needs must. Addie needs to listen to that baby of yours and I need complete access to your chest. Sorry, but that very attractive T-shirt is about to become ribbons. Jeans, too.'

'They're my...they're my gardening clothes,' Briana wheezed. 'We were going home...from helping my mother...spread chook poo on her roses.'

'Well, I'm very sorry, but your chook-poo-spreading T-shirt and jeans are no more,' Noah said gently. He couldn't touch her as he was already gloved, but Addie was doing the touching for him. 'But let's mourn them later. First let's get you safe.'

While Noah worked, Addie was fully occupied with her role, setting up a foetal monitor, trying to get a handle on the condition of the baby.

She wasn't liking what she was finding.

The paramedics had mentioned when they'd first tried for a heartbeat that they hadn't been able to find one. Given the roadside conditions, given the mother's distress, given their own stress, they could well have missed it. The second time they'd tried they'd found it but it was erratic. Addie took blood for cross-matching straight away as a precaution and then set up a foetal heart monitor. She studied the cardiotocography and found no reassurance.

There were dips in the baby's heart rate.

Briana had been hit, hard, and the placenta would have been slammed within the abdomen.

There was also vaginal bleeding. Not much, but enough for deep concern.

If this was partial abruption, it could turn to full at any moment. Or damage alone would be enough to cause foetal death. She needed to see this baby. She needed to be hands on.

This was a thirty-four-week pregnancy. Totally viable. The risks on leaving her in situ were enormous.

She wanted this baby born now.

Her eyes met Noah's and held for a fraction of a moment. It didn't take longer. He read the message.

He was working swiftly himself, with skill and precision, to establish a secure airway.

A local anaesthetic came first, then prophylactic antibiotics to prevent complications like pneumonia later. Finally the chest tube was inserted carefully, and at last Addie heard the blessed hiss of released air, the instant relief of a compressed lung.

Briana's short, frantic gasps eased.

Panic receded.

Then Cliff was in the room, swinging in with the casual air of a doctor who was there for a social visit. He was good, too, Addie thought, and thanked her lucky stars for such colleagues. His presence meant they had three doctors. It must also mean that Tom was safe. Her stress level dropped a notch.

'Greetings, all,' the anaesthetist said, smiling down at Briana. 'Mrs Danvers, you and your husband have interrupted my attendance at my son's under-twelve footie match. We're winning forty-seven to three and my Lucas has kicked seven goals. I need to get back for the riotous celebration of sausage rolls and soda. Meanwhile, I've been in to see your Tom. He's bruised and bumped and he has a sore shoulder but he's okay. I've given him a nice little something so he can be stitched up without pain and Dr Holloway has taken over. Now it's your turn. What do you need me here for, guys?'

'X-ray next.' Noah was adjusting the thoracostomy tube, responding to Cliff but still talking to Briana. Including her in the conversation. Holding her to him in a way that surely must settle her in the midst of pain and fear. 'Briana, your wrist is broken and needs to be reset. Dr Blair—Addie—also needs to run checks on your baby. What we plan to do is run you through X-ray, maybe do an ultrasound of your baby, and then make a decision.'

He hesitated but only for a fraction of a moment, a fraction that Briana wouldn't have picked up on but Addie heard it. It was a pause that meant he'd picked up on Addie's concern. And it was best to be honest.

'Briana, we'll need to put you under in order to treat your wrist,' he told her. 'You have a blocked blood supply to your fingers and if we leave that for long you might end up with long-term stiffness.' Paralysis, he meant, but that was a scary word to use. 'But more.' He nodded to Addie, an acknowledgement that she should take over the conversation if he got it wrong.

'Briana, we're also going to do a very careful assessment of your baby. She's been given a fair shaking. She's thirty-four weeks. If she's born now then she's hardly even classified as premature. She's a fully formed baby, ready to be born. Ideally she'd probably choose to stay where she is for a few more weeks, but she's had a bump and we'd like to see her, to make sure she's okay. Dr Blair thinks the safest thing is to perform a Caesar. Would that be okay with you?'

'You'll take my baby...' Briana quavered, and Addie stooped so her face was close to Briana's. She touched her cheek, wiping away a frightened tear.

'No, Briana, we won't take your baby,' she told her. 'We'll give you your baby. I am a little worried,' she conceded. 'You have a bruise on your abdomen, which means you've been hit. I can hear your baby's heartbeat so she's okay but I don't know if you have internal bleeding. For now, though, you and Tom and your baby are safe and we plan to keep it that way, even if it means we bring your little girl into the world a bit early. You need to trust us. Will you do that, Briana?'

'I...' Briana looked wildly around, at Addie, at the stern-faced Morvena in the background, at the now-serious Cliff, and then lastly at Noah. She looked at him for a long time.

What was it with this man? Briana instinctively looked at him with trust.

Whatever it was, she was taking it, Addie thought, because she saw the moment Briana relaxed. She saw the moment Briana decided she could abandon her flight-and-fight reflex and just...trust.

'Okay,' Briana whispered. 'Just do it.'

And after that there was no time for introspection, no time for thoughts of anything other than doing.

The X-rays showed a comminuted fracture of the wrist. There was an intermittent pulse. If there hadn't been, in probability she'd be looking at the loss of her hand, but the paramedics had done their job well. They'd stabilised it, splinting it as well as they could, which had allowed a tiny amount of blood to get through.

Not enough to stay viable for long, though, and the X-rays showed it wasn't enough to depend on. The fracture meant she'd need specialist orthopaedic surgery to make sure the hand was fully functional but they needed to reduce the fracture now to make sure her hand was viable until they could get her to Sydney.

Meanwhile, the information Addie was accumulating was growing increasingly worrying. The vaginal bleeding was sluggish but constant, and the baby's heartbeat…

'Anaesthetic now,' she said, as the world's fastest X-ray and ultrasound were completed. She stooped and kissed Briana lightly on the cheek. It was totally unprofessional but she'd been this woman's doctor for over two years. She'd seen the joy of Briana and Tom when their pregnancy had been confirmed. How hard was it to stay aloof in such circumstances?

She couldn't.

So she kissed her and signalled to Cliff to take over at the top end, but before he took her place she smiled down into Briana's eyes.

'Time to let us take over, Briana,' she told her. 'Time to relax and trust us. When you wake up you'll have your baby.'

'You promise?'

There was a risk… This baby had been shaken… She couldn't see the extent of the injury.

But who was she to say that now? If there was major trauma, if the unthinkable happened, a promise made and broken would be something Addie was prepared to carry.

'I promise,' she said, and as she said it she was suddenly aware of a brush against her arm, the slightest of pressures.

Noah.

It was a hug that was hardly a hug.

That was hardly professional either, doctor hugging doctor, but there it was and she'd take it.

'We all promise,' Noah said gravely. 'Briana, can Cliff

put you under now? Can we bring your baby into the
world?' And panic took an even greater step back. Briana searched their faces, one after the other, and finally
she sighed.

'Tom...'

'He's still making a mess of my emergency department,' Morvena told her. 'But the minute he's tidy we'll
bring him in to meet his daughter. I promise that, too.'

And they all smiled. The grumpy Morvena was no
one to argue with and Briana wasn't trying.

'So can I send you byebyes?' Cliff asked, and there
was only one answer.

'Yes, please,' Briana whispered. 'I want...my baby.'

It was a crowded theatre.

While Addie worked to deliver the baby, Noah stabilised the thoracostomy tube. He was deferring to Addie,
and that was a skill all on its own.

Egos often seemed something that came with the job
description of surgeon. They played with lives under their
hands every day, and without confidence they couldn't
go on. But Noah had the mix right.

They had the screen up, separating work spaces, working as if Briana were awake and wouldn't want to watch
the cutting process. In fact, it meant easier delineation,
with less likelihood of cross-contamination between surgery sites. But Noah wasn't going ahead to align the wrist
until the baby was delivered and the wound was closed.
That'd be too big a risk. He did what he could to main-
tain circulation. Not for a minute did he let Addie think
he was waiting. He knew she accepted the urgency.

They all did. Cliff was monitoring breathing, no easy
task for a patient as compromised as Briana. Rob, the

amily doctor who'd attended Tom, had appeared as sur-
;ery had started. 'Tom's okay,' he told them. 'Worried but
;ood. He's under obs and I'll head back if needed, but I
hought you might want someone for the baby.'

Morvena was there. And Heidi.

They had a warmed incubator. They had paediatric
resuscitation equipment.

Go.

Addie swabbed, then cut with the skill and precision
of years of training. She scooped in and lifted.

There was an audible intake of breath. Held. Until the
first weak cry…

Which grew stronger. Indignation a plus!

One tiny, fragile but already-turning-pink baby girl
had entered the world.

As Addie turned to hand her over to Rob—her priority had to be Briana as there was still danger of haemor-
rhage—she caught Noah's glance. Just for a moment. It
was a fleeting glimpse, a shadow of expression.

Care?

More than care. Involvement. Total empathy.

Despite the intricacy of this operation, despite the
concentration he had to apply, he had the whole room
under surveillance. Did he know what each of them was
thinking?

What made her believe he knew what she was thinking? She hardly knew herself. All she knew was that as
she handed over the tiny bundle of new life into Rob's
skilled hands, as she hesitated for just one fraction of a
second, as she felt the tug of letting go…

She knew Noah was with her.

'Hey, she looks great.' Rob had her on the pre-warmed
pad, using suction to clear the tiny airway, performing

a fast examination, looking for impact damage. 'She looks perfect.'

And for that tiny moment Addie's control slipped.

*Perfect.*

'Chopper's on its way with the neonatal squad,' Noah told Rob, but he was looking at Addie.

She got it.

He knew.

But the fraction of hesitation was past. She'd turned back to the operating table. Morvena was handing her the instruments she needed.

There was bleeding. Addie could see the damage to the uterus where the placenta had started separating.

They'd been so lucky. A new little life…

She was back at work, suturing, doing her darnedest to ensure that if Briana wanted future babies it'd be possible.

Doing her darnedest to make babies possible.

All the while she had a baby growing within her.

Noah's.

The helicopter took off an hour later. Aboard was a dazed but conscious Tom, an even more dazed but conscious Briana, and one tiny newborn called Alicia Adeline.

'Don't make any decisions until the drugs wear off,' Addie had told them when they'd told her the name, but Briana had smiled weakly and taken her hand.

'You were the last person I saw when I went to sleep and when I woke up, my baby was here,' she whispered. 'I'd like to use Noah, too, but that'll have to wait until next time.'

'And there will be a next time.' Noah stood next to Addie on the hospital veranda and watched as the chopper lifted. 'You've not only saved the baby,' he told Addie, 'I saw the way you stitched that uterus and I'd defy a second kid to rip that neat little bit of handiwork, no matter how hard he or she stretches. 'That's some skill you have, Dr Blair.'

'Speak for yourself, Dr McPherson.' She'd seen what he'd done with Briana's wrist. She'd seen the skill and surety of the thoracostomy tube. Most of all she'd seen the way he'd settled Briana's panic, and Tom's as well when he'd seen his wife and reacted with terror at the sight of the attached medical paraphernalia.

But now they were on their way to Sydney in the best of hands. Yes, tiny Alicia was prem and Briana would need further surgery, but all indications were that this was a happy ending.

For a moment Addie let herself relax. She closed her eyes and the emotions of the day took a step back.

She was standing on the veranda, with the feel of the afternoon sun on her face, the sound of the wash of the sea in her ears, the gentle talk of the oldies in the background...

The faintest of touches of Noah's body against hers.

And then his arm came around her and held.

'You're pregnant,' he said, and it wasn't a question.

# CHAPTER NINE

SHE DIDN'T OPEN her eyes.

This was just an extension of what she was feeling, she thought. God was in his heaven, and all was right with her world.

She was pregnant.

'I am,' she whispered. 'About two minutes pregnant. Far too soon to…'

Far too soon to be sure of anything. Too soon to know if it was a viable pregnancy. Too soon to know if it was ectopic.

Too soon to tell if it was anything other than hope.

He'd know all those things.

He didn't say anything. For a long moment they simply stood. His hand wasn't possessive. It was simply a touch in the small of her back. Contact. Warmth.

Strength?

She needed to pull away, to let him know she didn't need it. She didn't need him. So she would, in a moment, but just for now she let herself absorb his touch as part of the peace of this moment.

They'd just saved a little life.

There was a possibility of a little life between them.

There were, however, practicalities. Cliff and Rob

were cleaning up inside. There were case notes to be written up—they'd sent brief notes with the chopper but a fax with details needed to be sent to Sydney Central, hopefully to arrive before the chopper did. Then the normal Saturday afternoon bumps and bruises from Currawong would be waiting.

The world was waiting.

She made a move to step away but suddenly Noah's hold firmed.

'You're not in this alone, Addie. This is a shared journey.'

She blinked. What had she expected him to say?

Was he laying claim to her baby? Maybe he was, but the way he'd said it...

'I can manage,' she was able to get out. 'I... Even if it does...turn out to be viable...' she took a deep breath '...you know there's every chance I'll miscarry. Or it'll be another ectopic.'

'And there's every chance it won't.'

'I won't let myself go down that road yet. Maybe...in a couple of weeks...'

'Then we can find out whether it's in the right place.' He smiled down at her. 'A scan will be exciting—though it'll be too soon to tell if we're having a boy or a girl.'

*If we're having...*

*We.*

'It'll be too soon to tell anything other than whether the pregnancy's in utero or in the fallopian tubes,' she managed. 'At five weeks the pregnancy's just...a thing.'

A thing. Who was she kidding?

Her baby.

*He'd said we.*

'You don't need… Noah, if you want…this can be nothing to do with you. I never meant—'

'And neither did I,' he said. 'Neither of us planned this pregnancy, but it's happened and it's ours.'

'You didn't want this.'

'Did I say I didn't want this?' His gaze met hers, strong and sure. But there was a trace of something else. Implacability? 'Addie, you know darned well neither of us planned this—neither of us gave a thought to consequences. But it's happened, and you're feeling hope. And you know what? So am I.'

'But I don't want—'

'Me? Sorry, Addie, but you're stuck with me. You gave me assurances the night you didn't take the pill and I'm holding you to them. I'm darned if I'll be a sperm donor and back right out of your life. Out of our child's life.'

'But you're going back to Sydney. You have Sophie to care for. And if you lose access… You said England.'

'That might have to change.' He shrugged. 'Maybe it'd never happen anyway. Even if I don't have access… to walk away from Sophie…and now you…'

'Noah, you can't factor me into that equation. For one thing it's way too soon. It's crazy. And I don't need you. *I won't need you.*'

'So what do you mean by that?' he asked, and she was so out of control she told him.

'Noah, I can't,' she said. 'I told you… All my life my mum needed me. She needed me for everything. Her need controlled my life. I nearly married Gavin because of it. I was a doormat, a nothing. Need's no basis for anything. *I won't need you.*'

He stood and watched her, his face thoughtful. Kind? He was kind, she thought wildly. She could so easily…need.

No.

'That's why you went the sperm donor route?' he asked at last. 'Is that why you've steered clear of any relationship? Because you're scared of needing?'

'And being needed.' She fought for control, for sense, and managed a shamefaced smile. 'I'm sorry, Noah, I'm not making sense to you, but I'm making sense to me.'

'This baby will need you.'

'I can teach independence. I will.'

'Is that a priority? Independence?'

'It has to be. Noah…'

He saw her panic. She saw the moment he realised she was struggling for control.

She saw the moment he decided to back off.

'Let's leave it,' he said, gently now. 'It is too soon. We need to wait. We wait until the five-week mark until we find out for certain whether he or she is in utero or not. We wait until three months until we can do a decent scan and find out if our baby has all the right bits and pieces. And then we wait for forty or so weeks until we can welcome our child.'

*Our child.*

'Anything can happen,' she said miserably. 'You can't plan—'

'I won't plan,' he told her. 'I can only hope, as you're hoping. But whatever happens…' He sighed then and smiled but it was a tentative smile, a smile that said he was in unknown territory as much as she was. He put his hand up and traced her cheek with his forefinger, a feather touch that was maybe meant for reassurance but was maybe…much more?

'But whatever happens,' he repeated, 'you're not alone. Don't look so panicked, love,' he told her. 'I'm not about

to take control, holding you down while you act as an in
cubator for my child. Major decisions are yours to make
I'm with you, though. You'll need—'

'I won't *need*.' Anger surged again—or was it fear?
Emotions were threatening to overwhelm her. 'Don'
group me with Rebecca, Noah. Don't you dare change
your life because someone else needs you. I don't. I
won't.'

'Our baby might.'

'Then that's…that's a contract between you and this
baby. It's for you to work out in the future. Noah, I need
to get back on an even keel. I have case notes to write
and so do you. We need to get back to work.'

'But not ignore what's going on.'

'As best we can, yes,' she managed. 'Because I can't
allow myself to hope.'

'Well, there's a lost cause,' he told her, and that smile
flashed out again, the smile that was so dangerous it did
her head in. 'Because both of us are hoping with everything in our hearts.' He hesitated. 'Addie…you wouldn't
consider moving back into the doctors' house?'

'Why would I do that?'

'If it is an ectopic—'

'Then it's way too early for it to cause problems. Noah,
back off. I'm darned if I'll have you staring at my tummy
for the next forty weeks, waiting for something to explode.'

'I wouldn't do that. But I do care.'

'Then stop caring,' she said brusquely. 'Or maybe…
care a little bit but not that much, and only care about
the baby. Care from a distance and not for me. For now
we both need to put our heads down and move forward.'

'But not together?'

'There's no *together*.'

And that brought a matching flash of anger. Or frustration? Maybe a mix of both. 'Addie, we now have a relationship, like it or not. That's my baby you're carrying.' But then he paused, maybe having heard how he'd sounded. Deciding to regroup? 'No. It's *ours*,' he said, more gently but just as firmly. 'Yours and mine, and I will be involved. There has to be some sort of relationship for that to happen.'

'Fine,' she managed, but she knew she sounded scared. 'I meant...just not a man and a woman relationship. Not a relationship based on need. That's over. I'm never going down that road again, and neither should you.'

The late afternoon and evening were busy and Noah was grateful. Thomas Emmanuel, aged seven, had come off his roller blades and fractured his arm. The greenstick fracture should have been easy to treat but Thomas's mother was hysterical with anxiety and his father was threatening to sue everyone, right down to the council who'd planted the trees in the park because it must have been the gum nuts on the path that had caused Thomas to fall. Their reactions had been transmitted to Thomas. By the time Noah saw him, the little boy was vomiting in fear and pain, and Noah could scarcely get near.

It took patience, time and finally authority to settle things. 'If you can't be calm for your son, if you can't let me work without interference, then Thomas will need to be evacuated to Sydney to be treated by a paediatric team. Is that what you wish?'

It wasn't. They backed off. He then had to spend time calming the little boy, getting him interested in what was going on, talking of how they could decorate his cast, until he could finally set his arm without resorting to general anaesthetic.

Finally it was done. Thomas left between his parents, carrying his braced arm like a trophy. It had its first decoration—a motor bike sticker Noah just happened to have on hand for such an occasion, and the boy was asking where he could get more. The rest of the day's odds and sods were sorted and Noah was free to go home.

To the doctors' house.

Which was empty.

He'd shared this house with Addie for less than a week. He'd been alone in it for almost two months before that.

Why did it feel so lonely tonight?

He ate the casserole Mrs Rowbotham had left him, then snagged a beer and went and sat on the front veranda. There were still lights on in some of the wards. There were people moving behind the drapes.

People…

He abandoned his beer and walked out of the hospital grounds, down to the beach beyond.

He was done with people. Except for Sophie. Addie had it right when she said the last thing he wanted was someone else to need him.

He didn't.

But?

He was damned if he was going to leave her.

Why? Because he wanted this baby?

Yeah, okay, that was probably it. Something seemed to have died inside him the day Rebecca had told him he no longer had access to Sophie. Addie's news had been like a bolt from the blue, and now it felt like the most extraordinary gift.

And it wasn't all about the baby. In fact, it wasn't even mostly about the baby. The way Addie made him feel…

But he had to tread with care, he told himself. A woman he scarcely knew, a woman he'd...okay, say it like it was...a woman he'd shared a one-night stand with, was pregnant. She'd made her own decisions. He didn't owe her anything.

Except he did. She'd been vulnerable. She'd been... Addie.

He could see the lights from her cottage from where he stood on the beach. Was she still awake?

Surely it had nothing to do with him.

But it had to have something to do with him. He stood on the beach and let the shock of the day drift and settle.

There'd been too much emotion, he told himself. Neither of them needed it. What he needed was to be sensible.

If this pregnancy progressed to a birth then, regardless of what happened with Sophie, he couldn't go to London. He knew that.

But then he thought, even if this pregnancy didn't work out, how could he leave Addie? How could he walk away from her pain?

That was a bit of a blindsider.

Emotion... Back off, he told himself. Talk sense.

The light flicked off in the little cottage up on the cliff. She'd gone to bed.

She'd be frightened.

Of course she would. Even without the unknowns of her pregnancy, he'd threatened her. He'd seen it in her body language. She didn't need him. Or...she didn't want to need him.

But friends... If he could figure that one out...

Where to start?

His mind was in overdrive.

He paced a while longer. This was important.

He needed to get things right.

# CHAPTER TEN

ON SUNDAY ADDIE woke to Daisy going nuts at the door, almost turning inside out with excitement. She heard footsteps on the veranda. A knock.

She pushed back the curtains, just a little, and saw Noah standing at her front door. Casually dressed in jeans and T-shirt, he was grinning at the noise on the other side of the door.

Noah. Here.

She glanced at her watch and gasped. Ten! She'd slept and slept.

A first sign of pregnancy was often weariness.

Her hand flew instinctively to her belly. She was pregnant. She was still pregnant!

And her baby's father was standing at her front door.

It was no use pretending she wasn't home when Daisy was making mad dashes to her bedroom, to the door, to the bedroom, to the door, yipping in excitement. She shoved her feet into flip-flops, grabbed her glasses, then glanced at the mirror as she passed to check that her PJs were vaguely respectable. Her hair was a tousled mess. Her eyes looked too big for her face. She needed a shower, a hairbrush and some decent make-up.

She had time for none of them. Noah was waiting.

She opened the door, Daisy launched herself up into his arms—a leap she was getting better and better at—and Noah was smiling right at her.

What was there in that to make a woman catch her breath? Honestly, she needed to get a grip.

'Good morning, Dr Blair.'

'G-good morning,' she managed. Then, a trifle defensively because he was standing there looking cool, collected and gorgeous and she was in her PJs, she added a rider. 'It's Sunday. People are allowed to sleep in on Sunday.'

'Unless it's a medical emergency.'

'Is there a medical emergency?' She couldn't see it in his body language.

'Sort of,' he said. 'I've decided you may be deficient in Vitamin D. It's therefore my job as your consultant surgeon to remedy that situation.'

'Since when have you been my consultant surgeon?'

'Am I a surgeon?'

'I… Yes.'

'And do you consult me for medical advice?'

'Of course, but—'

'Then I'm your consultant surgeon.' His smile widened. 'And Mrs Rowbotham, as our consultant housekeeper, concurs. There's nothing happening at the hospital that Rob can't cover. We still need to be within cooee, but that can be arranged. Daisy spent a very boring day yesterday and our consultant oldies…'

'Our consultant oldies?'

'We consult widely,' he said smoothly. 'The residents of Currawong Nursing Home agree. You have a unanimous diagnosis. Danger of Vitamin D level dropping. Dog boredom. And the prescription is simple. My backpack is therefore loaded with Mrs Rowbotham's finest culinary efforts. Also beach towels, sun screen, flippers, snorkels and masks. In case you hadn't noticed yet, the day is glorious, and we have a task in hand.'

She was struggling to get her head around what he was saying.

She was struggling to get her head around the way he was smiling at her.

'A…task?'

'Agate,' he said.

She blinked. 'Agate? What…?'

'Moonlight Bluff. You must know it.'

She did know Moonlight Bluff. She'd investigated when she'd first moved here. It was a strip of coastline a couple of miles south of the town, where the cliffs rose steeply to make the beach almost inaccessible. But there were steps down, steep and narrow, carved into the rock by some long-ago person with time on his hands, and skill. Once at the bottom you needed to wade into the cove where it was said you could find agate. If you were lucky.

'Did you know you can find agate there?' he said.

'I had heard that,' she conceded. 'At least…gem-stones.'

'The agate's harder to find,' he conceded. 'The rocks have been pretty much picked over by centuries of fos-sickers. The word is that the best stones are to be found three quarters of the way up the steps when everyone's on their last gasp and ready to dump their loads just to get to the top. But I checked them out. They're okay, but nothing special.'

'Damned by faint praise.' She was feeling…totally disconcerted. She was still in her pyjamas.

He was still smiling at her.

'The locals make a fuss of them and who am I to argue? But, Addie, I've been diving around there...'

'Diving.'

'I swim,' he said, almost apologetically. 'The rock formations make diving a pleasure.'

'You carry your gear down those steps?'

'In my last life I was a mountain goat, bounding from peak to peak, so what's a few steps in this life? And once you're down it's magic. If you swim out around the headland the rock pools are stunning.' He paused as if a hiccup to his plans had suddenly interfered with his vision. 'You can swim?'

'I can.' Her response sounded ridiculously cautious.

'There you go, then. You're never more than a few metres from being able to stand up, and the sea today is mill-pond calm. And where I'm talking about... Agates, Addie. Black gold.'

'Black gold?' She was pretty much discombobulated.

'Okay, they're just gemstones,' he conceded. 'But they're beautiful. I saw them a few weeks ago. They're not everywhere but if you search the bottom at the far end of the cove you can find them. Tiny pieces of glossy black. Some have white lines, swirls, the most intricate patterns embedded. They're created by ancient volcanoes from liquefied silica. Agate's normally green, blue or amber. The black's rare and it's right on our doorstep.'

She was still confused but starting to be caught up in his enthusiasm. 'You found it.'

'I did.'

'But you didn't collect it?'

'Why would I?' He spread his hands. 'The beach has mostly been picked clean and I had no reason to take any. But this morning…' His face changed again and suddenly he was serious.

'Addie, it's a special day,' he said softly. 'It's the morning after you discovered you were pregnant. You should have something to remember this weekend. I thought… if we could find a few stones, maybe we could have a stone set in a ring for you. And maybe we could make some into a bracelet or a signet ring for…for whoever might come along…'

She looked at his face. He was smiling again—sort of—but behind the smile she saw doubts. Fear?

Fear that she'd say no, that she'd walk inside and slam the door, closing him out from this pregnancy? This baby?

Closing him out from sharing, as he'd been shut off from Sophie?

This was his need, she thought. It wasn't hers, so that was okay.

Black agate… She'd seen it, polished to high lustre, and she'd seen stones with white hearts.

If they could find it…

'What do you think, Addie?' he asked, and she knew the decision was all hers.

'We could get back to the hospital in an emergency?'

'Rob and Cliff are covering for us, but we could. We'll take the car.'

'But all those steps…'

'I can carry you if necessary, yodelling at the same time. I told you, mountain goat fits my job description.'

'Do mountain goats yodel?' She choked on laughter, but then fell silent. He let her be while she formed an answer. As if he knew this decision was about more than stones.

This wasn't just about finding an agate or spending the day at the beach. This was about so much more...

Sharing.

They really should have some sort of relationship, she told herself. As long as it didn't involve need, it should be okay.

'I think,' she said at last, and finally she managed a smile, 'that Daisy and I would love it. And I also think... isn't it lucky I bought new bathers?'

Noah might describe himself as a mountain goat but Daisy outshone him. What obstacle was a hundred or so steps? The pup hared straight down, then up again, down and up, almost pleading with them to go faster.

But Noah was carrying a pack and he was walking with Addie. There was no way he was going faster.

Once upon a time he'd read that gentlemen should precede ladies down stairs, to catch them if they fell. It made sense, but Addie had headed down in front regardless. She seemed steady. She seemed safe. And if he'd been in front he couldn't have watched her bouncy curls, her gorgeous legs in her cute shorts, the way she stooped to hug Daisy whenever the pup reached them on one of her loops, the way Addie's body language said she was out to enjoy herself.

He thought of the day she'd returned to the hospital with her brand-new suitcase, her brand-new puppy and her brand-new attitude. She was a woman prepared to take on the world.

This pregnancy could knock it out of her. If something happened...

But nothing was happening today. Please.

They reached the base of the steps. Here was another

reason why this place was generally deserted. The steps ended at a line of rocks, with no sand. To reach the cove itself you needed to wade around a rocky outcrop. But Addie obviously knew. She practically bounced down the last few steps, kicking off her sandals, then hauling off her T-shirt and shorts before she hit the water.

But not before he'd seen her bikini…

Of course it was a bikini—a New Version of Addie bikini. Skimpy, pert, bright crimson with white polka dots.

She beamed and stretched, holding her arms up as if to embrace the sun.

He believed he stopped. What man wouldn't have?

She took his breath away.

'Come on, slowcoach, the sea's waiting,' she called, and he gathered most of his wits and headed down the last few steps.

'Sunscreen,' he growled, because that was a practical thing to say and a guy had to mask his emotions somehow.

'Already on,' she told him. 'I'm a woman prepared.' And then she hesitated and her smile grew almost teasing. 'Or usually prepared. Apart from one major slip-up.'

The pregnancy.

'Was it a slip-up?' he asked without thinking.

Her smile faded. 'You still suspect I planned things?' That was an out-of-character snap. 'It takes two to tango and it was just as much your fault as mine.' But then she shook her head. 'Nope. I'm not thinking that. It was no one's fault. A fault means dire consequences and right now there don't seem to be any dire consequences at all. I'm not even morning sick.'

'It's might be too early.'

'Don't you dare be a killjoy.' She was suddenly bossy.

Let's get Daisy around to the cove. Then get your swimming gear on and hit the water. I'll see you in the deep
end.'

And she lifted Daisy into her arms and headed into
the shallows, wading around the rocks and leaving him
to follow.

She'd dropped a sandal. He carried it with him, be-
mused.

By the time he'd rounded the rocks she'd dumped
Daisy and her clothes on the sand. She'd adjusted a pair
of prescription swimming goggles. Then she'd bounced
through the minnow waves until a larger wave loomed
close.

She flipped forward into a neat dive that told Noah
she'd been swimming almost since before she could walk.

Daisy swam valiantly out to join her, but she was a
smart pup. There were seagulls to chase and seaweed to
sniff—and the sea was big. She headed back in.

And Noah was left…watching.

The sun was on his face. The cove was deserted and
the sea was a sapphire dream, calling him to swim now.

Addie was treading water, waving. 'What's keeping
you, slowcoach?'

He needed to catch his breath.

He took a couple of moments more, just to watch, as
she started stroking strongly across the bay.

And then…

*What's keeping you?*

Nothing.


Addie was a fine swimmer. There'd been a public pool
near her childhood home and she'd spent summer va-
cations enjoying it. She was therefore confident in the

water, but Noah… Noah was something else. He dived
into the oncoming waves and disappeared, the way a
sleek seal would hunt for fish. When he appeared again
he was further out, treading water, smiling.

And, oh, that smile…

'Race to warm up?' he demanded, and she had to catch
her breath before she could answer.

'I saw you dive. I'm not dumb enough to race without
a handicap,' she managed. 'So… To the side of the cove
and back, ten times for you, seven for me.'

'Are you kidding? I watched you swim.'

'Eight, then,' she conceded. 'Ready, set, go.'

And she put her head down and swam, hard.

The water was clear and crystal clean. The bottom was
sandy, with tiny fish darting out of their shadows. She'd
normally be entranced. She was…sort of entranced but
maybe not by fish.

For a while she thought he'd beat her. He did three
laps while she struggled to get two. But then he slowed.

Not because he was exhausted, though. He swam…
with her? He dropped back to pace her, swimming alongside her with strong, easy strokes that told her he could
go twice as fast if he wished.

He obviously didn't wish. After those first laps he
matched himself to her. Every time her hand sliced the
surface of the water, so did his. His body wasn't close
enough to touch but close enough so she could feel the
wash of him, so she was aware of him.

Entranced didn't begin to describe it.

She knew why she'd gone to bed with this man. It
hadn't been a moment of madness. There was something
about him… Some irresistible attraction…

It was almost as if…he was part of her?

Okay, that was a crazy thing to think and it wasn't exactly helpful, given the resolutions she'd made last night.

But a woman could fantasise…

A woman shouldn't, she told herself severely, trying to get her head to focus on her swimming. A woman would be very, very stupid to do any such thing.

But the matching of strokes was doing her head in.

She paused and trod water and Noah checked and did the same. 'Problem?'

'Just checking Daisy,' she told him, searching the shore. There was no need. Daisy was chasing seagulls, who seemed to have nothing better to do than to take off and land, over and over, forcing Daisy to run like a madcap.

'You just want a break,' Noah teased.

'Yeah, like there's a chance I might win if I cheat,' she retorted. 'I could double your handicap and still lose.'

'You wouldn't lose.' He smiled at her. 'Anyone less of a loser than you I have yet to meet.'

'Oh, *bleah*.' She shook her head in disgust. 'Did you get that out of some guy manual—lines for a pick-up? In case you've forgotten, the pick-up's already happened.'

'I didn't pick you up, Addie,' he said, smile fading. 'You know that. And this is no seduction scene.'

'It feels like it.'

'You think I want to seduce you?'

'It might be the other way around,' she admitted, deciding she might as well be honest. 'And that…scares me.'

'There's no reason why it should.' And he lifted his hand and touched her cheek.

She flinched.

Why? She wanted his touch. She knew she did.

It did scare her, though.

Why?

Because it was for all the wrong reasons, she told herself. He thought she needed him.

She would not be that woman. She shook her head, flicking his hand away.

'Where are these agates?' she asked, more roughly than she'd intended.

'So the race is off?' He was watching her. Like a shark watched fish? Prey? Oh, for heaven's sake, she told herself, get a grip. This was a nice guy, doing the right thing with no hidden agenda. Yes, there was a bit of sexual attraction. It had gotten out of hand and there were consequences but that didn't mean it had to continue. Practical Addie was down there somewhere. She just had to dredge her up and send hormonal, wanting-to-jump-this-guy Addie back to where she'd come from.

Except she didn't actually know where hormonal Addie had come from. She'd been hiding...well, for most of her life. All her life?

She'd never felt like this with Gavin. Maybe there'd been a spark for her French teacher when she'd been twelve but who wouldn't have gone weak at the knees for a guy who spoke her name like it was the sexiest name in the world? Adeline in French...

She shivered and Noah was all concern. 'You're cold?'

'Nope. Just remembering...something I should have forgotten.' She gave herself a mental shake, relegating M'sieur Gauthier to obscurity, then attempted to do the same with Noah. It didn't quite work. 'Yes, the race is off,' she managed. 'Racing you is ridiculous. Show me where the agates are.'

She sounded brusque, even angry, but he didn't seem to mind. He watched her for a moment, assessing?

She didn't like the way he looked at her. Or maybe she did but it had her totally…discombobulated? She felt twelve years old all over again, ready to stammer over her French primer.

'You need to swim around the rocks on this side,' he told her. 'It's deep water but at the far side there's a shelf where the agates seem to have collected. It's only about two metres deep.'

'I can dive that far,' Addie told him, and turned away to swim.

Two metres?

She was already way out of her depth.

Finding the perfect agate was a laborious business, because Noah was fussy.

He was right in that there were plenty of stones. He dived and spent a little time choosing before bringing a few special ones to the surface for inspection. Addie wasn't as good at staying under water. She dived, grab a handful of whatever she could grab, then dumped them on a rock ledge to sort, while Noah dived some more.

It was disconcerting, holding onto the ledge, sorting stones, while Noah dived underneath her.

It was more than disconcerting, though. She had to concede that it felt good. Or more than good. Gorgeous?

The sun was on her face. The water was cool and lovely. Daisy had discovered she could reach their ledge by clambering over the rocks, so she had a puppy in her face helping her sort.

Noah was diving like the seal he was, bringing up stones for her inspection.

And the stones needed very careful inspection. She didn't need to dive again with Noah.

She was scared to?

Oh, for heaven's sake…

She sorted and Noah dived until he was sure he had enough to check himself. Finally he heaved himself up onto the ledge.

He was wearing boxers. Nothing else. Lean, muscled, tanned…dark hair dripping water across his face…

She was still in the water, holding the ledge with one hand while she sorted with the other. He was right above her.

M'sieur Gauthier was relegated to even more obscurity.

'What have we got?' he asked, checking the pile, and she thought, trouble, that's what she had, but somehow she made herself answer.

'I think…there are some good ones… We could sort them back at the beach.'

'Let's do it here,' he said. 'We only need one or two. We should drop the rest back where they came from so some other couple needing special stones can find them.'

Couple…

Yeah, okay, her mind was ditzy. One word should not make her feel like this.

She didn't answer. She focussed on stones and after a moment's silence—a moment where the word *couple* seemed to hang over them—so did Noah.

The stones Noah selected were small, pea- to marble-sized, deep black with white flecks. They'd been smoothed by years of rolling in the surf, glossy when wet but already losing their gloss as they dried.

'They'll come up magnificently when they're tumbled,' he said, picking up a small stone, wetting it again and holding it to the light. 'This one… Look at the depth of the black and the purity of the white. But the hite forms a line, almost a division. I'm looking for white heart.'

'Tumbled?' she queried. She sort of knew what tumbling stones involved but it was easier than following the ther line of thought. Hearts…

Why was everything getting away from her? This was morning spent collecting precious stones. Why make something it wasn't?

'My grandpa used to collect gemstones,' he told her. He had a tumbler. I remember being awed at the way ie stones were transformed. Now I'm not going to London…' he abandoned the stone he was checking and icked up another '…maybe I could buy me a tumbler.'

'But… If you don't get custody of Sophie, you need ɔ go to London.'

'Why?'

'Because that's what you planned.'

'Nope,' he said easily. 'I planned on getting away. I ɔlanned on changing my life. Somehow that's already iappened.'

'Noah, I won't be responsible for—'

'You're responsible for nothing, Addie,' he told her, ;uddenly firm. 'I'm a grown man and I make my own lecisions. Staying in Australia? Buying a tumbler?' He iesitated. He glanced down at her and she saw the flash ɔf sudden uncertainty. Vulnerability?

'Maybe even falling in love?' he added, so quietly hat for a moment she thought she must have misheard.

She hadn't, though. The tiny waves washed in and out ɔf the cove. Daisy rushed across and pounced on the pile ɔf discarded stones, then rushed away again.

The words stayed where they were.

Falling in love?

'No.' She said it flatly. It was as if there was a shield somewhere within her that had to be raised. It was heavy, cumbersome, hard to raise but somehow she managed it.

'Why not? Other people do.'

'You wouldn't say it if I wasn't pregnant. If you didn't think I needed you.'

'You don't think I might say it despite the fact that you're pregnant?' He tucked a wet curl back from her eyes, setting it behind her ear. He did it with surgical precision, as if it was infinitely important that the curl be set just so. 'You're adorable, Addie.'

'Daisy's adorable.' She was having trouble catching her breath.

'So she is, but she's not someone I'd choose to marry.'

*Marry.*

Memories flooded back like a tsunami, the months, no, years, of planning the wedding of the century, her mother's joy, the culmination of the interminable car journey to church. And then… Her mother's pain. Gavin's mum's pain. No one knowing what to say. Standing in the sunshine in her stupid white tulle, dropping her over-blown bouquet at her feet, knowing she looked ridiculous, hating Gavin with every fibre of her being, Gavin who, minutes before, she'd thought was her best friend…

Gavin, who'd accused her…of needing him.

'You really think that's what I'd want?' she whispered, appalled. 'Marriage?'

'Um…possibly not,' he said ruefully. 'Can you forget I said it? It was a stupid thing to say and it's scared us both. Marriage doesn't have to come into it. Not for a long, long time, maybe not for ever. But love… Addie, maybe we could concede it's possible. I know it's too soon but…'

'Both of us have tried before.' Her voice was hard.

The armour was finally raised, hammered into place by shock and fear. 'Both of us know it's a disaster. Love comes with strings that break your heart. I don't need it.'

'Are we talking about need, or talking about love?'

'They work the same. I can't take the chance…'

'I'm not asking you to take a chance.' He was starting to sound exasperated. 'I'm asking you to drop your barriers for a bit because all they do is hurt. I'm asking to get to know you better. I want to see what makes you laugh, makes you cry. I want to learn what you like on your toast. I want to see you as I did this morning, rumpled, real. I've seen so many Addies…'

'Yeah, the white tulle…'

'And the workhorse Addie, and the frightened patient Addie, and the Daisy-toting, luggage-kicking Addie. And the Addie who lay in my arms. And, this morning, the rumpled, gorgeous Addie. And now the dripping, beautiful woman who won't get out of the water and sit beside me because she's afraid…'

'I'm not afraid.'

'Liar.'

'Okay, I am.' It was a yell, so unexpected that Daisy stopped dead in her quest to catch a seagull, and headed over the rocks at full pace to see what was wrong.

Only when she reached them she looked from Addie—still two-thirds in the water—and Noah, and made her choice. She shoved her nose under Noah's arm and made her allegiance clear.

'Traitor.' Addie hauled back on her fright—yes, okay, she was frightened—and summoned reserves to haul herself from the water. Noah put out a hand to help but she simply glared at it.

Did he smile? The toe rag. He'd better not be laughing.

'We have enough stones,' she said with an attempt a
dignity. 'I believe it's time to go home.'

'Mrs Rowbotham's made us lunch. It's in the backpack.'

'I don't want any.'

'Addie?'

'Yes?' She hauled herself up, standing, dripping water
on the rock beside him. It felt better standing up. Safer.

'You don't think you might be being a bit melodra-
matic? We haven't made a final choice of stones, and
lunch needs to be eaten.'

'Yeah, okay,' she muttered. 'Just don't say the L word
again.'

'Love?'

'Noah!' Drat it, he really was laughing.

'Okay.' He held his hands up in surrender. 'No L word.
Or even what seems to be more scary. The N word. Need.
For now all talk of future relationship is off the table.
But we still need to be colleagues. Daisy needs us to be
friends and, who knows, we might need to co-parent
one day. So let's start being civilised about it. Lunch and
stone sorting and maybe a wee nap in the sun before we
head home.'

'Okay,' she said grudgingly, and then, because she really had sounded grumpy and it was a gorgeous day and
he was a friend, she tried harder. 'Sorry. You gave me
a fright but I'm over it. Lunch, stone sorting but a nap's
out of the question. New limits.'

'Accepted,' he said, and gathered the remaining stones
and stood.

He was large. He was still wet. He was…

Don't go there. New limits. Lunch, stones and no nap.
Starting now.

* * *

Except she did nap and Noah was left staring out to sea wondering what he'd just said.

The L word.

What had he been thinking?

He suspected Addie had gone to sleep thinking he'd spoken in order to gain access to a child who was finally his. It was a reasonable thought. She knew he loved Sophie and might lose her. She'd guess now that he'd love this baby, too.

But what he felt for Addie was different. Far different.

Maybe she couldn't see it because almost every time he'd seen her she'd been at her most vulnerable. He couldn't deny it, but when the chips were down, that was when you saw the real person. The slap at the wedding. Her courage and fear in the face of an ectopic pregnancy. Her defiance and bounce as she'd returned, with a puppy and bright red luggage...

And a polka-dot bikini. She was wearing a crimson sarong now as she slept, but the polka-dot top peeped out. Her damp curls were splayed across her towel-cum-pillow. Her glasses were clutched in her hand. Her glasses were almost a line of defence, he thought. She could be awake and wary in seconds.

Wary of him?

Wary of talk of love? Of mutual need?

Was she right? Was it dumb talk?

Maybe it was, but it was the way she made him feel. She was vulnerable and needful but she was also feisty, skilled and strong. Fun.

To walk away from her now seemed unthinkable.

If this baby happened, she'd give him access. He knew it, but he wasn't thinking of a baby. He was watching a

woman sleep. *His woman. Part of him?* The sense of one
ness was so deep, so primeval it almost left him gasping
After Rebecca…the thought of another relationship had
seemed unthinkable, but somehow, some way, Addie had
breached defences he'd hardly known he had.

So… How to convince her to take a chance on more
than friendship?

It wasn't something she could be 'convinced' of, he
thought. It was simply the way things were—or weren't
If she didn't feel it, that was that. He was the last person
to try and force such an issue.

So back away, he told himself. You're scaring her. Be
a friend and take the pressure off. Like now. Go for another swim rather than sit and stare like a stalker.

But he wanted to sit. To guard his woman?

How corny was that?

He rose and headed for the water again, though Daisy
looked up as he left and whimpered a reproach.

Your place is here with us, her whimper seemed to
say, but he knew it wasn't.

But if not…he didn't have a clue where his place was.

Addie didn't…wouldn't…need him and the thought
left him bleak.

He dived under a wave and stayed under for a very
long time.

# CHAPTER ELEVEN

THE PREGNANCY WASN'T ECTOPIC. The pregnancy was safe in utero. Blood tests promised it. A scan at five weeks confirmed it.

She told Noah at the end of long day's surgery. She watched his face light up. She backed away as he went to hug her, and she went back to her cottage.

And closed the door.

Honestly? She was too frightened to do anything else. The thought of him falling in love… Of *her* falling in love…was terrifying. All the control she'd so carefully cultivated seemed to be as threatened as a house of cards in a wind storm.

As the weeks wore on, they settled into an uneasy pattern. Friends? Colleagues? Outwardly they were just that. And maybe it was true, she thought as she worked on. Noah was certainly respecting her boundaries. They worked together. They met in the staffroom and talked about shared patients, about dog training, about ordinary stuff. He shared some of her dog walking. He was friendly, warm…normal?

And yet there was part of her that knew that he was contained. Holding things back.

* * *

The phrase he'd used on the beach...*falling in love*. stayed with her. She woke in the night and it was there. She met him in the corridor and it was there. She saw him below the hospital, throwing a Frisbee for Daisy and it was there.

Love?

It was crazy, she thought. How could anyone fall in love so fast? The way he felt *must* be all to do with the baby. His relationship with her... He thought she needed him and he was honourable. How could it be more than that?

She should block out the emotion, but as the weeks went on another layer came into play.

It was getting closer to his court hearing for custody of Sophie. She saw him occasionally out on the veranda taking long calls, and his face was always set and grim

It was nothing to do with her, so why did her heart twist for him?

Her thoughts were all over the place.

She wanted to share his pain. If they were friends that's what she'd do, she thought, but the emotions he caused had her backing away.

*Falling in love...*

Impossible.

She moved from day to day, trying to block his unsettling presence. Trying to focus on her work and her pregnancy.

Her baby.

*His baby.*

How would co-parenting work? As her baby's father, he'd be in her life...for ever?

But just as her baby's father.

She'd worry about that when she had to, she told herself. Even though the pregnancy was where it was supposed to be, she was still barely allowing herself to hope.

She'd manage as she'd always managed.

She did not need Noah.

Fourteen weeks...

Not that he was counting. Not much. But this was Addie's pregnancy and he had to back off.

Eventually he wanted to be a part of this child's life. He knew enough of Addie not to fear being shut out, but shutting him out of his child's life was different to shutting him out of hers.

And that's what she'd done. It was her right, but still he counted.

Fourteen weeks...

And two more weeks until the family court case for Sophie. That was doing his head in.

If anything happened to Addie's baby... If anything happened to Addie... If he lost the court case as his lawyers told him he probably would... If he lost the right to see Sophie...

And then one morning he had a phone call.

He took it, and couldn't believe what he was hearing. He disconnected, then stared sightlessly out to sea while his world changed. And when it settled...

For some reason there was only one thing he could think of to do.

Sadly medicine had to come first, but he could deal with that.

He had two more patients to see before he could go tell Addie.

* * *

At fourteen weeks she'd finally booked in for the scan most pregnant women had at twelve weeks. She'd been... sort of scared to do it? The twelve-week scan would show arms, legs, a little face. Or not. It seemed like she was tempting fate to take the scan and find out.

At fourteen weeks she could put it off no longer but her scheduled appointment had to be set back. The radiologist who came to Currawong once a week was running late.

Addie headed into the staffroom. She made herself tea, put her head on her hands for a moment and closed her eyes...

'Dr Blair!'

She woke and Morvena was standing over her, looking astonished. Her tea was cooling in front of her.

She'd been fast asleep.

'What...?' It took a moment to collect herself. 'Sorry. Just...catching up with a quick nap between patients.' She checked her watch and relaxed. She had ten more minutes before she was due in Radiology.

But Morvena was still staring at her, and Addie could see calculations going on in her head. Fast calculations.

Uh-oh.

'There were no babies born last night,' Morvena said. 'No call-outs.' If anyone knew this, it was Morvena who had a finger on the pulse of the whole hospital. 'Why do you need to catch up on sleep?'

'I just...didn't sleep last night.'

'The lights were out in your cottage. All night.'

Honestly, was there anything this woman didn't know? Addie decided it wasn't worth a response. She rose and carried her mug to the sink, busying herself washing it. With her back to Morvena.

But she knew, reply or not, she was faced with the inevitable.

And here it came. 'You're pregnant again, aren't you?'

Go away, Addie wanted to say. This is nobody's business—nobody's baby—but mine. Admitting it to an outsider seemed fraught. Everything seemed fraught.

The scan just minutes away seemed terrifying, and now this...

She set her cleaned mug on the bench and held her hands to her tummy. She refused to turn around. She was holding her baby to herself. Holding hope.

'It's Dr McPherson's,' Morvena said.

It wasn't a question.

That took her breath away. She counted to ten, not because she needed to control what she was going to say but because she couldn't think of what to say.

'Leave it, Morvena,' she managed at last. 'Dr McPherson's due to leave in two weeks. It's hardly helpful to start rumours now.'

'I'm starting no rumours,' Morvena retorted. 'I'm stating facts. He's looking grim as death. You're falling asleep all over the hospital. I'm losing an excellent surgeon and I have an obstetrician who can't keep her eyes open. If that's not my business I don't know what is.'

'I'm fourteen weeks. I should be getting over fatigue soon.'

Oh, for heaven's sake, why had she said that? She should have denied it. Morvena had quizzed her before about the paternity of her ectopic pregnancy and she'd

admitted the IVF treatment. She should have implied i
was more of the same.

But it was too late now. Morvena's eyes narrowed
'Fourteen weeks...' She could see her doing mental arith-
metic and finding the answer. 'I'm right, then. And you
moved out of the doctors' house because...'

'Because it was a mistake. Because neither of us
want—'

'Well, that's nonsense,' Morvena said briskly. 'You
both want. Here you are, buying a dog that distracts the
running of the entire hospital, when what you want is
home and hearth and babies. And so does he.'

'Morvena, I don't. We don't—'

'Nonsense. I've seen the way you look at him. And
the way he looks at you.'

'He has enough on his plate. Do you know—?' She
broke off, aghast. The court case was definitely not for
public consumption.

'About his little girl? Of course I know. And not because I snoop,' Morvena said briskly. 'He takes phone
calls at the end of the veranda, and my office is just
through the window. I acknowledge I shouldn't know,
but I'm not stupid. I know why he's looking grim. I also
know why he's looking at you like he is.'

'Morvena, enough.' She didn't know whether to laugh
or cry. She glanced at her watch. 'I need to be in Radiology in five minutes.'

'For your own appointment. I saw.'

'You have no right—'

'I have every right. It's part of my job to check Frieda's
appointments. If no one's booked in, it's my job to tell her
not to come. When I saw your name I worried it was for
something serious. Until I thought about it a bit more.'

'Morvena…'

And then, amazingly the woman softened. 'It's okay, my dear,' she told her. 'I'm not about to shout it abroad. So you're off to have a fourteen-week scan. Is Noah going with you?'

'I… No.'

'You haven't told him you're having the scan?'

'It's nothing to do with him.'

'Why on earth not?'

'Because it can't be.' It was practically a wail, and suddenly it was as if a dam broke. 'Morvena, what if I'm in love with him? I won't let him take care of me because I need him. I won't. We've both been in relationships like that and it scares me stupid.'

Whoa.

How much had she exposed? What had she just said?

And to whom? Because suddenly…it wasn't just Morvena.

She stared blindly at the nurse manager, but as panic receded she became aware of a shadow behind. Blocking the doorway.

*Noah.*

What had he just heard? Beam me up, Scotty, she pleaded with the universe. Where was a time machine when she needed one?

'You know,' Morvena said, quite conversationally, 'I just remembered there's a rumour about a puppy in the kids' ward. If you'll excuse me, I have rules to enforce.' And she had the temerity to grin. 'Dr McPherson, I believe you have sense to enforce things as well. This woman's in love with you even if she won't admit it. Anyone who tells someone as grouchy as me that they might be in love…well, once upon a time I was foolish as well, and it got me a loving husband and a couple of children who are just as foolish as their mother was. Sometimes foolish is altogether sensible. I'll leave you both to it.'

And she had the effrontery to chuckle, a sound almost unheard of from Morvena, as she bustled away to do her duty.

Leaving Addie with Noah.

How long had he been there?

'I… Is Daisy…?' She was struggling to breathe, much less talk. Her fast-growing pup seemed the safest—the only option. 'Is Daisy in the kids' ward?'

'Daisy might have been in the kids' ward,' Noah said, his voice carefully neutral. 'I believe she might now be in Men's Surgical.' By rights Daisy should be in her playpen but increasingly the friendly pup was 'borrowed' at need. Keeping her out of the wards was a task even Morvena seemed to be giving up on.

'I…I have to go,' Addie tried.

'To have your ultrasound.'

'How long were you standing there?'

'Long enough. Sound carries down corridors and Morvena's never been one to lower her voice.'

'I…'

'Addie, would you like me to come?'

And it was exactly the wrong question. Or the right question?

*Would you like me to come*? No pressure.

All the pressure in the world.

If he'd said *I want to come,* she'd have handled that. But would she *like*?

'I don't need—' she managed.

'Let's leave need out of it,' he said, his voice suddenly rough with emotion. 'Let's focus on what we want.

Addie, you're about to have an ultrasound that is important. Fourteen weeks... It'll tell you if there are any problems you need to face—that *we* need to face. More probably, it'll tell us that we have a healthy, normal baby settling down to grow for the next two trimesters. I would like to be there. No, I want to be there. There's no need involved, only desire. But you're right, we've both been pushed in directions that weren't our choice and I won't do that to you. I will not. So trust me or not, this is the time to say it. What do you want?'

What did she want?

She wanted her baby. That was her one inviolate truth. Her hands were still on her belly, as if she could protect that truth from any outside threats simply by holding.

Was Noah a threat?

Somehow she'd made him out to be, but he was standing in front of her now and she looked into his face and what she saw...

It was just...Noah.

A colleague.

A friend.

An honourable man.

A man who'd held her and made the outside world disappear.

A man who could love her baby as much as she did. She knew that.

A man who could love her?

It was too soon to think that. Panic was still there, rearing its ugly head in the background. To let go...

But she didn't need to let go. Not completely. All he was asking was to say what she wanted right now.

Did she want him to be with her at the ultrasound?

The scan she'd had at five weeks had shown nothing

except the position of the pregnancy. Her baby had been the size of an apple seed. She had a chart of baby growth versus fruit sizes that she showed her pregnant mums. They liked it and so did she.

At this scan her baby should be the size of a lemon. Or a peach? Peach, she thought. She liked the image.

An image…

She'd see it. At fourteen weeks her baby could be sucking a thumb, wiggling toes. It'd be real. If everything was okay…

If something was wrong, could she bear it? Even now, the fear was still with her.

Did she want Noah with her?

And the answer came back, as clear as day. Yes, she did.

And more.

She didn't want him because she needed a support person. She didn't…need.

She wanted him because she knew he wanted this baby as much as she did. This baby meant love to Noah as well.

*Love…*

It was a concept she was having trouble getting her head around, but it was present, somewhere in this utilitarian staffroom with its noisy refrigerator and uncomfortable chairs and its unwashed coffee mugs. Mrs Rowbotham was always having forty fits about medics who grabbed coffee on the run and didn't clean up.

She'd cleaned hers, she thought inconsequentially.

*Love…*

Noah was waiting. Calmly. Whatever she said, he wouldn't push.

Did she want him to be there for the ultrasound? Did she want him to share?

'Yes, please,' she whispered, and then, more loudly, 'Noah, yes, please, I'd love you to come.'

Normal was a strange word. It sounded dull, plain. It didn't begin to describe how she felt as she lay and let the ultrasound wand stroke her belly.

Normal?

It was a fabulous word.

Frieda was talking them through what she was seeing, obviously enjoying their wonder.

'I'm counting vertebrae. Every single one in place. Gorgeously normal. Head circumference…within normal limits. Great. Head down, beautiful presentation, though there's lots of time to wiggle. Now sex… You know at fourteen weeks it's hard. I've seen a lot of ultrasounds and I could hazard a guess but—'

'No.' The word came from both of them at exactly the same time. Addie looked up at Noah and he looked down at her and then they both looked at the screen. And Noah's hand suddenly slipped into hers and gripped, hard.

She lay and watched the faint movement on the screen. Her baby—*their* baby—was trying to kick. And Addie was grinning like the proverbial Cheshire Cat, grinning and grinning because who couldn't grin in the face of such joy?

Normal.

What was normal about a perfect baby?

What was normal about a guy holding her hand? Her baby's father.

Noah.

Sharing her joy.

'I'll write the results up, but everything's wonderful,' Frieda was saying, and Addie thought 'wonderful' was an even better word than 'normal'. Or maybe they were the same. 'Would you like a print of the image? Or I could copy the file and send it to you.'

'Yes,' they said again, once more totally in unison, and Noah chuckled and Addie found herself doing exactly the same. Frieda was wiping lubricant from her belly. The scan was done.

Time to release Noah's hand?

No. And that was a unilateral decision as well.

His grip firmed. He helped her to sit up, then moved in to hug and Frieda had to manoeuvre past him.

'I do love a happy ending,' Frieda said. 'Or a happy beginning. Welcome to your second trimester, Dr Blair, Dr McPherson and baby.'

And that felt great, too.

Maybe all parents felt like this. Maybe this was normal?

*Normal.*

She was getting to love that word. If the feel of Noah's hand in hers could be...normal...

It was still too soon, she told herself, a trace of fear rearing its ugly head, so she didn't say it. But as she dressed, as Noah opened the door to the outside world, he took her hand in his again and she thought...

Normal could be just plain awesome.

But the outside world was waiting.

She was floating in a bubble of euphoria but the moment they emerged she felt Noah stiffen.

The X-ray department had two entrances, a door leading back into the hospital and another for outpatients, opening to the veranda. They'd emerged to the veranda because why wouldn't they? The sun was shining, the sea was sapphire and sparkling to the horizon, and the world was waiting.

But something else was waiting.

A car had just pulled into the staff car park, a white sedan with government number plates. A middle-aged woman, dressed in a smart black business suit, was emerging from the driver's seat.

She opened a rear door and helped a child out. A little girl dressed in blue dungarees and crimson trainers. She had deep black hair, tied into two pigtails with red-checked ribbon. Her face was broad, her big round eyes looking cautiously out to see where she was.

And even from the veranda, Addie could tell…

*Sophie.*

She knew even before Noah dropped her hand and strode—and then ran—down the steps, across the car park, to scoop the little girl into his arms. She knew, even before the little girl clung, her little arms going around his neck, her face burrowing into his shoulder.

'Papa…' the child said, wonderingly, and something very like a sob broke from Noah. His face was in her hair. He was holding her like she was the most precious thing in the world. Just holding.

*Love…* The word was all around them.

This child wasn't Noah's, Addie thought, dazed. This was Rebecca's child, foisted on him…

No, not foisted. He'd taken her willingly, more than willingly.

Because she needed him?

No. There was nothing even close to obligation on Noah's face. There was only joy.

He turned with the little girl in his arms. He smiled

across at Addie and she saw the glimmer of tears on his face.

She still wasn't sure what was going on. There was an official Government Family Services logo on the car. The woman—a social worker?—was standing back, smiling, but she was holding a clipboard. Official business?

'Sophie, this is my friend, Addie,' Noah told the little girl, and the child gave her a long, considering stare before burying her face in Noah's shoulder again. Noah kissed the top of her head and then turned back to the woman by the car.

'Thank you,' he said, and there was such fervency in the words that Addie could only wonder.

'I'll leave you to it,' she ventured, increasingly unsure of her place. 'I…I have patients to see.'

'Wait,' Noah said. 'Addie, this is important. Stay for a moment. Can you come and meet Sophie?'

So she allowed her legs to carry her down the steps, to where Noah stood hugging his little girl, while the woman in the suit beamed her approval in the background.

'Addie, this is my Sophie,' Noah told her. But as Sophie kept her face in his shoulder, he smiled and turned to the lady with the clipboard. 'And this is Dianne, Sophie's social worker. And risk taker and miracle worker.'

'Wow,' Addie managed, and was offered a hand in greeting and took it. 'That's some recommendation.'

'She deserves it and more,' Noah told her. 'She's won me my Sophie.'

'I don't understand.' There was a lot she didn't understand. The depth of her lack of understanding was bottomless.

'Sophie's foster father had a heart attack last week.'

Noah was still hugging Sophie, talking over her head, speaking softly so he wouldn't startle her. 'Her foster mother has been by his bedside ever since. There are no short-term carers available right now. I'm not permitted access, so Sophie had to go into a group home. She went into meltdown. As her case worker, Dianne had to make the arrangements but she hated seeing how confused and upset Sophie was. And she also knew I was here, loving Sophie, adoption papers lodged, court case pending, aching for access.'

'It was exceedingly unsatisfactory.' The social worker spoke briskly, holding her clipboard before her as if to make everything businesslike. 'Noah's been acting as much as a father as he's been permitted to for five years. We know he wants custody. He ticks every box as far as suitability goes, yet Sophie's mother has the rights. It was frustrating everyone, and when her foster arrangements fell through it became a crisis.'

'I can't bear to think…' Noah said, and his voice cracked.

'It was only for a week,' Dianne said soothingly, seeing the emotion on Noah's face. 'But things did become untenable. Sophie was disintegrating at the group home, withdrawn, not eating, sobbing her heart out, and there seemed nothing we could do. We're well overstretched in the department but finally I…*we*…took the time to go through her case notes since birth. I only joined the department eighteen months ago so a lot of it was new to me, but I realised there were inconsistencies between Rebecca's statements as to her ability to care for her, and Rebecca's obvious ability to function in the community. I made…subtle enquiries and exposed Rebecca's miscom-

munication. Finally the question solidified. Why don'
we simply take her back to her mother?'

'Because Rebecca hates her?' Noah said, softly
though, his hand ruffling the little girl's hair to muffle
her hearing.

'Be that as it may,' Dianne said primly. 'Rebecca's
never admitted that. Her case for fostering was based on
the extent of her disability, which I believe I've proved to
be less than she's previously implied. Our job then was
to make an immediate call on how to get Sophie out of
a situation where she was clearly failing. Once we had
the facts we called a case conference to decide whether
Sophie could be returned to her mother's care. There's
never been any hint that Sophie had been mistreated by
Rebecca. We decided we could keep constant supervi-
sion and that we could pull her out at need. So we rang
Rebecca and said we were bringing her home to her—
immediately.'

'I can only imagine how that went down,' Noah said
with feeling, and Dianne gave a tight smile.

'The child's welfare is paramount. We had no choice.
We knew that Rebecca was living with a new partner—
we'd done background checks on him before the case
conference. There was no hint he was unfit for the place-
ment but it seems *he* didn't know of Sophie's existence.
Maybe that would have been a deal breaker in their relationship—Rebecca's reaction seemed to suggest that.
Her first reaction was fury, then denial—and then panic.'

'Of course panic,' Noah said, hugging Sophie tighter.

'I admit we were concerned,' the social worker told
them. 'We were ready to back off. But we hung on long
enough for Rebecca to panic herself into another way.'

She gave a slightly shamefaced smile then, a crack

in the professional façade. 'And that was our success. It was the way I, *we*…had hoped. Rebecca was searching wildly for any way out and Noah was the only short-term alternative we gave her.' Once again that embarrassed smile. 'It may have been slightly unprofessional in pushing at this time, but by the end of the phone call the objection to Noah's adoption had been dropped. The papers were signed the next morning, while her new partner was at golf. The only stipulation is that Noah remains quiet about Sophie's parentage. Sophie will have that information from us when and if she needs it. Of course there'll be further formalities, but as far as we can tell there'll be no further problems.'

'And you have my undying gratitude,' Noah said, and then he couldn't say any more. His face was buried in Sophie's hair. He was just…holding.

Dianne and Addie looked at the little girl, clinging like a wee limpet. Dianne smiled but Addie couldn't even bring herself to smile. There was a lump in her throat so big she was struggling to breathe.

He wanted this little girl.

But Sophie wasn't his child. There was no need for him to get involved. There'd never been a need.

He loved her.

Love…

The word was all around her, singing its way into her heart.

Love.

Dianne was taking gear out of the car. Sophie was lifting her head from Noah's shoulder, looking around with caution at this new world she'd just been introduced to.

Noah met her gaze over Sophie's head and he smiled and smiled.

It was too much. Tears were sliding down her face and she couldn't check them.

'I... Excuse me,' she managed. 'I have... I have patients booked. I'll...'

She could think of nothing else to say.

She turned and fled back into the hospital.

But love stayed with her. Noah's smile. Dianne's triumph. The way Sophie clung.

More. The events of the morning were overwhelming. The grainy pictures on an ultrasound.

She needed Daisy, she decided. Where was a puppy when she needed one?

'Which room *isn't* Daisy in at the moment?' she asked Heidi as she met her in the corridor, and Heidi looked at her in concern.

'Is everything okay?'

'I... Yes... I just...need Daisy.'

'Daisy might currently *not* be in Room Seven,' Heidi told her. 'But—'

'Thanks,' she said, cutting off further questions. She headed for Room Seven and found one half-grown retriever puppy entertaining an elderly woman recovering from a fall.

'Hi, Mrs Crammond. Do you mind if I borrow my dog? I sort of...need her.'

'Of course you do.' Mrs Crammond beamed as Daisy scrambled off the bed and headed for her mistress. 'Everyone needs a puppy to hug.'

'Everyone needs a hug,' Addie concurred, and then added a rider. 'Everyone needs...love?'

# CHAPTER TWELVE

IT WAS EIGHT at night.

Addie had worked through, seeing one patient after another, and then organised a house call to a woman she suspected was at risk of postnatal depression. There was probably no need to go this evening, but it was on her list of things to do and she needed things to do.

She took Daisy with her. She sat at the woman's kitchen table and admired her new baby as she talked with her and her husband. She talked about how hard it was to adjust to parenting, to the demands of a totally different life. She talked about the lack of structure, of sleep deprivation, of fears of the future.

Addie talked of strategies. Of a plan, with sleep rosters starting that night. She helped a self-contained, controlled woman explore the idea that she needed to let go, to ask for help, to not have everything perfect.

She left them cautiously hopeful, facing challenges together.

Together was a good word.

She couldn't get it out of her head.

She drove back to her cottage, had tea and toast, tucked Daisy into her bed and then walked across to the doctors' house.

The word was still ringing in her ears.

Together.

Noah was sitting on the veranda step.

She'd known he would be. She'd just known.

Because she knew this man?

Because she loved him.

He didn't get up as she approached. He had a beer i
his hand. He put it down but went no further.

The night was totally, absolutely still. Or maybe
wasn't. She could hear the gentle hush of waves washin
in and out on the beach below. She could hear the call c
curlews, but nothing else. The world seemed at peace.

Waiting?

'I came to ask…' she said, and stopped. How to sa
it? How to take this giant leap?

He didn't help. How could he? she thought. He'd give
her so much. The control had all been hers.

He would never push, not this man. A man who'
taken on the care of a child who wasn't his. A man who'
entered a loveless marriage because how could he not?

A man who'd said the love word to her and seen he
back away in fright.

'I came to ask if you'd marry me,' she said.

Silence.

The silence was so deep it was terrifying. The curlews had stopped their calling. Even the waves seemed
to have stilled.

Had she got it so wrong?

'Why?' he asked at last, and his voice didn't seem like
his. It was distant. Faint. As if he, too, was facing a barrier he'd never contemplated crossing.

But there was only one answer and she had to say it.
Out loud. Right there and then.

'Because I love you,' she said.

More silence. Neither of them seemed able to move. He was still seated on the top step. She was a metre or so from the bottom step, looking up at him.

Holding her breath.

The whole world seemed to be holding its breath.

'I don't need you,' he said at last.

It could have been a rejection but it wasn't. She knew his man. She knew what he was saying.

'I don't need you either,' she told him. 'I can manage by myself and so can you. I can also give you any access to our baby that you want. We can co-parent without marriage. And you… Noah, I know you'll be a beautiful dad to Sophie without any help from me. So I don't need you and you don't need me. But today… It's taken me a while to figure it out but when I saw your face as you held Sophie… When I saw how much you loved… Noah, I'd love to share. I'd love…to love, too. If you'd let me…'

He stood then, but still he didn't come to her. She saw his face under the dim veranda light and she saw the wash of emotion.

'Sophie…' he said slowly, as if struggling to emerge from a dream. 'Sometimes… Addie, sometimes she's not easy.'

And there was only one answer to that. She said what was in her heart. What she truly believed. 'She'll be our daughter,' she said, and had to force her voice to rise above a whisper. 'Our family. Noah, I'm not asking for easy. I want it all. If you'll let me.'

'The full bells and whistles…'

'Not quite,' she admitted. 'Marriage with you? Yes and yes and yes. Co-parenting Sophie and my bump and a crazy pup called Daisy? Yes, please, to that, too. But Noah, I won't wear white tulle again. Not even for you'

'Not even a little bit?' He sounded so forlorn she had to chuckle, but a girl had to set limits somewhere.

'Not even a little bit,' she told him. 'I've sworn off the stuff for life. Noah…' She took a deep breath. 'The marriage thing…what do you reckon?'

And he smiled.

He smiled and he smiled, and his smile finally, finally carried him down the steps. Slowly, as if he couldn't believe what was waiting for him below.

Finally he reached her. He took her hands in his and he searched her face.

'You're sure, my Addie.'

'I love you, Noah.'

'And I love you,' he told her. 'If you'll do me the honour of becoming my wife, I'll be the happiest man alive.'

'But…you wouldn't be marrying because of need.' She was still anxious.

'See, there's the thing,' he said, almost ruefully. 'I would be. It's been a while now since I conceded that I need you. But it's you I need, Addie. Not anything you can do for me or mine. I just need…you.'

'Then I guess I need you,' she admitted, and as she said it something inside her seemed to crack. To melt. To disappear as if it had never been.

Years of building armour. Years of doing the right thing. Years of emptiness. They'd disappeared to nothing.

There was no emptiness now. Noah was looking into her eyes with such love, with such want, with such need…

Maybe need was a good word, she thought, and then, as Noah dropped to one knee she decided it was the best word she'd ever heard.

'Then let's do it properly,' Noah said, his voice husky with passion. 'Adeline Margaret Blair, will you do me the very great honour of becoming my wife?'

'How do you know my middle name?' she asked, weirdly sidetracked, and his gorgeous smile widened.

'I looked it up on staff records…just in case I ever needed it.'

She chuckled and she, too, dropped to one knee. 'Me, too,' she admitted. 'I sort of…needed the whole box and dice. So… Noah William McPherson, yes, please,' she whispered. 'And will you…?'

'Don't be daft, love,' he told her and his arms drew her into him. Firmly. Strongly. 'You've already asked. But, yes, please, too.'

And then there was no need—or space—for words for a very long time.

*Happy is the bride the sun shines on…*

But it wasn't sunny, Addie thought in satisfaction as she gazed out her bedroom window down to the beach below. The sea was covered in morning mist.

It was a far, far different wedding than the last one she'd tried.

They'd decided on a morning wedding because that's when Sophie and their newest addition to their family, Giles William, were at their most social.

They were being social now. Sophie was Noah's decreed 'best man'. She was dressed in so many pink flounces they almost enveloped her. She'd been practising for days, twirling and twirling, loving the way her dress flared when she spun, giggling at the sight of her pink self in the long mirror. It had been hard keeping it fresh but from today she could wear it whenever she wanted.

From today…

It really wasn't from today, Addie thought dreamil as Heidi fussed over her frock.

Addie was wearing a gorgeous, sapphire and whit dress, fifties style with a rainbow-coloured shawl. He dress hugged her to the waist, then flared out as Sophie did, so they could twirl together. Still breast feeding, he bust was two sizes larger than the last time she'd trie on a wedding dress.

She was a different woman from last time she'd wor a wedding dress.

She was totally, gloriously happy.

For, marriage or not, she and Noah were now perma nent in every sense of the word. Currawong seemed to be their for ever home. They were still living in the doctors house but a beautiful new home was being built up on the headland. They had friends. They had jobs they loved.

They had each other.

Noah…

He was waiting now, dressed in a charcoal suit, stand ing on the sand with his hand tucked into Sophie's. So phie…a gloriously contented little girl, her dad's friend.

Her dad? That was now definite. The adoption papers had come through three days after Giles was born. Giles, who was currently being held by Morvena. Morvena was standing with Daisy by her side. Waiting.

It seemed the whole town was waiting.

The promise was for heat later, but right now the sun was struggling to filter golden light through the haze hanging over the ocean. The sea itself was calm and still. Tiny waves washed in and out at the water's edge. Sandpipers scuttled along the shore, feeding at low tide, seemingly oblivious to the chairs, the ribbons, the flower-strewn makeshift altar and the myriad people waiting to see Noah and Addie married.

Any minute now…

She looked at her reflection one last time and her reflection smiled back at her. This was no bride turned out to be someone she wasn't. This was Addie. Mother of Sophie and Giles and a dog called Daisy. This was Addie, obstetrician to Currawong Bay.

This was Addie, beloved of Noah.

She turned from her reflection and Heidi smiled. 'Ready?'

'Ready,' Addie whispered, and smiled and smiled. And then she left her bedroom, she left the house and she walked the last few steps to the beach.

Where Noah stood waiting. Smiling. Her beautiful Noah.

'Will you take this man…?'

Of course she would. Of course she did.

Rings were exchanged, golden bands set with tiny slivers of agate. They matched the signet ring on Noah's right hand and the simple stone at Addie's throat, jet-black agate with the purest of white hearts.

They were just…right.

Finally the words were spoken. 'I now declare you man and wife,' and Addie's smile couldn't be contained.

And neither could the sun. It broke through the mist in a glorious shaft of golden light, to shine on bride and groom and all who loved them.

*Happy is the bride the sun shines on…*

*But who needs the sun?* Addie thought mistily. *Not when I have Noah and Sophie and Giles and Daisy.*

*Not when I have everything I need.*

*Not when I have love.*

\* \* \* \* \*

# COMING SOON!

We really hope you enjoyed reading this book. If you're looking for more romance, be sure to head to the shops when new books are available on

# Thursday 21<sup>st</sup> February

To see which titles are coming soon, please visit

**millsandboon.co.uk/nextmonth**

# MILLS & BOON

## Coming next month

### A WIFE FOR THE SURGEON SHEIKH
Meredith Webber

Malik saw what little colour she'd had in her cheeks fade, and the tip of her tongue slide across her pale lips.

And found himself wanting nothing more than to take care of her—this small, fiercely protective woman. Not only to keep her safe but to lift the burden of fear from her slim shoulders.

To hold her, tell her it would all work out.

To hold her?

*Get your mind back on the job.*

But guilt at how he'd hurt her with his words made him reach out and touch one small, cold hand, where it lay in her lap.

'I'm sorry, I shouldn't have threatened you like that—you look exhausted, and all this has been a shock to you. No one should make decisions when they're tired, but there's a way out of this for all of us. Don't answer now, we will talk again in the morning. I shall phone your Mr Marshall and explain you won't be in to work.'

But she'd obviously stopped listening earlier in his conversation.

'A way out for all of us?' she asked, looking at him with a thousand questions in her lovely eyes.

'Of course,' he told her, and felt a small spurt of unexpected excitement even thinking about his solution.

'We shall get married,' he announced. 'That way Nimr is both of ours and will be doubly protected.'

Her eyes had widened and although he hadn't thought she could get any paler, she was now sheet-white.

She stood up, and for a moment he thought she might physically attack him, but in the end she glared at him, and said, 'You must be mad!' before disappearing down the passage, presumably into her bedroom.

Malik realised there was no point in arguing, but the idea, which had come to him out of nowhere, was brilliant.

All he had to do was convince Lauren.

Her name rolled a little on his tongue and, inside his head, he tried it out a few times.

And his mind, for once, was not on Nimr, but on the woman he'd decided to marry…

Continue reading
A WIFE FOR THE SURGEON SHEIKH
Meredith Webber

*Available next month*
www.millsandboon.co.uk